The Ripple Effect

Sonali Gogate

Sonali has over twenty years of experience in the IT industry. She started her career as a software developer and after a successful and fulfilling career left the IT industry as a Technical Director last year. She has worked for some startups as well as global giants such as Microsoft and has lived in different parts of India as well as the US. She is now based in Pune.

She loves to read and has been surrounded by books from childhood. Her hobbies also include travelling and trekking/hiking. She has travelled extensively within and outside India; sometimes alone, sometimes with friends and sometimes with strangers. She has also trekked in different parts of the Himalayas. She has met interesting people from different walks of life and has been through some challenging situations, thanks to her adventures.

The Ripple Effect

Sonali Gogate

VISHWAKARMA PUBLICATIONS VP

The Ripple Effect

First Edition - March 2016
© **Author**

ISBN - 9789383572-96-0

Published by:
Vishwakarma Publications
283, Budhawar Peth, Near City Post,
Pune- 411 002.
Phone No: (020) 20261157
Email: info@vpindia.co.in
Website: www.vpindia.co.in

Cover Design
Milind Mulick

Typeset and Layout
Gold Fish Graphics, Pune.

Printed at
Repro Knowledgecast Limited, Thane

To my parents

ACKNOWLEDGEMENTS

I have had help from many quarters in writing my first novel and having it published. Many friends and family provided encouragement, and though I can't list all their names, there are a few who I have to specifically call out and thank.

First and foremost I thank my parents, Sharad & Shubhada Gogate. I wouldn't have dreamt of becoming a writer without them, I wouldn't have completed 'The Ripple Effect' without their constant encouragement and the work wouldn't have been accepted for publishing if they had not provided the critical feedback that I needed.

I needed help in understanding the legalities concerning an unnatural death and I turned to my friend Sunil Gokhale and my father Sharad Gogate for the same. I thank both of them for answering all my queries, some more than once.

I was pleasantly surprised and quite flattered when, in a casual conversation, Milind Mulick offered to make a painting that could be used for the design of 'The Ripple Effect'. I whole heartedly thank him for the beautiful scene he painted that is so suitable for the story.

When Subroto Bagchi, Chairman, Mindtree, heard that I am writing a mystery novel with the backdrop of the IT industry, he said he was delighted with the idea. I thank him for making it so easy for me to reach out to him and for providing support and encouragement.

I thank Anand Iyer, Arati Dabir and Chinmoy Bhagawat who read 'The Ripple Effect' patiently in very early stages and gave me important input and feedback. I also thank Ajit Patwardhan and Motiya Basargekar, who read when it was close to its final version and helped me fine tune the last hitches.

Special thanks to my friend Tapasi Ray, who gave me very detailed, point by point and specific feedback. She told me what she liked but also what she felt were the shortcomings of the novel and called out areas that she felt needed work.

When I asked her, Chaiti Bhagawat, in spite of her studies and exams, not only happily agreed to read 'The Ripple Effect', but having read it also gave useful feedback. I thank her for the valuable 'young adult' perspective on the novel.

I thank Suhasini Kirloskar for all the discussions and ideas regarding the story and publishing and marketing of the book; for long conversations at her place over tea and coffee and sumptuous meals; for fashion ideas and photo shoot.

Pradeep Singh, Chairman and CEO of VidyaNext is someone I have known and respected for a very long time. When I told him that I have written a novel, he was very encouraging; he even agreed to read it despite being extremely busy. I thank him for his encouragement and for finding time for my novel.

Finding a good publisher for your first book is difficult. I thank Vishwakarma Publications for taking my first work up for publishing. I thank Shivani Bail, my editor, who helped me improve the narration by clarifying and tightening as needed, ensuring logical flow and improving the language overall; I thank Abhishek Darekar for designing the cover based on Milind's painting and I especially thank Scharada Dubey for guiding and supporting me in the complete process of publishing the work.

PROLOGUE

16 Mar 2012

Manjiri walked down the path to the lakeshore and went right up to the waterline. She was unsteady on her feet thanks to all the alcohol she had consumed. She knew she needed to be careful; she had put a miner's lamp on her head and switched it on. But now, on reaching the waterline, she switched it off and looked at the darkness around her.

There was no moon tonight and when she looked up, the star studded sky made her nostalgic. It reminded her of a picnic from long ago, when she had looked at a sky just like this, with the man she loved by her side. They'd had so many dreams then, of the life they had thought they would share. But today, he was so far away from her; in every way.

She turned around feeling close to tears and noticed a boulder. She walked carefully and sat on it, then looked at the soft waves and sighed.

Manjiri sat there feeling forlorn, the reason she had come down to the lake almost forgotten. Should she just walk into the lake never to return? Earlier, she had thought about going to sleep never to wake up. She still had a lot of sleeping pills from four years ago. But she had not played with the idea of drowning so far. Actually, she had not thought about embracing death in quite some time; more than a year now. What had brought that to her mind tonight?

She looked at the trail going upto the camp site and wished Atul would come down soon. He would help her get out of her melancholic mood. Of course, she was here to talk to him about an important QSoft matter. They had to stop what was going on!

It was after about ten minutes that she heard footsteps and cheered up. But the person coming down the trail didn't see her and walked to the waterline. The person was not Atul, Manjiri realized; it was someone taller than him.

She must have made a noise, because the person turned startled and then saw her. But it was quite dark and she could not recognize him. Who was he? And what was he holding in his hand?

CHAPTER 1

15 Apr 2012

"I don't think there is any point in reopening this case," Commissioner Bakshi said. Then raised his hand when Neil was about to make his point and said, "But we will follow the orders and provide you all the support you need."

Neil understood the scepticism. Manjiri had died a month ago; her body had been cremated soon afterwards. There weren't any chances of collecting any new evidence at the site of her death or anywhere else.

Still he wanted to give it his best shot. He nodded to the Commissioner and said, "I understand where you are coming from sir, but if we put in enough thought and effort, and if we are lucky, we might be able to figure out what happened."

The Commissioner kept quiet for few moments and eventually said, "Luck will have to be on your side." Then he indicated that the meeting was over by saying, "Work out the details with ACP Sathey."

After a quick meeting with ACP Sathey and Inspector Pathare, both of whom seemed willing to help, Neil walked out of the Commissioner's office complex and got into his rental car. He thought back to the meeting in Delhi, after which he had agreed to take on this case. He had to get to the bottom of this; failure was not an option.

It was a warm Sunday afternoon and the traffic was light on Pune's roads as he drove towards his hotel.

Every investigation was like a puzzle. Some puzzles, you managed to solve, and others you gave up on, mostly because the budget ran out. Another factor that halted a puzzle on its way to a solution was political pressure, like in this case.

1

Now the case had been reopened but it was quite clearly an unusual one. While the state police would stay involved, the lead investigator would be Neil Bhargav, head of Detective Eye, a private detective agency in Delhi.

Neil had reached out to Abhijeet Desai, head of EnQuaiR detective agency in Mumbai, asking him to join the team. The two had worked together before and Neil had a lot of respect for the man. But Abhijeet was busy and Neil had to settle for someone else from Abhijeet's team.

When Neil reached the hotel, he checked the time and hoped that Abhijeet's detective had reached by now. As he approached the reception the girl behind the counter gave him a smile and said, "Yes sir?"

"Has Ishani Sohoni checked in?" He asked.

The girl nodded and said, "Yes sir. She checked in about fifteen minutes ago. She has asked us to inform her when you came in. Should I call her?"

Neil nodded and looked around as the girl dialled the number. After a few seconds she said, "Sorry sir, she's not picking up the phone in her room. Should I try on her cell phone?"

"No, it's OK," Neil said. He moved aside, pulled out his cell phone and was looking through his contacts when the girl at the reception said, "Sir?" He looked up and she said, "There she is, Sir".

Neil turned around to see a tall girl in a flowing skirt and a t-shirt, who must have stepped out of the lift. This was the detective Abhijeet had sent him? This young girl? Wasn't she supposed to be 31?

As the girl came closer, Neil recognised her as the woman from the photos that Abhijeet had sent him, but in the photos she had looked a lot more formal, serious and older.

Looking at her, Neil thought that the photographs had not done her justice at all. Ishani Sohoni was an attractive woman. He acknowledged that if he had run into her somewhere else, he may have turned around to get a better look. He liked the way she walked tall and the way her skirt swayed to her rhythm.

As Ishani came closer, she realized who he was. She stepped in front of him and offered her hand saying, "Hello Mr. Bhargav, I am Ishani Sohoni."

He shook her hand, collected his thoughts and asked her, "Were you heading to the coffee shop?"

"Yes," She said looking a little embarrassed, "I was not sure if I should call you; if you were in a meeting or something. I was planning to send a message at around 4 PM."

Neil nodded, "Let's go to the coffee shop and talk."

As they walked to the coffee shop, Neil said, "I believe you have come here directly from Himachal?"

"Yes, I was there on vacation with my family," Ishani said with a ready smile.

Once they reached the coffee shop, Neil let Ishani choose the table and was pleased when she selected a table in the corner that would give them a good view of the entire shop, along with its two entrances.

As they sat across from each other, Neil noticed how her shoulder length hair framed her face. He was still musing over this as the waiter approached them and Ishani asked for a chicken burger.

Once the waiter left, Neil went directly to the point, "What do you know about the case?"

"Very little," she replied. "Only that a 43-year-old woman, from the well-known software company QSoft, died about a month ago. The case was closed; her death was thought to be an accident. It has been reopened now and is being handled by Detective Eye."

"Yes. A group of senior managers from QSoft went for an outbound program at a campsite on the backwaters of the Mulshi Dam on a Friday. They were to return on Sunday but on Saturday morning, they found Manjiri Deshmukh's body in the lake."

"I see."

"There were no injuries on her body and though there were 18 people in the program no one knows anything."

"What does the post mortem report say?"

"That the death occurred by drowning and that she had consumed a fair amount of alcohol. There was water in her lungs and alcohol in her blood."

Ishani seemed to be absorbing this information. Then after a couple of moments she asked, "The case was closed within a week, I believe. Why was that?"

Neil looked around and then looking back at her said, "QSoft wanted it closed as quickly as possible, not dragged out and chewed on in the media."

Ishani tilted her head to one side and raised her eyebrows in question. When Neil didn't say anything, she asked, "Why?"

"A year ago, one of the four founders of QSoft walked out and said some nasty things about the other three. QSoft's response to the allegations was aknee-jerk reaction; as a consequence of the messy dispute, which played out in the media, they lost face and customers. You might have heard about their financial troubles since last year. If this case was to get dragged out, it would have been expensive, they felt. So they decided to do what was needed; close the case quickly, and prove that it was an accident."

They got quiet as the waiter came over and served their order. Then Ishani asked, "So how did it reopen?"

Neil knew this question would come up andhe didn't have an easy answer to it or a way to evade it. So he told her what he could, "Just the way political pressure was used to close the case, someone who wants to get to the bottom of this, has taken help from another politician to have the case reopened."

"Someone who wants to get to the bottom..." Ishani mused, "Manjiri's family?"

"Manjiri didn't have any close family. She was not married, was an only child and had lost both her parents in a car accident about four-years-ago."

"Oh!" Ishani exclaimed. "Then who?" She sounded perplexed.

Neil shook his head and said, "I am not going to be able to share that information. At least at this point."

Ishani looked stumped at this. Neil could guess how it must seem to her, but he went ahead, "For our work, that should not matter. Let's just focus on the investigation."

Both of them got quiet and after a few moments, Neil picked his cup and took a sip of the coffee that was not as hot as he would have liked it to be. Ishani, taking her cue, picked up her burger. After a couple of minutes she asked, "So where do we start?"

"I would have liked to start with a visit to the campsite, but we're going there later, so that we reach when there are no campers on site. We'll meet QSoft's HR Manager, Dheeraj Seth first thing tomorrow morning." After a pause, he also told her that he had called Dheeraj earlier and Dheeraj had been quite reluctant to talk. He expected resistance from other QSoft folks as well.

"I suppose we could begin by talking to all the people who were present at the offsite. What about the others? Like her friends, relatives, people she worked with?" Ishani was obviously thinking ahead.

"I'll give you the list of people when I give you the reports from the earlier investigation," Neil said.

Half an hour later they walked out to the lobby and Neil's attention went to the big TV screen. He had really wanted to watch this match. He was wondering what the score was when Ishani said, "Looks like we are batting: 60 for 3."

He turned and looked at her in surprise. She smiled and said, "You are eager to go and watch the match right?"

Neil was impressed with her ability to read his expression so accurately and when they came to the pool of lifts, for the first time since meeting her, he gave her a warm smile.

CHAPTER 2

'Oh wow!' Ishani was thinking to herself as they stood in the lift going to the fifth floor. She was dazzled by Neil's smile. She was a little surprised; why, she didn't know, but also a little nervous when she realized that they were staying in adjoining rooms. While she opened her room, Neil went into his to get the files with the police reports and other details.

In many investigations, when they had to go outstation, they had to make do with substandard accommodations. But this time, she had been put up at a high-end hotel that had all the amenities. Who was spending so much money on the investigation? And why was that a secret? Why couldn't Neil share that information with her? Why was it being investigated by Detective Eye, a private agency, in the first place?

She needed to talk to Abhijeet to get more details, she decided. She also wanted to ask him if he had any tips for her on how to work with Neil. She had been surprised when Abhijeet told her that she would be working with Neil on this case. She was also a little nervous, since Neil was such a well-known detective. But their first meeting had been good, she thought to herself and started going through the files.

She reviewed the list of QSoft senior managers in Pune. There were 23 in all, only three of whom were women. Atul Vaidya, the centre head was the oldest at 49 and Gautam Dhar a Marketing executive was the youngest at 32. Manjiri had been 43, this Ishani knew. The other two women were Sangeeta Pathak, 47 and Medha Panase, 40.

She then went through the reports and notes from the police investigation. The information she could gather was this –

On Saturday, March 17th, Jivaji Jadhav, in charge of the Wild Outdoors' campsite at the Mulshi backwaters went to the police station looking for help. He explained how the QSoft team was staying at the campsite for an off site and how one of the participants had gone missing.

6

Inspector Morey, who was present at the police station, went over to the campsite with a couple of constables; he also called the Fire Brigade. They conducted a thorough search and found Manjiri's body at a distance of about 75 meter from the shore.

The Inspector had talked to all the people present but they were in a state of shock and some were not even sounding coherent so he talked to them again, two days later at QSoft.

A search conducted underwater where the body was found yielded a Swiss knife and nothing else. Police were unable to establish the ownership of the knife; it could have belonged to Manjiri.

The post mortem report stated that death had occurred due to drowning between 11:30 PM and 1:30 AM.

There was nothing in the report to suggest foul play of any kind and no identifiable motives or inconsistencies in the descriptions of the events of the night of her death from all present. The police decided to close the case as an accident.

From the tone of the police report, it sounded like an open and shut case. Then why was it being reopened? Had she missed something? Ishani started going through the papers again.

On Monday morning, as Ishani got ready, she reflected on the previous night. Neil and she had discussed the reports at dinner and talked about what little they had found out from the notes about the QSoft folks present at the campsite.

Dinner had been quite enjoyable and the two of them had got to know each other a little. As they walked from the lift to their respective rooms, Ishani had started yawning and Neil had even teased her a little about that.

Ishani felt pleased about the camaraderie they had developed; it should make working together comfortable. With that thought she stepped into her neatly pressed jeans and put on her favourite olive green shirt. She then tied her shoulder length hair into a pony tail and applied lipstick in a natural shade.

Making a note that she needed to call Geetika sometime during the day, she walked out of her room and pulled the door shut. Geetika Singh was a close friend. She had been Ishani's room-mate when they were studying in Pune and was now happily married to a banker named Rishi Kapoor. She worked as a technician at a big pathology lab.

Thinking about a conversation she'd had with Geetu a few months back, Ishani walked across to the lifts with a smile on her face. She saw Neil waiting there, so quickly schooling her features she called out, "Hi Neil, good morning".

As they drove towards the IT Park, they got stuck in bad traffic. Everyone and their uncle seemed to be driving to the IT Park! Sitting in the passenger seat, she watched Neil drive with ease. He seemed to know the city well and Ishani couldn't help comment on it.

"Yes," He said turning to give her a quick smile. "I did part of my schooling here. Even afterwards, I continued to visit my grandparents here. But now it's only for work."

As they got closer to QSoft in the IT Park, the traffic got thicker and they moved at a snail's pace. Finally after about 45 minutes in which they had driven less than 15 Km, they reached QSoft's gate number 1.

After an elaborate security procedure, they were given a badge each that said "VISITOR" in bold and were escorted to the reception lobby. The lobby was a rectangular area with a high ceiling, decorated in beige and brown. There was a rich mahogany reception desk right in the front, with matching panelling on the back wall. Comfortable looking sofas were arranged in clusters on either side of the desk.

They approached the receptionist and told her that they were there to meet Dheeraj Seth, who was expecting them. After a quick call, she told them that he would be down right away and asked if they would like water, tea or coffee. They declined the offer and sat down on the sofa closest to the reception desk.

Ishani was impressed by the security procedure, the reception lobby as well as the smart, well dressed and efficient receptionist. All these seemed to indicate that QSoft was an organization that was financially sound, and had a happy talent pool..

Fifteen minutes later, they were still waiting for Dheeraj Seth. When she saw that Neil was also getting restless, Ishani asked, "Should we call him?"

"Let's give him another five minutes," Neil said.

Just before Neil lost his patience, Dheeraj Seth walked out to the reception. He was about 5ft9 or 10 inches tall, broad shouldered, fair and balding. He was wearing well cut, expensive clothes but he managed to look as if he had thrown on the clothes at random. He was 38, but he looked older. He came over and smiled saying, "Hi. I am Dheeraj Seth. Sorry for being late, but there was something important to take care of."

After a series of quick introductions and handshakes, they followed Dheeraj through the access-controlled glass door, then up a flight of stairs, to his office on the first floor. They sat across from him at the big table and Ishani noticed that the décor of this room matched the shades she had seen in the reception. Dheeraj's table was cluttered with a lot of papers, files and other things. There was a laptop open on the sideboard behind him.

Dheeraj opened the conversation with, "Like I told you on the phone, Manjiri's death was an accident. The case was closed after a thorough investigation. I am sure, you have seen the reports." Then as an afterthought he said, "We were all very sorry about what happened. She was a very important member of the QSoft family. We lost one of our best."

Neil bent forward putting his forearms on the table top and said, "Mr. Seth, the case has been reopened because the investigation was completed hurriedly the first time. Don't you think Ms. Deshmukh's death deserves a proper investigation?"

"QSoft would be happy to help, but really there is nothing more we can do," Dheeraj said with a displeased expression.

Neil nodded and said, "We want to talk to all the QSoft folks who were present at the campsite. We also want to talk to other people who Manjiri worked with."

"If you think even for a minute that someone from QSoft is responsible for Manjiri's death, I can assure you that you are mistaken." Dheeraj seemed genuinely agitated. "We are confident about our people."

Before Neil could reply Ishani had jumped in to say, "Mr. Seth, Manjiri died an unnatural death. The only way to know whether it was really an accident, as it is believed to be, is to do a thorough investigation. That's why we want to talk to people who can tell us more about that night and also about Manjiri."

Somehow that seemed to calm Dheeraj down a little and after a couple of moments, he said, "Well, alright. But you should also talk to her friends and her aunt."

"Yes, we will definitely be talking to them as well," Neil said in a cordial tone. He was not perturbed; he had anticipated resistance, Ishani realized.

Dheeraj suggested meeting the folks at QSoft and Neil agreed. On reaching this agreement, Neil said, "We would like to start with you, Mr. Seth. What can you tell us about Manjiri?"

Dheeraj had relaxed a little. "Please call me Dheeraj. We are not formal in our industry," he said and smiled at both of them.

They smiled in response and he said, "I didn't really work with Manjiri. Of course as head of the People Care team here in Pune, I interacted with her."

Ishani had pulled out her notepad and the list of QSoft folks from her backpack. Now she went through the list and said, "I am sorry, Mr Seth", then she corrected herself, mostly to please Dheeraj, "I mean Dheeraj, which team did you say you head?" He was listed as 'Head HR' in her list.

"People Care team. Here at QSoft, we don't treat people as resources; they are very important to us. We are not just a traditional HR team; we are here to take care of our people in every possible way. So the HR team at QSoft is called the People Care team. And I head the team for this location."

He seemed to be rattling off a rehearsed speech. His attitude towards the investigation of the death of one of his 'people' didn't seem to indicate any 'care' to Ishani!

"So tell us about Manjiri. Whatever you can," Neil said.

"OK," Dheeraj said but seemed rather unsure of what to say. Then he began with, "She was with us for 8 years. Overall a good person, I would say."

Obviously he was going to need more prodding. Ishani nodded and said, "Tell us about her personality. What was your overall impression of her? Was she a good manager?"

"Yeah, well. She was a good manager, overall. She could make a very good impression in meetings. She was articulate and spoke her mind, no matter what."

Ishani probed further, "Did anyone have any problems with her?"

"She was quite aggressive sometimes. She also complained a lot about many things. Sometimes, she used to be quite harsh with people. But I guess, generally people working with her, the managers who reported to her were OK with her. Well mostly. Only Lokesh Mehta, had issues with her. That too only recently; she had said no to his promotion and he had come to us asking us to intervene."

"So then what happened?" Neil asked.

"I had a joint meeting with them. To start with Lokesh was angry and aggressive but by the end he had calmed down. Manjiri had come prepared to cut him down to size. Towards the end of the meeting she presented us with data that revealed his incompetency and gave several examples to prove her point. He had left feeling cornered."

"Did he complain again?" Neil asked.

"He didn't complain again officially. But I am sure, his ego was hurt. He didn't like to be put down like that; especially by a woman," Dheeraj said and then looked away.

That last statement touched a chord in Ishani's heart. She had her own share of trouble being a talented woman detective in a field that was considered male territory. She had seen incompetent men react strongly and negatively to her.

Dheeraj looked at her and said, "No offense to women really, but some women try to prove they are better than men. That is not a good thing; men don't like it. It is a fact of life."

Then he turned to Neil and said, "Later, I told Lokesh that maybe in the next cycle he would be reporting to another GM and could get a chance to get promoted. I had to motivate him you know. Manjiri had just not thought about that when she was proving her point about why she had not promoted him."

Ishani asked, "Is that a common problem? You needing to handle disappointed people?"

Dheeraj made a face and said, "Umm, yes to some extent. But people like Manjiri make our lives difficult. You know, honesty and all is fine in theory. But, if you want people to remain happy, you can't be so blunt about their shortcomings. You have to put a positive spin on it."

"Did anyone else have any complaints about her?" Neil asked.

Dheeraj thought about it and then replied, rather quietly, "No, no one else had complained".

Ishani looked at the list she had and asked about other managers who had reported to Manjiri.

"Well, they never complained to the People Care team about her. The overall impression everyone had was that they were happy with her management style. Ajit & Sandeep had been working with her for over three years and I guess had become very comfortable with her style." Dheeraj paused but it was obvious that he did have more information. It almost seemed like he was deciding whether to say anything more or not. Thankfully, he did continue, "Then there is Dilip. She was rather too fond of Dilip. In fact, people talked about that behind her back. It was like she was in love with the guy!"

After some moments of silence, Dheeraj continued without any prompting, "When the promotions were discussed everyone expected her to make a case for Dilip's promotion; quite surprisingly she didn't. But he didn't complain either."

When Dheeraj seemed to have said all he wanted to, Neil asked, "How were Manjiri's interactions with your team?"

"Like I said, she was very aggressive... and unforgiving. If someone made a mistake, she would be quick to point it out and then she would want that person to accept the mistake; say it in so many words, not just correct it. She was harsh with my team; exacting. One person in particular found it very difficult to work with her."

"Who is this person?" Neil asked

"Nisha Khanna. She was scared to work on any project in which Manjiri was involved."

Dheeraj talked about Manjiri and her wrong attitude for a few more minutes. Then finally Neil asked about the mishap, "Dheeraj, now, can you please tell us what happened on the night of March16th?"

Dheeraj kept quiet for some time, probably collecting his thoughts. Then he started in a sombre tone, "We all went to have dinner around 9:00 PM. A buffet had been set up and we ate at leisure. I think it was around 9:50 PM when Gautam, Jayant and I went to watch TV in the recreation centre.

We watched news for some time and then started playing cards when a few others sauntered in. When I went to my tent, it was past 1 AM. I was very sleepy, so I hit the bed right away."

"Who were you sharing the tent with?"

"Hemant. Manjiri's boss. He had left the recreation centre earlier in the evening. When I went to my tent, he was already asleep."

"When did you find out that Manjiri was missing?" asked Neil.

"Next morning I was the first one to go for breakfast. I think it was just before 7 AM. I was chatting with the Wild Outdoors folks as our team slowly trickled in. We were to start the session at 8:00 AM so everyone was expected to finish breakfast by then. Everyone got there by 7:30; except for Manjiri. When I asked around, no one knew where she was and no one had seen her. Sangeeta and Manjiri were in the same tent so I asked Sangeeta. The night before, Sangeeta had gone to bed right after dinner; she had a headache. She said she didn't know when Manjiri had come in or if she had come in at all. She said when she got up in the morning, Manjiri was not there. She had assumed that Manjiri had already gone for breakfast."

"Then what happened?" Ishani asked in a sympathetic tone.

"We started searching for her; calling out to her and looking around everywhere. We kept searching for a while, thinking she must be somewhere on the campsite.

"When we had been searching for over an hour, we began to worry. I tried to call her on her cell phone to see if she would pick up. As expected, her phone was out of reach. She of course would have been able to receive the call only if she had gone away from the campsite. The only phone network that worked on the campsite was BSNL. Atul and I were the only ones from QSoft who were carrying BSNL phones.

"Then Jivaji came to me and asked whether we should call the police. On taking stock of the situation I agreed with him. Jivaji went to the local police station and within a short while a police jeep came over, followed by afire truck. Once the police arrived, they took charge. They took a small row boat from the shore. One of Jivaji's men, and two firemen along with a constable got on it and rowed in. Some distance from the shore, the firemen dived in. They kept disappearing underwater and coming up for air after short intervals of time. It seemed as though they were moving in a circle. We were all waiting on the shore. Then one guy shouted, 'Here, down here.' Before we could understand what exactly he was talking about, he and the other guy both disappeared underwater. In a short while they came up and they were holding something. They got on that boat and came back." He paused and then continued, "By that time we had all guessed what was going to happen but still it was quite a shock when they brought Manjiri's lifeless body ashore."

"It was such a shock! Everyone was stunned and didn't know what to do. Then the police wanted to talk to each one of us. When did we see Manjiri last? How well did we know her? Could she swim? And on and on and on."

"After some time, I talked to Atul and we made a call to Surya, my boss, who is the overall head of People Care for all of QSoft, to inform him."

Ishani and Neil kept quiet, waiting for Dheeraj to come out of his memories ofthat fateful day. Finally, it was Ishani who broke the silence to ask, "As per the post mortem, Manjiri had consumed alcohol. Can you tell us about that?"

Dheeraj looked annoyed and said, "QSoft does not allow alcohol on any of its official outings, like this one was. We didn't supply any alcohol and we didn't encourage people to drink."

"Who else, apart from Manjiri had had alcohol that night?" Ishani tried a different approach.

Dheeraj looked away and said, "I don't know. I don't know how Manjiri managed to get alcohol. I didn't see anyone drink."

Neil signalled to indicate that she should drop the topic and instead asked, "One more question. Do you know if Manjiri was a good swimmer?"

"She was not a good swimmer but she was taking swimming lessons. She had recently boasted to me about how she was able to swim about 50 feet now." Dheeraj said. Then he added as an afterthought, "But Manjiri was rather reckless. She would not have thought about the risks and would have decided to just swim by herself. She was quite capable of that."

So according to Dheeraj, Manjiri was working at a senior position in a big company, handling different responsibilities, handling so many senior managers and yet so reckless that she would not think about the risks of swimming out alone when she wasn't a good swimmer!

"But, if she intended to go swimming, wouldn't she have changed into a swimming costume?" asked Neil.

Dheeraj shook his head and said, "She might have decided to go swimming after she went down to the lake and it would have seemed like too much effort to go back to the tent to change. Anyway, she was in shorts and a t-shirt, not flowing clothes."

After a couple of minutes, when Dheeraj realized that Neil and Ishani had become quiet and were not asking him any more question, he asked them if they would like to go to the canteen and have a cup of coffee. Both Ishani and Neil said yes, almost simultaneously. Then they looked at each other and smiled.

In the canteen, Dheeraj sat them at a table and went to the counter to get coffee for them. When he was out of the earshot, Ishani said, "You know, I was mulling over the stuff that Dheeraj mentioned—about the three people who disliked Manjiri, a woman, because she was exacting. They found her harsh."

Neil looked at her and raised his eye brows in question.

"Well…. You know, men in her shoes would have been admired for their 'brutal honesty' and 'focus on quality'," Ishani couldn't keep the sarcasm out of her voice.

Neil gave her a sardonic look and said, "Let's keep our feelings about the unfairness of the world out of this. Let us focus on the case and what has happened."

CHAPTER 3

As they stepped out of the air conditioned premises of QSoft, they were hit by a wall of heat. It was the middle of April (the 16th to be precise) and temperatures had started climbing towards the 40° mark. Compared to Delhi's summers, this was quite mild and didn't bother Neil. But he could see that Ishani was feeling the impact, though she didn't say anything about it.

As he drove out of the Tech Park, Neil looked across to Ishani, who had been rather quiet since his cutting remark to her. He opened the conversation with, "Hey there partner! I hope you're not mad at me."

Ishani seemed taken aback by his words, his tone and looked at him in surprise.

Neil smiled and said, "I understand where you are coming from, but we do need to keep our feelings a side."

He was relieved to see her smile in response and say, "Yes, of course. You're right. Let's focus on the case."

Now that Ishani seemed to be back in the right frame of mind, he turned the conversation back to the case, "So what do you think of our Mr. Seth?"

She said, "Mr. Seth was quite obviously unhappy with Manjiri. He clearly disliked her."

"You are right. He is also unhappy that the investigation has been reopened. That could be because he thinks it will hurt QSoft."

Ishani was quiet for a while and when Neil turned to look at her she seemed deep in thought. "Ishani?" he prompted.

"Sorry, I was trying to think back to our conversation with him. To be honest, I am unable to make up my mind about him as a person. He seemed to be spouting lines he didn't really believe in. Makes me think that he's not a very honest person…"

She was making a good point. "I don't know if it would be useful now since it's been a while since the incident, but could we have people followed? And could we tap their conversations?"

"I suggested shadowing to the Commissioner. Yes, it has been a while but when people know that we are investigating again, they might get jittery." Neil liked the way she thought but he wanted to be cautious. "Tapping phones is a very sensitive topic and we can't do that."

He turned to look at Ishani when she said, "Could any of Manjiri's co-workers actually have murdered her? These are people from a high-profile industry, working in a very well-known company, earning very high salaries. What reason could they have to murder any of their own?"

Neil shook his head and replied, "I am sure you must have come across some weird cases in the last six years that you have been working with Abhijeet. As they say, truth is stranger than fiction. People are not always rational; individuals who seem absolutely harmless and docile are capable of some horrible actions and crimes."

After tackling the unruly traffic in the IT Park, driving got easier as Neil hit the highway.

"By the way, I forgot to mention that we are going to be able to go through Manjiri's personal belongings that police picked up for investigation; things like her laptop, cell phone and some handwritten notes etc., that they got from her flat."

Ishani looked surprised and said, "Why are they still available to us? Weren't they returned to her family?"

"No one came to complete the legalities and take them back. So the police still has custody over them."

After a few seconds Ishani asked, "What about her flat? Is someone staying there? Can we go and look at the place? And who owns it now?"

"Manjiri had made a will soon after her parents died four years ago, leaving the flat to her aunt and two cousins. But then she made another will just a few months back. As per the latest will, she left the flat to two of her friends. Her aunt is going to court to dispute the new will. We can discuss this in detail when we meet her advocate, Ms. Aditi Kulkarni."

Both of them got quiet after this and Neil switched on the radio. They were headed to meet Inspector Morey, who would accompany them to the campsite, on the backwaters of Mulshi dam.

CHAPTER 4

As they got out of the city, the traffic thinned considerably and the landscape seemed to get a lot greener. Ishani marvelled at the landscape that seemed to defy the scorching heat of the sun shining so brightly.

They reached a small dhaba where Inspector Morey was supposed to meet them. While waiting for the Inspector they asked for some tea. Ishani looked around the place and saw a corner full of pictures of various gods. Ganapati was placed right next to Ram and Sita; then there was Shiva, with six-pack abs and Parvati seated on his lap. There was Balaji there and Vitthal Rakhumai too.

"All the gods you can think of are here," She said turning to face Neil.

Neil turned his head to look at the corner. "I am not really into Gods," he said and smiled when she raised her eyebrows at his words; then said, "I know all the important ones in their original forms."

Ishani found herself laughing at that and then wondered if he had said it only to get a reaction from her, because he was smiling a big, satisfied smile now. He was actually able to identify all the ones displayed there and they entered into an interesting conversation about gods and their various forms.

Inspector Morey reached in about ten minutes on his motor bike. He looked younger and fitter than Ishani had thought a police inspector would be.

Sitting there at the dhaba, Inspector Morey explained to them how it had all happened. He explained how one of Jivaji's men, who had taken out a canoe to test its water-worthiness, had jumped in the water some distance from the shore and had seen what looked like a human body underwater. Jivaji had not mentioned the body to Dheeraj because he didn't want to raise an alarm unnecessarily, but had suggested that they should go to the police. Inspector Morey happened to be there when Jivaji reached the police station and had decided to call the fire brigade as well. It had been easy to find the body, as they had looked in the very spot pointed out by Jivaji's man.

He then talked about the investigation; how they had been talking to people, but had to stop abruptly. He mentioned that the last person to see Manjiri alive was Mr. Atul Vaidya, QSoft's head for the Pune centre. Also, the next time they spoke to everyone from the program was at the QSoft premises. By that time, all of them had probably been coached and maybe even coerced into answering him in a specific way. All of them had provided the Inspector with a matching story. Inspector Morey found it very suspicious that their stories matched so perfectly!

Their conversation with Dheeraj and Inspector Morey's description of the investigation were good enough reasons to reinvestigate, Ishani thought.

They headed out to the campsite; Inspector Morey on his bike followed by Neil and Ishani in the car. As they drove around the lake towards the campsite, Ishani was mesmerized by the beauty and the serenity of the location. Continuing to look outside the window, she said, "Oh wow! What a perfect setting!"

Neil snorted and asked, "For what? Murder?"

She turned around to look at him and saw that he had said it only to create an impact. Looking at his smiling face she smiled herself and said, "Yeah! One can kill off one's husband here! Maybe with the help of a secret lover."

She loved seeing him taken aback. Getting carried away she asked him with a sweet smile, "Neil, can you swim?"

He laughed out loud and said, "I feel sorry for the poor fellow who will end up marrying you!"

"What do you know? Any man I decide to marry would be the luckiest guy in the whole world!" She retorted.

It was so easy to get into this kind of banter with Neil, even though she had known him for less than a day. Ishani was smiling to herself when they reached the entry gate of the campsite.

They were met by Jivaji Jadhav of "Wild Outdoors". He had a certain simplicity about him. He had innocent eyes and spoke with a soft voice, "Namaskar sir, madam. Welcome to this campsite of Wild Outdoors. I, Jivaji Jadhav. I will show you the campsite. First we can go to the recreation centre."

Jivaji pointed to an octagonal building and they all walked towards it. It was right in front of the entrance gate. Anyone coming from the gate would have to pass by the recreation centre to go anywhere else on the campsite.

Inside the recreation centre, Jivaji showed them a plaster model of the place and explained its layout. The campsite was spread over a few acres of land right next to the lake but it was on a higher level from the lake. The lake was formed by the backwaters of the dam. The shore was quite peculiar, forming a "wide N shape made up of an inverted 'V' and another 'V' juxtaposed together. The inverted 'V' was quite wide and had a shallow, gradual incline. The other 'V' shaped section of the shore was like a cliff, with a sudden drop on both sides. Wild Outdoors had setup river crossing equipment on the cliff section of the shore and they took people down to the shallow section of the shore for water activities like canoeing. While the recreation centre was right at the entrance, the dining hall was at the rear end of the campsite. The recreation centre, the dining hall, the kitchen attached to the dining hall and the conference/meeting hall were the only constructed buildings. The residential arrangements consisted of tents that were setup in clusters of three or four tents. It looked like there were two clusters of tents along the lake and the remaining six clusters were close to the conference hall. Having seen the model, they had a fair idea of what to expect when they started walking across the campsite. There was a winding dirt path, which they were following to the dining hall. The lake was on their right and it offered a serene backdrop to the unsettling mystery they were trying to solve with a view that seemed to go on forever. You could see the other shore, but it was quite some distance away.

Jivaji was pointing out things to them as they walked along.

"This is open ground which we are using for physical activities and games."

"We are sometimes setting one outdoor classroom under this mango tree."

"This is conference hall with all required facilities like big screen and projector. Forty people are seating comfortably."

The said hall was on their left and had big glass windows, through which one could see the lake.

"We are having 16 fixed tents, twelve are two people tents and four are four people tents",

Jivaji spoke English with the grammar of Marathi, something that Ishani had heard a lot in her line of work. She wanted to switch to Marathi so that Jivaji would be more comfortable, but then Neil would not understand the conversation.

She was surprized when Neil asked in Marathi, "Didn't the model show more tents than there actually are?"

Jivaji, too looked at Neil in surprise. He expressed his relief with "Sahib, you speak Marathi, is it? That is very good. Then I can explain in Marathi." And he proceeded to answer in Marathi, "When needed, we can setup other tents. But they are smaller tents and don't have toilet & bath facility inside the tent. The model shows those kinds of tents also as part of the setup."

The last cluster of permanent tents was on a slight incline on the side of the lake. A dirt path went down to the lakeshore from between this cluster and the dining hall. The climb down to the lake was about 35 to 40 feet away from this point.

They walked across to the dining hall which was about 150 feet away, from the track going down to the lake. While there was a good amount of shade, thanks to all the trees around the campsite, it felt good to enter the dining hall. It was a big and airy room with a high ceiling. The right side of the hall was completely taken up by French windows that opened on to a deck. On the left side, close to the entrance was the cashier's desk. Right in the front, by the kitchen entrance was a row of serving tables where they must have kept the buffet. Next to that was a water cooler.

They made their way to a table and sat down and Jivaji got them water from the cooler. Neil opened the topic of the fateful night by asking, "Jivaji, please tell us exactly what happened on March 16th and 17th when the QSoft people had come over for their program".

Jivaji explained how they came in a bus, how the registration was done and how the tents were allocated to them before going to lunch.

"Tell us more about the tent allocation. Did they stay in two people tents or four people tents?" Ishani asked.

Jivaji nodded and answered, "There were only 18 of them and we have 12 two people tents. So they all stayed in two people tents. That Manjiri madam was in that tent", he said pointing to the tent right next to the dirt path going down to the lake. "And there was another madam with her in that tent".

"Who was in the tent next to theirs?" Neil asked.

"No one was in the tent next to theirs."

"I see. What happened after lunch?"

"Some walked around, some sat here saying they wanted to be indoors and some went to the lake shore. We always tell people that they will not get cell phone range except for BSNL. But people always bring their phones and check if they can get range. Some of the people from QSoft also did that."

"Did any of them…" Neil and Ishani said at the same time. Neil looked at her and indicated that she can go ahead, so Ishani asked, "Did any of them have BSNL phones?"

"Dheeraj sir had a BSNL phone. And Atul sir also had. They had told everyone at lunch that if anyone needed to make any calls, then they could borrow the phone from either Dheeraj sir or Atul sir".

"What about the others?" Neil asked.

"We are not knowing about others sir." Jivaji said. Looking at him, it seemed like he wanted to share something but was unsure. Inspector Morey too noticed and said, "Jivaji, what is it? Don't hesitate to share information."

Jivaji looked at Neil and then at Inspector again and said, "Sir we found a BSNL SIM card two days back. It was found in the sand on the shore. We didn't know if it was from QSoft group or someone else. Three other groups came after the QSoft team."

Inspector Morey looked at Neil, then back at Jivaji and said, "Where is the SIM card? Bring it."

Jivaji walked over to the cashier's desk, unlocked a drawer, picked out a small envelope and brought it over. He handed it over to Inspector Morey and said, "We put it in one of our phones, but it is not working."

Inspector Morey shook his head and said, "Jivaji, you should have informed me."

Neil asked, "Has anyone enquired about the SIM card?"

Jivaji said, "No sir, no one has asked about a SIM card. But we think it must be from the QSoft team only. That time the water level was higher and maybe it fell in the water."

Inspector Morey took out his white handkerchief and spread it on the table. Then he opened the envelope and dropped the SIM card on the handkerchief. If it had been in the water for some time, it was probably useless to take so many precautions. In addition to that, the Wild Outdoor guys had already handled it.

Even so, the Inspector put it back in the envelope with the same degree of care and said, "Jivaji, I am going to take this with me as possible evidence in our case. You will need to come over to the police station and write a report for finding this."

Neil turned to Jivaji and said, "Let's get back to the QSoft team. Tell us what happened after they had lunch."

Jivaji then explained how they had a session in the conference room, tea was served there and then they all went for the river crossing exercise. After that, around 7:00 PM they all went to the open ground.

"We had setup a camp fire in the open ground. The QSoft people wanted a barbeque. They had brought everything with them and only asked us for some coal, which we provided. They all sat around the fire and sang and danced. They also started drinking beer and also whisky."

Ishani stopped him and said, "You don't allow people to drink here, I thought."

Looking a little embarrassed Jivaji said, "Madam we don't allow general people. But when groups come from these big companies, they always bring alcohol and drink. We don't stop them; otherwise they will not come for outings."

25

Neil asked, "Did you get a chance to see who was drinking? Was Manjiri drinking?"

"Sir, there were three ladies but Manjiri madam was the only one drinking. Amongst the men, most of them were drinking."

"All of them were drinking?" Ishani couldn't help asking.

"Most of them were drinking, madam. Some two, three people were not drinking. Dheeraj sir was drinking but Atul sir was not drinking. He was only drinking water or Thumps Up." Jivaji kept mentioning Atul and Dheeraj, looked like he knew only the two of them well.

Neil turned to Inspector Morey and said, "When you came here the first time, did you ask people about alcohol?"

Inspector Morey looked a little sheepish and said, "Jivaji and his men did say once or twice that people had been drinking. So we enquired, but when everyone we spoke to at QSoft said that they had not been drinking, we went with it. We went through the tents to look for anything that might be relevant. We didn't find any bottles anywhere.

"We found two-three empty beer bottles. But they were in the lake. Only later on, when the post mortem report came, did it became clear that alcohol was definitely involved."

Neil nodded to acknowledge this new piece of information and then turned to Jivaji, "Where did all the bottles go?"

"Sir, one sir had a car. He had driven out at night and came back early in the morning. He took away all the bottles. We had told the police."

Inspector Morey looked down at that. Ishani didn't blame him; the police had done what they were asked to do.

Neil went back to Jivaji and said, "Tell us what happened after the drinking session."

Jivaji continued, "They came in to the dining hall for dinner at around 9:15 PM. Many people ate very little but the dinner went on for a long time. After dinner Manjiri madam said something to Atul sir and then went out. We saw her walk down to the lake.

"Some people went to the recreation centre. Atul sir waited in the dining hall. Then he made a phone call which went on for a long time. We were waiting here for him to finish. From here, I watched another sir go down to the lake. In a few minutes we saw him come up and go towards the recreation centre."

"Who was it?" Neil asked.

"I don't know sir. From here, I couldn't recognize him." Jivaji said. He looked at Neil almost apologetically. Ishani made a note about this and Jivaji continued his story, "As soon as Atul sir finished the call, we locked up the dining hall. We wanted to go and sleep. We had to start early the next morning as QSoft had asked breakfast to be served from 6:30 AM and tea even before that."

Inspector Morey said, "They have tents for the staff behind the kitchen."

Neil asked, "How do we go there?"

Jivaji said, "You can go this way sir, through the kitchen. This is a short cut. Otherwise, from outside also we can go."

They all walked out through the backdoor of the kitchen, to see four staff tents setup in a row. At the other end, there were toilet and shower tents.

From here, you could see the conference hall and you could also see the recreation centre in the distance.

"I didn't notice these tents in the model." Ishani mused.

Jivaji smiled and said, "Madam is correct. Staff tents were setup much later, much after the model was made."

"How many people from the Wild Outdoor were here that night, Jivaji?" Neil asked.

"Six of us; there were the cooks, the people who take care of all the different activities we offer like river crossing, canoeing and the general service staff."

"What about security staff?"

"There are four guards who stay here. Two work the day shift and two the night shift. All of them were here."

"Where do they stay?"

"They stay in the last tent, sir. If there are more staff people, we setup one more tent."

They made their way back but from the outside, around the building. Instead of entering the dining hall, Neil walked towards the lake and the others followed him. Till you got to the point from where you would start climbing down, you didn't see the lakeshore itself. From there, it was a gradual and easy climb down. Once you got to the lake shore, you could only see the dining hall and the two tents that were right next to the path coming down to the lake. So only someone standing at the French windows of the dining hall or on the deck or right by the two tents would have been able to see what happened down here.

They walked the length of the shore till the sharp uphill turn. It looked to be about 60 to 70 degrees incline, impossible to climb up. The canoes were all turned upside down on one side of the shore. There were also three row boats, one of which was turned upside down.

"Last month when the QSoft people came, water was up till here", Jivaji pointed to a rock on the shore. It was about eight feet away from the present water line and about one and half feet higher. "We found the SIM card somewhere here," he said, indicating four feet outside the current water line.

Inspector Morey said, "The incline is gradual for another 30 feet, I think; then it's a sudden dip."

"If we assume that Manjiri went into the water, and drowned on reaching the sudden dip, she should be somewhere within the range of about 40-45 feet inside the water line at that time." Neil said.

"Yes. I think someone must have taken her in, either in a boat or maybe swimming." Inspector Morey said.

"Is it possible that she could swim a little, so she did swim out and then got a cramp or felt really ill in some way and so could not continue to swim? She could not return and even if she tried calling for help, no one could hear her, and she drowned," Ishani asked.

"250 feet?" Neil asked incredulously.

Remembering that Jivaji had talked about the river crossing, Ishani asked him, "That evening were you present when they did the river crossing exercise?"

"Yes, madam."

"Some people get scared while they do it for the first time, right?"

"Yes, a lot of people get scared but many will tell that they are not scared or it is not a big deal. Only some people say they are scared."

"Did all the QSoft people participate in the exercise? And were any of them scared?"

"All of them did it. Some said they were scared."

"What about Manjiri?"

"Madam, mostly women would be more scared. Sangeeta madam and that third madam, both were scared. But not Manjiri madam."

"She was not scared at all?" Ishani wondered if Manjiri had a lack of fear bordering on recklessness, which could have proven to be very dangerous.

"She had done it earlier. Many times she said. She was not scared, she knew how to wear the harness, and she knew how the carabiners worked."

"We found out that she used go for a lot of adventure activities like mountaineering, river rafting, even bungee jumping", Inspector Morey pitched in.

When they walked back to the dining hall, Ishani noticed that a table for four was setup by the French windows, under a fan. Jivaji urged them, "Sir, madam, we would like you to have lunch. We make simple, but very good food."

Inspector Morey was the first one to speak, "I bring my own lunch, so I'll head back. Neil sir, Ishani madam, you please go ahead."

Ishani was in two minds about it but she was really hungry. She looked at Neil; he too seemed to be in two minds.

"OK. We will have lunch but we will pay for it." Neil said.

"No, no. We want you to have lunch as guests, sir. We are not going to charge you." Jivaji replied.

But Neil was firm about it. He said, "Jivaji, Ishani and I will be able to have lunch with you only if you charge us for it. We will need the bill and we will be getting the company to pay for it. Like the Inspector, we too are working. We can't eat here as your guests."

Ishani was glad when Jivaji agreed and asked the person hovering in the background to serve lunch.

It was nice to sit by the French windows and savour the simple food. They also kept the conversation away from the case. Jivaji entertained them by telling them about a film shooting that had recently taken place in the vicinity.

After the meal they talked to the security guards, and around 4:00 PM, made their way back to the city. Neil drove quietly and Ishani decided to call Geetika. She put the call through and smiled listening to the caller tune, Dil chahata hai… Kabhi na beete… Finally Geetika picked up just as Ishani was about to hang up.

"Hi Shani! How are you?! Back in Mumbai or what?" Geetika was her exuberant self.

"Hi Geetu, I am in Pune actually."

At first, Geetika insisted that Ishani stay with her. But when Ishani explained that she was working on a case, she settled for meeting her as soon as possible. They agreed to meet on Thursday evening and talked a little more, before ending the call.

"An old friend?" Neil asked when the call got over.

"Yes. A very old friend; we studied together. She is like the sister I never had", Ishani said with a smile. "She works at a pathology lab here. We plan to meet on Thursday evening. I know you warned me that our evenings would be busy and not to make other plans, but I would really like to meet her."

Neil looked at her, smiled and said, "That's fine. Call her over to the hotel. You can sit and chat, away from her hubby and son." He had used the same words that she had in her phone conversation.

"They are going out of town, hubby and son, that is. We'll see."

They both got quiet for some time and as they reached the city limits, the traffic had thickened to the point that Neil was constantly driving in second gear. Ishani was glad that she was not the one driving. Then remembering her earlier surprise, Ishani asked, "I never knew you spoke Marathi!"

Neil shrugged and said, "I know a lot of languages. I have been speaking, Marathi, Bengali, Gujarati and Punjabi since childhood." Then looking at her expression, he smiled and said, "My grandparents came from four different states. My mother's father was a Punjabi Sikh, her mother is Maharashtrian. My father's father was Rajasthani but from Bengal and his mother Gujarati. And all of them spoke to us in their own languages. So my sister and I picked up all these languages. I studied languages for my graduation before going into law."

"Wow", Ishani didn't know what else to say.

CHAPTER 5

When the alarm went off at 5:30 AM on Tuesday, Ishani had a very strong urge to turn it off and go back to sleep. But she forced herself to getup. She had a cup of tea; that always helped. Now she was completely awake.

She went to the gym thinking she would run on the treadmill for a while and do some weights. She entered the gym and just stood there. There was only one other person there, Neil! He was running on the gym's only treadmill; dressed in shorts and a vest, he looked really fit. Tall and slim; running at a good speed, he looked graceful and at ease. She knew he was 37 but in those shorts, his muscular arms swinging as he ran, Ishani felt he looked very energetic and much younger. He saw her in the mirror, smiled and waved at her. She waved back and got onto the stationary cycle.

She had been cycling for about twenty minutes and had begun to wonder if Neil was ever going to get off that treadmill, when he finally slowed down. Then he said, "Great minds and all that…" and gave her another smile. Ishani said, "Yeah… all that," but felt like saying, 'Forget the mind! You have a great body!'

When Neil got off, she went to the treadmill and started running. She could see him in the mirror as he started working the different machines.

Boy, this was going to be difficult. She didn't want to feel attracted to him! 'He is a married man!' she told herself. But her mind was not listening to her. She ran only for about ten minutes and then went to the free weights kept on the other side. Fortunately, she didn't see Neil from here. She worked the weights for a while and then came around. She wanted to do some ab exercises, but the only place for that would be right next to where Neil was doing crunches. Being so aware of him physically, she just could not bring herself to do that. So she did some pushups against a wall and decided to call it a day. She said, "Bye Neil" and was about to walk out of the door, when he said, "Bye, partner. See you at breakfast at eight."

She walked back to her room and just sat on one of the chairs for a few minutes. She needed to collect her thoughts. She switched on the TV and selected a news channel. That would help take her mind off Neil and his physique. Taking off her workout clothes, she went into the bathroom and got into the shower. It felt good to let the water run over her body. When she came out the TV news reader was running a report about the Law minister accusing the Minister of State for Industries of meddling in the affairs of the law ministry. Ishani found herself laughing. Politicians were such good entertainers, she thought! She had been absolutely right in turning on the news channel.

She felt cheerful as she got ready. She wore a cream coloured shirt with her jeans and like the previous day, tied her hair into a ponytail. Today, they would be going over to see Manjiri's aunt and if time permitted, her lawyer. So, instead of the canvas shoes she had worn the previous day, she put on flat sandals. They were easier to take off if required.

Ishani went down for breakfast five minutes before eight. Neil was nowhere to be seen yet, so she chose a table close to the window overlooking a small garden. She put her backpack on a spare chair, and asked for a cup of tea. She had just gotten up to go and get some food from the breakfast buffet, when Neil entered the coffee shop. She waved to him and he walked over. He looked formal and very good in brown trousers and a light green shirt. If she closed her eyes she could still imagine him in his shorts and vest but it was not bothering her as much now. He smiled at her and said, "I am not late, you are early." She smiled back, nodded and said, "Yeah and I am really hungry! Let me go get something."

They drove over to meet with Mrs. Rekha and Mr. Vikram Panday, Manjiri's aunt and uncle. Mrs. Panday was Majiri's mother's younger sister and claimed that she had been very close to Manjiri. She was the one disputing the new will.

Mr. & Mrs. Panday lived in a penthouse in one of the developments that boasted of three 12-storied towers. After a brief security check at the gate, they made their way to the Panday penthouse. The door was opened by Mr. Panday and they entered the living room. Mrs. Panday was in the bathroom, they were told. Mr. Panday was a well-dressed man. He wore crisply ironed blue jeans and a maroon, collared T-shirt. He was of average height and his hair was mostly grey. He was more than eager to talk to them. So in the ten minutes they spent waiting for Mrs. Panday, they had heard about how Mr. Panday had retired from a very high position in a company in the Oil & Gas industry and moved to Pune only two years ago. He found it difficult to be retired; they had to get used to a different lifestyle, even though they had made an effort to maintain their lifestyle as much as possible. They had made sure that the apartment they bought for themselves was in the right locality and came with all the right trimmings. Each room in their four bedroom apartment was air-conditioned and had a flat-screen TV. They had a separate room for the servant. He added how it was essential to have a live-in servant if they wanted to continue to live at the standards they were used to. Ishani was getting bored listening to the man. She looked at Neil and guessed that he too was bored but was making an effort not to show it.

Ishani was wondering how long she would have to listen to this "lifestyle" drivel, when Mrs. Panday came in. She was a chubby woman of medium height, a round face with a double chin and short hair that was dyed pitch black. She walked as if she was in a hurry. She wore a pink salwar suit with no dupatta. She looked like a middle class housewife; a poorly dressed one at that. Somehow her overall appearance was contradictory to the whole high-end lifestyle spiel her husband had been giving them.

Mrs. Pandey sat down on the chair next to her husband and smiled at them. "Hello, hello. I am Rekha Panday. And you must be the detectives who wanted to talk to me." She talked like she walked, in a hurry. "I had planned to be all ready but what to do, my son called from Australia unexpectedly.

"Today was not our usual day to chat. We chat on Skype twice a week. My son and daughter-in-law are very busy. They are near Brisbane; both working, but today is a holiday for them. And they have a small son, so they need help, you know. So when they call, I can't say no. And my grandson then has to talk to me."

Ishani was waiting for a pause in Mrs. Panday's hurried monologue to cut in and steer the conversation to the investigation. But the woman just seemed to go on at breakneck speed.

Everyone turned around in alarm, when Neil started coughing. Mrs. Panday got up saying, "Let me get you some water", and walked to the kitchen. When Ishani looked at Neil, he winked at her and she realized that he had done that just to stop the tirade. Taking the cue, as soon as Mrs. Panday came in with the water, while Neil was taking a glass from the tray, Ishani said, "Mrs. Panday, as you know, we are here to talk about Manjiri, your niece who died last month."

"Yes, yes, of course." Mrs Panday said and then continued, "You know, it was such a shock for me and my family to learn about her death. She was only 43 and quite healthy. Who would expect her to just swim out on her own like that and drown?"

Neil had stopped coughing after sipping some water and he was all ready to start asking questions.

"You are Manjiri's closest relative, Mrs. Panday. So we would like to hear about her from you", Neil said.

"Yes, yes. I am her mother's younger sister. We were always close. I was only 17 and studying when Manjiri was born. I saw her grow up, you know. After I got married, I couldn't meet my sister as much as I would have liked. My husband was in a transferable job and we were posted to remote places. But I tried to come over as much as possible, and I had them come over to our place many times. You know, we have always had a high standard of living, we stayed in big houses, always had servants. I wanted my sister and Manjiri to also be able to see all that and enjoy the luxury. My sister used to come to visit often till Manjiri went to college. Then, we didn't get to meet as often. But we always talked on the phone. Every week, we would talk and tell each other about the day-to-day happenings in our respective households." She was saying a lot and it was more about her, not about Manjiri.

Ishani was wondering if Neil was going to start coughing again, when she heard him literally cut in and say, "Mrs. Panday, can you please tell us about Manjiri? We need to know her as a person."

That seemed to do the trick. Mrs. Panday stopped and asked, "So when you say you want me to tell you about her, what you want to know?"

Ishani looked at Neil wishing that he would ask specific questions and not let the woman talk freely like this. He looked at Ishani once as though she had said it out loud and then turned back to Mrs. Pandey, "Was Manjiri a reckless person?"

"Manjiri was very adventurous, you know. From the childhood, she always wanted to do these kind of crazy things only. Always doing something or the other like going for treks in the Himalayas or bungee jumping even."

"But she used to be rather scared of water. I don't know why she just went into the deep water like that. If she was alone, she wouldn't go swimming in our society's pool also. But every summer she used to go off to Himalayas and…"

"Is it possible that someone else was there with her and that's why she went into the deep water?" Neil asked. He had taken control of the situation now. He asked the next question when he had heard what he was looking for, even though Mrs. Panday was still talking.

Mrs. Panday looked confused, "But police said she went in alone. That is what they told us".

Ishani jumped into the conversation and said, "That is what was believed. But now the case is reopened to investigate from other angles. One of the possibilities we are considering is whether there was someone with her when she went into the water."

"Oh! Oh, I see. I thought you wanted to talk to me because of the will. You know, Manjiri's lawyer is playing some game. She is now saying that Manjiri made a new will. But we know that can't be true. Manjiri made her will when my sister and brother-in-law died suddenly; four years ago. We were in Assam that time, but of course we came over immediately. Then Vikram helped Manjiri make the will before we went back." Though Mrs. Panday had gone off on a different track, this was useful information.

Surprisingly it was Mr. Panday who brought her back by saying, "Rekha, they are asking a different thing. Whether Manjiri would have gone in the deep by herself."

"But Vikram, I don't know. You know she never went swimming on her own."

Neil then addressed the next question to both of them. "When did you know about Manjiri's death?"

Mr. Panday replied, "On 17th March, at around 4:30 PM, a police inspector and a constable came home. They asked us if we knew Manjiri. When we told them that she was Rekha's niece, they told us that she had drowned that morning and her body had been sent for post mortem."

"What did you do, then?"

"They told us we had to go to Sassoon hospital to take the body once the post mortem was over." He paused for a few seconds and then went ahead, "Rekha was beside herself. I didn't know how to manage everything. So I called a friend of mine over. Manjiri's body was released to us on 18thand we performed the last rites on the same day."

"Did you know that Manjiri had gone for the outbound program?"

Mrs. Panday spoke very quietly, "Yes, I knew. I had talked to her on the morning of the 16th, when she was leaving for the campsite. She had told me that she would return on the 18th and that her phone would not work at the campsite."

"Do you know any of the people she worked with?"

Mrs. Panday thought for a bit and replied, "She had taken me to Hemant Joshi's place once. He was her boss but they were also very good friends." Then she went ahead, "But I don't think Hemant's wife had liked our visit. She wouldn't come out. When Hemant went inside saying he will call her, we could hear her yelling. He was trying to calm her down but she would not listen. She wanted us to leave."

"So did she come out?" Ishani asked.

"No. After a few minutes Hemant came out and told us that she was not feeling well so she would not come out." She hesitated for a moment and then said, "I had felt very awkward and wanted to leave, but not Manjiri. When Hemant came out and said his wife was not feeling well, she actually had smiled and said, 'I can understand her not feeling well.' I found that strange and even asked Manjiri about it."

"What did Manjiri tell you?"

"She said that Hemant's wife was jealous of working women and especially of Manjiri because she worked closely with Hemant and he respected her."

"Could you hear what Mrs. Joshi was saying when she refused to come out?"

"We could hear it partly. She was saying something like, 'I want her out of my house' and 'I refuse to meet them'."

"Do you remember when this was?"

Mrs. Panday did remember. "This was last year. Sometime in January, I remember because we had first gone shopping and seen a sweater just like the one I was wearing; mine was from Australia you know."

As Ishani made a note that they needed to talk to Mrs. Hemant Joshi, Neil asked, "Mrs. Panday, can you tell me why you think the new will is fraudulent."

Mrs. Panday looked at her husband, but he just nodded to her indicating that she should go ahead and say what she wanted to. "See after my sister died Manjiri made a will. As per that will, she had left everything to my daughter, me and a paternal cousin. Now, suddenly where did this new will come from? She had not told me anything. If she was changing the will she would have talked to me. Why would she want to hide it?"

Mr. Panday added, "Look, it's not as if my wife needs Manjiri's property. It is nothing compared to what we have. My daughter too is quite well off. But we think this new will is all fraud. Manjiri's advocate is making it up. My wife is Manjiri's closest relative and Manjiri would have told her if she had changed her will."

Mrs. Panday wanted to make another point, "See basically we want to stop wrong people from getting Manjiri's property."

"Where is your daughter Mr. Panday and what does she do?"

"Rashmi is married and settled in Delhi. Her husband is a businessman and she works with him. They are quite well off. They have their own house in Paschim Vihar. It's a very high-end locality". Mr. Panday said proudly.

"What is his name? Your son-in-law, that is. And what kind of business does he have?" Ishani wasn't sure why Neil was asking for this information.

"Vishal Bhatnagar. He has three different dealerships and he invests in various businesses."

CHAPTER 6

15 Apr 2012

They made their way to the IT Park. This time the traffic was not as bad. At QSoft, they would first be talking to Atul Vaidya, the Centre Head. Then Ishani had to talk to Nisha Khanna, while Neil went ahead and met some of the other folks.

Ishani was quiet for some time, thinking over the meeting they had just come out of. Neil laughed softly and said, "Those two were quite a pair. I don't know who I feel sorrier for!"

Ishani found herself laughing in agreement. "He talks a lot, but when she started talking, I didn't know how to stop her".

"But I don't think they have anything to do with Manjiri's death. Mrs. Panday seemed really sad about losing Manjiri and they genuinely believe that this will is fraudulent." Then after a pause, she asked him, "Why did you take down the details of their daughter and son-in-law?"

Neil turned to look at her, smiled and said, "Like you, I think that they are idiotic, silly and pompous and have nothing to do with the death, which is my gut feeling. However, I had to ask a few more questions even though they did not really fit with all the evidence."

"While my gut feeling is important here have been times when it has misguided me and I have ended up making big mistakes. So, even though I follow my instincts, I also make sure to collect all information possible".

Ishani just kept looking at him. Finally, Neil asked her, "What? That made you speechless?"

She said, "I am surprised to hear someone like you accept that you have made mistakes. And accept it so easily. And to someone, that I am sure, you look at as just a junior."

Neil was quiet for so long that Ishani thought that he was not going to reply at all. Then he said, "We all make mistakes Ishani. Life is all about making mistakes, learning from them and then going and making some more. I have made a lot of them; not just in work but in many of my choices.

"A few years ago, I would have had difficulty accepting my mistakes so easily, but now it does not bother me. Maybe because I have come to understand that, accepting one's mistakes is the only way to move ahead. It is the only way to not let the mistakes define whoI am. And for a person to accept their own mistakes is tough. Once that's done, it is not difficult to accept the min front of someone else."

Both of them were quiet for some time. Neil seemed to be deep in thought and when he spoke next, Ishani thought he had been thinking about what to say. "I'll be absolutely honest with you. I am not yet sure, what I think of you. But 'just a junior' is definitely not how I think of you".

Ishani sat quietly reflecting on how in this short conversation, Neil had gone from being a smart and sexy detective to so much more in her eyes.

They reached QSoft and just as they got out of the car for the security check, Neil's phone rang. As she made an entry for Neil and herself and got their "VISITOR" badges, Ishani couldn't help over hearing his conversation.

"Good morning.

"Yes, yes, started well. It got pretty late last night so I didn't call you.

"Yes, of course. I'll call you this evening. Will 10–10:30 be OK?

"Right, talk to you then".

Like the previous day, they were walked to the reception lobby. They told the receptionist that they were there to meet Atul Vaidya and sat on the same set of sofas as before.

Ishani was curious about who Neil had talked to. She contemplated whether she should prod him or not and finally gave in to her curiosity, "Neil, it seemed like you were talking about the case. Wasn't it? Who are you reporting to? Who is checking on our progress?"

Neil looked at her with a serious expression and then said, "Ishani, hopefully soon, I will share all these details with you. But for now, I am not going to answer your questions. It is not because I don't trust you or I don't want to share the information with you."

Ishani sat quietly for a moment. Then she thought about the conversation in the car, and what she thought about Neil. She smiled and said, "OK. I'll wait for you to tell me."

Today they didn't have to wait very long. Barely five minutes had passed since they had come in, when Mr. Atul Vaidya walked in to the lobby. He was a short, balding and chubby man, with a round face and sparkling eyes.

He came over, shook their hands and then accompanied them inside. He took them to the cafeteria for coffee. While having coffee he talked to them about a lot of things, from the weather and cricket to QSoft, their cultural club, movies and the current news. He talked a lot, but it was never one sided. He gauged their interest, their response and turned his conversation to suit them.

The way he talked about QSoft, it was very clear that he cared about the organization as well as the people. He also came across as very mature and responsible. One could easily see why he would be popular with people.

After about ten minutes, he looked at his watch, then said, "Let's go to my office so that we can talk without being overheard or interrupted", and got up.

When they entered Atul Vaidya's big office on the top floor, Ishani looked around and saw that the office was designed beautifully. It had a big table in mahogany and comfortable chairs in brown and beige. There was an arrangement of sofas by one wall, made cosy under the cover of venetian blinds. Atul went to the venetian blinds and opened them to reveal that the wall was made completely of glass. The view outside was quite something. You could see the mountains in the distance and thanks to being so high up you could also see a large water body in the distance.

"Right now, it's all brown and dried up. But come monsoon, the view is absolutely breath taking", Atul said.

"I can imagine", Ishani said, "Even now it's beautiful".

"Let's sit here on the sofas", Atul said.

Neil and Ishani sat opposite Atul Vaidya and Neil asked, "Mr. Vaidya, tell us about Manjiri, as you knew her."

"Please call me Atul. As you would have heard, in this industry we are all on first name basis with everyone. Mr. Vaidya would be my father", Atul smiled as he said this and then started talking about Manjiri. "I knew Manjiri long before she started working here at QSoft. She was a friend of my cousin and I had known her since her college days. She used to come over to my aunt's place quite often. In fact, I was the one who suggested that she join QSoft. I treated her like my cousin. I think she treated me like an older brother. She never really worked directly with me, but she used to come to me for advice".

Neil said, "What was she like? Was she a good employee?"

"She was a very good employee. But she was not very good at creating favourable impressions. People who worked in her teams always liked her and would hate being moved to any other team. But she ended up rubbing the senior executives, the support teams like the admin team and HR team or IT team, the wrong way. She would question too much. She would need things in black and white.

"Of course, I am not saying she was wrong in what she was doing; just that her way of doing things didn't go very well, with the culture of the organization". He was quiet for a few moments.

"She was a very interesting person, taking part in different activities, getting her people involved in many things apart from their projects. She had very high energy and was always cheerful".

Atul seemed to have a lot of good things to say about Manjiri.

"How were her interactions with her peers? And their families?" Neil asked.

"Her peers had mixed feelings about her. They admired her for a lot of things, but like I said, she didn't fit into the culture. I think her peers felt this way on more than one occasion. They didn't always voice their grievances, but they distanced themselves from her when she went out of her way to question certain norms or practices.

"As for the families, I can tell you that my wife liked her a lot. She treated Manjiri as a member of the family. She would call Manjiri over for lunch or dinner many times. They used to have a great time together and would end up ganging up against my sons and me."

"She was like a family friend?" Ishani wanted it stated clearly.

"Yes, very much so!"

"What about others? What about Hemant, her boss?"

Atul didn't say anything so Neil prompted him, "Atul, it would be best if you told us what you know."

Atul looked at Neil, nodded and said, "Hemant's wife was unhappy with him. I think she was also unhappy about Manjiri working with Hemant. I am not sure exactly what the equation between Hemant and Manjiri was, but there was something there. Everyone thought they were having an affair. But then things changed about a year back. They weren't together all the time, like they used to be. She tended to avoid him and he used to be nasty to her. I never asked Hemant or Manjiri directly about it."

"Tell us about the night of 16thMarch" Neil said.

"After dinner, Manjiri came to me and said she needed to talk to me. I had an important client call, so I told her I would see her after the call.

"When the call was over, I went down to the lake where she had said she would be. She was sitting on a rock there and looking at the sky. I could see that she was still quite high. Maybe she had had some more to drink after dinner."

Neil interrupted and said, "I believe you folks had drinks by the camp fire. But Mr. Dheeraj Seth has categorically denied it".

"On our official programs we are not supposed to drink. The company policy states that. So Dheeraj, as the HR manager feels responsible to say that there was no alcohol.

"But yes, there was alcohol. There always is when there is an outbound program. At the campfire, Manjiri had had a lot of beer and some whisky. She was already quite drunk when we went for dinner."

Atul continued without any prompting. "So when I went down to the lake and saw her drunk, I suggested that she go back to her tent and sleep. That we could talk the next day. She didn't agree right away. She was saying, 'he has a phone. I saw him. I am telling you Atul, he has a phone!' But when I asked her who she was talking about, she could not tell me. She said, 'that guy, you know.' Then she took two three different names and said, 'no, no, not him. That guy...' But I could not figure out who she was talking about.

"I then got her to climb down from that rock and walked her very slowly to her tent. But she refused to go in and sat there on a tree bark, right outside her tent. I thought she was safe there; that she only had to walk into her tent when she wanted to sleep. I went to the recreation centre for some time and then retired to my tent."

Atul looked quite sad and serious. This person really must have cared for Manjiri.

"You were the last person to see her alive", Ishani said after a few moments.

Atul was looking down at his feet. He slowly raised his head to look at them both and then said, "If Manjiri walked down to the lake again by herself and got into the water and drowned, then yes, I was the last person to see her alive."

"You don't believe it was an accident," Neil was not asking a question.

Atul sighed and put his hands over his eyes. He then moved them slowly to his head, opened his eyes and said, "No I don't."

After a couple of moments he went on, "Knowing Manjiri, she would not go into the water by herself. She was not reckless. In all the adventurous activities she participated in, she was very careful. She would go well prepared. She did whatever was necessary - training, equipment, procedures, precautions."

"If that is your belief, why have you not talked to the police? Why have you let them close the case as an accident?" Ishani asked.

He smiled a sad smile and said quietly, "I have been helpless to stop that happening. Our senior executives wanted to close this chapter and move on.

"I am really glad that the case has been reopened for investigation. Many people think I might have been instrumental in getting it reopened." Then after a pause, he continued, "I know that some QSoft senior executives are not very happy that it has been reopened. I also know that they think I have something to do with it. But that is OK."

Neil nodded and said, "One last question for now. Do you remember the names Manjiri had mentioned? The two names you said she mentioned and then said, 'not him'?"

Atul shook his head and said, "She was very drunk that time and was not able to think of the right name. She mentioned Dheeraj and Lokesh as the names. But honestly, I don't think she meant to talk to me about either of them."

"OK, thanks. I think that is all for now. If we have any more questions later on, we will call you. If you think of something, please call either of us. Here are our numbers", Neil said handing him a card with Ishani's number written in hand.

Atul nodded and said, "Do you folks want to grab lunch before your next meetings?" Ishani looked at the time for the first time that day and realized it was almost 1:00 PM. She looked at Neil, shrugged and said, "I am OK either way." But Neil was obviously in favour of the food. He said, "Let's eat and then continue."

So Atul accompanied them to the cafeteria where the three of them had lunch together. Ishani noticed that like the previous day, Neil talked very little while eating. He concentrated on his food and seemed to really enjoy it. Atul was the one who kept the conversation going. He was in the midst of a description of a painting he had seen recently, when he looked up, and seeing someone enter the cafeteria suddenly said, "Oh God, I had forgotten he was here today."

Neil and Ishani turned around to see who he was looking at. It was a dark man of average height, rather thin with a small face. He was balding but he had combed his long kept hair over his bald spot, from one side to the other. He walked as if he was in a hurry. He noticed Atul and walked over to their table and said, "Hello Atul. How are you?"

Atul got up and said, "Hello Pramoda. Are you just coming in?"

"Yes, yes. Coming from the airport directly. It is quite hot here in Pune, no? Bangalore is much better," Pramoda said. Then he continued, "Good I caught you here. Are we meeting all the managers at 4:00 PM as planned?"

Atul said, "Yes, we are meeting. I confirmed the meeting with Nisha this morning."

At that moment Pramoda noticed that there were two other people seated at the table and said, "Sorry to disturb your lunch, please carry on." But he didn't move and it was very obvious from his expression that he was curious about them.

Atul smiled and said, "Let me introduce you. These are the detectives investigating Manjiri's death; Ishani Sohoni and Neil Bhargav." As Neil and Ishani were getting up, Atul continued, "And this is Pramoda R. L. from our Bangalore Head Office. He handles the Quality Engineering group."

"Hi. I am a Senior VP, actually", Pramoda said. "I have been hearing a lot about you lately."

Hearing about them? From whom? And what? Ishani was wondering what to say to that when she heard Neil say blandly, "Don't pay any attention to what you have been hearing. It's all made up."

"No, no. Only good things" Pramoda said laughing as if it was a big joke.

Neil smiled and insisted, "Still".

Then Pramoda looked at his watch and said, "Actually, I would like to talk to you guys for a few minutes. Do you have time now?" Then before either of them could answer, he went ahead, "Actually, my calendar is packed. I have too many things lined up. But this is also important. So, ten minutes? Yes? Atul, if you don't mind."

Was he expecting them to leave their lunch and go and talk to him? Ishani said, "Sure. How about as soon as we finish our lunch? Where can we meet you?"

"Yes, OK, OK. Finish your lunch. Atul, if you can bring them over to the executive offices after lunch?" Pramoda said looking at Atul with a false smile on his face.

Atul smiled back in a similar fashion and said, "I'll do that." Then watching Pramoda walk over to the cashier, he sat down with a sigh, and they continued their meal in silence for a few minutes.

Neil's phone on the table started vibrating. He looked at the screen and quickly picked it up. "Hello sir."

He listened for some time and then said, "Sure, I'll come over right away." Then after another gap, "No, not a problem. Ishani will take care of those here." And finally, "Right sir".

Then he put it down, looked at Ishani and said, "I'll have to go over to the Commissioner's office right away. You go ahead with the meetings here. We'll sync up in the evening at the hotel."

Great! Ishani thought. She would have to meet Mr. Pramoda all by herself now! She just hoped she didn't blow her fuse…

It seemed like Atul wanted to say something. There were a few moments when he appeared to be on the verge of saying something but had stopped himself. Neil stopped eating, looked at Atul, smiled and said, "Don't worry, Ishani can handle the joker."

Atul laughed at that and said, "He likes to think he is very important."

After their meal was over, Atul walked Ishani to the executive offices on the second floor. He shook her hand and said, "In the evening, one of us can give you a ride to your hotel, if you like. Or we can order a taxi." Then, after a moment, he said, "I wish you all the best; for this meeting, but more importantly for the investigation. Let me know if there is anything that I can help with", and with a warm smile he was gone.

CHAPTER 7

Ishani knocked on the door, and then after a couple of moments entered the room. It was a smaller office, but it had the same kind of décor and finishing that they had seen earlier in Dheeraj and Atul's offices.

Pramoda looked up and said, "Oh it's you", as if Ishani was the last person he was expecting. He gave an exaggerated sigh, as though she had interrupted something very important, then said, "Please be seated."

She sat opposite him in one of the two chairs that were on the visitor side of the table. He turned to his laptop and started typing. She waited for a couple of minutes and then said, "Mr. Pramoda, you asked to meet us?"

"Yes, yes. Just give me two minutes, OK? This is very important. I need to reply to an email from the CEO."

Ishani was getting annoyed; she looked straight at him and said, "Maybe if you are busy now, we can meet later."

"No, no. Ishani. I hope I can call you Ishani? I am done. And this is also very important." Pramoda said and then finally closed his laptop and gave her his full attention.

"So you are investigating Manjiri's death" he said. Then, finally noticing Neil's absence he asked, "Oh your boss didn't come?" Ishani didn't correct him about Neil not being her 'boss'. She only said, "He had to go to the Commissioner's office. But I am here, you can talk to me."

He started off, "Hmmm... You know, this case, it was all investigated and closed. It was very obviously an accident. Now, someone wants to dig it all up again. We know who is behind this; they want to do this in the hope that it will harm QSoft. But that is not going to work.

"I know, it's not your decision. You are only working on the case. I will talk to the CEO, and let him know that I have met you. And I will make sure

49

that QSoft people here give you all the support you need. But keep in mind that it's not going to reveal anything new. It was nothing but an accident. If you knew that woman, you would understand. She was like that, you know. She wouldn't think twice about being risky and aggressive. She didn't want to follow any norms or conventions.

"I have nothing against women managers as such, but there has to be a way to behave. She was drunk when she drowned. Why was she drinking? And that too when she had gone for an official program. It creates a bad impression about women don't you think?"

Talk about character assassination, Ishani thought! That too of a dead woman! Ishani realized that this guy was an idiot. But he was a Senior VP who considered himself important. So she asked the question that could be logically deduced from what he had said, "Do you think that perception or impression could be the cause of her death? Do you think someone who didn't like how she was behaving would want to put a stop to it like that?"

"No. No. I am not trying to tell you that one of our people would be like that. No one would murder her because she didn't behave properly! I am just telling you that she was that kind of a woman, nothing else."

Then he changed his track and said, "This reopening of the case will be difficult for Atul, you know. Everyone said he went to talk to her and then after that no one saw her alive. He must be worried that it has been reopened. He is a good guy and I am personally worried... for him."

When Ishani didn't respond to that, Pramoda changed the track once more and said, "So your hotshot boss, Mr. Bhargav, is I believe a star detective! Very successful in all the investigations he gets involved in. But I think he made a mistake by taking this case. This case is not going to look good on his record, let me tell you. You know, you are trying to dig out dirt on a good company like QSoft; you are not going to find any. You are going to have to close this case as an accident, because that is what it was. That will not look very good then will it?"

Ishani smiled, more to herself than at Pramoda and said, "Mr. Pramoda, thanks for thinking about us. I will let Neil know that you are worried about him and check if he would like to meet you to discuss this further." Then she got up and said, "I'll take your leave then. If there is anything more, please let Atul know." Looking at Pramoda, Ishani felt like laughing. He was getting up looking a little lost. She shook hands with him and walked out.

The security guard on the floor helped her find the office she was supposed to use and Ishani called the first person on her list.

Nisha took time coming over; when she came over, she said a very hesitant 'Hello'. She was a slim girl of average height. She was thirty, but looked younger, maybe about twenty five. Except for her eyes. They looked old and tired. She was a good-looking and well-groomed girl. Her hair was done up in a French plait; she wore dark maroon lipstick and dangling gold hoops in her ears. She was dressed in tight blue jeans, a crisp white shirt and high heeled sandals. She had multiple rings on both her hands, a bracelet on her left and a slim watch on her right wrist.

After a quick preliminary introduction, Ishani came to the point, "Dheeraj mentioned that Manjiri was rude to you and that is what I wanted to talk to you about."

Nisha spoke in a very soft voice, "Actually, I quite admired Manjiri. She was a senior leader and we all learnt a lot from her. I personally learnt a lot."

"But she also was difficult to work with, I believe?" Ishani said.

Nisha seemed to be thinking what exactly to say and how to answer that. So Ishani prompted her, "Did you have trouble working with her?"

"I didn't have to work with her regularly. But there were some initiatives in the organization for which I had to work with her."

"Go on".

"Once she had asked me for some details and I replied to her email. But I had missed out a few things. She asked me so many questions about that and I got scared. I replied back with details but that only made her angry because some of the details I sent the second time didn't match the ones I had sent the first time. I was in a hurry to leave for the day, and so had not got a chance to check that everything was correct. The next day, she came over to my place and asked me to prepare the complete list all over again, and give it to her by lunch time.

"When I was working on something for her, she would always want to know what time it would be completed. And then she would be watching for that time. It was not enough if I said I'll give it to you in two or three days. She had to know the exact date and time.

"There are so many things we have to take care of that sometimes I would forget something she had asked me to do. And that used to really make her angry. She would tell me again and again that I should note down all the things I needed to get done. But I have my own way of working; her way did not work for me."

Nisha continued to speak in a low and soft voice. The overall impression Ishani had about Nisha, was that of a very hesitant person. She probably was not very confident and based on the issues she was talking about, in all likelihood not very competent.

"So you had trouble working with her, didn't you?" Ishani asked.

"Yes, I didn't like working with her at all."

"But she is gone now. You don't have to work with her anymore." Ishani said, watching Nisha for any kind of reaction.

"It's not like that. It's not like I wanted her dead or anything."

While her words seemed appropriate and some level of uneasiness was to be expected Ishani could sense that Nisha had gotten very nervous.

Nisha had gone to Bangalore on March 15thon work and returned on Sunday, the 18th. So why was she so nervous?

Ishani bent closer to Nisha and asked in a stern voice, "What do you know about what happened at the outdoor program, Nisha? What do you know about Manjiri's death?"

Nisha looked down at her feet and said, "I really don't know anything. I got to know about it only on Monday, when I came to work. Dheeraj called a meeting to inform all of us."

"Why didn't you get to know earlier? It was in the local news on the 18th. And I am sure, people from your company would have called each other and talked about it. How is it that you didn't hear about it till the 19th?"

"The people who were on that program were all senior people, not my friends. And somehow other friends didn't call. I only heard on the 19ᵗʰ from Dheeraj." Ishani could see that Nisha was definitely uncomfortable now. She had perspiration forming on her forehead.

"But you must be working closely with some of these senior managers as you are from the HR team. Also, how is it that Dheeraj didn't inform his entire team before the 19th, when he would have to inform everyone else?" Ishani insisted on this point only to increase the pressure.

"Actually, you know I am now not sure if someone called me and informed me before the 19th."

"This would be very big and upsetting news. You don't remember?"

"It was very sad and upsetting. That's why I am not able to remember." Nisha was close to tears.

Ishani decided to stop for the time being. But there was something quite fishy about Nisha Khanna. She made some notes and then let Nisha go.

She sent a quick message to Neil before calling over the next person on the list—Lokesh Mehta. He was a fair man with curly, black hair; about five feet ten, and slim. He had a pleasant personality and was dressed in simple clothes. He was forty-two-years-old and Ishani thought that he certainly looked his age. She changed her mind soon after he started talking because he spoke fast, and seemed to have a peculiar way of saying things, that made him seem immature, and as a result, younger.

"Yeah, Hi. Myself Lokesh Mehta", is how he opened the conversation.

Spending minimal time on introductions, Ishani said, "Lokesh, I want to hear from you about Manjiri. How was she as a manager? What was your experience working with her? And what happened at the outdoor program?"

"Yeah. So, I was working with Manjiri for more than two years. She was very good. She would correct me in many things, but it was all useful. I was always willing to learn, and so we got along really well."

"You had some issue with her not promoting you." Ishani made a statement.

"Yeah. So, I had thought I deserved to be promoted. When I wasn't promoted, I went and talked to People Care, probably a mistake, I think. Dheeraj setup a meeting and we talked about a lot of things. Manjiri told me about the things she had considered when she had made her decision not to promote me." Lokesh seemed to be stating it all in a matter-of-fact manner that was disarming. He didn't seem emotional about it.

"I was not completely happy even then, and I mentioned that to Dheeraj. I also mentioned it to Manjiri in a separate conversation. Then, she talked to me at length on various points. She and I reached an agreement, to work on three important areas so that I could be a candidate for promotion in the next cycle.

"Manjiri was very good at that kind of thing. Identifying areas to work on, defining what should be achieved, then helping the person put together a plan and the timeline to achieve the same." Lokesh was talking earnestly. "Her death was a shock but it was also a big loss for us. I definitely feel like I lost the best manager I had the opportunity of working with."

Ishani then asked him to describe what had happened at the campsite. Lokesh went on to describe their arrival, stay, finding Manjiri missing on the morning of the 17th, the police coming over and finally her body being brought out. He got a little emotional towards the end when he described how they had tried searching for her, and then, about the shock when the divers found her body and brought it up.

On the night of the 16th, after dinner he had gone to the recreation centre, watched the news for some time and then played carom for a long time. He went to his tent with Gautam, his tent-mate, at around 12:30 AM. They got up at around 6:30 AM the next morning, quickly got ready and went to the dining hall at around 7:15 AM.

He went on to mention that mostly everyone had gone to the recreation centre that evening, at least for some time. But many people had left only to return after a while. He couldn't say exactly who was there at what time. Ishani closed the conversation with, "Thanks Lokesh. That is all for now. If you think of something else, remember something else, please contact me."

By the time Ishani was done for the day, it was past 6:30 PM and Ajit Ketkar was waiting outside the meeting room for her. Atul Vaidya had stopped by earlier, and she had gone to the cafeteria with him for a cup of tea at around 4:45 PM. He had talked at length about Manjiri and from some of the anecdotes he mentioned, Manjiri appeared tohave a very good sense of humour. Atul had also introduced her to Ajit Ketkar, who would drive Ishani to her hotel, as he was anyway going that way. When she saw him she quickly grabbed her backpack and they went to the basement together.

On the way to the hotel, she got a chance to talk to Ajit about Manjiri. His overall description of Manjiri was similar to Lokesh's. Moreover, Ajit mentioned that he had been Manjiri's close friend. They had worked together for a long time and knew each other really well. He also told Ishani that Manjiri would go over to his place, to spend time with him and his wife quite often. Ajit had not gone on the outdoor program. He had got to know about her death on the 17th. Lokesh had called him from the bus, when they were on their way back and had come close to the city. Ajit had not been able to believe it. He had gone and met the police and given them the address and phone numbers of Manjiri's kin.

Like Atul, Ajit too seemed glad that the investigation was reopened. He too, believed that Manjiri could not have gone into the deep water by herself, since she couldn't really swim.

Towards the end of the conversation he said, "Manjiri had wanted to talk to Atul for a while but he had been busy. Just the day before they went for the offsite, she had gone and asked Dheeraj for some details. She had also said that, she would definitely talk to Atul at the offsite.

"When I asked her what it was about she had said that it was really big. And that it would be best for her to talk to Atul before talking about it to anyone else."

"So you have no idea what it was about?" Ishani asked.

"No, unfortunately, no idea at all." Ajit said. "Now I wish I had insisted at the time that she give me some clue."

CHAPTER 8

On reaching her room, Ishani put her backpack on the centre table. Neil had messaged her and said that he would see her at 8:00 PM. So she still had about 20 minutes. She freshened up and made herself a cup of tea. Oh the luxuries of a good hotel, she thought! Then she started going through her notes.

She looked up in surprise when there was a knock on her door. She looked at her watch and saw that it was 7:55 PM. It must be Neil. She got up and opened the door saying, "Hi—"

Before she could finish, she found a big hand covering her mouth. She was then pushed and shoved back into the room by a man. He shut the door behind him with a kick and pushed her all the way into the room.

Ishani forced herself to calm down, and stop resisting. He was a big man, tall and hefty. She would be no match to him in physical strength. She needed him to think that she was not going to fight so she could catch him off guard. She observed him carefully; she wanted to be able to identify him later. He was dark and had spots on his forehead; had a big nose and big teeth. His curly hair was cut short and he had bushy eyebrows. He didn't look like a hotel guest, but she could be wrong about that.

She would have to engage him in a conversation somehow. He tentatively lifted his hand from her mouth and when she didn't scream, he pushed her on the bed. She tumbled but quickly sat up and said, "Did you want to talk to me?"

The man was taken aback by that. His surprise was written all over his face but in the next moment he recovered and said, "Don't try to be smart with me! I am warning you! Go back to Mumbai! You are digging up old corpses! If you don't go back, you will join the one that was found in the lake!"

Remembering how Neil had coughed in the morning, Ishani started coughing violently. When it didn't have much of an impact on the man she said in between the coughing spells, "Can you" cough, cough, "please get me" cough, cough, "some water?" cough.

The man continued to look at her for another moment and then started looking around for water. Luckily he could not see any in the room. Ishani pointed to a glass on the side table behind him. He turned and picked it up and went into the bathroom. She continued to cough but got up behind him and ran to the door and managed to open it. Just as she stepped out in the corridor she heard him yell behind her, "You bitch! You will pay for this!" She looked over her shoulder as she ran as fast as she could. She ran directly into something that jabbed her in her ribs. Looking ahead, she realized that she had collided with a waiter carrying a serving tray. She looked down and discovered the toppled tray lying on the carpet surrounded by broken plates, some kind of fish curry that was spreading fast, and an upside down wicker basket that had tandoori rotis.

She looked at the waiter and said, "I am sorry for that. But did you see that man chasing me? Where did he go?"

The waiter said, "It is OK madam. Yes, I saw a man behind you, but could not see him clearly. He turned and went in another direction."

"Is he staying at this hotel?" She asked.

"I don't know madam. But he is not on this floor; that I know."

"So where can he go?" Ishani asked him.

The waiter was shaking his head to indicate that he didn't have a clue, when she saw Neil get off the lift and start walking towards them. He came over to where they were standing, looked down at the food on the floor and said, "Aah fish… I see!" Then he looked up at her, took in her ashen face and tousled hair and asked, "What's wrong?"

The waiter said, "Madam, can I go please? I will have to go and again bring this order. You should tell our manager what happened."

Ishani nodded to him and said, "Yes, I'll do that. Thanks."

She started walking towards the other end of the corridor. Neil followed and said, "You want to tell me what is going on?"

She said, "Yes, of course. But, before that I want to see where someone can disappear to from this side of the building". She would not have felt so brave to go figure out where the man had vanished if she had been alone. She was quite grateful to have Neil's strong presence next to her.

Neil was nodding his head and walking along with her. They went to the other end of the corridor and saw that on the left side of the corridor, at the end of all the rooms there was a big window, and it was open. Outside the window they could see scaffolding, the kind that is setup when there is work to be done on the exteriors of big buildings.

Ishani just waved her hand towards the scaffolding and walked back towards her room. Neil looked at her curiously, but walked quietly by her side. When she came to the room she realized that the door was locked. She turned to Neil and said, "My room got locked. We'll need to call the reception." He nodded at her and then opening his room, turned to her and said, "Come in. I'll call the reception."

She went into his room and sat on the comfortable chair. Now that the incident was over, she was feeling quite shaken. While Neil talked to the reception, Ishani was mentally going over everything that happened. She had worked on many investigations but she had not had to face anything like this before. She was surprised that she had managed to handle the situation. She was also surprised that she had been able to get away so easily.

Once the call was over, Neil asked, "What happened?"

When she explained everything, he said, "You look shaken."

"I am. A little." She agreed with him.

He walked closer to her and patted her on the shoulder, "Relax. It will not happen again. We'll make sure of that." He looked at her closely and then walked over to start the electric kettle to make tea.

Ishani said, "I am surprised I got away so easily. I mean, I asked for water and he just obliged?"

Neil shook his head, "The idea probably was to just scare you a little." Then he also said, "We'll take this up with the hotel. I'll also talk to ACP Sathey."

"This silly attempt to scare me, suggests that someone is desperate to stop the investigation," Ishani said after being quiet for a few moments.

"True." Neil said. He then picked up the hotel phone and called the manager. He also called ACP Sathey and updated him. It was agreed that the ACP would come over to the hotel in the morning and Ishani would look at the video recordings of the security camera the next day.

There was a knock on the door and he called out, "Who is it?"

"The key, sir", came the reply.

The person outside was from the reception and he unlocked Ishani's room. She took the key card and came back into Neil's room.

Neil had made tea for both of them. He handed one mug to her and said with a smile, "Did you see what I did when there was a knock on the door? You ask the person to identify themselves, then you look through the magic eye, which lets you see who is standing on the other side. Then and only then, you open the door."

Ishani knew he was just teasing her so she said, ""Now that you have demonstrated how that is done, I am sure I will get it right!"

She had been too eager to see Neil and had opened the door in a hurry. Of course, she was not going to tell him that. So she opted for, "It was almost eight. I thought it must be you and we could go for dinner. I was very hungry."

Neil gave her a big smile. She had known that he would be able to relate to this reason without any problem. The guy really liked everything about food, even just the thought of it! He was a tall man and she had seen him work out that morning, but it still didn't explain how he managed to stay so slim when he devoured so much food anytime he got a chance!

It was no surprise then when the next thing he said was, "Let's go down to the restaurant." Then he looked at her and said, "You might want to change your shirt though. I don't know if having fish curry smears on your shirt like that makes for a good fashion statement!"

Ishani looked down at herself. She had not even realized that her shirt was dirty!

As soon as they were seated in the restaurant, she asked, "So why were you summoned to the Commissioner's office?"

Neil smiled at her choice of words and said, "The Commissioner wanted to discuss different approaches; rule out some of my ideas and impose some of his own."

"You know you are not sharing any information right? Only giving me your theory of his intentions," Ishani said.

The meeting must have gone well and Neil must have managed to convince the Commissioner because he smiled and said, "But that is a very important input". After this he finally started talking about what they had discussed. "When investigating the first time, the inspector had felt that Mr. Hemant Joshi was hiding something. What Mrs. Pandey described also indicates that there might be something unusual about Mr. Hemant Joshi's relationship with Manjiri. So we talk to both Hemant and his wife tomorrow. Independently."

He got quiet as the waiter came over with their order. Then he attacked the food and for some time ate without talking.

"If Hemant had an affair with Manjiri, like everyone thought, that would explain why Mrs. Joshi was unhappy and refused to meet Manjiri and her aunt." Ishani said breaking the silence.

"Right", saying just that one word, Neil continued to eat.

"We could just talk to Hemant, grill him even. Why bring Mrs. Joshi into the picture unless it is necessary?"

Neil looked up from his food, sighed and said, "During the first round of the investigation, Hemant looked very suspicious. He did everything possible to stop the police from talking to his wife. He behaved as if he had a lot more than a casual affair to hide. We want to talk to her to see if there was anything more."

"OK", Ishani conceded and then focused on the food herself.

"By the way, the SIM card that Jivaji found did not have any finger prints but inspector Morey was able to get the name of the owner. It's one Arun Mandhare," he said, after which he again got quiet. Ishani waited patiently. After a few moments he looked up, smiled at her and continued, "You would never guess who he is! He is a driver, works as a cab driver for one of the call centres."

"So nothing to do with QSoft?"

"As per Wild Outdoors, that call centre has never gone on any official program to their campsite", he said, "The police are bringing Arun in for questioning. We should know more tomorrow."

After his update, he asked Ishani what had happened in QSoft. She told him about Pramoda and his response was, "Idiot!" Ishani laughed softly and said, "First he was a joker. Now he is an idiot?"

Neil gave her an insolent look and said, "I am sticking to the censored version around you. You don't want to know what I really think of him!"

Ishani smirked and said, "Don't restrain yourself on my account. I don't care if you use bad words; I am used to hearing them."

"Well, I mean what I said. If I was not being careful, I would have said 'dickhead', but basically an idiot!" Neil said.

"That's the word that came to my mind," Ishani said smiling.

Neil raised his eyebrows in surprise and then turning back to his food said "I thought good girls didn't use such words."

Ishani gave him a steady look, waited till he looked up at her and then said, "First of all, that is a very archaic line of thought. Secondly, I am busy working as a detective, I don't have time to worry about whether I am seen as a good girl or not. And thirdly, I don't even care."

Neil nodded, "Alright, I'll keep that in mind." Then he focused on the case again. "What about other meetings?"

She updated him about all the meetings and said, "I got the strong feeling that Nisha Khanna knows something. She was so jittery." After a pause she said, "The documents we have from the police have minimal information on all these people. Didn't they compile files on each of them like they normally do? And Nisha doesn't appear on that list at all. I would like to see all the details on her." Neil nodded and Ishani continued, "Lokesh Mehta was very forthcoming and had only good things to say about Manjiri."

After their dinner, as they walked towards the lobby, Neil asked her, "Are you going to be OK in your room? Or will you be scared to be alone?"

Ishani stopped mid-stride and looked at him to see if he was serious. "What?" he asked.

She answered with a question of her own, "In my place, would you be scared?"

He found that absurd and said, "What? Of course not!"

Ishani smiled and said, "Neither am I." Then she went ahead and said, "Neil, keep this evening aside. Believe me, I am quite capable of taking care of myself. I have been working as a detective, not as some clerk in Abhijeet's office."

As they entered the lift, Neil gave her a solemn look and said, "Alright. I just thought that, that would be a normal woman's reaction." Then he raised his hand to stop her saying anything because he had said it wrong, and said, "Sorry, I meant average. Not normal."

Ishani was starting to enjoy this. "Haven't you worked with women detectives before?" She asked.

"Well, I guess you would classify them as 'clerks' in our office. They normally participate in analysis or get involved when we need a woman to be questioned or shadowed."

Ishani was suddenly feeling very tired, "I'll be alright. If it makes you feel better, we can inspect my room together before I turn in."

They walked to her room and Ishani opened the door. Neil did a thorough check of the room and then at the door, touched his hand to his head as if he was saluting her and said, "Good night, Detective."

CHAPTER 9

In his room, Neil switched on the TV, thinking he would watch one of the movies to try and relax. He had too many things going through his mind.

His meeting with the Commissioner had not been an easy one. To start with, the man had seemed so stubborn. But eventually he had listened to Neil and agreed to let him continue the way Neil had planned. At the end of the meeting, the Commissioner had softened up quite a bit and indicated that he liked Neil's approach.

Neil considered what they had learnt about Manjiri so far. A different picture was beginning to emerge. What he had been told about her before taking this case contradicted with what they were beginning to understand. She had been strict and demanding. As per Ishani's interviews she had also been a very good manager; Lokesh and Ajit had only praise for her. Atul too, had said very good things about her. In his words she had been a misfit in the culture of the organization.

Neil knew that she had loved with abandon but she had not been able to marry the one she loved. That had been more than 20 years ago. But she had chosen to remain single.

Unknowingly, his thoughts drifted to his own married life; something he avoided as much as possible. Thinking about it was a sure shot way to lose focus and get depressed. He had realized within a year of his marriage that it was a mistake. It had taken him another four to finally talk to Divya about getting a divorce. And for the last year, she had been making all kinds of demands before she agreed to go ahead with a divorce with mutual consent.

Fortunately they didn't have any children. Deciding to take the divorce route would have been complicated in that case.

He realized that the TV was still on. He flipped a few channels, just so he had something to do. He stopped at a channel showing a Hindi detective serial. The woman detective looked like she was dressed to make a fashion statement. Her clothes, sandals and makeup could have given some of the Bollywood actresses a complex. She also looked as intelligent and smart as a card board box! He laughed out loud and found himself relaxing a little. He should ask Ishani how she liked these so called detective shows. She would have something really interesting to say. He found himself smiling thinking about her.

Ishani was so different from all the women he knew. Even the girls in his office who worked on some of the investigations, were nothing like Ishani. He had been right when he had said that Ishani would have thought of them as clerks. He found himself thinking how Ishani had surprised him multiple times.

On Sunday, when he had talked to her about the case, she had been a little nervous. There had been a distance between them, probably because she saw him as an experienced senior. But now, while she still looked to him to define the overall plan and steer the investigation, she was treating him as an equal. She was not hesitant and she was not nervous around him.

She was one strong and confident woman! The way she had handled the situation this evening was amazing. Of course, the intentions of the intruder must have been only to shake her up mildly and it wasn't only her smartness that had made it possible for her to run out of the room, like she had described. Obviously, the man had been taking it easy and had played along when she had asked for water. Still, she had managed to think on her feet and not panic. And now she was in the next room, all by herself.

Her reaction when he had asked her if she would be fine being alone had been completely unexpected. She had almost felt offended. He smiled thinking about how she had asked him if he would have been scared!

Of course, what would he have suggested if she had said that she was scared of being alone? That she sleep in his room?

He imagined her sleeping on the bed next to him and right away he found himself getting hard thinking of having Ishani in his bed. He groaned and tried to stop thinking about her. But the more he tried to stop, the more he thought about her.

It had been a long time since he had been with a woman. Though he had been tempted to, he had not been with anyone since Divya moved out more than a year ago. Even before that, sex had been minimal for a while. But, so far, he had not been besieged by thoughts of a woman like this. Of course, he had fantasized about strangers and faceless women, like most men did. The only thing he was thinking of in those fantasies was the female body, and not about any particular person. But now, he was unable to stop thinking about this specific woman. A strong, confident and beautiful woman who was right next-door!

He felt torn between two strong feelings. On one hand, he desperately wanted to stop thinking about Ishani. On the other hand, he found it almost impossible to stop thinking about her and he didn't want to!

He told himself to stop it. "Take a cold shower," he muttered! After a few minutes he got up and walked into the bathroom...

Neil woke up with a start at 7:00 AM. He looked at the watch and swore. He had not been able to sleep; the last time he had checked the time, it had been 2:47 AM. The ACP was coming over at 8:00 AM and he had not mentioned the time they were to be ready to Ishani. He decided to knock on her door and see if she was there. He put on an old t-shirt, and opened his door, without bothering with the slippers. He knocked on her door and heard her call out, "Who is it?"

This early in the morning she could remember to ask, but last night she couldn't! He said, "Your friendly neighbour".

She opened the door and said cheerfully, "Hi neighbour!" She looked all bright and cheerful. She was wearing dark blue tight pants, the kind women wore when exercising, and a light grey fitted t-shirt. He found himself just staring at her, not saying anything.

Ishani was the one to break the silence, "What's wrong?" She said and then looked down at herself to see if there was something amiss.

He pulled himself together and said, "Nothing. I forgot to tell you last night that ACP Sathey is coming over by 8:00 AM. So we need to be ready by then."

Ishani shrugged and said, "I can be ready in 20 mins."

Neil felt he had to explain why he was standing at her door, bare feet and in his night clothes, "I thought of calling you but then was not sure if you were in the gym. So I thought I would check if you were here."

Ishani shook her head and said, "I didn't go to the gym. You didn't go either?"

"Why don't you go down for breakfast when you get ready? I'll join you there," Neil said and returned to his room. As he walked towards the bed, he saw the hotel phone and said to himself, "You moron! Why couldn't you just call her on that?!" He shook his head and went to brush his teeth thinking that he seriously needed to get a grip!

CHAPTER 10

As she got ready, Ishani found herself thinking about Neil. He had seemed a little unsure. She wondered what could be the reason. Once she started thinking about Neil, her mind lingered there. There was so much about him that was so unpredictable.

He was great to work with. Even though he was supposedly the hotshot detective, he was very simple and grounded. He also treated her as someone who knew her job.

He was quite well dressed. But not this morning. When he had stood there outside her door, he had been in old shorts and an even older brown t-shirt which at some point must have been saffron or orange. As she combed her hair and tied it into a ponytail she found herself smiling, thinking about how he liked to eat.

It was 7:25 AM and just as she was about to put her phone in her backpack, it started ringing. It was her mother. She had a quick two minute conversation with her and promised that she would call later. She walked to the lift telling herself that she needed to call Abhijeet too.

When ACP Sathey and Inspector Pathare walked in to the lobby at 8:05, Ishani and Neil were already there. The ACP first talked to Ishani about going through the hotel's security cameras and then got down to the case.

"We questioned Arun, the driver last evening. He said he had lent his card to his brother, Sagar Mandhare and that Sagar lost the card. He had given it to Sagar on 15th March and Arun registered a lost card complaint on the 19th of March. So the SIM card was lost between those three days?" He looked first at Ishani, then at Neil and said, "We asked him for his brother's address. He did give us the address, but said that his brother has been missing for the last two weeks. He even went to the police for help. When we checked, we founda missing person's report for Sagar Mandhare, dated April 10th. But we still don't have any leads on where he is."

"What did Sagar Mandhare do?" Neil asked.

"He also worked as a driver. But as a personal driver for someone who lived in Sahakar Nagar. We will get more details and question his employer." The ACP said.

When the ACP got quiet, Inspector Pathare took over. He said, "The last call from the SIM card, before it was reported lost, was on the night of 16th March, at 10:22 PM."

Ishani asked, "Any idea who was the recipient of the call?"

Inspector said, "We don't know yet, but will definitely get to know today."

Neil asked, "Anything else about the SIM or the owner that we know at this point?"

When the Inspector looked at the ACP and shook his head Neil said, "OK then let's go through the hotel security cameras first. Then we can head out to talk to Hemant and his wife."

"I have information that Hemant is going to go to office only in the afternoon," Inspector Pathare said.

Neil thought for a minute and said, "In that case, after we are done here, let's go through Manjiri's personal belongings; her phone, laptop, any diaries; whatever is still in police custody."

Twenty minutes later, Inspector Pathare, Neil and Ishani were seated in a small office behind the reception and going through the recordings with the hotel's head of security. They started with the recording of the camera focused on the main entrance of the hotel from about ten minutes before Ishani came in the previous evening. Finally after about an hour of going through the different recordings of two other cameras, Ishani said, "That's him!"

There was a separate entrance to the restaurant and they were looking at the recording of the camera focused on that entrance. They watched him come in and it looked like he stopped by one of the waiters very briefly before moving out of the frame. Inspector Pathare said to Ishani, "We will be questioning the restaurant staff and we'll figure out who that is." Then the security head and the Inspector got up and went out in search of the restaurant manager.

Ishani had not realized how tense she was about this, but knowing that the search for him had begun, she felt relieved. She looked at Neil and found him looking at her. "You will be relieved", she said to him and smiled.

He took her hand in his at that and caressed it softly before saying, "Very!"

Ishani was surprised by his action and unsure of what it meant. But it felt nice to have him hold her hand like that. He kept holding her hand a little longer and then finally dropped it with a sigh.

Ishani was going through the text messages on Manjiri's phone. There were messages from some of her friends, her cousins and aunt. There were messages from various people at work. The ones from Hemant were old, more than a year old. But apart from the fact that he seemed to love dirty jokes, there was nothing extraordinary in his messages to her. Most people's messaging history would be similar.

Then she started going through the call record history that the police had taken from the cell phone company. In the three months prior to her death, there was one particular number that she seemed to have called at a regular interval. Ishani searched for that number in Manjiri's phone and found it stored under the name "Deena".

She looked up to find Neil looking intently at the laptop screen. He was going through Manjiri's emails. "There is one number she has called regularly, at a defined frequency," Ishani said.

Inspector Pathare said, "Deena".

"Yes!" Ishani said and then asked, "Who is Deena?"

Neil turned around and looked at the Inspector. The Inspector shook his head and said, "We don't know. We stopped the investigation before we figured that out."

Neil turned to Ishani and said, "I would like you to look at these emails and tell me what you think."

Ishani got up from her chair quickly and walked over to where Neil was seated. She felt extremely pleased that Neil was asking her opinion on something. When she got close to him, he got up and vacated the chair for her. When she sat down, he bent down, showed her the email exchanges he wanted her to go through and then walked over to the other side of the room.

The three email threads that Neil had kept open were all work related. In one of those, Manjiri had asked Nisha for some information. There was a lot of back and forth with Manjiri asking for information and promises from Nisha about when she would provide it to her, followed by Nisha either not being able to provide it or providing partial information. After that, Manjiri had written to Dheeraj about not getting the information. The next mail in the thread was from Dheeraj, asking Nisha to give the information to Manjiri on priority. The mail thread seemed to have gone on for more than two weeks. After going through the complete email conversation, Ishani felt sorry for Manjiri. The woman must have been so terribly frustrated about not getting the information even after asking for it repeatedly.

The other two email threads were between Manjiri and Hemant. The first one was from December 2010 and the second one from October 2011.Both the exchanges were about the same project and in both they were discussing how to handle a customer expectation. In the first one, Manjiri seemed to be stating a problem but didn't seem worried about it. Hemant's tone was friendly. He was asking Manjiri to relax and not worry about it. He was telling her he had confidence in her ability. But in the second thread, he was sounding angry. In a couple of places it almost seemed like he was accusing Manjiri of not taking care of her projects, not giving them the attention they needed. She was trying to defend her actions, stating everything she had done, etc. She sounded annoyed, but restrained.

Ishani looked up and found that Neil was standing by the window looking at her. She said, "Something changed between them. Changed drastically. Hemant's tone changed completely." Neil nodded.

Inspector Pathare's phone rang shrilly startling them all. Inspector took it out of his pocket saying, "Sorry. My nephew must have changed the ringtone and settings again." He looked at the number and took the call. "Yes, OK," he said into the receiver. Then he turned to Neil and said, "Hemant Joshi left his home about 15 minutes back and we have confirmation that he is on his way to QSoft."

"I'll head out to QSoft then," Neil said.

Inspector Pathare nodded, turned to Ishani and said, "We can go on my motor bike, if that is OK with you."

It was quite hot and the traffic was no help. But the motor bike was a good mode of transport for Pune roads and they were outside Hemant Joshi's housing complex within fifteen minutes. They stopped at a small tea stall near the complex and waited.

The tea stall owner paid special attention to the Inspector. Asked him if he and 'madam' wanted tea or coffee. Or if he could get them some biscuits. Finally, Inspector Pathare asked for some tea so that they could relax.

It was a good fifteen minutes later that Ishani's phone finally vibrated. She quickly took out the phone and checked the message. "Talking to him. His phone is now switched off," Neil had written. Ishani and the Inspector walked the short distance to the housing complex and thanks to Inspector Pathare's uniform entered the complex without any questions from the security men at the gate.

Three minutes later, they were standing at the door with the name plate, "Hemant Joshi & Uttara Joshi". The Inspector rang the doorbell and the door was opened within a few seconds by Mrs. Uttara Joshi. She was in her early to late forties and wore a simple but well ironed salwar suit. She looked at them with a worried look in her dark brown eyes and asked, "Yes?"

The Inspector introduced Ishani and himself, and then told her they wanted to talk to her about Manjiri. This took Mrs. Joshi completely by surprise. She looked hassled, as if she was unsure about what she should do about them. After a little hesitation and a strong push from the Inspector, she said, "Come in and have a seat."

71

About twenty five minutes later, they were at the tea stall again. Mrs. Uttara Joshi had finally broken down and told them that her husband had an affair with Manjiri. That is why Uttara hated her. But she believed that her husband was basically a good man; he was good to their children as well as to her parents. She of course knew that the affair had ended; Hemant had been quite mad with Manjiri after that, for some time. Ishani came out of the meeting feeling really sorry for Uttara.

Neil had messaged, asking Ishani to call him after the meeting with Uttara Joshi. He had got Hemant Joshi to reveal the same – that he had had an affair with Manjiri.

Ishani called Neil and he picked up on the first ring as if he was waiting for her call, "Hi!"

"Hi," Ishani replied.

"The Commissioner heard from the ACP about your visitor. He is upset because he thinks we haven't taken it seriously enough. He asked me if it makes sense to move you off the case." Neil told her without any preamble.

"Move me off the case?" Ishani couldn't believe it! "What did you tell him?" She asked rather angrily.

"I told him I don't see why. It was only a half-hearted effort, at best. That you had handled it well and were not letting it affect your work."

Ishani felt calmer. "OK." She said. Then, after a moment, "Thank you".

Neil seemed to be smiling when he said, "You are welcome, partner," and Ishani found herself smiling at his words. "But please call him. He has not met you and he thinks he should."

CHAPTER 11

After a very brief call with the Commissioner, Ishani made her way to meet him. Inspector Pathare rode the bike expertly through various short cuts and got Ishani to the Commissioner's office complex in about fifteen minutes. She had to go through the security routine, but it was quick since she was with Inspector Pathare. They walked to the main building in the complex and Ishani went to the Commissioner's office. His PA asked her to wait and called the Commissioner on the intercom. Ishani looked around and noticed various trademark symbols of a government office, photographs of old leaders on the wall, the solid wooden furniture and row upon row of box files.

She was told that the Commissioner was in a meeting and would see her as soon as he got done with that. Ishani sat down in one of the solid wooden chairs and pulled out her notepad. She started going through her notes of the events of the night of March 16th.

She looked at her note about Sangeeta. She was no longer working at QSoft. She had left the company just a week after Manjiri's death. That looked rather suspicious.

She was so involved in what she was doing that when the PA said, "Madam", she was quite startled. "You can go in now."

When she knocked on the door, a voice boomed from inside, "Come in."

Ishani entered and said, "Good afternoon, sir".

Commissioner Bakshi stood up and stretched out his hand to Ishani, "Afternoon Detective Sohoni". He was a big man; tall and broad with a rounded middle. He had a round face, small eyes, bushy eyebrows and a bushy moustache. Ishani felt he looked like a character actor playing the role of a Commissioner. They shook hands and he said, "Please be seated." He watched her sit down and put her backpack on the second chair.

Then he said, "ACP Sathey told me about what happened last evening at the hotel. I asked Neil if we should move you out but he said he does not think so." He stopped talking but continued to watch Ishani; she kept quiet. "I don't want to make this matter more complicated. I think whether half-hearted or not, the thought of threatening you occurred to them only because you are a woman. They wouldn't dare do that to Neil or another male detective."

"Sir, if I am moved from the case, we would be confirming that they were right in thinking that a woman detective could be easily scared and removed from the case." Ishani said as quietly as she could. "I personally don't want to be moved from the case and I don't think it would be the right thing to do for the case."

"Let me be clear. I don't want to have to provide police protection to a detective! Anyway, we don't have the bandwidth. So if it seems like you are in any kind of danger, the only option is to move you out."

Ishani nodded and said, "Sir, I believe it will not happen again. I will also be more careful."

"Were you scared?" the Commissioner asked.

"Yes, I was. But I didn't panic. And I was able to stay calm and think."

"Are you trained in self-defence?" was the next question.

"Yes I am, sir. But in last six years I have never had to use it."

Ishani felt a change in the Commissioner's demeanour. He smiled at her and said, "I think people are quite used to seeing women in the police force now. But a woman private detective is still a novelty."

Apparently, such a thing was novel even to the Commissioner of Police. Ishani was annoyed at the whole thing. The Commissioner was looking at her, so she said, "Sorry sir. I was just thinking that the only way to get them to see that a woman private detective was as tough as a police woman was to let me continue on this case."

"You might be right at that. But we want to ensure your safety too. I think we should bring in the media. That way everyone will be watching what happens in the case."

"Media?" Bringing in the media would make things difficult for the investigators.

The Commissioner knew that of course. He said, "Yes, we will bring them in, in a controlled manner. We'll figure that out. We'll make sure it will not hamper the investigation in any way."

"Sir, we have nothing much to go on. The evidence collected is minimal." She paused for a moment before saying, "My fear is that if we go to the media, and they start following the case, they might make us look like fools."

Commissioner Bakshi almost smiled and said, "Let's not worry about that. It will not come to that." The Commissioner indicated that their meeting was over by saying, "Well, let me not keep you. I am sure you have a lot to do."

Ishani shook hands with him and walked out. She was feeling the pangs of hunger. She had not had anything to eat since breakfast that morning and it was past 4 PM now. Walking out of the big building and towards the gate, she was thinking about getting a quick bite, when Inspector Pathare came out of one of the offices and walked over to her saying, "You want to go for chai and wada pav?" When she said an eager 'Yes', he laughed and said, "We have a nice place right around the corner. Let's go there." They walked out of the gate to the corner, and had couple of wada pavs each along with tea.

The chai and wada pav helped Ishani feel better. She took out her phone and sent a message to Neil, asking him to call her when he could. It must have been less than a minute before the phone rang. Ishani took the call and said, "Hello".

"Hi. How did it go with the big guy?"

"OK. Just came over for wada pav with Inspector Pathare." Ishani wanted to let him know that the Inspector was with her and she might not be able to talk freely.

"Why don't you go over to the hotel? I am done here; I'll reach the hotel in about 40 mins. Manjiri's lawyer's office is close by and we can meet her only after six."

Ending the call, Ishani turned to Inspector Pathare and asked, "Did we get to know more from Arun Mandhare?"

The Inspector said, "Yes. But it will not help us."

Ishani raised her eyebrows at him and said, "Why?"

He looked around to make sure no one could hear them and said, "Sagar Mandhare worked as a driver with Prof. or Prof. Ashok Dhotrey. And the last call from his number before it was lost was also to Prof. Dhotrey."

"So we need to talk to Dhotrey, don't we? Where do we find him?" Ishani asked.

"Prof. Dhotrey is part of the S. J. Gaikwad group of institutes. He handles a lot of different responsibilities for the whole group. We can't really go and question him because he is very close to Vasantrao Dabhade. We need something substantial to question him."

"So? I mean I know Dabhade is a very powerful politician, but why can't we talk to this Prof. Dhotrey about his driver who has gone missing and about the call he received?"

"See, he has already given his statement to the police about his missing driver. And now if we were to go and ask him about one call from his driver, he will not be happy. We don't want that unless we have some clue about how, if at all, this is linked to Manjiri's death."

"Well, we might be able to figure that out if we question him! Maybe he knows something. Maybe he has some connection to this. We have to investigate this!"

Inspector Pathare was shaking his head. He said, "That is not going to be possible."

Ishani could not believe this! But Inspector Pathare was not the one who needed to be convinced. She would have to talk to Neil so that he could take this up with the Commissioner.

She took an auto rickshaw and reached the hotel in less than twenty minutes. As a result, she had time to freshen up. As she did that she decided that it was such a luxury to be able to go to your room and freshen up in the middle of the day during an investigation like this!

She had been waiting in the lobby for fifteen minutes, when her phone rang. It was Neil, "Hello detective Sohoni, detective Bhargav reporting at the hotel."

Ishani made a face but then smiled and said, "And you are late!" Then she shook her head and said in a neutral tone, "I am in the lobby."

"OK. I am ..." Before Neil could finish the sentence, Ishani heard someone else saying something to him. Then she heard Neil's voice but could not understand what he was saying. She could only figure out that he was talking in Marathi. It seemed like he told the person to wait for a minute and then he talked to her, "Ishani, I am just outside, but I am going to take a few minutes."

Ishani walked to the entrance and saw that a man was talking to Neil in Marathi. It seemed like the person was hassled and Neil was trying to calm him down. The person kept looking around as though to check if he was being watched. The man noticed her standing just inside the entrance and said something to Neil. Both of them turned to look at her. Then Neil said something to him and both of them walked over to the entrance.

When they entered the lobby, Neil pointed to the sofas in the corner and said, "Let's sit over there".

Once they were seated, Neil said, "Ishani this is Arun Mandhare. Arun you know detective Ishani Sohoni."

"Yes, yes. I am seeing madam", Arun said.

Neil then turned to Arun and said, "Don't worry. I'll find a way. I will not tell the police." Arun nodded and said "Thank you, sir. I didn't know what else to do."

Neil patted him on the shoulder and said, "Have some tea. You will feel better."

"No sir. I will go now."

Neil took out his card and gave it to him and said, "This is my number. You can call me if you need to. You are not using the BSNL card anymore you said. Do you have another number?" Arun nodded and rattled off the number. Neil noted that down on his phone.

Arun got up thanking Neil and then also said, "Thank you madam" before departing.

"What was that?" Ishani asked.

"Let's go up and talk. I would like to freshen up." He said.

"Go up? Aren't we going to see the advocate?"

Neil shook his head, "I called Adv. Kulkarni. We don't need to meet her right now. Manjiri's new will states that a trust is to be formed and two friends have to take care of that trust. Her entire wealth will be held in the trust. The trust has to work for education and art. They have to choose the charities they will donate to, scholarships to be given to educational institutes etc. It all sounded very sensible. So I decided that we should start working on putting the pieces of the puzzle together first. If we miss a piece and think it will help if we were to meet Adv. Kulkarni, then we can meet her at that point. Sound good?" When Ishani nodded, he went ahead, "I got a white board setup in my room. We can start putting the pieces together and see what picture emerges."

"OK." Ishani said and got up. Neil asked her, "Are you hungry?"

"No. I had wada pav just before coming to the hotel," she said smiling at him.

They took the lift to the fifth floor and walked to his room in silence. Ishani decided to change out of her jeans and said, "I'll be over in five minutes," then walked into her room.

She changed into her favourite track pants and a soft t-shirt. She pulled off her scrunchy and her hair cascaded down her back. She then began to comb it out. It felt good not to have it all tied up. Precisely five minutes later she knocked on Neil's door. He was smiling when he opened the door. "You must be the only woman who says five minutes and means it". Ishani noticed that he too was in track pants and an old, faded t-shirt.

She walked in behind him and went and sat on one of the two sofa chairs. The white board was on a stand in the corner. Neil put down his notepad and sat on the other sofa chair.

"Tell me about Arun Mandhare" Ishani said.

"He is worried about his brother. He has been going to police but they won't do anything. According to Arun, Prof. Dhotrey did a lot of underhanded things for Vasantrao. Sagar got to know about some of these activities. He recently saw something. He had called Arun and said he was scared, that he wanted to get away. A couple of days after that, Sagar went missing. Arun talked to his uncle, who is somewhere near Jabalpur, two days ago, and he thinks his brother has gone there. But he is scared to reveal this to the police. Sagar, it seems, was scared for his life."

"Why did he come to you?" Ishani asked.

"When police questioned him regarding the SIM card, he got to know that we are investigating some murder case and that the SIM card was found somewhere close to the site. He wanted to talk to us and give us some information. He was scared to talk to the police about it because it involved Prof. Dhotrey.

"He didn't know where we were staying or how he could reach us. Today he saw you on Inspector Pathare's bike and waited outside the Commissioner's office. He followed you here but he couldn't bring himself to come and talk to you. He waited outside gathering courage and finally walked in deciding to ask about you at the reception. I was handing over the car to the valet when he was near the entrance and heard me talking to you on the phone and realized who I was."

"Oh! I see" Ishani said. "What information did he want to share with us?"

"So the lost SIM card, he says was borrowed by Prof. Dhotrey. According to him, Prof. Dhotrey borrowed and used his brother's SIM card all the time. Arun had this BSNL card for a while. Nowadays he has a phone given to him by the taxi company so he was not using the BSNL card. His brother had borrowed the BSNL card sometime back and he had been in the habit of giving that BSNL card to Prof. Dhotrey quite often apparently.

"According to Arun, Prof. Dhotrey used it when he didn't want to call people from his phone. When the card was lost, Sagar told Arun that Prof. Dhotrey had given it to someone else and that person lost it. Prof. Dhotrey insisted that a complaint be lodged for the lost card and a new card with the same number be acquired.

"He also insisted that his name should not be mentioned anywhere in the report."

Ishani said, "And he couldn't tell this to the police because he thinks it would reach Prof. Dhotrey! Hmm…"

Neil nodded in agreement. Ishani went ahead, "You know this is very interesting because, today when I suggested that we talk to Prof. Dhotrey, Inspector Pathare very categorically said that, unless there was a clear sign of his involvement in the case, we can't question him!"

Neil whistled, and then said, "The last call from the card before it was lost went through the Mulshi tower."

"Moreover, the last call was to Prof Dhotrey! Isn't that substantial enough? You need to take this up."

Neil said, "Politicians are a difficult lot to handle. Police have enough trouble with them. I can understand their reluctance to get tangled with a powerful politician but if it is a must for the case then we'll have to find a way. Let me think about this a bit."

What was there to think about? Ishani was getting annoyed with everyone, including Neil, trying to pussyfoot around the issue.

"Ishani?" She looked at him and he went ahead, "What else did you find out today? How was your meeting with the Commissioner?"

Ishani said, "He has agreed to let me stay on the case and he wants to involve the media. He thinks if they are watching then it will be difficult for someone to harm us."

Neil said, "Oh you mean 'you' not 'us'."

When Ishani looked at him, though he had a straight face, he had a twinkle in his eyes. She didn't rise to the bait; instead she made a face and nodding her head from side to side, said, "Yeah. Me. The weak, helpless female playing at being a detective." She found herself smiling a big smile when Neil laughed out at her comment. Then she schooled her features and said, "So what do you think? I wasn't sure about involving the media. Their involvement can be good or bad or both at the same time, actually."

"Hmm. Let's think about it a bit. I'll talk to the Commissioner," said Neil.

He was closing off every lead saying they were things to think about later! "Boy, you are going to have to do a lot of thinking!" she said.

"Yeah. I do that sometimes. Think, that is," he said and smiled.

CHAPTER 12

Ishani told him about her meeting with Mrs. Uttara Joshi, ending with, "But nothing really came out of it that could be useful for the case. Did you find anything from Hemant?"

"Hemant went to the recreation centre after dinner that night and was there till 11:30 PM. He says he went to his tent after that. Dheeraj went to the tent at 1:00 AM and found him there, asleep. But what he did between 11:30 PM and 1:00 AM can't be confirmed.

"He was angry when Manjiri ended the affair. He was quite besotted with her. But that was more than a year ago. He admitted that he gave her very high ratings in her yearly appraisal when they were having an affair. That made him even angrier when she ended it. They continued to work together after that. Things had not been easy; he had gotten harsh with her, very critical too. But it had not gone beyond that level. In fact, he showed me some recent email exchanges in which their tones were a lot calmer than the ones we saw this morning."

They started going down the list of names to see who they had already covered. Ishani had kicked off her slippers and was seated cross legged now.

When they came to Dilip Araghade's name, Neil said, "Today, I talked to Dilip. He had all good things to say about Manjiri. When I quizzed him about her being sweet on him, he said she acted as if she liked him but he was not sure about that. He pointed out that she had not promoted him, even though others believed he was ready for the next level.

"He said, because it seemed that she liked him a lot, sometimes people made fun of him. At other times, they preferred to keep him at a distance and sometimes they looked to get information from him, which they felt he would have gotten from her. He said it made him feel uncomfortable.

"On that night, he went to the recreation centre right after dinner; then went to his tent at around 11:30 PM but he could not sleep so he returned to the recreation centre at around 12:55 AM, just when Atul was leaving. He said he didn't see Manjiri at all after dinner."

"How did he come across as a person?" Why had Manjiri like him?"

"Smart. Confident. Speaks well and a lot!"

"Good looking? Attractive?"

"Not to me." Neil said and when Ishani looked at him with annoyance, he winked at her, smiled and said, "I guess he would be categorized as a guy with a good personality. Pleasant mannered, well groomed, polished. Does that answer your question?"

"Yes," Ishani said smiling a fake smile.

Neil got up smiling and as he walked over to the coffee maker, he ruffled her hair.

"Hey!" She complained and he just smiled at her again.

"Coffee?" He asked.

"Yes, OK," she said.

He got busy making the coffee for both of them. Ishani asked, "Who else did you meet today?"

"Talked to six other people who had gone for the program. So between you and me we have covered sixteen people now. Only Sangeeta, who is no longer with QSoft, is left." He focused on the coffee preparation for a few moments then said, "I also talked to two people who worked with her but were not on the program. Dinesh worked closely with Manjiri. He is from the HR team. He seemed neutral about Manjiri. Then there's a guy called Yogesh, who moved from Manjiri's group recently. He had a lot of complaints about Manjiri. Mostly along similar lines. She expected too much, didn't let go easily, etc."

Ishani suddenly remembered something. She got up and then turned to Neil and said, "Where are those reports that the police gave us?" He looked at her and raised his eye brows. So she repeated, "The docs the police gave you."

He said, "I have them locked in the safe. What did you want to see?"

"I want to see the tent allocation list. When I looked at it the first time, these were just names on a paper. Now it should be more meaningful."

Neil looked at her for a few seconds and then shook his head. He said, "I thought about that list when talking to Hemant. I have a copy in the notepad in my backpack." He was pointing to his backpack. Ishani went to where the backpack was kept. Then she turned to look over her shoulder and noticed him watching her. He saw her look at him and said, "Go ahead. Open it. The front pocket."

Ishani took out the notepad in question and brought it over. She sat back in the sofa chair and flipped through the notepad. A single sheet of paper fell out.

Tent Number	Occupants
1	Lokesh, Gautam
2	Medha
3	Rajesh Nadeem
4	Hemant Dheeraj
5	Atul
6	Sanjay Thomas
7	Milind Krishnan
8	Jayant Nitin
9	Manjiri Sangeeta
10	-
11	-
12	Dilip Ajit

Neil came over with the coffee and handed her a cup. He sat down in the other sofa chair and said, "If you remember, there were more tents along the conference hall – sort of in two rows. And there were four tents along the lake. Since all the tents had not been setup, all these tents were separated from each other kind of in pairs. So tent 1 and 2 were neighbours, but the others were far away from this pair. Again 3 and 4 formed a pair. And so on.

"As we know there was no one in the tent next to Manjiri's. Moreover the closest tent to their pair, tent 11 too was empty. Dilip and Ajit were in tent 12."

Neil got his laptop from the backpack and sat down again. "I jotted down things about all the people I talked to." He opened the spread sheet he had created and put the laptop on the table between them. As they went down the list, Neil provided a running commentary.

"Gautam, a Marketing Executive, was at recreation centre till 12:30 AM. So was Medha. Medha is a Project Delivery Manager. You'll notice that she and Gautam were in neighbouring tents. They walked back from the recreation centre together. Lokesh, you had talked to him."

"Yes. He said that he too returned to the tent with Gautam." She remembered that clearly. Her conversation with Lokesh had surprised her.

"What about Rajesh, you talked to him, didn't you?"

"Yes, I did." Ishani said and flipped open her notepad. "He works in a group called 'Technical Presales'. He and Nadeem, who heads the training group for Pune, were tent mates. Both of them went to their tent right after dinner, didn't go to the recreation centre at all."

"Hmm. Nadeem gave me the same story today. Then…" He looked at the list and went ahead, "Dheeraj we know, Hemant I told you. Atul was alone in the tent." He was ticking off the names from the list. "Did you talk to Sanjay the other day?"

"Yes. He heads the Finance function for Pune. He went to the recreation centre and was there till the end. He went back with his tent mate, Thomas. He told me that they could hear Atul snoring. They had talked about how loud the snoring was and wondered whether they would be able to sleep.

"I also talked to Thomas that day. His story matched Sanjay's. And I talked to Krishnan," Ishani had wondered how a person with such poor communication skills could be effective in a customer-facing senior manager's role. "He went to watch the news and then immediately went to his tent so he must have left the recreation centre between 10:15 and 10:30 PM."

Neil picked up from there. "Milind, who heads IT for Pune, must have followed right after. He told me that he went to his tent at 10:30 PM and that Krishnan was already there." Neil said. Then he mentioned what he had noticed about Milind, "Milind is a very quiet guy. Didn't come across as confident, like the other managers. For someone to be heading a function for the location, he seemed very low-key."

Ishani nodded as if to say, it was expected. When Neil looked at her and raised his eyebrows, she said, "That's because he is not part of the customer-facing groups. Normally, people in the non-delivery groups like training and recruitment and sometimes even IT & HR, are seen to be of lower class in the industry. They don't get the same kind of importance and respect. They themselves don't really believe they deserve it. Of course, many times they don't have the focus on quality that they should and so it becomes easy for people on delivery projects to point fingers and look down upon them."

Neil looked surprised and said, "You sound like an expert, Ishani."

"Yeah, well. I know this because my fiancé used to work in a software company."

Neil looked taken aback. He went quiet, but after a few seconds asked, "Oh? What does he do now?"

Ishani needed a couple of moments to grasp what he was asking, "Oh! He still works in the same software company. But he is not my fiancé anymore. We broke up last year."

"I see." Neil said. Then as an afterthought he added, "I am sorry."

Ishani shrugged her shoulders and said, "No need to be. It was not going to work out. I took that decision after giving it a lot of thought."

"Still. Ending a relationship is painful."

Ishani sighed and said, "Yes it is! It was... But knowing that it was the right thing to do, helped."

With effort she collected her thoughts and brought herself back to the present. They needed to focus on the case. She looked at Neil and felt herself blush when she noticed that he was staring at her intently. She suddenly felt that maybe she had shared a little too much about herself. She shook herself mentally and said, "OK. Coming back to the case, what about Jayant?"

She felt he had not heard her question. Or he was not going to answer. Then he said, "Right!" and after a pause, "Jayant... Jayant. Yes, Jayant is an architect, I was told. He did have a tent allocated to him, but he never stayed there. He is the guy who had a car. He drove back to the city in the night and went back in the morning. He said that he had to come to the city as his uncle was seriously ill and in the ICU. He left the campsite right after dinner, around 10:00 PM."

Ishani, who was looking at the spread sheet, looked up and said, "I see that you managed to convince him to accept that he had carried away all the bottles with him."

"Yes," Neil said smiling. "I had to do some arm twisting, but it wasn't too difficult."

Ishani looked through her notes again and said, "Nitin didn't tell me that he was alone in the tent. He said he walked back to the tent with Milind. I got the impression that Milind was his tent mate."

"What do you make of Nitin?" Neil asked.

Ishani looked at her notes and thought back to the conversation before saying "He is also a Delivery Manager. He came across as someone desperate to make a good impression. He, I felt, was trying too hard. But he didn't have much to say about Manjiri. They had not worked together at all. They were in different groups and different hierarchies. Even their interactions were limited."

"OK. Just add a comment on his name to say that he had not shared all the details." Ishani nodded and added the note.

Neil looked at the list and said, "Next is Ajit Sinha. Talked to him today. Ajit Sinha, handles recruitment for various business groups. He didn't go to the recreation centre till past 11:00 PM but then was there till everyone left."

"Where was he before he went to the recreation centre? What was he doing?"

"It seems he had some important work to complete so he sat outside his tent and worked on his laptop for a while before going to the recreation centre."

"Did anyone see him there?"

"No one saw him outside his tent. But Medha saw him walk over to the recreation centre from the general direction of his tent. She had stepped out thinking she would go to her tent but he convinced her to go back in with him and play cards."

That completed the list. Ishani said, "I think we should look at people who don't have alibi for parts of the night."

Neil nodded and said, "Right."

Neil got up, went to the white board and picked up a marker. He thought for a bit and then started writing on the white board. He started putting down people's names and the times for which they didn't have any alibi, in a table. They discussed every name and the time for which that person was missing before he wrote it down. In a short time they had a table with seven names.

Hemant	11:30 PM to 1:00 AM – He went to his tent at 11:30 PM. His tent mate, Dheeraj got there only at 1:00 AM
Atul	11:00 PM to 11:35 PM – He had gone down to the lake shore and as per his statement, had brought Manjiri up and then goneto the recreation centre.
	12:55 AM to 1:30 AM – He went to his tent around 12:55 AM and was alone in the tent. But at 1:30 AM, his neighbours went to their tent and could hear him snore.
Jayant	10:00 PM – 7:15 AM – He said he left the campsite at 10:00 PM and went to the city and returned the next morning.
Nitin	10:30 PM – 7:15 AM Jayant was his tent mate so no one had seen Nitin after 10:30 PM till 7:15 AM the next day.
Sangeeta	9:45 PM to 7:15 AM – She had a headache and so went to the tent right after dinner. No one was with her till the next morning when she went for breakfast.
Dilip	11:30 PM – 12:55 AM – He left the recreation centre but couldn't sleep, so came back.
Ajit	10:00 PM to 11:00 PM – He was not with anyone for about an hour after he left the dining hall. He said he was working outside his tent on his laptop but no one saw him.

Once the table was ready, Ishani copied it into Neil's laptop. Then she checked the time and was surprised to find that it was past seven thirty.

She looked at Neil wondering how he had not mentioned food yet. On cue, as if he had read her mind, he said, "Should we order food? They will take some time getting it and I am hungry."

Ishani found herself grinning and saying, "Yes, sure."

"You OK with butter chicken?"

Ishani made a face and said, "Can we eat something other than Punjabi?"

"You don't like Punjabi food?" Neil sounded offended.

"I like it. But not all the time. And I also like other stuff."

"So what did you want to eat? Dosa or something?" He sounded displeased with the thought.

"You don't like dosa?" It was now Ishani's turn to feel offended by his lack of taste for good food.

"I quite like it. But not for dinner. It's too light; not filling enough."

"Sandwiches?" Ishani asked.

"I can have a couple of sandwiches if you really want to have sandwiches, but they are not really something I would choose for myself."

"Why don't you order butter chicken?" Neil looked pleased when she said this but then she continued, "I'll have my dosa or sandwich."

Neil shrugged and said, "OK". He picked up the phone and ordered his butter chicken and naan and then turned to Ishani and said, "Dosa or Sandwich?"

"Chicken sandwich and coke."

He ordered that, put the phone down and turned to her. "They are going to take about forty minutes."

Ishani needed to talk to Abhijeet and she decided that this would be a good time to do so. "I'll come back when the food gets here," she said getting up.

"OK", Neil said, "I'll call you when the food gets here." Ishani thought he seemed rather eager for her to leave.

CHAPTER 13

Ishani called Abhijeet as soon as she got to her room.

"Hello Sohoni. You sure must be busy. Haven't called me since getting to Pune."

She felt good to hear his familiar, calm voice. "Yes, I have been busy. But I should have called earlier. Sorry about that."

"So? How is the case coming along?" Abhijeet asked.

"We have got one lead, but police are reluctant to take that forward because the person we want to question is very close to Vasantrao Dabhade."

Abhijeet whistled and said, "Be careful, Ishani." Ishani didn't mind this coming from Abhijeet. She had worked with him for six years and was very close to him and his wife, Uma.

They treated Ishani like family but respected her independence. Though they both were fifteen years her senior, they didn't think that gave them right to advise her on everything. She knew that when Abhijeet expressed concern, he wanted her to be more focused and attentive; he was not going to try to pull her off the case or be over protective.

"And I had an unexpected visitor last evening; he had come to tell me to stop investigating." She would not be telling this to her mother for a very long time, but she didn't mind telling Abhijeet.

"What kind of a visitor?" Abhijeet asked. Ishani explained in brief what had happened. "What?!" Ishani had not expected a reaction like that. "How did that happen? What was Neil doing?" He sounded angry.

"Neil? He was not at the hotel. He came back after the thug ran away. But don't worry. I am going to be more careful now."

She could hear Uma say something to Abhijeet and then he said, "Uma has just come home. She says hello."

Ishani could hear her say something else and finally Abhijeet handed the phone to her. "Isha, how are you?" Before Ishani could say anything she went on to say, "I don't know what you and Abhijeet were discussing but he is looking worried now. I hope everything is going well?"

"Yes, Uma. Everything is just fine."

"Are you sure? I hope you are not doing something silly or dangerous."

"No, auntiji", Ishani said smiling. She called Uma auntiji whenever she wanted to indicate that Uma was behaving like an aunty.

Uma laughed and said, "OK. Let's not talk about the case. How about we discuss that hotshot detective you are working with? Neil Bhargav?"

Ishani was not sure she wanted to discuss Neil. But she didn't want to tell Uma that she didn't want to discuss Neil. So she forced herself to sound very casual and said, "One thing I can tell you for sure is that he is a big foodie."

"You know, I met him once about three years back. He was here in Mumbai working on a case with Abhijeet. It was some case involving quite a few folks from the movie industry." Uma pitched in.

Ishani remembered it well. It was a very high profile case and Abhijeet had asked Neil to come over and help him. They had wrapped it up within a week. Neil had come over to EnQuaiR detective agency only twice and the only person from the agency who had worked with him, had been Abhijeet.

"We went out for dinner to the US Club", Uma was continuing her story. "He was very charming." Ishani could imagine that. She didn't quite know what to say. Thankfully, she didn't have to say anything.

"You can talk about Neil's charms some other time, Uma. I need to talk to Sohoni about the case." Abhijeet could be heard loud and clear in the background. "Oh OK Abhi! Isha, we'll have to catch up some other time. Your boss is breathing down my neck!" She was saying something to Abhijeet in the background as she handed the phone to him.

"I want a complete update, Sohoni." Abhijeet said.

So Ishani went ahead and gave him the complete update. After hearing the whole thing he said, "I suggest you do involve the media. Ask the police to tip off a couple of newspapers. Ask them to say that they have got new evidence and that the new evidence has given them a clear direction for the investigation. The news should be made big enough to make the person responsible for the death nervous." Ishani felt, as she did many times after discussing things with Abhijeet, that she had a clear path to follow.

"But you'll need to discuss this with Neil." Abhijeet was saying.

"Yes, I will do that, sir. I am glad I called you. Talking to you has helped." Ishani said earnestly.

"Don't hesitate to take decisions. And call me as often as you need." He said reassuringly.

"Sir, do you know who got this case reopened?" Ishani could not help asking.

"I know this got opened from the highest level; someone from the law ministry." Abhijeet said.

"Law ministry? Really?"

"Hmmm. That is what I know. Who exactly and why, I don't know. You need to talk to Neil about it. By the way, how are you getting along with him?"

"We are getting along really well. For the hot shot detective he is supposed to be, he does not act like one. I mean, he is simple and all that but also, he seems to approach the case more like a game or a puzzle he is working on, and less like a serious murder investigation."

Abhijeet laughed softly and said, "Yes that is what I felt the first time we worked together. But then I realized that he is also actually very good at it. How is he treating you? He had some concerns about having you on the case, you know."

"He did? Why? He didn't even know me!" Ishani felt offended.

She could hear him chuckle before he said, "No, no. Not you personally. He was not sure about having a woman detective on the case. He wanted a very good detective, but when I suggested your name, he was taken aback."

"OK." Ishani smiled. "Yes, he does not have much experience working with women detectives. But isn't that strange? He does have some girls on his team. What do they do?"

They talked for a few more minutes on some other investigations before closing the call.

Ishani looked at the time and found that it was only eighteen minutes since she had left Neil's room. She picked up the small notepad by the phone and noted down open threads on the case. They had only one real lead, the SIM card. What else could they look at?

She remembered that there were a few small villages scattered around the shoreline. Had police tried talking to people in those villages? Hadn't Jivaji talked about a film being shot near the campsite? When was it that they had been shooting? Where had those people been staying?

She looked at the time again. It was exactly half an hour since she had come to her room. She picked up the receiver and dialled the number for Neil's room. It rang for a while but Neil didn't pick up. She called on his cell phone and found it was busy. She tried again after five minutes but his phone was still busy. Maybe he was talking to his wife, she thought.

She felt curious about his relationship with his wife. She had heard that his wife was very beautiful. Was she a house wife? Did Neil have children? She tried imagining him as a father. He would be a fun father, she thought.

She decided it was ridiculous to sit here and think about Neil's family life! She switched on the TV and selected her favourite news channel. The news reader was talking very excitedly about how a divide in the ruling coalition was becoming apparent. The law minister was accusing the minister of state for Industries of meddling in the working of the law ministry. Ishani had heard that yesterday morning. But now, Ishani felt a little uneasy. Abhijeet had said that the case had been reopened by someone in the law ministry. Would this tiff between the two affect the case?

She looked at the room phone in surprise when it rang. She picked it up and said, "Hello?"

"Sohoni, you were trying to call me," Neil said. He must have talked to Abhijeet, Ishani realized from the way he addressed her. She could almost hear him smile.

"Yes, I was, Bhargav." She replied in kind. He laughed at that and said, "I have been on phone with various people, the last person being your boss." She heard his cell phone ring in the background. Then heard him say something under his breath that sounded like "Oh hell". Then to her he said, "I am going to have to take this call. But it shouldn't take too long. I'll call you back in ten." He had cut the line before she could say "OK."

Ishani looked at the receiver as if it was Neil and made a face at it before putting it down. Then she went back to the news she had been trying to watch. But the news was in the last segment and so she had to listen to gossip from the movie industry. Feeling quite annoyed with everything in general, she switched off the TV, put her head down on the pillow and closed her eyes.

She woke up with a start when the phone started ringing. She felt disoriented. Where was she? It took her a few moments to gather her thoughts and pick up the phone. "Hello", she said.

"Ishani? What's the matter? Are you not well?" Neil sounded concerned.

"Me? I am fine! Why?"

"You didn't pick up the phone the first time. Didn't pick up your cell either. And now you sound like you have a cold or something."

"No, I am fine," she said smiling. "And hungry. Is the food here yet? What's the time?" She picked up her cell phone and exclaimed, "Gosh its 9:30?" It had been around 8:45 PM when Neil had told her he would call in ten minutes.

"Yes. And the food is here. Why don't you come over?"

"OK." She said and put the phone down. She had slept for a good forty minutes! She had also been dreaming about something. She could not remember clearly what the dream was, but Neil had been a part of it and it was related to the case. She went into the bathroom and washed her face, then came out and combed her hair. She shook her head at her image in the mirror, then picked up her cell phone and left her room.

Neil opened the door when she knocked. Then as she went inside, he put his hands on both her shoulders and looked at her closely as if to make sure she was OK. She shook his hands off and smiled at him saying, "I am OK!" Then she walked in. She was both pleased and annoyed at his concern. She really liked it when he touched her, even briefly, she acknowledged and then sighed.

Neil walked towards the table with the food tray saying, "Let's eat. And I have a story to tell you."

"Story?" Ishani said with raised eyebrows.

"Yes, a story."

Ishani went over as Neil opened the cover on the tray. She picked up the plate that had her chicken sandwich. Neil looked at her plate and said, "That looks good. Are you going to eat all those fries?"

She smiled sweetly and said, "Yes. All of them. I love them."

Neil looked longingly at the fries and then again at her. She turned her head to one side and picking up a couple of fries, put them in her mouth. Then she couldn't resist his look anymore and smilingly said, "Did you want some?"

He looked pleased, like a small child given an extra toffee. "A few," he said. He picked up the empty plate from the tray and held it in front of her. Ishani put a few fries on his plate and then sat down on the sofa chair, with her plate. Neil served himself and sat in the other sofa chair. Both of them were really hungry and they ate in silence for a few minutes. Then Neil looked at her and asked, "Are you ready to hear an amazing love story?"

Ishani wasn't sure what he wanted to tell her. Was he going to tell her how he met his wife and how they fell in love? Why was he telling this to her?

"Is the story going to help us with the case? Whose love story is it?" She asked.

"This is Manjiri's love story." Neil said sombrely.

"Oh!" For Ishani that was rather unexpected. She paused to collect her thoughts and said, "Of course. Tell me the story."

"When Manjiri was studying engineering, she fell in love with a guy who was two years her senior. He too loved her and they spent as much time with each other as they could. When she finished her engineering and he completed his master's program, the two wanted to get married. They told their respective parents and all hell broke loose. He was from Bihar, from a family of politicians. Manjiri's parents didn't want her to marry a non-Brahmin, that too someone from Bihar. Manjiri was sure that if she gave them time, her parents would come around. But the problem on DK's, Deena's side was larger."

Ishani suddenly became very alert. "Deena?" She asked. She remembered the name from Manjiri's contact list.

"Yes," Neil said confirming what she was asking. "His father didn't want his son to marry some nobody from a middle class family. His father, at that time was getting established at the state level and he wanted his son to marry the right girl. Right girl, in his opinion was the daughter of a big industrialist from Patna.

"There were a lot of arguments and fights. DK and Manjiri were thinking of various options. Manjiri had suggested that the two of them run away and get married. DK knew he could not afford to do that. His father and uncle would have gone after them and destroyed their chances of any happiness. Manjiri suggested they both go to US, and the two were working on that front. But DK's father found out and he made sure that Deena didn't get a passport.

"When DK found out that he was not likely to get a passport, he had been so frustrated with the whole thing that he had thought of committing suicide. And it was Manjiri who had steered him away from that thought. She had convinced him that even if they had to part ways and lead their lives away from each other, life was still worth living. And that they would always live in each other's memories.

"They parted ways and Deena went to Patna. He did marry the girl his father wanted him to. She was a very nice girl and she became a good wife to him. But she was not the one he had loved. He continued to miss Manjiri and think about her. Manjiri never got married. The two lost touch. DK went on to become a big industrialist. Manjiri did fairly well in her career.

Then about fifteen months back, Manjiri was in Bangalore for a technical conference and DK happened to be staying at the hotel where the conference was being held. He saw Manjiri there after a gap of about twenty years.

"They had dinner together and chatted long into the night. A lot had happened in twenty years and the two of them were different people now; light years away, it would seem, from the two young lovers who had been prepared to give everything up to be with one another. But they found that they still had very strong feelings for each other.

"A lot had changed since. Manjiri's parents had passed away and she was living an independent life. DK was a powerful industrialist and didn't have to fear his politician father or uncle. But he also had responsibilities. He had a wife, who had been by his side all these years, a daughter and a son.

"Since that meeting in Bangalore, they were in touch with each other. They talked regularly; shared their lives as much as they could. They talked about what was happening around them, what they were thinking and feeling."

Ishani was listening mesmerized. So far, Manjiri was just the dead woman who people had either very good or very bad opinions about. This story showed her a different side to her.

Neil looked at her expression, and gave a smile of understanding. Then he continued, "DK was in Europe when Manjiri died. He had talked to her two days prior to that. When he came back he got to know about her death through Atul Vaidya. It came as a big shock to him. He had lost her a second time and this time it was much worse and final.

"When he started enquiring about the investigation, he was horrified to know that it had been closed off in a week's time as an accident. He then decided to involve a private detective agency to find out how the case had got closed off in such a short time. That is when I got involved.

"DK was willing to go to any level to get the case reopened. He had feared that his uncle, who happens to be the Law minister, was the one to close the case. But luckily his uncle didn't have anything to do with it.

"We found out that QSoft had used their connections and the minister of state for industries had helped them close the case. Now, DK as a strong industrialist, was someone the Law minister was more than happy to please. So the case got reopened."

When Neil got quiet, she said, "That is one amazing story!" They both were quiet for a few moments and then Ishani said, "DK is Deenanath Kumar."

"Yes." Neil confirmed.

"You know him personally."

"Yes, I know him." Neil acknowledged. "DK is very wary of the story getting out and the media going after him. He is not too fond of the media. He didn't want his and Manjiri's story to be made out to be a torrid affair and he didn't want his wife to be hounded by them, asking her how she felt about it.

"He had asked me to keep the information to myself. But things have changed in the last three days. Considering a lot of things, including your visitor, I agree with the Commissioner on involving the media. So I talked to DK and explained to him how we would go about it."

Ishani nodded and realized that Neil really had a lot to think about!

"He had told his wife about Manjiri all those years ago, before they got married. He had also told her about running into Manjiri last year. But he had not told her that he had been in touch with Manjiri on a regular basis. When he talked to me and asked me to lead the investigation, I suggested that he talk to her about Manjiri's death. I also suggested that, he tell her about him getting the case reopened.

"Now, he has talked to her. But he is still wary about the media. Still, he has agreed to let us involve them. We'll have to make sure we are very careful though."

"And he is the one who is funding the investigation now?"

"Well, he is funding it partially. The case is reopened. The police would have taken it ahead at their pace but he wanted me to handle it. So he is funding our expenses."

They both had finished eating but were still holding their plates. Neil was the first one to get up and start cleaning up. As Ishani got up with her empty plate, and he said, "If you want to use the wash basin or the bathroom, go ahead."

Ishani washed her hands and stepped back into the room to find that Neil had neatly piled the plates and serving bowl on the tray. He carried the tray and opening the door, put it outside. Then he went into the bathroom. Ishani went and sat back on the same sofa chair she had occupied earlier.

She found herself thinking about Manjiri and Deena, DK. Manjiri had lost the love of her life in her youth; she never married. Then she had lost both her parents in an accident. Ishani felt very sad for a woman she had never known alive.

How had Manjiri felt meeting DK again? Did they only talk on the phone or did they meet?

Ishani looked up and found Neil standing across the room, his right shoulder popped against the wall. He was watching her quietly. She felt uneasy about his scrutiny but didn't know what to say. Neil asked, "Running it all through your mind?"

Ishani just nodded and was quiet for a few moments. Finally she said, "It does not change anything for our investigation really."

"True. But now you know more about the investigation." Neil said. Then he walked across the room to the window. He straightened the curtain and turned around. Then he said, "DK is absolutely sure that Manjiri would not go into the water by herself. He says he knew her too well. She was not rash at all."

Ishani lifted her feet up onto the chair and sat cross legged. Then she said, "You know, the Manjiri from that story seems like another person altogether. Someone who was so much in love with DK, seems like a contrast to the one that would have an affair with her boss, without caring about him being married."

Neil shook his head and said, "I got to know tonight that DK knew about her affair with Hemant. She had talked to him about that. After her parents died suddenly, she was very lonely and depressed. That is when Hemant started going over to her place. That is when the affair started. She was kind of grateful to Hemant, for being there with her in her time of need but then when she got in touch with DK again, she broke off the affair. According to DK, she had always felt guilty about it."

"Does DK know any of the people she worked with?" Ishani asked.

"He knows Atul from his college days, when Atul's cousin and Ishani were friends. He also knows few others. He had met a couple of them when he visited her in Pune a few months back. She had talked about some of them, like Ajit Ketkar, Sandeep and Dilip. It seems, Dilip, in some ways, reminded her of DK, which is why she couldn't help liking him."

Neil went and sat on the bed with his head against the headboard and legs stretched out in front of him, ankles crossed.

Ishani said, "It's a great love story."

He turned his head and looked at her. "Great or sad?" He asked.

"It is very sad, but also great. Like one of those tragedies from literature," Ishani clarified.

Neil shook his head, crossed his arms and closing his eyes said, "Reading them as part of great literature is one thing. Having to live them..." He sighed and kept quiet.

Ishani kept looking at him. He looked tired and his brows were drawn together as if he was trying to concentrate or focus. What was he thinking about? Different thoughts kept running through her mind, but she found it impossible to look away from him. Would she like someone because the person reminded her of someone else? Would she like some guy because he reminded her of say, Neil?

Her eyes were drawn to his mouth and she found herself wondering how it would feel to kiss him. Just then, Neil suddenly opened his eyes and caught her staring at him. She felt herself blush and looked away quickly. She didn't quite know what to say. She felt embarrassed when she turned back to find him still looking at her. He didn't say anything. Now, she could not look away. She felt as if he was holding her captive, their eyes locked. After what seemed like forever to Ishani, Neil put his feet down and got up. He walked over to her chair and stopped as if he was unsure about what to do.

"Ishani", he said huskily.

She opened her mouth to say something. Anything. She could only manage, "I…" Then she tried once again. "Neil, I…"

He suddenly bent down and rested his arms on the two arms of her chair. His head was now close to hers. She rested her head against the backrest and found herself looking into his eyes. He moved almost in slow motion and stopped when his face was barely an inch from hers. "Ishani", he said in that husky voice once again. "Umm?" was her only reply as she kept looking into his eyes.

"Stop me," he said softly. But she didn't. Something had definitely short-circuited in her brain and made her incapable of logical reasoning. In fact, her lips were waiting eagerly for the touch of his. She couldn't stop her hand from lifting and touching his cheek. Very softly, she said, "Neil."

He groaned and finally closed the distance between them to cover her mouth with his. For some inexplicable reason, it was as exciting as experiencing the very first kiss of her life.

The kiss started off gentle, his mouth shaping itself to hers, exploring her lips. Then his lips moved, probing hers to open up and one of his hands slid to her nape, holding her head gently. The kiss was insistent and when his tongue slid against her lips, she moaned and gave up any hope of holding onto her sanity. Lost in the kiss, she wrapped her arms around his neck and moaned. He got bolder with her response and his tongue plunged into her mouth, stroking hers.

After a long time, or it could have been just a few moments, when Neil finally lifted his head and looked into her eyes, Ishani quickly removed her arms from around his neck. They both were breathing as if they had been running. Neil withdrew his hand and straightened. He turned away and muttered something.

Ishani could still taste that kiss. If he had not stopped, she would not have been able to. She shook her head to clear her thinking. 'But this is so wrong', she thought to herself.

"Exactly!" Neil exclaimed and turned back to look at her. She realized then that she had not just thought the words, but actually said them.

"You are a married man…"

"We are here for the investigation…"

Both of them spoke simultaneously.

"Yes, of course that too," Ishani said. But she was surprised that for him the foremost reason, why this was wrong, was the investigation. Shouldn't his first reason be the fact that he was married? She thought angrily. She was getting teary eyed and hoping to hide it from Neil, she looked away.

Neil was quiet for so long that finally Ishani turned to look at him. She found him standing at the other side of the room, reclining against the wall and looking up at the ceiling as if he was lost in his own thoughts.

Ishani decided that she should leave. As she got up, Neil looked at her. It seemed like he was going to say something, but then changed his mind. Then he cleared his throat and walked towards her.

He stopped at some distance from her, ran both his hands through his hair and said, "We still need to talk about a few things for tomorrow." He laughed mirthlessly and said, "It is dangerous being here with you. Can we go down to the coffee shop and finish this talk?"

Ishani knew what he was asking was the right thing to do. Yet, at that moment, the fact that he was back to being business-like made her sad.

CHAPTER 14

Neil walked into the coffee shop fifteen minutes later, wearing blue jeans, a khadi kurta and chappals.

What exactly should he say to Ishani? Why had she looked at him with longing, the way she had? Till then, he had managed to keep his distance. But that look in her eyes had tipped him over. And the way she had responded had completely blown him away. His mind kept going back to those few moments when she had had her arms around his neck and her tongue was playing with his. Breaking off that kiss had been one of the hardest things he had done.

They should just focus on the case for now. He sincerely hoped that Ishani would be sensible about it. Ishani was seated at the same table where he had met her for the first time three days ago. Why did it feel like he had known her forever?

She noticed him as he got closer and stopped what she was doing. He sat down across the table from her and said, "I am sorry I took so long."

"That's OK," Ishani said. She must be feeling uneasy after what happened upstairs, but she managed to sound quite calm. Would she be worried that he could decide to have her moved from the case?

A crazy part of his mind was wishing that they were upstairs in his room. He almost groaned and accepted that he was not going to be able to sleep tonight. Making an effort to get a grip on his errant mind, he said, "I am going to have some coffee. How about you?"

Ishani nodded and said, "Yeah, sure."

Neil ordered coffee for both of them and then as the waiter left, turned to Ishani.

She opened the conversation with, "So tell me about how we get the media involved".

Neil blinked once and then smiled. He shook his head and laughed softly. She had managed to amaze him once more. "Yes ma'am", he said. Without any apparent discomfort, they could go back to discussing the case.

"The Commissioner's office will tip off news reporters; provide information but informally. That was your boss's suggestion and the Commissioner agreed. The information will get into a couple of newspapers and maybe even on some TV channel. It will not be official information. More like an 'our sources tell us', kind of story.

"Officially they will not talk about our involvement, but the reporters will be able to say, 'we also believe there are private detectives working on the case'."

Ishani nodded without saying anything.

"We go over to the Commissioner's office in the morning." He said finally.

"Why is that needed?" Ishani asked.

"Going over to the Commissioner's office?" Neil asked, looking confused.

"No. Sorry. I mean why do they need to talk about our involvement?" Ishani clarified.

Neil gave her a brief smile and said, "Both the Commissioner and your boss want to let the media know that someone tried to threaten you." Had she forgotten that?

When the coffee was served, Neil sipped his and looked at Ishani with raised eye brows, when she suddenly put her cup down and sat up as if something had struck her. She said, "You know, if this is made to be a big story then QSoft will not be able to hide it anymore. Then the best way to save face for them would be to cooperate in the investigation."

The discomfort and the unease that Neil had feared would hamper their work, had not lasted. Ishani was able to keep their close encounter aside and think about the case. He admired that. At the same time he could not help feel a pang of disappointment. Did that kiss mean so little to her that she could put it aside so easily? 'She is doing the right thing,' he had to tell himself.

"So do we meet Sangeeta tomorrow or not? I am really interested in what she has to say?" Ishani said interrupting Neil's musings.

It was one thing to be able to focus on the work but did she have to be so high energy and excited about it?

"You can go talk to her after the meeting at the Commissioner's office," Neil said curtly. Then, from Ishani's expression, he realized that his tone had come as a shock to her.

"I have something else that I need to take care of, so I'll not be able to join you. But yes, you should go," he said in a softer tone. He sounded almost normal.

CHAPTER 15

On Thursday morning Ishani woke up to the shrill sound of the alarm. She had to get up; it was 7:30 AM!

She'd had been an unusually late night, had not been able to sleep for a long time. She kept tossing and turning; unable to stop thinking about Neil.

As a result, she had to force her lethargic body and her reluctant mind to start functioning. She slung her legs down and sat up. She decided to brush her teeth and splash some cold water on her face to shake herself out of slumber.

Twenty minutes later, she was in the shower when her cell phone started ringing. She ignored it and started washing her hair. The cell phone stopped ringing and before she could sigh in relief the hotel phone started ringing. The only person who called her on that phone was Neil. She groaned. 'Leave me alone!' she felt like saying. But when the phone stopped ringing after just four rings she found herself think, 'Well, you could at least wait for a few more rings!' She had wrapped a towel around herself and was just stepping out of the bathroom when she heard a knock on her door.

"Who is it?" She asked.

"Neil", Neil said and stopped her in her track.

"I am up. Getting ready," she called back.

"Can you please open the door?" he sounded annoyed.

"Umm… In five minutes." She called out as she started drying herself.

He had gone silent. She waited for a few seconds to see if he would say something. But he didn't. She was wondering about his strange behaviour when the phone started ringing again. She picked it up and tentatively said, "Hello".

"I had called earlier but you didn't pick up your cell or this phone. That's why I came to knock on the door. I wasn't sure if you had gone to the gym," Neil explained.

"No I didn't go; was in the shower when the phones rang." She said and then when he went quiet wished she had not mentioned the shower. "Why did you call?" She asked hoping to get to the case and leave the awkwardness aside.

"Yes. I got a call from the Commissioner's office. We need to be there at 9:00 AM so we need to leave by 8:30 AM."

"OK. I am almost ready. I can meet you downstairs in ten minutes", Ishani said.

"I'll go ahead and start with breakfast then," Neil said.

She smiled at Neil's enthusiasm for breakfast in spite of all the craziness, "Yes, do that."

When she went down in ten minutes, she piled a few things on her plate and went to the table where Neil was having his breakfast. They ate quietly and Ishani could feel Neil watching her from time to time. Was he remembering their kiss? 'Think about the case!' she scolded herself.

Neil's phone started ringing and Ishani almost felt relieved. He looked at the phone but didn't pick it up right away. Why wouldn't he take the call? Finally he picked up the phone and said, "Excuse me" to Ishani. He got up and walked towards the reception area as he put the phone to his ear.

Ishani had almost finished when she felt someone approach the table. Assuming that it was the waiter, she said, "Can I get another coffee please?" and then turned to look at the person. She found Neil standing at the table.

"Yes, ma'am", he said and she could see the twinkle return to his eyes.

"I am sorry. I thought it was the waiter." She said unnecessarily.

"Well, you would know differently, if you looked at the person before placing the order", he said. But there was no sting in his words and half a smile on his face.

Ishani gave up on the coffee in the interest of time and got up saying, "I don't need the coffee. Let's go."

"Sure?" Neil asked her with raised eyebrows.

She didn't bother answering that. She walked to the reception and then outside to the porch. Neil followed and asked the valet for the car.

As they waited for the car, Neil's phone started ringing again. He pulled it out and frowned at the screen. Then he connected the call and put it to his ear. "Hi", he said and then got quiet. He just listened for a few moments. Whoever was on the other side, was saying a lot. Neil had gotten uncomfortable and Ishani felt, the reason was her presence.

"But isn't that what you wanted?" he said sounding exasperated. He listened for a few moments and then said, "I can't do this right now."

That probably was not the right thing to say. Ishani could hear a woman's high pitched voice, though she could not understand any words. Neil's brows were creased and he had closed his eyes, as if he was in pain.

"Alright. But I can't talk right now. I'll call you later." He said and looked a little relieved. Then almost as an afterthought he said, "Bye" and cut the call.

It was obviously a very personal call and the conversation had been disturbing. Ishani found herself asking, "Everything OK?" without thinking. She also felt like reaching out to touch his shoulder or arm.

Neil turned to look at her and said, "Hmm. I am trying to do what's right. It's not always easy."

It seemed like he wanted to say something more, but he didn't. They could see the valet driving in with their car. Since Neil still looked annoyed and unhappy, Ishani asked him, "Would you like me to drive?"

"What?" Neil asked as if he didn't understand what she meant. Then he said, "Are you a good driver?"

"I am not answering that question," Ishani said and walked over to the driver's side, even before the car stopped. The valet was surprised but politely said, "Here you go ma'am". Opening the rear door, Ishani threw her backpack in. Then she got in the driver's seat, closed the door and adjusted the seat. When she looked up she saw that Neil had not moved from his spot. She stared without saying anything. He shook his head and smiled. Then he walked over to the passenger side.

As they drove out, Neil said with a smile, "Sohoni, your boss did say that you can drive things really well, but somehow I didn't think he meant automobiles."

"Bhargav, he has kept us in the dark on many things. He didn't tell me that you are a chauvinist at heart or that I'll have to keep proving my abilities all the time," Ishani retorted. Then she wished she had not said it with a sting like that, just when he was getting back to being his friendly, teasing self.

Neil didn't say anything for a few moments. Then as she was getting uncomfortable with the silence yet wasn't sure what to say, he said, "You sound angry."

He had this habit of going silent and making the other person think he was not going to say anything. Then just as the other person was about to give up, he would say something. Ishani thought, it was very annoying but it must be very useful when he had to question people.

"Ishani?" Neil prompted.

Ishani found it funny that she herself had gone silent now and Neil had to prompt her. Smiling as she turned to look at him she said, "No. Not really. Anyway I can't stay angry for long and I don't hold grudges." Then she looked ahead and focused on the road.

"I am glad to hear that." Neil said rather seriously. He was in an odd mood this morning.

After a few minutes, he said, "I am not a chauvinist you know".

Ishani shrugged and repeated his words, "I am glad to hear that."

"I was only playing on the words when I mentioned driving things." Then after a pause, he said, "I thought you would find it funny too." He sounded like a petulant teenager.

Ishani was smiling as she said, "Well. It is funny actually. And I am sorry, I reacted strongly. But we see chauvinism around us so much, that sometimes we see it even in places where it does not exist."

"You as in, all women, you mean." Neil asked.

Ishani nodded and gave him a quick look. He raised his hands and said, "Just trying to get clarity. Not disagreeing and definitely not ridiculing!"

Ishani giggled at that and said, "Good for you." She felt really good when she found Neil chuckle in response.

She remembered something that she had forgotten last night, thanks to their misadventure in Neil's room. "Neil, have Inspector Morey and his team talked to people in the villages around the lake?"

Neil shook his head and said, "They did ask a few people, in the first couple of days after the incident, but nothing came up at that time."

"You know, Jivaji had said that there was a film being shot nearby. If they had stayed somewhere close to the campsite and had been there on 16thand 17thMarch, maybe they would have seen or heard something?" Ishani said.

Neil turned to look at her. He didn't say anything, just kept looking at her. She got uncomfortable and said, "What?!"

"Sorry. Yes, we should ask the police to find out." He again looked ahead, but looked back at her to say, "Good point, Sohoni," and smiled warmly.

They reached the Commissioner's office at 9:05 AM and went to the press room, where the Commissioner's office interacted with press. The first person they met was Inspector Pathare. He took out a piece of paper from his pocket and handed it over to Neil. "ACP Sathey has prepared this. We will give this to the press, though not as an official statement."

Neil read it and then handed it over to Ishani.

Manjiri Deshmukh case:

On 17th March a woman called Manjiri Deshmukh was found dead in the back waters of Mulshi dam. She worked at a well-known software company and she had gone on an official program to a campsite on the west bank of the dam along with seventeen other people from the same company.

After the first round of investigations the case was closed as an accident. But now more evidence has come to light and the possibility of it being a murder can't be ruled out.

The new evidence has given the police a clear direction to follow, to complete the investigation. They hoped to solve the case soon.

The police department hopes that Manjiri's colleagues and her relatives will cooperate and will provide the information that the police need, without hesitation.

At the bottom of the page, there was more matter –

It is believed that there are two private detectives working on this case; though it is not clear at this point, who has hired them. Neil Bhargav from Delhi and Ishani Sohoni from Mumbai seem to be working with Pune police.

It is also been said that on Tuesday evening, someone tried to attack Ishani Sohoni at the place where she is staying at present. This could not be confirmed.

"Are you sure these journos are reliable?" Neil asked. "I don't want us to be dodging reporters."

"They will not be any trouble, we'll take care of that," Inspector said.

ACP Sathey joined them in a few minutes and they all moved to the adjoining small room and talked about the case over tea.

"The Commissioner will be here any minute," the ACP said when he saw Ishani check her watch.

The Commissioner came in at 10:05 AM and called all of them in. He went over the statement and the additional information. He looked at the ACP and said, "Who are we giving this to?"

The ACP mentioned a Marathi and an English daily.

"What about the TV channels?" the Commissioner asked. He mentioned the name of a news channel and said, "Give this to them. They are very good at running it again and again, proclaiming exclusivity."

Then he looked at Ishani and back at the ACP, "Make sure Ishani here is not hounded by reporters. While we try to save her from goons, we don't want to make her a target for the media!"

Why was he singling her out? She looked at Neil and found him looking at her. He smiled and said "Please make sure I am not hounded either!"

The ACP said, "We'll do our best. These guys are OK. They will not bother you." After a pause he said, "We manage to control the impact most of the times. But sometimes the story tends to take a life of its own." Then he smiled grimly saying, "These days media wants to play investigator, police, lawyer and judge!" He sounded quite bitter about it.

After the brief meeting, when ACP Sathey, Inspector Pathare, Neil and Ishani walked out, Neil asked the Inspector if they had got any information on Ishani's visitor.

Inspector shook his head and said, "The waiter, who the visitor had talked to, didn't know the name of the person. But he did confess accepting money from the visitor, who had asked about you."

Neil then addressed the ACP, "When Ishani and I visited the campsite, Jivaji talked about a film being shot nearby. We need to get details of who was filming there and when."

CHAPTER 16

After a call to Sangeeta, Ishani made her way to see her. When she left the Commissioner's office, Neil was still there. He had insisted that she take the car, he didn't need it.

Sangeeta now worked at Infinity Software, a QSoft competitor. They had a big building in Kalyani Nagar, another part of the city that had a lot of IT companies. Sangeeta had suggested meeting at a coffee shop close to Infinity Software.

Sangeeta was waiting outside the coffee shop. When Ishani walked up to her and introduced herself, she asked Ishani if she had any identification. Ishani liked that, the woman was being careful.

In the coffee shop, they ordered the coffee at the counter and walked to a corner table. As soon as they sat down, Sangeeta opened the conversation with, "I have about 40 minutes, hope that will be enough."

Ishani gave her a cursory smile and said, "Let's get started right away then. Tell me about Manjiri. What was she like?"

Sangeeta shook her head and said, "You know even now I find it hard to believe that she is dead. Some people are just so lively and active. Manjiri was like that. Very smart and independent. Her teams loved her. Her peers, especially men, they actually admired many of her qualities but some never acknowledged that. Some men hated her, I think just for being more successful than them or just being smarter. But those who saw her good qualities, wanted to work with her and learn from her."

"Did you two work together?" Ishani asked.

"We never really worked together, except for a technical paper competition. Both of us were on the panel for evaluation. We got along really well. We were quite different from each other in every possible way, our working style, family background everything. The only thing common between us was that we both loved to travel. So we talked about different places we visited. Oh! And for a long time, we were the only two women in senior management at QSoft in Pune." Sangeeta was talking from the heart and she seemed to have a good opinion of Manjiri.

"Tell me about the night of March 16th. What happened?" Ishani got to the point.

Sangeeta went ahead and talked about the fateful night; her story was only a little different than what Ishani had heard so far.

"Can you tell me about the drinking session?" Ishani wanted specifics.

"Well, as always these folks sat around and had a drinking session," the way she said it, Ishani got the feeling that it was something Sangeeta disliked.

"Did everyone drink?" Ishani asked.

Sangeeta was quiet for some time, as if she was trying to remember back to that day. Then she said, "Hmm. Now that I think back, I think I didn't see a few people who would normally drink, drinking that day. But I am not sure I remember accurately." Sangeeta said.

"Who were the usual drinkers who didn't drink that day?" Ishani asked again.

"I don't remember seeing Dheeraj drink that evening." Sangeeta said closing her eyes. The waiter came and served their coffee and Sangeeta spent a couple of minutes sipping it. Then she said, "You know, I think Ajit Sinha didn't drink." She sipped some more coffee. "Actually, all of us were there and there were lot of things going on. People were singing, joking about. I don't remember exactly about everyone. But I think Jayant also didn't drink. He would normally drink a lot. That evening he said he had to drive back to the city as his uncle was in the ICU. I don't remember about others now."

"OK. Tell me about the dinner time." Ishani said.

"People had already had a lot to eat at the barbeque, so no one was looking for a proper meal, except for us vegetarians. But anyway, we all went to the dining hall. Manjiri was quite drunk that time.

"Just looking at her one couldn't know. But she came and sat by me and asked me why I was so quiet. I told her that I had a headache and so wanted to quickly eat and go lie down. That is when she told me that she felt high, so she would spend some time in the fresh air. She asked me if I would be ok with that. I of course had no problem. Asshe sounded quite drunk, I insisted that she eat something, which she did."

Sangeeta seemed to be thinking back to that night and remembering Manjiri. Her expression had changed to one of sadness.

"When I was leaving the dining hall, Manjiri was talking to Atul. Atul was not just the Centre Head for her; he was a very close friend. She went to him for advice."

"When did you know that Manjiri had not been to the tent?"

"I got up in the morning around 6:15 AM and got ready. Her bed was empty that time. I was quite surprised because it looked unused," She paused and then said, "I mean…. umm…. Well, Manjiri had something going on with Hemant and at some point people had talked about how he would go over to her place many nights a week. I don't know if it was all true but I thought about that when I saw the empty bed. I did wonder if she was with Hemant. But then I immediately rejected the idea.

"I thought maybe she had not come in because she had been sitting outside or slept in the hammock. I only got to know that she was nowhere to be found when I went for breakfast. Dheeraj asked me where she was. After a while, everyone was looking for her."

"It seems Manjiri had sat outside your tent for some time in the night. Did you hear anything?" Ishani prompted.

Sangeeta closed her eyes as if in pain. Then she opened her eyes as if she had some clarity and said, "I heard someone talking outside the tent when I got up to take a tablet for my headache. I think a man and a woman. I think the woman was Manjiri. The guy was asking her if she was OK and if she was sure she wanted to sit there. Then the voices stopped and it was all quiet for some time.

"Then I got up again to go to the bathroom. When I went into the bathroom, I didn't hear anything. But when I came out, I could hear someone talking in a very soft voice. I didn't understand what was being said."

"What time was that?" Ishani asked.

"I saw the time on my phone when I came out of the bathroom. It was 11:47 at that time."

"Why did you not tell this to police?" Ishani asked.

"When they asked us questions at the campsite after Manjiri's body was found, I was very upset. And I didn't think about this at the time. Later on I wanted to talk about it. But Dheeraj had called a meeting of all the people who were at the offsite and told us that QSoft needed to have this case closed quickly. That we should all stick to the basic story and not talk about anything more than the specific questions the police would ask. He also kind of defined the exact story that should go to the police from everyone."

"Everyone from the offsite was at this meeting?" Ishani asked.

"Everyone was there except Atul. He had gone to Bangalore on work when the meeting happened.

"I went and talked to Dheeraj. I told him that I had heard someone talk outside my tent in the night. He asked me if I was sure and knew who it was. I didn't know who it was and he told me to shut up." Sangeeta looked down at her hands as if she felt guilty. She seemed to be struggling with herself and finally said, "He also agreed to release me within a week, if I kept quiet."

"Sorry, what was that?" Ishani didn't understand what she meant.

"The notice period in QSoft was recently made three months. I interviewed at Infinity before that. But before they made an offer, the notice period at QSoft changed from one to three months. So I had been trying to get released as soon as possible, and QSoft was holding me to the three month notice period. After the offsite though, Dheeraj agreed to release me within a week of the meeting.

"I needed to start at Infinity as soon as possible so that I could take time off in another three months. I need to travel to the US for my daughter's graduation. So I kept quiet."

Ishani tried to control her anger, but she couldn't guard her expressions completely. Sangeeta was already feeling guilty and she rushed ahead to justify her actions further, "I was sorry that something so terrible had happened to Manjiri but I convinced myself that she was not going to come back, no matter what." Then after a pause she said in a small voice, "She also didn't have a family who was going to suffer."

Ishani felt lost for words. After a pause, she finally asked, "Why didn't you go to the police after you had joined Infinity?"

"I got really busy with work here. And I didn't think about it again, till two days back when I got a call from Inspector Pathare." Sangeeta explained as one would explain forgetting to buy a gift for someone or exchange a book at the library.

Focusing on the case, Ishani asked "So you heard someone talk outside first when you got up to take a tablet and then again when you got up to go to the bathroom. The first time you heard two voices, a man's and a woman's, right?"

"Yes," Sangeeta confirmed.

"What time was that?"

"Not sure. It was some time before I got up to go to the bathroom."

"How much time before that? Twenty minutes, half-an-hour, an hour?"

"Maybe twenty minutes to half-an-hour. Not more than that."

"And the second time you heard a very soft voice. Only one voice at that time? Was that a man's voice?"

"It was a soft voice. And yes, it was a man's voice."

So, according to Sangeeta, the first time she heard voices was around 11:20 to 11:25 PM. Ishani remembered that Atul Vaidya had said that he had brought Manjiri up and left her outside her tent around that time.

"Sangeeta, try to think back to that time and tell me, if any of the voices you had heard were familiar. Think about the people who were there and if the voices could belong to any of them." Ishani said.

Sangeeta looked at Ishani and seeing her serious expression, she nodded. She closed her eyes and was quiet for a while. Ishani could feel her focus.

Then suddenly Sangeeta opened her eyes and said, "The second time, I heard a woman giggle and say, "OK". I am pretty sure it was Manjiri's voice. I think then she got up and walked away; maybe with the person who had come to talk to her."

"So you heard two voices both times—Manjiri's and an unknown man's. What about the man's voice? Was it the same voice both times?" Ishani asked.

"No, I don't think so. The first one was calm and mature. It could have been Atul. The second time, I am not able to place that voice at all. It was very soft." Sangeeta gave a sad smile and said, "I wish I could help more. But that's all I remember right now."

Sangeeta had been quite forthcoming so Ishani asked, "If you were told that it was definitely a murder and someone from QSoft had killed Manjiri, would you believe it?"

Sangeeta sat up at the question. She looked at Ishani and then looked away. Then she shook her head, turned back to Ishani and said, "It was no accident; that I am now, sure of. That is a very scary thought, you know. One of my colleagues, one of Manjiri's colleagues killed her! Why would someone do that? I don't know."

"Based on what you knew about them and about her, who would you suspect? Could it have been more than one person?" Ishani asked.

Sangeeta shook her head and was quiet for some time. Then she said, "You know, I didn't like the way Dheeraj handled it later on. Maybe he was doing what was best for the company, like he said, but his attitude at the time was such that I now wonder if he was trying to cover-up for someone." But she could not come up with any names.

Before leaving she said, "I feel much better now that I have told you what I know. I took the easy way out to leave QSoft quickly but I couldn't help harbouring a nagging doubt at the back of my mind that I should have come clean to the authorities."

Once Sangeeta left, Ishani called Neil. He picked up on the second ring and said, "Hi!"

That one small word, made her think of the previous night.

"Hi," she felt breathless saying just saying it.

"Ishani?" He prompted after a few seconds of silence.

She collected her thoughts and said, "Just done talking to Sangeeta. She was quite forthcoming. I can update you when we meet."

"OK. You heading back to the hotel now?" he asked.

"Yes. I'll check with Inspector Pathare about Nisha Khanna's file."

"Alright. I'll see you later in the evening then." He was about to cut the call.

"Oh. Neil?!" She said and kicked herself for sounding like an idiot.

"Yes?" he said with his usual calm.

"My friend is coming over this evening. So I hope it's OK."

"Yes, of course."

"Are you going to be at the Commissioner's office till evening?" Ishani asked.

"No. I need to step out for some time. I'll update you about it later, when we meet."

"Do you need the car?" Ishani asked.

"No. Not at all."

"OK then. See you in the evening."

"Bye, Ishani," he said softly and cut the call.

Their reality had not changed since last night but right now she felt very happy at how his tone towards her had softened. She was not feeling as guilty about the whole issue now as the previous night. She smiled to herself and forced her crazy mind to come back to the case.

Ishani opened her notepad. She went to the list they had made last night of the people whose whereabouts between 11:30 PM and 1:00 AM could not be vouched for. She wanted to know who it could have been outside Sangeeta's tent when she heard the second voice at 11:47 PM. She eliminated Jayant from the list. The security guard had seen a car leave the campsite that night and noted the car number. It was Jayant's car alright. That shortened the list but there were still three names she could work with—Hemant, Nitin and Dilip.

She left the coffee shop ten minutes later thinking about ways to convince Neil to push the police to question Prof. Dhotrey.

Thirty five minutes later, as she entered the hotel lobby, she looked at the wall clock and noticed that she was just in time. She didn't see Inspector Pathare anywhere. As she made her way towards the lifts, a person got up from one of the sofas and walked over to her with a smile. It took her a couple of seconds to register that it was the Inspector. He was dressed in civilian clothes and though it was true that clothes didn't make a man, sometimes they made it difficult to recognize a man.

She quickly walked over to him and said, "I am sorry. Did you have to wait long?"

Smiling at her he said, "No, just got here and I am early." He was holding a folder that he held out to her and said, "The file you wanted."

She took it from him but before she could open it, he asked her, "Have you had lunch?"

"No, not yet", she said.

"I am off duty now and I am heading for lunch. I wanted to go for some simple, south Indian food. Would you care to join me?"

She was eager to go to her room and open the file. She was thinking of ordering something from the room service. But she didn't want to appear rude... It would help to have a good rapport with the Inspector.

"OK, sure", she accepted the invitation and then said "I'll keep all this in my room and come back."

They made their way on the Inspector's bike to Vaishali, a place Ishani had frequented in her college days. They placed their order and Ishani said, "Inspector, I wanted to…"

He stopped her mid-sentence and said, "I am off duty now so it would be nice if you didn't refer to me as Inspector". He laughed a little before saying "My name is Nikhil."

"OK," Ishani said and smiled in answer.

Over lunch, Inspector Pathare or rather Nikhil, turned out to be good company. He completely surprised her by talking about poetry. He quoted a few couplets by famous Marathi poets. He then told her that he had written some poems himself. Ishani smiled and thought how one person had so many different facets. A tough police inspector by profession was a poet at heart. And he was in a talkative mood today. She also found out that he was not married and his mother pestered him regularly to get married and settle down. He had an elder brother and he too was a police inspector.

She had been reluctant to go for lunch with Inspector Pathare but by the end of the meal she was quite glad she had joined him. The food was as good as she remembered, the service was still as efficient and the crowd as vibrant. And Inspector Pathare had turned out to be good company.

As they were walking out of the restaurant, Inspector Pathare asked, "Did you talk to Neil since this morning?"

"Yes. Around noon. Before coming to the hotel. Why?" Ishani replied.

Inspector gave a wry smile and said, "The Commissioner has decided to involve him in a different matter."

"What different matter?" Ishani didn't know what he was saying.

"I am not sure. But I think he wants Neil to be kept away from this investigation."

"Why?" Ishani was confused now. What was the Inspector telling her? Nikhil shrugged and gave a lopsided smile.

She got to her room and called Neil but heard the irritatingly familiar recorded message of the phone company, "The number you are trying to reach has been switched off".

"These phone companies are crazy!" she said. Sometimes when the call didn't connect, you got some random message. She waited a couple of minutes and called him again and was surprised to hear the same message once more.

'Trying to call you but am told your phone is switched off. Call when you get the message', she wrote and pressed the send button. She waited for a few seconds to receive the message delivery notification, but it didn't appear. Had Neil actually turned off his phone?

"Get to work" she told herself and opened Nisha Khanna's file. Nisha had two brothers, both older than her. Her father had expired many years ago and Nisha had lived with her elder brother till she moved into her own flat three months back.

Nisha had done BA and then MBA in HR and started working with a small software company about 6 years ago. She had joined QSoft four years ago.There was some information in the file about her passport and some mention of her travels. The last time she travelled was in March. On 15thMarch, Nisha had travelled to Bangalore and retuned on 18thMarch.

Ishani looked at the financial details mentioned and was quite surprised to see that Nisha's yearly salary was quoted to be 7.2 Lakhs but the flat which she had booked last year and moved into this year, was valued at 80 Lakhs. Yes, Nisha had a bank loan on the flat. But strangely, it was only for 38 Lakhs. Where had the remaining money come from?

There were some photographs of Nisha in the file, some from various ID cards, and some that looked like photos from parties or weddings. The woman was very photogenic; even her ID photos showed a beautiful face. Then, there was one that looked like a photo taken by a professional photographer. Nisha was wearing a lot of makeup in that one. It almost looked like a picture from a glossy magazine.

Ishani picked up her phone, selected Inspector Pathare's number and then changed her mind. It was rare for an Inspector to get some time to himself these days so she called ACP Sathey instead.

"Hello Ishani", he said.

"Hello sir. I was going through this file on Nisha Khanna and I wanted to as you about something. I don't know if I should talk to you about it or someone else." Ishani said.

"Depends. What did you want to check out?"

"Nisha bought a flat last year. The valuation of that is about 80 Lakhs. Her salary is 7.2 Lakh a year. Somehow it does not add up", she said.

"Is there a mention of a loan?" ACP asked.

"Yes, there is a loan. But it's only for 38 Lakh. Where did she pay the remaining amount from? Or is some information missing?"

He was quiet for a few seconds. Then he said, "You mean if she has borrowed the money from someone?"

"I was wondering if there was any inheritance; if she had come into some money. But yeah, she could have borrowed it too", Ishani said. You would borrow that kind of money only from someone very close.

"Hmm. We put that file together quickly in a couple of days so we have not been so thorough," he said a little defensively.

Ishani was not trying to find fault with the police. "Yes sir, I understand. In fact I was amazed at the information the police have managed to put together in such a short time."

That pleased the ACP. "I'll get someone to look into getting more information on the woman."

Around 4:30 PM, Ishani called Neil once again and was again told that his phone was switched off. She had not slept well last night and it was beginning to affect her now. She should make some tea for herself, she decided.

She was pouring hot water over a tea bag in a cup when the hotel phone rang. She smiled thinking that Neil was back; he was the only one who would call her on that phone. She picked up the phone and said, "Hi!"

"Good afternoon madam, I am calling from the front desk".

"Yes?" She was taken aback.

"There is a visitor here for you."

"Who is it?" Ishani asked.

"Mr. Harpal Singh."

"Who?" Ishani didn't know anyone by that name.

"Mr. Harpal Singh, from Delhi."

"Can you put him on the line, please", Ishani asked.

"Sure madam," The person said obligingly and there was a short pause.

"Ishaniji, helloji. Harpal this side. I would really like to meet you. I will not take too much of your time." The person said in a strong Punjabi accent.

"Hello Harpalji," Ishani replied politely.

"I was in Mumbai and since I was coming here, Uma Desai has given a package for you. She wanted me to give this to you as soon as possible," Harpal said.

"OK. I'll come down to the lobby. Give me a couple of minutes", Ishani said.

"OK ji. I am waiting here".

CHAPTER 17

Ishani got out of the lift on the lobby level and walked towards the reception desk. As she got closer to the reception desk, a person got up from a sofa on the other side and walked over.

"Ishani ji. I am Harpal Singh", he said.

He was a tall man with a full beard and typical Sikh pagadi. He was probably in his early fifties or maybe a little younger, it was difficult to say. He was not exactly fat, but he looked quite well fed, on the chubby side. He had rounded cheeks and a big, flat nose. His eyes, for some reason, reminded Ishani of Neil's eyes; though Neil's eyes were hazel green and Harpal's eyes were almost grey.

"Hello Harpalji", Ishani said with a smile.

"Thank you ji, for meeting me."

"Sure".

"Can we go to the coffee shop ji? I would like to sit down and talk to you," Harpal asked.

He looked harmless. And even if he was not, what could he do in the coffee shop? "OK, sure. It's over there". Ishani said pointing in the direction of the coffee shop.

They walked to the coffee shop side-by-side. At the table, before the waiter could come over, Harpal pulled out a chair for Ishani. "Oh, thank you!" she said and smiled. Very well mannered, she thought to herself.

"I will have some tea and something to eat. How about you Ishaniji?" Harpal asked.

"I'll have coffee", she replied.

Harpal looked around. Noticing his gesture, a waiter came over.

"Ishaniji here will have coffee. I will have tea and something to eat. What are you serving?" Harpal said.

"Sir, I'll get you the menu card," the waiter said.

But Harpal stopped him. "No menu card. Just tell me. What do you suggest?"

The waiter was well trained; he didn't hesitate. "Sir, would you like a sandwich or a burger?" he asked.

"OK. Bring both. Chicken," Harpal said.

"Sir? Do you mean one chicken sandwich and one chicken burger?" the waiter confirmed.

"Yes, yes. And coffee and tea," Harpal repeated.

Once the waiter had left, Harpal turned to look at Ishani and said, "Ishaniji. Or should I call you Ishani? After all you are much younger."

"Yes, sure. Ishani is fine."

"Ishani." Harpal said the name softly, as if he was trying it out. "It's a very nice name, it suits you".

"Thank you". What else could she say?

He looked around the coffee shop and Ishani followed suit. The coffee shop was completely empty at this time. The waiter had taken their order and gone inside. Right then, there was no one other than the two of them in the coffee shop.

Harpal looked at her and surprised her by saying, "Ishani, I didn't tell this to the hotel staff but I am related to Neil."

She looked at him carefully. From a distance, he didn't look anything like Neil, but at close quarters, she could believe that he was related to Neil.

"Neil and I are related from his mother's side," he stated. Ishani remembered Neil telling her about his grandparents. He had said that his mother's father was Sikh.

"His great grandfather was also my great grandfather," Harpal said.

126

Ishani thought about that for a moment and then said, "I see. So you are second cousins?"

"Not exactly. But let's not get into that", Harpal said and then went ahead, "One thing I can tell you. Neil and I are good friends." He looked around and then back at her. "So I was in Bombay on work. Then I decided to drive over to Pune. Then while I was driving over, I got a call from Neil's mother. She said he was here in Pune and staying at this hotel."

"OK, but you said Uma has sent something from Mumbai", Ishani said.

"Oh, that", he shook his head. "It was only to make sure you would meet me."

"I would have agreed to meet you even if you had told me that you are related to Neil".

"I didn't want to mention that to the hotel staff."

"Oh?"

"It's complicated. Neil can explain it."

"Neil? He knows?"

"Yes. Of course," Harpal gave a smile that made Ishani feel like she was missing something.

Before she could think what she could or should say, he asked, "So is Neilhere on a case then?"

The question put Ishani on her guard suddenly. Why was he asking her that? On one hand, he was saying Neil knew he was here and in the next sentence, asking her if Neil was here on a case!

"I can't tell you that", Ishani said but with a smile. She didn't want to annoy him, if she could avoid it.

Harpal looked surprised. He stared at her, then shrugged his shoulders and said, "As you wish. It does not matter".

That stare upset Ishani. It was a penetrating look. It made her think that he could read her thoughts.

"I tried calling Neil. But his phone is switched off," Harpal complained.

He was right about that. "Yes, his phone is off", Ishani agreed. "I don't know where he is right now, but he should be returning in some time, I think. So if you want to wait for him you could or just call him later, you should be able to reach him then."

"I am staying at Sun n' Sand hotel. Can you ask him to call me when he gets back? He has my cell number."

"I'll tell him to call you, but why don't you drop him a message?"

"Yes, yes. I can do that." Harpal agreed.

He took out his cell phone and got busy with it. His phone, Ishani noticed was a simple model, not a smart phone. It surprised her a little; most everyone who led a busy life these days used a smart phone. What did Harpal do? He had not said anything.

"If you don't mind my asking, Harpalji, what do you do?"

"I don't mind at all, Ishani. I work for a construction company. I am a general manager. I travel to different locations where our company has projects. I came to Bombay to review a new site. Then since I was already so close, I decided to make a trip to Pune."

"I see." Ishani said. She was still thinking about his phone. He had not offered her his business card and she had not looked for any other identification. Now she felt uneasy about him.

"Harpalji, can you give me your business card?" She asked.

He put his phone down and said, "No. I have run out of my cards."

How could she confirm his identity? She could ask to see his license; but he would feel offended by that.

She came out of her thoughts when Harpal asked her, "So how long have you known Neil?"

She could not, not answer. "Not very long", she chose to say.

"So what brought you to Pune, Harpal ji?" Ishani decided to start asking questions herself.

Before Harpal could answer, the waiter arrived with their order and spent some time making sure everything was served correctly.

Once the waiter left, Harpal focused on the food. Just like Neil would have, Ishani thought.

As she spooned sugar in to her coffee, she asked once again, "So Harpalji I was asking what brought you to Pune."

"Yes. I am here on some personal work, for my son. I want to check out some engineering colleges here."

"I see."

"Are you and Neil close?" She asked the next question that came to her mind. She wanted to keep him busy answering her questions.

"Yes. We are very close. Always have been," Harpal answered with a strange smile and then without giving her a chance asked a question himself, "How long have you been in Pune, Ishani?"

"Not very long," Ishani said.

After a few moments of silence, she looked up from her cup and found Harpal looking at her. Again, the way he was looking at her reminded her of Neil. "You seemed lost in thought there Ishani. What are you thinking about? Are you worried about something?" he asked.

She was startled. She sat back in shock and stared at him. He had suddenly lost his accent.

"Harpalji, I don't know what you are playing at! Till now you spoke with an accent and now suddenly it's gone", she said, deciding quickly to address the issue directly.

Harpal shook his head and said, "Ishani. It's me."

She looked at him. He sounded like… "Neil?" She asked incredulously.

"Yes, it's me! Neil."

"What?!" She looked at him carefully now. "What is going on?"

"I'll tell you everything. Let's finish here. Then I am going to leave the hotel as Harpal and go to Sun N' Sand, where there is a room booked for Mr. Harpal Singh. Few hours later, I'll return as Neil. Then I'll tell you everything." He slid the folder towards her "Can you get the bill? Put it on your room tab?"

"I need you to prove that you are Neil. I just want to be careful. I am sure you will appreciate that," Ishani said.

"You are being careful, which is good, especially after what happened two days back. By the way, did Inspector Pathare have any information about your visitor?" he asked.

So he knew about her visitor. And Inspector Pathare. With that, could she conclude for sure he really was Neil? She felt a little unsure. "Why don't you have your phone? Why is your phone switched off?" She asked.

"That is because I am Harpal right now. I don't want to be tracked by my phone. I will switch it on only after I am back to being Neil."

"Tracked? By whom?"

"The police."

"What?!" Ishani exclaimed. "Why would the police be tracking you?"

"It's a long story. I don't want to discuss this here, right now. When I come back as Neil, we can talk."

Then probably guessing her continued dilemma, Neil said, "OK. Let me tell you something that no one other than Neil would know."

"Good idea," Ishani said sceptically.

"We, you and I had dinner in my room last night. You had some sandwich, which came with fries. I had butter chicken with naan."

Ishani started smiling even before he completed what he was saying. Of all the things that he could have told her to establish his identity, he had chosen to talk about food!

"OK," she said. "Why don't we go to my room and you tell me what's going on right now?"

"You would not have taken Harpal Singh to your room in the normal course of events. We need to have people think that someone you didn't know came here to meet you." Neil kept his voice low. "I only came here to test the getup."

Ishani raised her eyebrows but didn't say anything. Neil went ahead, "If after half-an-hour, you could not figure out, that it's me under this disguise then I think it's very good!"

"You mean I failed some test? You know, I kept thinking that Harpal reminded me of you."

"It's not your failure, Ishani. It's the success of the disguise," Neil said, shaking his head. He smiled at her and said, "You have a very good eye for detail. And if you could not catch me in half-an-hour, the people who I will meet as Harpal tomorrow will have no clue."

"Who will you meet tomorrow?"

"All in good time," he said and gave a big smile. "I agree that this empty coffee shop is safe enough for us to talk but I need to be leaving now. I have to go and check in at Sun n' Sand. Then change and head over to the Commissioner's office and then return here as Neil," he said.

"You don't want to take the car right?" Ishani asked.

"I have my car and driver waiting outside."

"Your car and driver?"

"Yes, the car in which I have arrived in from Mumbai".

"Whose car is that?"

"I rented a car and driver in Mumbai."

"Mumbai?"

"Harpal flew into Mumbai and then drove down to Pune. He rented a car in Mumbai to drive to Pune". Neil explained very patiently.

Ishani thought about it for a minute and then said, "So it's a car and driver from Mumbai. It came and picked you up from someplace. Where?"

Neil sighed, scratched his beard and said, "OK. In short, the Commissioner arranged for me to go to Lonavala as a constable from his office along with a makeup artist. I became Harpal in Lonavala. The car came from Mumbai. The driver knew that a Mr. Harpal Singh had got stuck in Lonavala and he was to drive this Mr. Harpal Singh to Pune, stay one or two days and then drive Mr. Harpal Singh back."

What was all this? Ishani was quite confused. But she could see that Neil was getting frustrated. Whatever the plan was, she needed to cooperate to make sure it succeeded.

"OK. Mr. Harpal Singh. If you are sure you need to leave, then what can I say?" she said and smiled.

They got up together and walked through the lobby. At the exit she offered her hand for a handshake. Neil shook her hand and smiled. "It was very nice meeting you Mr. Harpal Singh," Ishani said.

"Pleased to meet you Ishani ji. You will be back in Mumbai in a few days right?" he said, his accent back in place.

Back in her room, when Ishani checked her phone, she saw a message from Geetika. 'C u @ ur hotel–7ish. Shaani, m so lukin 4ward!' Ishani smiled at the message. She thought to herself about how she really hated using cryptic SMS short forms but Geetu on the other hand, had really gotten the hang of it.

She had a lot of things whirling in her mind after that conversation with Harpal. Why would police be tracking Neil? That made her restless and she started pacing the length of her room as she thought.

Her phone started ringing, startling her. She picked up the phone, saw who it was and said, "Hello darling." She called her mother darling only when she knew she had not done something that her mother was expecting her to.

"Don't hello darling me! You were supposed to call me yesterday. Is it too much to ask for?" Her mother was in no mood to be cajoled.

"You left Shimla in a hurry and went directly to Pune to work on a case. You didn't bother to call me. When I called you, you were busy, I understand. But then you didn't call back. Now I switch the TV on and there you are in the news!"

"Oh!" Ishani was lost for words. She had not expected the news to be on TV this quick.

"Someone came over to your room and threatened you? And I have to find out about it from the TV news?" Her mother was very upset.

"I am so sorry, Ma. I didn't tell you because it would worry you." Ishani said. "Don't worry. It was not very serious, I was able to outsmart him and run out."

"How did you open the door without checking who it was? You are normally quite careful. What's happened now? Are you tired? Troubled by the case?" Her mother sounded worried.

"I made a mistake Ma. But I am being very careful now. I am not troubled about the case; nor too tired to think straight. I know it sounds really bad but it was actually not so," she said trying to pacify her.

"Ishu, I am really worried about you." Her mother sounded close to tears.

Ishani felt lost when her mother got emotional. She herself had been emotional like her mother, but slowly she had learnt to stop her emotions from determining her actions. She made an effort to calm down and then said, "Ma, don't worry. I am safe. Neil Bhargav, who is leading this investigation, is in the room next to mine. The local police are alert. Nothing will happen to me." Then to distract her mother she asked her, "Did you talk to Anil uncle? How is his arm now?"

That worked. Though her mother allowed for the topic to be changed with some reluctance, she went ahead and talked about her brother at some length.

After a few minutes, when Ishani was sure that her mother had calmed down enough she asked, "Ma, which channel did you see the news on?"

She was surprised to hear that her mother had heard the news on a well-known English news channel that would definitely be watched across the country. The news was made even bigger than what Neil or she had believed it would.

After promising to call her mother the next day she ended the call and switched on the TV to check the news.

Sure enough, towards the end of the main news, the newsreader spoke about the case. The newsreader made it sound like someone had hired the private detectives and instead of helping the investigation they were getting into trouble. Ishani's photo was put up on the screen while the news reader sceptically said, "Ishani Sohoni was allegedly attacked in her room." She made a face and switched the TV off.

At 7:10 PM Neil called from his cell phone. She picked up the call on the second ring and said "Hi".

He didn't give her a chance to say anything more, "Hello Ishani. Did you try to call me? I saw a message from you just now. I am sorry. My phone had some problem so I had to switch it off. Strangely, when I switched it on just now, it is working fine."

"Oh ok", Ishani said. There must be a reason why he was stating all this on the phone.

Neil went ahead, "I have been in meetings and discussions with the Commissioner all day long. Now I am heading back to the hotel."

Ishani asked the question that she would have asked if she didn't know what Neil had been up to, "Well! You could have at least called me and told me. I have been wondering about you! Anyway, where are you right now?"

"I am at the Commissioner's office but am walking out as we speak," Neil said. "I'll see you in half-an-hour," he said and ended the call.

Ishani was extremely curious to know about the whole Harpal thing. But it would be some time before she could talk to Neil about it. Geetu had called from the airport to say she was on her way and that she hoped to stay with Ishani for the night.

CHAPTER 18

As Neil walked towards the rickshaw stand, he smiled to himself. The day had not started very well but had gotten better with every passing hour. It had had many surprises; most of them pleasant.

His call with Divya in the morning had been like what calls with her were these days. She was angry, upset and accusing. Probably at that point the fact that he was agreeing to most of her terms had not registered clearly.

Later on when he was waiting for the Commissioner at his office, after talking to his lawyer once again, on a whim he had called Divya back. She was quite surprised by the call and said so multiple times. She had calmed down since the morning and talked to her lawyer. She had surprised him by telling him that she didn't mind dropping some of her asks. It had been a very amicable conversation. In fact they ended the call, on a decidedly friendly note.

Neil had gone into the meeting with the Commissioner on a very positive note. When Neil had explained that he wanted to meet Prof. Dhotrey and if required he could go in disguise, he had expected a lot of resistance. He was prepared to spend a considerable amount of time to convince the Commissioner. To his astonishment the Commissioner had been readily agreed to this idea.

The Commissioner had warned Neil that he had a very strong suspicion that Neil and Ishani's every move was being watched. He also thought that there was a leak in his office. He didn't know who was providing the information, but Vasantrao was definitely getting to know what the police were planning. He did think it was someone at a senior level based on the kind of information that seemed to be reaching Vasantrao. He felt it had all started after they thought of questioning Prof. Dhotrey.

When Neil explained that he had already thought about the disguise he could use, a Sardar named Harpal Singh, the Commissioner suggested that they don't wait, even for another day, to put the plan in action. He had decided to bring in his best makeup man to make Harpal look quite different and older than Neil.

The two of them had then planned all the steps they would take to create a completely different identity that would be very difficult to trace back to Neil.

They defined the person, his job and the background to his visit to Pune. Harpal was forty-eight-years-old and had two children. He was worried about his elder son, who seemed to not be doing well in his studies. He was looking for an engineering college for him. Since colleges in Pune had a good reputation he was interested in colleges there. The Commissioner said that the Gaikwad group of institutes had a reputation of having a lot of rich kids of businessmen and politicians. For Harpal to get a meeting with the principal, Harpal would have to be either of the two and willing to spend a large sum of money.

They had decided to take DK's help to make a hotel reservation in Harpal's name. The booking was made under the name of a construction company in Delhi and had been pre-payed. The Commissioner trusted very few people in his office when it came to sharing confidential information about this case; only his driver and a couple of constables. He had asked one of these constables and Neil to exchange clothes. Then Neil had waited for the makeup man, in a small room, which had an inconspicuous door opening into a side street. He was wearing a constable's uniform and so he was not likely to stand out if he stayed inside.

The Commissioner along with the constable, who was wearing Neil's clothes and big shades, had gotten into the Commissioner's car in a hurry. While getting in, the Commissioner had taken care to say very loudly, "Neil, this meeting could take the whole day and you will not be reachable. If you want to inform someone, do it now." People watching from a distance would have seen a tall man in Neil's clothes and heard the Commissioner address him as Neil. The Commissioner had also told all the senior police officers earlier in the day that he was involving Neil in another case.

The makeup man and Neil wearing the constable's uniform had left for Lonavala in a different vehicle half-an-hour later. Neil had taken care to switch his phone off. He had not informed Ishani even when he had talked to her just before leaving for Lonavala, since he didn't want to talk about it on the phone.

In Lonavala, the makeup man had changed Neil's look completely. In a formal light brown suit, and burgundy turban he looked about fifty. He was made to look a little rounded, especially around his middle. His cheeks too were made to look chubby. His nose now looked wider and flatter. He wore lenses to change the colour of his eyes. It had taken a lot of time to get the makeup in place. The makeup man had made sure Neil could put it all on himself. He would have to be able to do it the next day.

The car had arrived from Mumbai for Harpal Singh, who the driver knew was stranded in Lonavala and needed to go to Pune.

As the car got closer to Pune, Neil had decided to take a detour. He had a strong urge to go and see Ishani as Harpal Singh, because if Ishani didn't catch him, then no one else would be able to. He knew he was right about that. But at some level, he knew he was making an excuse to go and see her in disguise.

He had quite enjoyed playing the role of Harpal for her benefit. But she kept giving him looks that made him wonder if she suspected something. And at one point, he had felt that she knew it was him. So he had dropped the pretence and told her it was him. Then he had felt stupid.

After meeting her, he had gone to Sun n' Sand and checked in. He had put the "do not disturb" sign on his door, changed into the constable's clothes again and left the hotel to go back to the Commissioner's office. There he had changed back into his clothes and had a quick word with the Commissioner before leaving.

He was looking forward to seeing Ishani again. He knew she would have a lot of questions. He smiled thinking about the way she had looked at him when he had revealed his identity. He was also eager to meet Ishani because after the conversation with Divya and the lawyer in the morning, he felt like a free man.

He had been attracted to many different women and he had dated a few. But none of them had been able to hold his interest for long. Then Divya had come along. She was very beautiful and his parents had liked her so he had gone along with their suggestion and married her. Even during their short courtship he had felt that she spent too much time on looking good, but he had not said anything because he had thought all women did that.

Ishani was different. She was not obsessed with her looks. He had noticed that she dressed well; her clothes were of good quality and they fit her well. He had also seen her wear some amount of makeup but it seemed effortless and throughout the day she focused only on work. She didn't seem to think about her looks at all. Her hair, either tied up in a ponytail or lose on her shoulder did get messy and her lipstick faded by the evening but that didn't bother her.

She came across as a warm person with a keen eye for detail. While she focused on work, she didn't lose her good humour. She smiled easily and genuinely. It was a pleasure to see her smile. It made one feel that everything was just the way it should be.

He found her very beautiful; especially her big dark brown and very expressive eyes. Every time she smiled, her eyes shone. They twinkled when she was thinking of something witty to say. She was tall and lithe and she walked with an easy grace. For the first time in his life, he had come across a woman who he found very sexy and also intellectually stimulating. Funnily, she didn't seem to be aware that she was attractive and sexy.

She had opened up his mind to the possibility of a different kind of a woman. In her he could see a sexy lover but also a witty and warm friend.

His divorce proceedings had been in a suspended state for a while and till Ishani came into the picture, he had not felt any eagerness to get that moving. Knowing Ishani had made him want to be free of the ties that were broken long ago.

"Hotel Deccan Pride", he told the driver when he got into a rickshaw. All the way to the hotel he looked outside at the traffic and though about Ishani.

CHAPTER 19

At 7:20 when Ishani opened the door to Geetu both of them had big smiles on their faces. Geetu hugged Ishani right at the door and said, "Oh Shaani! It's so great to see you!"

"I know! It's been too long!"

"You and your work!"

"Don't blame my work! It's all because of your husband and son!"

They came in and sat on the bed laughing with excitement and happiness.

"That is a big bag!" Ishani said looking at Geetu's bag.

"I told you that I am staying here with you, right? And tomorrow I'll go to work directly from here."

"Alright. Do you want to freshen up? Want a cup of tea?" Ishani asked.

"What? This tea bag kind of tea? No way! We can go down for dinner after some time." Geetu said getting up. She picked her bag up and put it in the closet. Then she turned to Ishani and said, "So how come you are staying at this fancy place? What kind of case is this?"

Ishani explained briefly.

"Wow." Geetu said, her eyes getting bigger in surprise. Then she came over to the bed, took off her sandals and sat on the bed cross legged. "So your team is here? Your boss too?" She asked.

"No. This investigation is led by a detective from Delhi. Neil Bhargav. From EnQuaiR, I am the only one working on this case."

"Shaani! It all sounds so high profile!"

Ishani laughed and said, "We are also in the TV news today."

"What?!" Geetu said, "Why?"

Ishani gave her a brief lowdown on the whole thing. Geetu got worried and Ishani had to talk to her like she had talked to her mother earlier. She squeezed Geetu's had and ended with, "Don't worry! Neil is in the room next door and I have promised him that I'll be more careful."

Geetu seemed to be considering what she was saying. She was having trouble digesting it all. Then she said, "OK. I'll take your word for it." She gave a small smile and then said, "So this detective from Delhi, is he a good detective? Old? What did you say his name was?"

"Neil. Neil Bhargav." Ishani said with a smile. "He is one of the best. Not very old, less than forty."

"Good looking?" Geetu asked, her eyes sparkling.

"Very good looking" Ishani said. Then she laughed at Geetu's expression and went ahead, not giving her a chance to say anything, "And very married!"

"Are you sure?" Geetu asked wrinkling her nose. She was always considering every single man in the age group of 25 to 45 as a possible match for Ishani as well as for a couple of her, Geetu's, cousins.

"Am I sure about what? His looks or him being married?" Ishani teased her.

Geetu picked up a pillow and hit Ishani with it. "Yeah, yeah. I am sure! He is married," Ishani said laughing.

It was so good to have Geetu come over! Ishani felt her tensions and worries about the case, as well as her guilt about her crazy attraction to Neil, diminishing in the span of a few minutes.

"Tell me about your Rishi and Adi. Why are they going to Delhi and not you?" Ishani said changing the topic.

"I want to take time off later on. Rishi's mom and sister are both going to be there so Adi will be fine. Rishi was very nice about it. He said I needed the break." Geetu said with a smile.

"Your husband is really awesome! You know that right?" Ishani said.

"He is ok. Well mostly," She said nodding her head. Then she also said, "But sometimes he can be a real pain".

Ishani raised her eyebrows and Geetu knew she meant, 'Oh really?'

"Well most husbands, even good ones, are sometimes... you know!" she said.

Ishani laughed again and said, "I don't know anything about husbands but I can tell you that most men can be a pain sometimes. Some men can be a pain most of the time." Then to change the topic she said, "Forget grown men! Tell me about your little man, Adi. Show me some pictures, like a good doting mother!"

Geetu didn't need any more encouragement. She started talking about her son. Like any mother of a three-year-old, she was extremely proud of her son. She kept telling Ishani anecdote after anecdote.

The knock on the door brought their chat to a sudden halt. Ishani looked at her watch. It was exactly 8:00 PM.

"Why aren't you picking up your phone?" Neil asked as soon as Ishani opened the door.

"Not picking up my phone? It didn't ring." Then she said, "Can you come in? My friend Geetika is here. Let me introduce you."

He strolled in lazily behind her. She said, "Geetika, meet Neil Bhargav."

"Hi Geetika," Neil walked past Ishani, offering his hand to Geetika. Geetu shook his hand and said, "Hi."

"I hope you don't mind if I join you two for dinner," Neil said looking at Geetu and giving her his most charming smile.

"No, not at all," Ishani heard Geetu saying completely charmed by him. "Actually I should thank you," What? Ishani wondered if Geetu knew what she was saying!

"Thank me?" Neil asked sounding surprised himself.

"Yes. You know, for involving Ishani in this case and bringing her over to Pune for a few days. Otherwise, even though she lives in Mumbai and I in Pune, we hardly ever get to meet," Geetu explained.

Neil laughed softly and said, "I see." Then he turned and looked at Ishani and said, "So should we go down for dinner?"

"Yes. I am really hungry," Ishani replied. She decided to carry only her phone with her and started looking for it, but couldn't find it. Then she remembered that she had taken it into the bathroom with her. She opened the bathroom door to look inside and heard Neil say, "Ishani, I think that's the wrong door."

Did he have to keep making such jokes? She would have said as much if Geetu had not been there. For now, she just made a face at him and said "I think I have left my phone inside."

She found her phone on the counter in front of her. She found multiple missed calls listed on it, three from Neil, two from Abhijeet and one from Atul Vaidya. She also found a message from Abhijeet, 'Saw the news. Seemed to have gone well. Call tomorrow.'

She walked out with the other two, wondering if she should call Atul Vaidya right away. As they made their way to the lift, she let Neil and Geetu walk ahead. Falling back, she dialled the number and heard it ring. The phone rang for a whole minute, but Atul didn't pick up. Did he have more information for them? Had he heard the news? She decided to call, first thing in the morning.

She reached the lifts and realized that Geetu and Neil were talking about some Delhi restaurant. They didn't seem to notice that she had fallen back. When Ishani had almost reached them, Neil stretched out his arm and pulled her closer, "Ishani here doesn't like Punjabi food."

"Of course she does! Don't you Shaani?" Geetu turned to her for confirmation. Ishani smiled at her and said, "I do, of course. I was just telling him, that I don't like it all the time. Sometimes I want to have a dosa or something."

When the lift arrived they got into it and got quiet since there were other people with them but when she looked at Neil, he was looking at her and his eyes were twinkling. What was he thinking now?

From the lobby they made their way to the restaurant. The buffet table had already been laid out. In the restaurant while Geetika and Ishani went to find a table, Neil went to check out the buffet.

As they sat at the table, Geetu said, "Shaani he is really handsome! And so charming! And well-mannered too!" Ishani looked at her and shrugged her shoulders. She was not going to say anything about being madly attracted to him.

"Even if he is married, he must be great company while working, right?" Geetu suggested.

Ishani laughed at that and said, "Well, yeah. But sometimes he gets annoying with his silly jokes."

"I thought we have already established that all men are annoying sometimes," Geetu said.

They were both laughing when Neil came over and sat at the table. He looked at Ishani on his left then at Geetu on his right and said, "What did I miss? What are you laughing about?"

Neither Ishani nor Geetu replied. Instead, Ishani asked, "How is the food? Do we want to go for the buffet?"

That was the right thing to ask. "Oh the food looks good. They have butter chicken," he said with enthusiasm.

Ishani shook her head, turned to Geetu and said, "He had butter chicken just last night".

"So?" Neil asked. "I also had naan last night and plan to have it again tonight. But there is no dosa. No sandwich either," he informed her. "You might want to order that instead of going for the buffet," he told her with a smile.

"I think I'll manage to find good stuff in the buffet, thank you", Ishani said to him and then turned to Geetu, "Geetu, what do you want to do? Buffet? Or should we order something?"

"I am happy with butter chicken and naan," Geetu said.

Neil gave a big smile as if he had scored a point against Ishani. She ignored him and said to Geetu, "I am sure they'll also have ice cream in the deserts." Geetu loved Ice cream.

"I am trying to avoid deserts!" Geetu wailed.

Ishani looked at Geetu with raised eyebrows.

"I need to lose weight. My baby is three years old but I have not lost any of the weight I put on in pregnancy," Geetu said making a face.

"You can do that from tomorrow", Neil said and both the girls turned to look at him. "The deserts looked very good. We should do them justice," he explained with a smile.

The conversation was light and the food was good. Neil was being exceptionally charming. Geetu and he seemed to be in agreement on various things. They talked about the many things peculiar to Delhi but then Neil changed the topic and looking at him Ishani felt, it was because he had realized that she was getting left out.

He then asked the two girls about their college days. He listened with interest and laughed at their stories. Geetu was doing most of the talking. Ishani was only providing small additions here and there. She slowly got quiet and started watching Neil. Whenever he looked at her, and it was often, his look was warm and caring.

Ishani was lost in her thoughts, just soaking it all in, watching two people she really liked, getting along and making this evening so special for her. Then she heard Neil say, "Ishani? Ready for ice cream?" She looked up to find him looking at her curiously.

"Yeah, I am going to get some ice cream!" She got up and looked at them with raised eyebrows.

"After you ladies", Neil said.

"Really?" Ishani said, "You must be really full!"

She felt warm all over when he winked at her. She looked at Geetu and then walked towards the ice cream counter.

Geetu came after her and said, "Shaani!" Then she turned and looked at Neil before turning back to Ishani, "He is really wonderful! And he definitely likes you!"

"Geetu! Not now!" Ishani said in a tone of warning. Then she forced a smile and said, "Let's go get chocolate ice cream!"

Geetu made a face, "I am going to visit the rest room before getting the ice cream."

Ishani laughed and said, "Oh God! Even now?" She remembered well, how Geetu had to visit the loo anytime she had a heavy meal, how she would always take a break before the deserts.

"What to do, Shaani?" Geetu said with feeling and made her way to the rest room.

Ishani came back to the table with two scoops of chocolate ice cream. She sat down and asked Neil, "Want some?"

He looked at her for a moment. Then he nodded and picked up one of the two spoons from the plate and took a spoonful of ice cream. Ishani did the same. "Good, right?" She said.

"Yes. Very," he said. But it seemed like he was not talking about the ice cream at all.

He then looked around, "Where did you lose your friend?"

"She's gone to the ladies room."

"We need to talk", Neil said.

"Yes, I know! I want to know what's going on!"

Neil gave her a big grin and said, "It must be killing you right now not to know!"

"Do you find that entertaining?" she said sarcastically.

"It is!" Neil chuckled looking at her.

She changed the track, "You seem to be in an exceptionally good mood this evening. What's the reason?" Then before he could reply she said, "I mean, yes the food is good but you don't seem to be having a lot of it. You have not even gone for the desert!"

"It's not the food. And yes, I am in a very good mood. I'll tell you when we talk about it tomorrow."

"I can ask Geetu to go ahead and we can sit here and talk before going up," Ishani said, thinking about a way to avoid going to his room. Surely, he too would not want a repeat of last night.

"Let's go up. You can chat with Geetika for some time and then come over to my room. We have a lot to talk about."

Ishani didn't say anything right away. Then, because she could not let it go, she said, "Don't you think we should discuss it in the coffee shop?"

Neil stretched out his hand on the table and caught hers. She looked at their linked hands in surprise and then up at his face. "Come over to my room in an hour. I'll explain everything then." He said with an earnest expression.

She thought of snatching her hand away but she loved the way it felt in his. He seemed to be telling her something more than his words, but she wasn't sure she understood it.

He then looked up and removed his hand saying, "Geetika is back".

Ishani was glad for the warning. By the time Geetika came back with ice cream, Ishani had got her wayward emotions under control.

When Geetu and Ishani reached her room, Geetu opened her bag and started getting ready for bed. Ishani realized that she had left Nisha Khanna's file on the table. She scolded herself for being careless, picked up the file and put it in her backpack. Then she switched on the TV. If their news was going to be shown again, she wanted Geetu to watch it.

When Geetu came out of the bathroom, she took a look at the TV and said, "Oh are they going to show you in the news?" She sounded excited.

"I don't know. But maybe they will. I thought you might want to watch."

"Yes!" Geetu came and sat on the bed.

Ishani went into the bathroom and brushed her teeth. Then as she was washing her face, Geetu said, "Shaani I know this girl!"

Ishani tried to figure out if it was their news yet, but it didn't sound like it. What girl was she talking about? Must be some celebrity.

When she stepped out of the bathroom, Geetu said again, "I was saying I know this girl." She was looking at something on the table by the side of the bed.

"Which girl?" Ishani asked walking over.

"This is Reema Kulkarni".

Ishani was not sure who she was referring to. "Who is Reema Kulkarni?"

"This girl! You have a photo here. This is Reema Kulkarni".

The photo Geetu picked up was that of Nisha Khanna. It must have fallen out of the file.

"That is a photo of a girl called Nisha Khanna," Ishani said with a smile.

"No, no. This is Reema Kulkarni," Geetu insisted. "I have met her".

"You have got the wrong person, Geetu. This is a Punjabi girl, called Nisha Khanna."

"Yeah, yeah, she is Punjabi but her husband is a Marathi guy called Ravindra Kulkarni." Geetu said.

"She is unmarried," Ishani said shaking her head, "You're obviously thinking about someone else."

"Can you tell me why you have her photo with you?" Geetu asked.

"She works at QSoft. I am going through her file to check if there is any connection with our case." Ishani didn't mind telling Geetu. "But that is Nisha Khanna."

Geetu looked at the photo again and then said, "In January, Rishi and I had gone to Mahabaleshwar. The hotel we were staying at, Table Top Inn, is in a secluded area; very tranquil, very remote. It is also known as couples Inn because their clientele is mostly couples. They don't have a lot of entertainment at the hotel and it is away from the main town. It was also the low season, so they had only a few rooms open. Apart from Rishi and me there were only four other couples there at the time. So I remember all of them. Especially Ravindra Kulkarni and his wife Reema. They were in the cottage next to ours. They seemed to prefer to stay to themselves, but we ran into each other three times. Once we were sitting on the swing outside the cottage and they both came out. We chatted for a while. The next day we met over breakfast. Reema was wearing the same top and same earrings she is wearing in this photo."

Ishani knew her friend well. Geetu was not likely to insist that she knew the person unless she felt absolutely certain. Two people who looked so alike and wore same clothes? Was it possible that Nisha was married? And she had not informed the people at work? But the file that police had compiled on her also mentioned her being a single woman.

Ishani suddenly found the TV too loud. She picked up the remote control and switched it off. Then she turned back, "What can you tell me about her husband?" she asked.

Geetu thought about it and said, "He was average height, had a dark complexion. He talked a lot more than her. They said they had been married only for a couple of months and it showed. They sat close together, held hands all the time. He was always whispering something to her."

"You really seem to know them well," Ishani said with a smile.

"They were so much into each other! That's why I remembered." Geetu explained.

"Do you happen to have their contact details by any chance?"

"No. I don't. We didn't exchange contact details. We didn't really get to know them. We chatted about the hotel, the food, not being able to take time off."

"Does she work? What does Ravindra do?" Ishani was very curious now.

"They said both of them worked in a software company in Pune."

"Give me that photo. I should put it back in the file", Ishani said stretching out her hand. She took the photo from Geetu and put in the file.

"What are you going to do?" Geetu asked.

"We'll have to find out more about her."

"But how is all this connected to the death of that woman? Is Reema a suspect?"

Ishani sighed and said, "I don't know if this is connected to the death at all. She is not a suspect. But talking to her, it seemed like she knew something. She was in Bangalore when Manjiri died. And yet she was very nervous talking to me. I was going through her file to see if there was something that could tell us why she was."

After a few moments, Ishani asked "What hotel in Mahabaleshwar did you say you stayed at? Do you have their address and contact number?"

"Table Top Inn. I don't have the details but Rishi might. I can get it from him."

"Can you call him now?"

Geetu looked unsure but then probably because she realized the importance of it, she nodded and said, "Yes, of course. He was going to call me once he landed so I'll wait for his call for a few minutes and then call him."

Then she picked up the remote control and switched on the TV saying, "Let me watch the news and see if you are there."

When the headlines were over, just before the break, the newsreader mentioned their story in the upcoming news. Ishani dialled the number for Neil's room.

"Hi Shaani!" he said almost in the same tone that Geetu used. Ishani found that annoying and amusing at the same time. She was still thinking about what to say when he went on, "Are you calling me to make an appointment, to come over Sohoni?"

"I am calling to tell you that they are showing our news. In case you would like to watch", she said.

"Which channel?" He asked and she told him.

"Oh and there is something more. But I'll tell you when I come over in a while."

"I am waiting," he said.

When Ishani turned around after putting the phone down, she found Geetu looking at her.

"Shaani! What's going on? Neil Bhargav likes you. A lot! And you obviously like him! I can see that."

Ishani shrugged and said, "I told you he is married right?"

"Yeah!" Geetu said and made a face, "How sad is that?!"

Ishani laughed at that statement. Then she said, "Anyway, let's watch the news."

Geetu watched attentively but before the news got over, Geetu's phone started ringing. She picked up and said, "Hi" with a big smile. "How is Adi doing?"

Then she laughed a little and asked, "Alright. How are you doing?"

Ishani signalled to Geetu and Geetu said, "Hold on a sec" into the receiver, she looked at Ishani and whispered, "This will take some time. I have to talk to both of them and maybe even my mother-in-law."

"I'll be at Neil's room. We need to discuss a few things." Geetu nodded. Ishani could not help remind her, "Please ask Rishi about the phone number and address of the hotel."

Geetu smiled and said, "Yes madam detective!"

CHAPTER 20

When Ishani knocked on Neil's door, her heart was galloping in anticipation. Neil opened the door and smiled before stepping back to let her walk in.

"Did you watch the news? Your photo was flashed on the screen and you looked quite good, I thought", he said.

"Yes, I watched. And you need to get your eyes checked!" Ishani said, being in this room again, alone with him, made her feel a little uneasy.

"We have about half-an-hour," she said.

"To do what?" Neil asked with a twinkle in his eyes and a big smile.

Exasperated, Ishani closed her eyes. Then she stared at him and said, "Look Neil. We both agreed that last night was a mistake! And that we need to avoid a repeat. Can you please not say things that….."

He prompted, "Say things that?"

"Never mind. Can you tell me what the plan is for tomorrow?" It was best to get to the heart of the matter.

Neil considered that and nodded. Then he said, "Why don't you sit down? I'll make some coffee. Let's discuss the plan for tomorrow but I also have something else to tell you."

"I'll make the coffee. You sit down." Ishani said. It would be better if she was doing something with her hands.

Neil looked at her for a moment but then agreed, "OK. Make it strong".

Ishani got busy making the coffee and Neil went and sat on the bed. She felt his eyes on her. She forced herself to think about the case and said the thing that was fresh in her mind, "Geetu found a photo of Nisha Khanna and she says she knows her but by a different name. Reema Kulkarni."

151

"Does Nisha have a sister?"

"No. There is no mention of a sister in her file. Geetu is absolutely sure it's the same person." She explained what Geetu had told her about Nisha.

"That is interesting," Neil said.

"I have asked her to give me the details of the hotel," Ishani said.

"Yes. Good," Neil replied.

"OK. Now tell me about tomorrow", Ishani was eager to know what he planned to do.

"Right. Tomorrow I am going to meet the principal of S. J. Institute of Technology as a father of a rich kid who needs admission and degree from a reputed engineering college. The person I need to really meet is Prof. Dhotrey. So Harpal will have a lot of questions about the job prospects, about companies that recruit from their college and about the process. This should get me a meeting with Prof. Dhotrey. I think I would be able to steer the conversation in the right direction to find out if there is any connection with QSoft."

"You think, recruitment from the Gaikwad group of institutes is the connection with QSoft?"

"Well. That is what I was able to think of. What else could it be?"

"QSoft recruits from many colleges," Ishani said. "Maybe they recruit from the Gaikwad group too but so what?"

"I don't know if it will lead anywhere but we have to talk to him. We can't question him directly, so I have to do it under disguise," he explained.

Ishani thought about it a bit and then said, "Alright but be careful. If the principal or Prof. Dhotrey suspect something, you could get in big trouble."

She brought two mugs of coffee over and handed one to Neil. He took it and took a sip. "Perfect!" he said and took another sip before putting the mug down on the side table.

Ishani sat in the sofa chair and sipped her coffee. Then she said, "So you go as Harpal. Before that you go to Sun N' Sand and turn into Harpal."

"Hmmm. I have an appointment in the college after 10:00 AM, but I'll vanish from here before 7:00 AM.

"You and I are being watched, fortunately from a distance. The Commissioner has managed to find out that they watch us from the time we leave the hotel in the morning till we get back. Someone will be outside the hotel from around 8:00 AM.

"This evening when I came in, I think I figured out who our watch dogis. He is a short, thin guy with thinning hair. Very non-descript, one would not notice him easily."

"One wearing an old khaki shirt and dirty, fawn pants? Who smokes?" Ishani had noticed the guy.

"Yes", Neil confirmed and smiled. "So you know the guy. He will be here by 8:00 AM and I want to be gone much before that. I'll have to get into my room at Sun N' Sand unnoticed and put on my disguise. I'll checkout from there before going to the college. After my meetings in the college, I'll head back to Mumbai. I'll get off in Lonavala and return in another disguise.

"I got another magnetic card for my room from the reception. I'll leave one with you. I'll be leaving my cell phone here in the room. After I leave, you are going to tell everyone that I am down with high fever.

"When I return, I'll act like I have just started feeling better."

Ishani was listening attentively and nodded in agreement. "What is this about police tracking you?"

"The Commissioner thinks that someone from his team is passing on information to Vasantrao Dabhade. As part of another case, he had discovered that Vasantrao had moles in cell phone companies and he was able to track people by their phones.

"I switched off my phone so that my whereabouts could not be tracked using that, when I was under disguise."

"Is there any way to know if our phones are actually being tracked?" Ishani asked "And what is Vasantrao's interest in us?"

"Well the Commissioner believes that Vasantrao's interest is due to Prof. Dhotrey." He paused and then said, "It's possible that Prof. Dhotrey may divulge information that can hurt Vasantrao."

153

They sipped their coffee in silence for a couple of minutes. Then Ishani remembered, "The QSoft guy who heads recruitment for the centre is Ajit Sinha."

Neil nodded in agreement and Ishani went ahead, "If there is a recruitment connection between Prof. Dhotrey and QSoft, then Ajit Sinha would know. Should I talk to him to see what I can find out?"

While Neil was thinking about that Ishani continued, "Atul Vaidya tried calling me today. When I tried returning his call, he didn't pick up. I'll call him in the morning. Should I try and talk to him? He seemed really interested in helping us in the investigation."

"Don't try talking to Ajit Sinha yet but do call Atul back. See if you can talk to him. See if you can find out anything about their recruitment from the Gaikwad group of institutes. But don't divulge any information."

"What time do you think you'll be back tomorrow?" Ishani asked.

Neil got up and yawned. He picked up his empty mug and headed for a refill. "The meetings at the college could take a couple of hours so taking into consideration the time I would need to get rid of Harpal in Lonavala, I think I should be back by 4:00 PM." He stood by the coffee maker sipping from his mug.

Ishani got up and walked over with her mug. Neil extended his hand for her mug and said, "Want more?"

"A little."

As he turned to pour coffee for her, he said, "When I get back, I'll call you from my phone. Leave it here in the room. Don't try to contact me before that."

He yawned again and Ishani said, "Are you OK Neil? You are yawning a lot. Are you not well? Too sleepy?"

He turned with her coffee mug in his hand and giving her a sardonic look said, "I am very sleepy. I have not been sleeping well".

She took the coffee mug and went to turn. But he held her arm and said, "I hardly slept last night." It seemed like he meant that he had not slept because of her.

"Look Neil…" She started but he stopped her with a finger on her lips and asked, "Did you not think about us at all last night?"

Of course Ishani had stayed up thinking about him. But she didn't really want to tell him that. If she didn't want to get involved, she should not be having this conversation with him.

"Ishani?" Neil prompted. When he was asking her specifically, how could she lie?

She sighed and looked at him. He lifted his finger as she went to say, "I did. Of course I did."

He then took her coffee mug from her and put it on the counter top next to his. Turning back he said, "I am sorry".

Before he could go ahead, she said, "Sorry? For what? For the kiss?"

"No. Oh no!" he replied with a gentle smile that made her heart do a summersault. "Definitely not for the kiss! But for letting you think later on, that it was wrong. For letting you believe that I am a married man."

What was he saying? "What do you—" Before she could complete her question, the hotel phone started ringing. "It must be Geetu," Ishani said and pulling her arm from Neil's grip walked over. Then she felt a little awkward. What would he think? It was after all, his room and his phone! So instead of picking up the receiver, she put it on the speaker to receive the call and said, "Hello".

"Shaani, are you coming back or have you decided to give in and spend the night with him?" Geetu asked. Ishani turned red in embarrassment and didn't quite know what to say. She was quiet for long enough for Geetu to notice. She said, "Shaani?"

Ishani wanted to yell at Geetu for her inappropriate behaviour. Shouldn't she have at least made sure that Ishani was the only one listening to her? Then she noticed that Neil had walked over with a wicked smile. She could not bring herself to look at him. As she went to pick up the receiver, Neil held her hand realizing her intention and said in the speaker, "Geetika can you please help me here? Ishani has been trying to have her wicked way with me, though I am telling her that I have a headache." Then when he heard Geetu mutter "Oh shit!" he burst out laughing.

Ishani waslivid; she wanted to kill him! Neil took one look at her and said, "Alright girls! I am sorry. Geetika, just in case you are wondering why I am suddenly apologizing, it's because your friend is hopping mad. If looks could kill, I would be dead a couple of times already!"

Ishani pulled her hand free from Neil's grip, picked up the receiver with her other hand and said, "Geetu I am coming over in a few minutes." Then she cut the call and turned around to look at Neil. But before she could say anything, he said, "OK. Maybe it was not the best thing to say, but I am sure you can see how tempting it was!"

When she just stared at him, he said, "Come on Ishani! Can't you see the funny side to this situation?"

"Is everything a joke to you Neil?" Ishani asked seriously.

He sighed and said, "No. It is not. But why are you so angry about this?"

When she looked at him incredulously, he went ahead, "So Geetika is teasing you about being with me! What is the big deal?"

What he was saying was true enough. What was the big deal? Didn't Neil already know that she was attracted to him?

Ishani was an honest person and she could express her thoughts without hesitation. But one's expressions often get coloured by society's norms. She could be honest about her opinions and ideas but it was not always easy being honest about one's feelings. As a woman she was conditioned to hide her feelings, especially the ones involving sexual desire.

She was not a blushing virgin and yet when she felt exposed about her desire for Neil, her instinctive reaction had been that of anger. It had felt as if her crime had been exposed.

Ishani thought about the situation a little more calmly. Only Neil and Geetu were teasing her. And she had not committed any crime. She calmed down and acknowledged that the situation was quite funny actually.

Neil realized that she had calmed down. He smiled at her and she found herself give him a shy smile. Neil's smile broadened and suddenly Ishani was giggling. He laughed softly and reaching out pulled her to him. That sobered her and she tried to pull herself free. But he would not let her go.

"Ishani, listen for a minute. I am not a married man. Not the way you think."

Ishani stopped struggling and said, "Which way?"

"I mean, I am getting divorced."

"What?"

"Yes. Divya, my wife and I have been living separately for more than a year. We stopped being a couple long back."

So why had he not told her this last night? Why was he telling this to her now?

"Last night…" he said and stopped. Neil wrapped his arms around her waist slowly and pulled her closer. She rested her hands on his chest and stopped him.

Neil said, "Last night I didn't know what I was doing; I couldn't think of the appropriate explanation. I didn't know what to do," Ishani accepted that. She had felt like she had been swept away by a storm. He read the change of her expressions correctly and feeling encouraged said, "I have been thinking all day today that I need to tell you. I am not cheating anyone."

Ishani's mind had stopped functioning. She wanted to ask him something about what he was saying, but just could not remember what it was anymore. Instead, she found herself looking at his lips. She wanted to trace them with her finger. She wanted to touch his face, put her lips on his cheeks and his eyes. She looked up and found him looking at her intently. He searched her face and obviously found something that he was looking for. Bringing his left hand up, he held the back of her head and bent down slowly, looking into her eyes. She struggled to breathe and when he seemed to take forever, Ishani closed the gap to put her lips to his. Just as her lips touched his, he very softly said, "Ishani". She moved her hands from his chest with one going around his neck, the other in his hair. She traced his upper lip with her tongue and he groaned. He tightened his hold even more and turned her face to angle it properly for a deep, all-consuming kiss.

When Neil pulled back Ishani found herself feeling desolate. Neil dropped his arms and stepped back. "No, don't look at me like that." he said and reaching out, caressed her cheek with his knuckles. Ishani closed her eyes and sighed. Then she made a physical effort to snap out of the spell. She opened her eyes and he said, "We can't go beyond this right now," Ishani nodded and he went ahead, "Not only are we working together, but for this case, I am your superior. We can't openly be a couple. And I don't want us to have to sneak around like thieves. This is not going to be a sordid affair. I don't want anyone to be able to point fingers at you, at us."

Ishani felt overwhelmed. It was a combination of having to stay apart, knowing he was right and feeling happy that he cared. Neil saw that she was closed to tears and said, "Ishani? Did I say something wrong? I didn't mean to…"

"No. You didn't," She stopped him and then with her hand held the wrist of his hand that was still on her cheek. "You are right." She said and gave him a teary smile and pulled his hand away from her cheek. She held it in both hers and said "And don't worry. I am not going to start the water works."

He laughed softly and shook his head, "It is going to be very difficult to stay away from you, Ishani!"

Ishani smiled and nodded in agreement. She dropped her hands reluctantly and said, "Alright. I better go and face Geetu now."

She turned and walked towards the door and he followed just a step behind her. As she opened the door he said, "Alright Sohoni! I'll be calling you early in the morning, before I leave. Now, for what it's worth, good night!"

CHAPTER 21

Ishani was up and doing stretches on the floor when the phone rang in her room. She went over to Neil's room and found him dressed in track pants, a dull grey t-shirt and running shoes. He had a hooded light jacket in his hand. As she entered, he closed the door and turned. He looked at her from top to toe and took in her dark blue tights and light grey fitted t-shirt and said, "I can't wait for this case to be over!"

She blushed at the look he gave her, and felt lost for words. Then making an effort she asked, "Where is that spare key? And your phone?"

He pointed at the counter where both the things were kept. She said, "Have you got everything you need? The other phone? The key to that hotel? The key to this hotel?"

He said, "Got all those. Just need one more thing." He walked over to her with a purpose and then gave her a quick hard kiss on the lips and said, "For good luck." Then he was gone.

She went back to her room and got ready. At 8:10 AM, she told Geetu that she would go check why Neil was not taking her calls. She let herself in using the spare card key. Then she arranged the pillows and bolsters on the bed and covered the arrangement with the comforter. She checked to make sure that from the door it would look like a sleeping person.

She called housekeeping and asked if they could give her a thermometer, Crocin and Vicks. She then called room service and asked for hot tea and Parle-G biscuits.

She waited till the things she had asked for were delivered by housekeeping and room service. She told the house keeping staff how Neil was running a high fever and should not be disturbed. Even to make his room.

She was about to walk out, when Neil's phone rang. She walked back inside and looked at the phone screen. "DK" it said. Making up her mind, she connected and said, "Hello, Neil is not well. I am Ishani Sohoni. I am working with him right now. Can I take a message?"

"Hello Ishani. I am Deenanath Kumar, calling from Delhi."

After the call she put Neil's phone on silent mode, but didn't switch it off. When she walked out of the door, she made sure to hang the "Do Not Disturb" sign on the door.

She went back to her room and said, "Neil is not well."

"Oh? What happened?" Geetu sounded surprised, as expected.

"High fever. Nothing too serious, I hope." Ishani said, making an effort to sound worried. "But I think he will stay in bed."

Geetu looked at her and Ishani knew she wanted to say something, but was hesitating because of the 'talk' Ishani had had with her the previous night. So Ishani smiled at her and said, "And no I am not going to go and keep him company in bed!"

Geetu relaxed and laughingly said, "But you want to!"

Ishani punched her playfully and said, "No! Not today!"

"By the way, have you seen today's papers? You are there. With your photo too!" Geetu informed Ishani.

Ishani picked up the paper and looked at the page Geetu opened for her. It was the local section, but the news was given prominence.

After they had a quick breakfast, Geetu gave Ishani a tight hug and before leaving said, "Shaani! Come over on Saturday or Sunday, if you have time. I am alone and am going to take it easy."

Ishani drove to the coffee shop where Atul Vaidya had agreed to meet her on his way to work.

After ordering coffees for both of them, Atul opened the conversation with, "I saw the news last evening. I was sorry to hear that someone tried threatening you."

Ishani gave a tight smile and shrugged.

"In the news yesterday, they said that police have got new clues and a clear direction for investigation. Is that true?" Then before she could say anything, he went ahead, "I hope so. I would like to see this case solved."

He got up and got their coffee, which was kept on the counter. He spent a few moments neatly arranging the cups on the table, making sure they had sugar and spoons and the tray was kept out of the way.

Sitting down, he said, "There is a party this evening to honour QSoft's top performers. Our CEO Sivshankar Venkatesan, SSV for short, is coming over from Bangalore for that. He would like to meet the two detectives working on the case." He sipped coffee for a couple of moments, nodded as if he was pleased with the taste and then said, "I thought it would be a good idea for the two of you to come for the party. A lot of people from QSoft will be there. It would be a good chance for you to observe people, even to talk to them."

Ishani thought about it for a minute. Getting media attention, it seemed, was working. She said, "Neil is not well. He is running a high fever. So I don't know if he can make it, but I will come over."

"Great! It starts at 7:30 PM at Holiday Inn." Atul said. "Do you need a ride?"

"No. I'll drive." Ishani said. Couldn't he have told her this on the phone?

He sipped some more coffee. Then looking at his coffee cup he said, "There was something else that I wanted to tell you. This is something that should have struck me earlier itself."

Ishani waited patiently for him to come to the point. "I think Manjiri wanted to talk to me about Ajit Sinha that night." He said and sighed.

"You had said she was in no state to tell you the name." Ishani remembered clearly.

"That night she was very high. She couldn't tell me the name. The only thing I could understand was that the guy she wanted to talk about was there and she thought he had a phone. So I wondered if she meant Dheeraj."

"So now, why do you think that she meant Ajit Sinha?" Ishani asked.

"Earlier in the week, she had called me and said she wanted to talk about Ajit. I had assumed she meant Ajit Ketkar; he is a manager who reported to her. But Ajit Ketkar was not on the program." He turned his head and looked outside for a couple of seconds then turning back to look at her he said, "I think even earlier she meant Ajit Sinha. I just didn't realize that."

"So what made you realize this?" Ishani asked.

"You need to talk to Dheeraj in detail, but in short, Manjiri had gone to Dheeraj about two weeks or so before her death, complaining about Ajit Sinha. This was about some engineering students we had hired last year. Two engineers had moved to her team in February after their earlier project ended and according to her they were no good. She felt they should not have been hired in QSoft. She had earlier talked to Ajit Sinha and they had ended up having a fight. She had then gone to Dheeraj.

"She had insisted on knowing the details of their recruitment. She wanted to see who had interviewed them. Both of them were from M.V. College of engineering and one was actually interviewed by her. She had written very good comments about him in the feedback form. She couldn't believe it. Then she went back to Dheeraj after a couple of days and insisted that the student she had interviewed was different from the engineer in her team. She said she had 'interviewed' him again and he could not solve the most basic problems. But the photograph in the file from the time of recruitment was of the engineer in her team. To appease her, Dheeraj had said he would check the other files, but he didn't really buy her story. The files were all in order."

They were both quiet but Atul read Ishani's expression correctly and shaking his head said, "I didn't know anything about this. It was only yesterday when I went and talked to Dheeraj about Manjiri wanting to talk to me about Ajit, that he finally said it must have been about Ajit Sinha. And he then told me all this."

"When we asked Dheeraj about people who might have had problems with Manjiri, he didn't say anything about this." Ishani said.

"He thought he was acting in QSoft's best interests," Atul said.

"Dheeraj should know that withholding information in a crime investigation is a punishable offence," Ishani stated sternly. Atul closed his eyes and nodded briefly.

"You should talk to Dheeraj," He said. "I have asked Dheeraj to pull out files of all the students from M.V. College. We will review their performance. We have ten engineers from M.V. College who joined us last year and three from the year before. We are also expecting about ten from that college to join this year." He waited for a moment, "I don't know if I should involve Ajit Sinha in carrying out the exercise or do it without letting him know. What do you suggest?" He asked.

"Don't let him know. In fact inform as few people in QSoft as possible. Dheeraj and you. Don't involve anyone else." Ishani advised. Then she also said, "The investigation should be for all the engineers recruited last year." She could see Atul feeling the pressure and went ahead to say, "Neil and I can help you investigate. Or turn it over to the police."

"I will need to inform a few folks; at least the CEO and his team. Hardly anyone will be in office tomorrow and the day after that. It would be a good time to do this," Atul said.

When the meeting ended, Ishani made a quick call to Inspector Pathare and made her way to the Commissioner's office. She parked in the underground parking across the building and walked around the building to the entrance. Outside the gate, there were a few reporters who must have just come out of the compound after a briefing. One of them seemed to recognize her and made his way over to her, "Detective Sohoni, are you here in connection with the Manjri Deshmukh case?" He asked. Ishani just walked on but as she walked, more reporters came her way, "Can you tell us more about the person who attacked you?" "Did he hit you?" "Did he grope you?" "Did you scream?" "Were you really attacked or is that a made up story?" She entered through the metal detector, made an entry in the register and waked in, leaving the reporters shouting questions at her.

"Hello Ishani", Inspector Pathare said coming out to the reception area. Then he took her through to his small cabin and even before she was seated, he said, "I have been calling Neil but he is not picking up."

"Oh! That is because he is not well. He is running a high fever. So I have left him to sleep." Ishani explained.

"Really? High fever? Suddenly?" It sounded like he didn't believe her. "How come?"

"I don't know. But when I checked before leaving the hotel, his temperature was 102 deg." She said, making an effort to sound normal. "I gave him paracetamol before leaving."

"I see," he said. Yesterday he had been asking about Neil, when he had turned off his cell phone and 'gone missing'. Today he was checking up on him. Was he the one keeping track of the two of them?

Keeping that thought aside, Ishani told him about Ravindra and Reema Kulkarni and the Inspector said, "We should be able to get information from the hotel quite easily."

He looked up some number and called the Mahabaleshwar police. He gave them the name of the hotel and the dates of the stay.

"They will get back to us by afternoon," he said after the call.

Ishani saw a pen knife on the Inspector's table and remembered the Swiss knife found near Manjiri's body. She had seen it a couple of times. Its logo had been a little different than other Swiss knives she had seen. She said, "The Swiss knife is one unsolved piece of the puzzle."

The Inspector nodded at that and she asked, "Of what make is it?"

"It's made by a company called Wenger. On the handle of the knife it says 'Wenger Titanium'". For Ishani the name was unheard of.

"We should check with some adventure sports shops that sell international brands," she said.

"Adventure sports shops?" Inspector asked.

Where else would you look for it? She got her answer when Inspector sheepishly said, "We looked in shops that sold men's accessories." Then he got defensive and said, "Look, I have seen them selling Swiss Knives. There is one brand called Victorinox. They make many different models. I have seen them in men's stores."

Ishani nodded saying, "Yes. I have seen that brand too."

"And then before we could think more about it, the case was closed," he explained.

"We can also run some searches on the Internet," Ishani said.

"I'll run some online searches and let you know what we find," the Inspector said.

Should she tell him about her conversation with Atul Vaidya? Till yesterday, she would not have hesitated. But she had not liked the way he seemed to keep tabs on Neil.

Before she could make up her mind, the Inspector asked, "Do you think we should pick up some QSoft people and question them in a proper manner?"

"Some people? Who?" Ishani wasn't sure who he meant.

"Atul Vaidya may be?"

Ishani's suspicion got stronger when he said Atul's name. Maybe Inspector Pathare knew that she had gone to meet Atul Vaidya in the morning.

She forced herself to stay calm and said, "Atul? I didn't think he is hiding anything. Did you get that feeling from his statement? We should probably ask Neil. I might have missed something." Then deciding that it was best to mention meeting him, so that the Inspector didn't feel she was hiding anything, she said, "I met him this morning before coming over. He wanted to invite Neil and me for the QSoft party this evening. He felt it would be a good opportunity to meet their CEO and other folks." She looked at him and noticed him relax visibly. "I don't know if Neil can go, but I think I will."

The inspector had to step out for something but he let Ishani wait in his cabin. About half-an-hour later, a person came in and told her that the Commissioner was in the office and he would like to talk to her.

She saw Inspector Pathare near the entrance of the main building, talking on the phone. As she approached he looked up, then ended his conversation quickly and came over. "What happened? Where are you going?" he asked.

"The Commissioner wants to see me." She said.

"For what?" he asked.

Ishani shrugged, "I don't know."

As she was entering the building she saw the same person approach Inspector Pathare and say, "Sir the Commissioner wants you to come to his office with the files for the builder's case".

In the Commissioner's office, Ishani was surprised to hear the Commissioner say, "There is nothing urgent really. But I thought since you are here and I have a few minutes to spare, we should catch up." Surely he must be a very busy man! How does he have time for a casual conversation?

"So Neil went off as per the plan?" he interrupted her train of thought.

"Yes." Ishani assured. She then told him about Nisha being mistaken for a Reema Kulkarni. She also talked about the information she had got from Atul.

"I see," he said. Then he called someone on the intercom, "Bring in the information Inspector Morey has sent."

As they waited, Ishani told him about the party that Atul had invited her and Neil for.

"You should go", the Commissioner said.

"Yes. I plan to. Neil might have to skip," she said smiling.

"No, not at all. Especially if he manages to get the kind of information he is looking for. He can start getting well quickly and meeting the CEO would be important enough for him to go."

A guy brought some papers and handed them over to the Commissioner. He shuffled through them and then said, "Inspector Morey has found out which production house was shooting near that camp site. It's a company called 'Sai Sapne Movie Company'. We called their production manager. They shot at that location for a movie for a period of seven days. But the first day they shot there was about two weeks after the incident. They had first gone there two months before that, to look at the location. So on the night of the incident none of the unit members were present there."

"Oh," Ishani said, sounding disappointed.

"Yes. But the production manager said that they had got to know about the location from a naturalist, who has been going to that area for some time. It would be a good idea to check with him if he was around at that time.

"His name is Sameer Ranade and here is his number. You should call him," he handed her the piece of paper.

While Ishani looked at the name and number, the Commissioner went ahead and warned her about not trusting anyone from his office.

Ishani nodded and then said, "Yes, today I got the feeling that Inspector Pathare was keeping a track of our whereabouts. He knew I had met Atul before coming over."

"That is quite possible", he agreed.

The intercom buzzed and the Commissioner picked it up, "Yes?" he barked into it. Ishani could see that he was annoyed at whatever he was hearing.

"Alright. Tell him, he can come in."

To Ishani, he said, "Inspector Pathare is here. I didn't want to give him an impression that we were keeping anything from him."

Ishani nodded. The inspector walked in with a bunch of files in his hand. "Sir, here are the files you asked for. But you had said, we should wait for the report from the arbitrator."

"Have you followed up with the arbitrator's office? Why is it taking this long?" the Commissioner asked.

"I have not followed up. I thought we should wait at least this week."

"Inspector, while Manjiri Deshmukh's case is important, we can't be neglecting other work," the Commissioner sounded quite stern.

"Ishani," The Commissioner turned to her and said, "I would request you and Neil Bhargav to not involve my people unless it was absolutely necessary. Wherever you need help from the police, let us know. But for things like going over documents and talking to people, don't expect the Inspector or others to spend too much time."

It was a very clear message to keep the Inspector out of the investigation as much as possible but she didn't want to offend the Inspector in any way. So she said, "Yes sir, we'll keep that in mind but I must say, everyone, especially Inspector Pathare, has been a lot of help to us so far."

"That they will continue to be," Commissioner said. Then he looked at his watch and said, "Inspector please follow-up with the arbitrator's office for the report. We can talk about it tomorrow." He then pressed the button on the intercom and said, "Ask the driver to be ready in five minutes".

He turned to Ishani and said "Ishani, I hope Neil feels better soon. Tell him to call me once he is better. If he is not better in the evening please let us know."

"Sure sir. I'll take your leave then," she said and got up.

The Commissioner's demeanour had changed completely from the time the Inspector had entered his office; he had assumed a sterner stance.

Ishani and the Inspector walked out together. The Inspector said, "Sorry about that. He reprimands us regularly. I didn't think he would do the same to you. And don't worry; I'll take care of all other pending work. So feel free to involve me. You don't need to do anything different."

Ishani felt relieved because there were a lot of things that they would need to depend on the police for. "Alright but do let us know if anything is taking too much of your time," she said to end it on the right note.

As they got near his office, he asked her, "Why don't you join me for lunch? I have brought food from home but we could get something for you from here."

It was past two. Should she just go back to the hotel? She had a good excuse… "I think I'll go and check how Neil is doing."

The Inspector seemed disappointed. He looked at his watch and said, "Let me check with the Mahabaleshwar police. See if they have any information for us."

In his office, the Inspector went to his desk and right away dialled the number.

After what seemed like a long time he said, "Hello. This is Inspector Pathare. I had talked to Jawale in the morning." He listened for a few seconds and then said, "Yes. That hotel. Did you get any information?" As he listened, he started making some notes on a writing pad. "Tell me the number again." He wrote some more after that. He ended the call and looked down at the writing pad.

"There were very few guests staying at the hotel that time. There was a Mr. Rajendra Kulkarni. The address he wrote in the hotel register is from Nagpur. He made full payment, in cash. He and his wife had been walk-in guests, no advance booking."

Nagpur? But hadn't Geetu said they both worked in a software company in Pune?

"They had a car. A Tata Indica. This is the registration number." The inspector said. "We can get the details from the RTO." Ishani nodded and he went ahead, "I'll also run a check on the Nagpur address. But I think it's a bogus address."

"Bogus?" Ishani asked.

"'Maya', 22/11 Dharam Pet, Nagpur", he read out. "We'll check it out, none the less."

Ishani walked out of the gate and was relieved that there were no reporters. She shook her head and smiled to herself. She had not become a celebrity overnight for them to wait for her!

The hotel reception was quiet at this time. As she made her way through the reception, the young, well dressed receptionist called out to her, "Madam, as you instructed us we didn't disturb Bhargav sir. But we tried calling him half-an-hour ago to see if he would like some lunch. He didn't pick up the phone. We are getting worried."

"Oh!" Ishani said. "I'll check now."

She went upstairs and saw the housekeeping trolley in the corridor. As she walked towards her room, she saw a maid come out of the room opposite Neil's and open the door to Neil's room.

Ishani almost ran and got there before the woman could enter. "What are you doing? Don't you see the 'Do Not Disturb' sign?" She asked the maid, rather angrily.

The maid looked startled. "Sorry miss," she said.

"Poornima," Ishani read out her name from the name tag.

"Madam, please do not complain about me. I made a mistake. I came in late and got late doing the rooms. In hurry I missed the sign," she pleaded. Ishani was not sure she could trust her. "Please madam. Please do not complain." The maid said again.

Ishani didn't want to make a big deal out of it and attract attention. "Alright. I will not complain. But make sure to be careful."

She turned and looked inside Neil's room. Looking in from the door, it did look like a person was sleeping on the bed facing the other side. She went in and closed the door. Instead of going over to her room, she would stay here.

She called the reception and told them that Neil was feeling much better; that his temperature had come down. That should keep them out of her hair for the time being.

She then freshened up and called room service. She ordered two soups and a sandwich. Would that be too much? But she needed to make people think that there were two of them eating...

She then called Sameer Ranade, the naturalist, introduced herself and told him how they had got his number. Then she said, "I was hoping you could help us with a case we are investigating," she explained.

"Sai Sapne. Ok," he said. "What case?"

Ishani explained. Then she asked, "Were you near the Mulshi dam on 16th and 17th March?"

"Umm", he paused to think. "I think I was there from 13th to 18th March."

"Did you stay in the small house where the film unit was staying?"

"Yes. In fact, I put the owner in touch with Shivan," Sameer said.

"Oh good!" Ishani exclaimed. "Mr. Ranade, we would like to meet you and ask you a few questions. Can we meet tomorrow morning?"

"Yes, sure. You can come over to my house. I live in the city", he gave her the address. "I hope 9:00 AM is OK with you."

She was startled when she heard a knock on the door. Then she remembered that she had ordered food. She went and opened the door. As the service guy made to come in, she stopped him, "Give me the tab you need me to sign".

He looked at her in surprise, so she clarified, "He is still not up. I don't want to disturb him."

The soups smelled very good. She took the tray to the centre table and took off the cover from one bowl. She tasted from it and said, "Mmm!". It was really good. And she was really hungry!

She sat cross legged on the sofa chair in front of the table and finished one bowl of soup. Then she opened the other bowl and uncovered the sandwich. She polished off the sandwich and ate more than half the soup from the second bowl. This was more than enough to create the illusion that two people had eaten that meal.

She looked at the time. It was 3:27 PM. She decided to take a quick power nap. She sat on the empty side of the bed, pulled out one pillow from the pile she had made on the other side, and rested her head on that. She sighed and closed her eyes. Just a few minutes, she thought to herself.

She spent some time on the edge between consciousness and dreamland. She didn't realise when she entered the dreamland; and yet, she knew that she was dreaming. She was also thinking how strange the dream was. In the dream, she was in her grandparents' attic. She was looking for something but not finding it. She kept looking and kept finding things that she had lost - a doll with golden hair; a jewellery box containing tamarind seeds. She smiled at that. She didn't know what she was looking for, only that she must keep searching. She heard the attic door open and saw Neil walk in. What was he doing there? She smiled when he called out to her softly. He came over and touched her cheek softly and said something really nice, but she could not hear him clearly. She felt his lips on hers and she moaned; enjoying the caress of those warm lips. Then she felt something tickle her and realized that the person kissing her had a thick moustache! She panicked and opened her eyes while at the same time trying to push the person away, a scream forming in her throat.

"Shh… It's OK. It's me, Ishani," Neil said.

She stared at him wide eyed for a few moments; then slowly her panic receded. He was sitting on the edge of the bed in a constable's uniform, including the cap. His nose looked a little crooked; he had bushy eyebrows and a thick moustache.

He smiled down at her and said, "Hi sleeping beauty."

She smiled back at him and said, "Hello constable," making him grin.

She wrinkled her nose and said, "I hate that moustache!"

"Do you now?" He asked playfully and bent down to tickle her with it.

"No Neil!"

He lifted his head and looked at her. "Do you know what I wanted to do, when I came in and saw you asleep with a smile on your lips?" He asked her huskily.

She could not look away. She shook her head and he said, "You are making this very difficult Ishani!"

She didn't know what she should say to that. She looked away, then sat up and ran her fingers through her hair. He looked at her, tucked a tendril behind her ear and said, "Alright! Sohoni, Lets go back to the original game!"

She looked at him in confusion. "What?"

He sighed and said, "To solving the case!"

"Oh, yeah." She said sheepishly.

He smiled and said, "I am feeling much better now. The fever is gone, I think. I plan to freshen up. Can I have the room to myself for some time? We can then talk about what happened today."

Ishani put her feet down on the floor and got up swiftly. She looked around, picked up her backpack and slipped her shoes on. She stood in front of him and said, "Fifteen minutes?" Then since she could not resist it, she picked up the cap from him head and put it on hers.

Neil laughed and said, "That is a strong fashion statement, Sohoni!"

She made a face at him, dropped the cap in his outstretched hand and said, "Oh by the way, we have to go for a QSoft party this evening at around 7:30 PM. At Holiday Inn." She looked at her wrist watch and said, "That means we have about two hours." Then she saw the twinkle in his eyes and said with annoyance, "To exchange notes!" When he laughed she asked, "Are all men the same?!"

"I wouldn't know," he said.

She got angry and said, "You insist that we focus on the case. Then act as if you don't care about the case! Say things which are nothing to do with the case!" She pointed the index finger of her right hand at him and said, "You better make up your mind Bhargav!"

Neil held his hands in front of him in defeat and said, "I am sorry." Then when she seemed to calm down he asked, "What party?"

She explained and he said, "Alright Sohoni, fifteen minutes", he said.

She walked to the door, turned and said, "By the way, not right now and not if you don't want to, but I would like to..."

"You would like to?" Neil prompted.

She wrinkled her nose and said, "Actually it is not about the case, so I don't know if I should..."

"That is OK." He walked over smiling. "What would you like?"

"I would like to understand about your divorce," she said. Then she pressed the bridge of her nose with her thumb and forefinger. That didn't sound quite right. "I mean, not just that. I would like to know more about you."

"Yes," he said and smiled. "I want to get to know you too. Let's go on a date when the case is over."

CHAPTER 22

Neil ran his hands through his hair as he paced restlessly. He was losing his mind over Ishani. When he had come in and found her sleeping there, all he had wanted to do was go curl himself around her and start making love to her slowly. He had stood there watching her sleep for a few moments, fighting this urge. Then he had sat next to her on the bed and softly touched her cheek. Her smile had broadened and he had bent to catch that smile on his lips.

Did cold showers really work, he wondered walking into the bathroom. He ended up spending more than fifteen minutes under a really cold shower. When he stepped out, he actually shivered. He even sneezed a couple of times. 'Great! A real cold is all I need', he thought. By the time he got dressed in his jeans and t-shirt, he had managed to collect his thoughts and he felt ready to focus on the case again. He put the moustache, eyebrows and the stuffing he had used to look thicker around the middle, along with the constable's uniform in a bag and stuffed it all in his suitcase. He would be calling the reception and asking them to get the room ready so he needed to clear all evidence of his disguise.

The day had gone pretty much as planned. In his meeting with the principal he had spent a lot of time talking about his son's job prospects. Whether he would be able to work for a good company, how would the college help him get a job in a good IT company, which companies recruited students from their campus and so on...

The principal had suggested that Harpal talk to Prof. Dhotrey regarding all his concerns. He had told Prof. Dhotrey to show Mr. Harpal around the campus and answer all his queries. He had looked quite pleased when the two had walked out of his office.

Prof. Dhotrey had been on his guard for a few minutes but then he had relaxed and talked for a long time. Neil had managed to video record some of that conversation.

When he knocked on Ishani's door, she opened it and said, "Come in. I am making tea. Would you like some?"

He said, "Sure".

He sat in one of the two sofa chairs and watched her moving about making tea. She arranged the cups and tea bags. Then she looked up and found him watching her quietly. She blushed and gave him a shy smile. For someone who was so smart, capable and confident, she blushed very easily.

She poured the hot water in the two cups and brought them over. She put the cups on the table between the two chairs and sat in the other chair saying, "Alright Bhargav. Tell me what you got Prof. Dhotrey to reveal!"

"Prof. Dhotrey can guarantee a job in QSoft for an additional fee of Rs. 8 Lakh!"

Ishani raised her eyebrows questioningly.

"So firstly, my son can get admission in their engineering college through management quota. The fees for a seat through the management quota are only Rs. 6 Lakh a year."

"As opposed to? What are the regular fees?" Ishani asked.

"The regular fees are Rs. 2.5 Lakh a year. So for the management seat its only Rs. 3.5 Lakh more a year." He paused to sip his tea. "Then in the 7th semester there the Institute hosts a campus recruitment drive for which it invites many companies. Most of them offer jobs that start from Rs. 3 lakh a year and some go upto Rs. 10 lakh a year.

"Prof. Dhotrey assured me a job for my son in QSoft and two or three other companies if I was willing to pay an additional fee of Rs. 8 lakh, in the 7th semester. Of course, these fees are 'special fees' and will have to be paid in cash… to Prof. Dhotrey directly.

"Oh and there is an option of paying Rs. 4 lakh in the 7th semester and Rs. 4.5 lakh in the 8th semester. But if you fail to pay the special fees, your job with QSoft or the other company will stand cancelled."

"How does he guarantee a job? People from these companies will be conducting tests and interviews, right?" Ishani asked.

"Let me show you the recording!" Neil said.

He switched on the laptop and plugged in a flash drive. He selected one version from various versions of the recording that he had created.

"I was hoping for an audio recording, but actually managed to get a video," he said. He was really pleased with what he had managed to get.

He started the video. He knew that the angle was really strange. He saw Ishani look at it, "I had a video camera in the bag with a small, unnoticeable hole for the lens." He answered the question she had not asked.

She looked up at him and said, "Oh! Wow!"

In answer, he reached out and ruffled her hair. He liked doing that.

Then they concentrated on the video. The edited clip he was showing her was about three minutes long.

Prof. Dhotrey was saying 'Which company does he want to work for? We can guarantee a job with QSoft and' Neil had edited the names of the other companies. 'Leave it to us. I can't reveal how we do it but we have managed to place many students so far.' Neil looked at Ishani. She turned to him and said, "And this guy is a professor? He is a crook! He even looks like a crook!"

Prof. Dhotrey was saying, 'No, it does not matter what percentage he has scored in Class 12. In his engineering exams he will score good marks. We can guarantee that'.

In the later part Dhotrey was talking about the 'extra' fees he collected from 'special' students. All the things Neil had already told her about.

The video didn't explain how he claimed to do it but it was hard evidence against Prof. Dhotrey. Now they had proof that he accepted bribes of Rs. 8 lakh to guarantee jobs in well-known companies.

"Which other companies does he promise jobs in?" Ishani asked.

He told her the names though for their case they were not important.

"I have sent a copy of this recording to the Commissioner. He should be getting it by this evening." He explained.

"Should you call the Commissioner?" She asked.

"I will. What did you do today? Did you find out anything important?" He asked. Then he listened as she talked about her meeting with Atul Vaidya and her visit to the Commissioner's office.

"I see." He said. "Good job, Sohoni!" Ishani smiled at that. "Alright now I am going back to my room. I'll call the Commissioner and DK".

Ishani said, "He had called in the morning."

"OK." He nodded, "We can leave by 7:15 PM."

He walked out of her room feeling that things seemed to be finally moving on many fronts.

CHAPTER 23

Instead of wearing a skirt as she was tempted to, Ishani chose to stay in her jeans. She wore a light yellow top with delicate lace around the Chinese collar and cuffs; that was the only slightly dressy thing she had. She wore the strappy sandals and as she applied some makeup, she wondered if she was going overboard. Yet at the last minute she changed her ear studs for golden hoops.

Five minutes later, Ishani looked at Neil standing at the door. In blue jeans, a white shirt, blazer and leather shoes, he looked striking. He gave her a look and whistled, making her glad that she had dressed up. "Thank you" she said. "You are looking very good yourself."

He too seemed pleased at that and looked down at himself before saying, "Well, as they say, clothes make a man."

"Yeah, right!" Ishani said and stepped out.

Neil was sneezing as they walked across the hotel lobby. He also seemed to have a runny nose.

"How have you managed this?" Ishani asked him.

"What?" he asked, turning back to look at her.

"This cold is a good touch. The fever is down but you still have a cold. That works."

He shook his head smiling a tight smile and said, "I got lucky!"

As they went out the entrance Ishani said, "I'll drive," and was surprised when he didn't say anything. Was he actually coming down with something now?

The traffic was thick and they moved slowly. Neil seemed to get irritated at the RJ rattling off her 'knowledge' on the FM station. He tried different stations and finally switched it off. Then looking at her he said, "So the parcel has reached the Commissioner already!"

"Oh! That was fast, wasn't it?"

"I had paid to ensure it would reach by 7:00 PM," Neil explained.

"What will the Commissioner do with it now?"

"I talked to DK from Lonavala after sending out the courier," Neil said. "He will make sure the right politicians start putting pressure on Vasantrao."

"Why couldn't he do that earlier?" Ishani wondered aloud.

"You can't put much pressure on someone, especially a politician, till you have something significant that could go against that person. Now, with Prof. Dhotrey seen asking for money on camera, Vasantrao could be persuaded easily not to shield him."

They had got stuck at a signal for over ten minutes.

She thought about what Neil had said. "So now we get to question Prof. Dhotrey?"

"We can…" he stopped mid-sentence and both of them became aware of the sound of a phone ringing.

"Oh, it's my phone!" Ishani exclaimed. She was carrying a small purse and she had put it on the back seat. Neil took off his seat belt, twisted in the seat and picked up her purse. "Can you please open it? It's in the front pocket," Ishani said. He nodded and opened the front pocket and pulled out her phone. But before she could take the call, it stopped ringing.

She looked at the number and said, "Nikhil." She used Inspector Pathare's first name just to tease Neil. When he looked at her blankly, she said, "I mean Inspector Pathare."

She felt thoroughly satisfied by Neil's reaction. He raised his eye brows and said, "Nikhil? You and he are on first name basis now?"

"He has been calling me Ishani right from the start! You know that!" She protested.

Finally the traffic started moving and once they made it to the other side of the crossing, the traffic thinned. They were moving at a good speed now.

"So when did he become Nikhil?" Neil asked with a lopsided smile.

"Yesterday. When we went to Vaishali to have lunch and he recited two of his poems to me," she said with a smile.

"Poems? He writes poetry?" Neil asked scornfully.

Ishani nodded and Neil asked, "Were they any good?"

Ishani shook her head, wrinkled her nose and said, "Not really."

"Thank God!" Neil said with feeling and Ishani laughed. "I mean, he is an eligible bachelor. He could woo you easily. If he was a good poet, I am sure I would have no chance against him!" He sounded half serious.

Ishani sobered, "For some strange reason, he doesn't seem to be making much of an impression. I guess something to do with this guy from Delhi who is my neighbour at present."

Neil looked really pleased. He smiled and then started whistling a tune.

Ishani stopped at the Holiday Inn gate for the cursory security check and then drove in. She handed the keys to the valet and joined Neil at the entrance. As they entered the air conditioned lobby, he started sneezing again. She looked at him and he said, "It's the change in temperatures and the air conditioning."

She needed to call Inspector Pathare. Neil was obviously thinking the same thing. He said, "You better call your Nikhil before we go in."

"My Nikhil?" She asked. "You mean our Inspector Pathare."

"He is not my anything!" Neil said with a smirk and sneezed a couple of times.

Ishani smiled and called the Inspector. It seemed like he was waiting for her call because he picked up on the first ring. "Hello. Where are you? Where is Neil? I called you and when you didn't pick up I called the hotel and was told both of you were out!"

She explained about the party.

"Neil is well enough to attend the party?" He was sarcastic.

"His fever is down. And meeting the CEO was important. He is still sneezing like crazy though," Ishani explained.

"I was calling to tell you that I got the information from the RTO. The car is registered to a Jitesh Taneja. He has a car rental agency called 'Rent Easy'. I got his number." He paused and then said, "I thought I should pass this on to you folks and not call him myself. I don't want to displease the Commissione run necessarily."

She was about to close the call when he said, "Ishani?"

"Yes?"

"There is a video recording that has come to the Commissioner this evening. I don't know who sent it and I don't know if this will be useful for the case, but it is about Prof. Dhotrey. The Commissioner called ACP Sathey and me to see it."

"What recording?" Ishani said looking at Neil.

"You should ask the Commissioner to show it to you and Neil." He seemed to be changing his mind. "I said we couldn't question him because he is close to Vasantrao. I still don't think we should do anything to upset Vasantrao. But you should see this video."

She put the phone back in her purse and turned to Neil and told him about the car rental agency.

They climbed the stairs to go up one storey and walked towards the big banquet hall. Dheeraj Seth and Atul Vaidya were at the entrance. Neil and Ishani walked up to them and Ishani said, "Sorry, we are late. We got caught in the traffic."

They shook hands and Atul said, "No problem. We just got started."

"Hello Neil. Hello Ishani," Dheeraj said and quite surprisingly gave them a big smile.

"Are you feeling better?" Atul asked Neil.

Neil sneezed before he said, "Sorry. Yes, much better."

Inside the hall there was a dais setup and a good looking, young woman was making an announcement, "… so please welcome SSV!"

Sivshankar Venkatesan was of medium height and had a round face. He was not fat but definitely not slim. He had bushy eyebrows which were almost hidden behind the frame of his glasses and he had a thick moustache. His eyes were not clearly visible, but he seemed to have a genuine smile. He started his speech by addressing everyone as, "My dear friends".

"Excuse me. I will need to be at the stage," said Dheeraj and he walked towards the dais.

"Why don't you two go in and sit down?" Atul suggested. Ishani and Neil walked over to sit in the last row.

SSV spoke about the company, its culture and how every employee was important. He then talked about the company's philosophy behind honouring top performers. Finally he talked about how a person's family played a huge part in their success and that's why when QSoft honoured its best, the families were always invited.

Ishani thought it was a very good and sincere speech. She looked at Neil. He felt her watching him, turned to look at her and said, "Good speech." She smiled and nodded.

Dheeraj went on the dais and then read out names of the top performers and their achievements. There were more than twenty achievers who were honoured and reading out about each one took some time. Then Atul too was called to join and there was a photo session.

Neil and Ishani started looking around. Ishani saw some of the people she had talked to. Neil pointed out some of the people he had talked to. But beyond that there was nothing they could do but wait. Ishani checked her watch and saw that it was almost 9:00 PM. "We could have come an hour later" she whispered. "And miss out on this entertaining evening?" Neil whispered back mockingly, "No way!"

People had started getting up and moving about. Neil and Ishani too got up and as they walked towards the door, Ajit Ketkar saw Ishani and came over.

"Hello Detective," he said.

Ishani introduced him to Neil and said, "It was a very nice speech".

"Yes. SSV is a good speaker," Ajit said. He looked around and said, "I am guessing you are here to meet some people regarding the case. Who do you need to talk to? Do you want me to call those people over?"

"Atul Vaidya asked us to come over and meet your CEO," Neil said.

"OK. That can take some time. Would you like something to drink?" He pointed to a counter serving drinks.

As they walked towards the counter, a good looking guy walked over to them. He stretched his hand out to Neil and said, "Hello Detective. I hope you remember me."

Neil shook his hand and said, "Yes, of course." Then he turned to Ishani and said, "Ishani, this is Dilip Araghade."

"Hello" she said and shook his out-stretched hand.

"How is the investigation coming along?" He asked casually.

"Going on," Neil said.

"I heard you are from Mumbai, detective Sohoni," Dilip said.

"Yes, I am", Ishani said with a smile.

"So tell us if we can do anything to make you feel comfortable in our city," Dilip said.

"I know this city well," Ishani said.

"Someone tried to attack you at the hotel?" he asked next.

"Yes," Ishani acknowledged.

"It's amazing to see you not getting scared. It can't be easy to continue to work when you are being threatened like that," he said.

Ishani only smiled at that.

"Did you manage to catch the person or did he run away?" he asked.

"We are working on it," Neil said. His tone indicated that he wished to end the topic.

When Ajit went to the drinks counter, Dilip said, "Ajit was very close to Manjiri. He found it very difficult to accept that she was gone." Then after a pause he said, "Actually all of us struggled for a while. She was an important part of our lives. That is why we all want to help this investigation."

They stood around for a few more minutes but at least now they had drinks to sip. When Ishani turned to keep her empty glass on the small table behind her, she saw Atul Vaidya approach them along with SSV. He came over and introduced them, "SSV, these are the two detectives investigating Manjiri's death. Ishani Sohoni and Neil Bhargav."

"Hello Detective Sohoni," SSV said and shook her hand. Then he said, "Hello Detective Bhargav" and shook Neil's hand.

Atul said, "Excuse us folks" to Ajit and Dilip. Then he turned to SSV and said, "There is a meeting room on the other side of the banquet hall. Let's go there".

They all walked towards the other end of the hall and around it to enter the meeting room. They all sat around the small, oval table and SSV said, "We would like to help the investigation in every way possible. It might have seemed otherwise earlier but I am giving you my word now. Whatever help you need, whatever it takes, we will provide all the support."

Neil cleared his throat and said, "I appreciate that but Detective Sohoni and I would not be here investigating this case right now, if it had not gotten closed in such a hurry."

"Sometimes, the best of us make mistakes in our judgement. We end up taking advice from the wrong people. But we want to do what is right. So tell us how we can help," SSV said.

"We will need to look at some QSoft data," Neil said, "We will be bringing in some QSoft folks for more questioning. Someone might be put in police custody. You will need to be ready to handle that."

SSV thought about this and then turned to Atul and said, "Let us make sure we are providing them access to the data they need." Then he turned to Neil and said, "We are holding a news conference tomorrow morning to announce our full support to the investigation."

Neil was sneezing but he nodded and agreed that it was a good idea. SSV then said, "I am here only till tomorrow, but I am sure Atul will be able to take care of everything. Right Atul?" He put the question to Atul.

"Absolutely, SSV," Atul said and nodded.

SSV got up and said, "I'll need to go mingle now. I get few chances to meet our people, and so I would like to make the most of it." He sounded sincere about it. Atul, Neil and Ishani too got up. SSV said, "Please do stay for dinner. As you can hear, there is music and people will start dancing soon. You young people should let your hair down and enjoy." He smiled and walked out.

"We would like to talk to Dheeraj Seth about the complaint Manjiri had against Ajit Sinha," Ishani told Atul. Then she went ahead and asked, "Is Ajit Sinha here by the way?"

"No. He's been in Bangalore for the last two days, for recruitment related meetings. He is returning on Sunday night." Atul said. Then he looked at his watch and said, "Why don't we have dinner and then talk to Dheeraj?"

"Sure," Neil agreed.

As Atul led the way, Ishani looked at Neil and smiled. "What? I am hungry woman!" he said.

They had dinner while chatting with Atul, who was great company. From time-to-time people came over to talk to him. He made sure to introduce Neil and Ishani though he didn't tell everyone they were detectives. He included everyone in the conversation and kept it lively.

Few of the folks Ishani and Neil had talked to, stopped by. Ishani noticed that Nisha was keeping her distance from them.

Dheeraj came over and said, "I believe you folks want to talk to me. I'll grab something to eat quickly and then we can meet."

"Sure," Neil said.

"We'll go to the meeting room behind the hall," Atul told Dheeraj making it clear that he would be there too.

When the others had dispersed leaving only the three of them, Ishani said to Atul, "Dheeraj seems to have changed his stance. He was rather reluctant to talk to us. Now he seems eager."

Atul said, "He needs to be told by someone what course of action he should choose. Sometimes he listens to the wrong kind of advice. He rarely has his own opinion. But he always has the company's best interests at heart."

They finished their dinner in silence and then went back to the meeting room. Dheeraj was already there waiting for them.

"I talked to Detective Sohoni this morning," Atul said addressing Dheeraj. "They know the background but they need a few more details from you."

"Yes, of course," Dheeraj said.

"Can you please tell us about it once again?" Neil asked Dheeraj.

Dheeraj told them what Atul had shared with Ishani in the morning. The only additional information he gave them were the dates on which these conversations took place.

"Did you speak to the managers of the teams that had engineers from M.V. College?" Ishani asked.

"I didn't take it very seriously then," Dheeraj said sheepishly. He tried to defend himself by saying, "See Manjiri was always complaining about things. Everyone had started to feel like she couldn't see the good in anything; that she only found faults all the time. So we tended to not take her complaining very seriously."

"When you say everyone, who do you mean?" Neil asked.

"Well, everyone in the People Care team," Dheeraj clarified.

"But in this case, she had made a very strong accusation, hadn't she? That the engineer in her team was not the same person she had interviewed." Ishani pointed out.

"Yes, but I thought she was mistaken. I had checked the engineer's file myself. His papers were all there. His photo was also there," Dheeraj clarified. "And no one else had ever complained about Ajit Sinha ever!"

"So tell us about the fight that Ajit Sinha and Manjiri had." Neil prompted him.

"When she saw that the file was in order, she started saying that Ajit was somehow responsible for doing something underhanded! The engineer in her team just could not have passed our entrance test, forget clearing the interviews.

"Ajit had got very angry. I had never seen him so angry. He came to me and told me to control Manjiri. He said he couldn't do his job well if he didn't have support from the People Care team. He said he had the tough task of hiring 60 engineers from engineering colleges around Pune. He had a lot to worry about, without having to answer to people like Manjiri."

"What was his reaction when Manjiri's body was found on March 17th?" Neil asked.

Dheeraj was quiet for some time. Then he said, "I don't remember exactly. But like everyone else, he seemed shaken." Then after another pause he said, "I don't think he had anything to do with her death."

"But..." He started and then got quiet again.

Neil sneezed couple of times, and said, "Excuse me." Then he prompted Dheeraj since he had gotten quiet "But...?"

"Maybe there is some problem with the recruitment from colleges." Dheeraj said. Neil didn't say anything. Ishani began to say something to which Neil responded by lifting his hand to signal her to stop. So they waited. Finally, Dheeraj said, "I talked to a few managers casually over coffee yesterday and today, after my conversation with Atul. Three of them said that the engineers we had employed last year as part of our campus recruitment drive were not good performers. They don't seem to know the basics and are not able to carry out even simple tasks independently.

"I made a list of names that managers said were not good. There were four names. This is apart from the engineer Manjiri was complaining about. I checked their files and discovered, quite surprisingly, that only one of them is from M.V. College. Two are from S. J. Institute of Technology and one is from HIT.

"I then looked at who had interviewed them. Each one had been interviewed by a different QSoft manager."

Atul's reading about Dheeraj was spot on. He was now genuinely interested in doing the right thing and had already started investigating.

"Anything else?" Neil prompted him.

"Normally, the fresh engineers are allocated to teams managed by the managers who interviewed them but these four recruits and the one Manjiri complained about, were all allocated to the teams of other managers. I don't know why that was done. I wanted to ask Ajit but Atul told me not to discuss any of this with Ajit.

"The engineer Manjiri complained about was earlier in another team but that project closed and Manjiri's team needed an engineer urgently so he was moved to her team."

"How many fresh engineers were hired last year?" Neil asked.

"Fifty-five joined QSoft last year." Dheeraj said.

"And Ajit Sinha handles the entire recruitment process?"

Dheeraj nodded his agreement.

"So would Ajit be seen as being responsible for hiring bad engineers?" Neil asked.

"Umm," Dheeraj considered this for a while. "Not really." He looked at Neil's raised brows and said, "I mean, he is responsible for making sure we meet our quota of new recruits. The interviewers are responsible for the actual hiring. Ajit does very few interviews himself, compared to the number of people we recruit."

"So for the engineers hired from the campus, there is an entrance test and then an interview with a manager?" Ishani asked.

"There is an entrance test. Then there is one interview with a manager. It is a technical interview. If the manager is not able to decide then there is a second interview with another manager. Finally there is a HR interview." Dheeraj explained.

"Who does the HR interviews?" Neil asked.

"For campus hiring, Nisha Khanna, is the HR person. Of course, Ajit Sinha also does some interviews. He can do technical interviews and also HR interviews," Dheeraj said.

"Dheeraj, can you arrange for us to go through the files of all the fifty five new recruits? We would like to go through those tomorrow. We might also want to talk to the managers who interviewed them and the managers they are presently working with." Neil said.

Dheeraj looked uncomfortable. He turned to Atul, who said, "We should be able to share the files. I have talked to SSV. He wants us to provide whatever data these folks need." Then he sat up and said, "But you should do it yourself. Let us not involve anyone else."

"Should Ishani and I come over by 11:30 AM?" Neil asked.

"Can you make it 12:30 PM? I have a meeting with my team at 10:00 AM. By 12:30, I can make sure that everyone leaves and the People Care section is made available to us. I will also take out all the files and arrange them by college."

"OK," Neil agreed.

"I'll see you tomorrow then." Dheeraj said. Then he turned to Atul and said, "Atul we should go out and mingle. People will start leaving soon and it would not look right if both you and I are not around."

Atul looked at Neil and Ishani, and said, "Why don't you folks stay for some more time? Enjoy the music? Dance a little."

Ishani didn't want to party but Neil was already accepting, "Sure. We'll stay for a short while."

They all made their way to the main hall. Both the big doors of the hall were closed but one could hear the music. Dheeraj pushed one of the doors open and loud music poured out. Ishani walked in behind the three men and resigned herself to the craziness in the room.

The dais had turned into a dance floor. A lot of young and some not so young people were dancing on it to loud Bollywood music. There were also a lot of people watching from the side lines. But a conversation was impossible. Ishani looked at Neil in exasperation. He shrugged his shoulders and bending down he shouted in her ear, "Do you want to dance?"

"No. I would like to leave, actually," she shouted back looking at him.

"OK," he mouthed. Then he waved to Atul who was looking at them and steered her outside with his hand on her elbow.

Once outside, he closed the big door and sighed. As they walked towards the staircase, he asked, "You don't dance?" He sounded surprised. "I thought you must be a good dancer," he said.

She stopped and looked up at him. "I must be a good dancer? Why?" she asked.

He gave her a warm smile and said, "You are very graceful. You move with such ease," he said.

She gave him a shy smile saying, "You think I am graceful?"

"Extremely graceful!" he said. He noticed her blush and added, "And you blush easily." Now he was teasing her.

"Neil!" She exclaimed.

He laughed out loud. As they started climbing down the stairs, she placed her right hand on his left arm and said, "I love dancing."

"Good. I will take you out dancing someday!"

"For our date?" She smiled.

"Maybe," he said.

"What would you like to do for our date?" she asked, as she thought about the time she would spend with him, getting to know him better.

"We will not be doing what I would really like to do," he said with a sideways glance at her.

"Why not?" She asked curiously.

"Because what I would really like to do is to collect on the promise you have been making me," he said.

"Promise? What promise?" What was he talking about?

He bent his head sideways towards her. "The promise, Ishani, that you have been making me every time I kiss you," he said softly, his meaning being very clear.

Ishani sucked in air, suddenly feeling warm all over. She knew she was blushing to her roots but she didn't know how to stop it.

Neil laughed softly when he realized that she had understood him correctly and patted her hand resting on his arm. She looked at him and he winked.

"Let me drive," Neil said. She nodded, unable to say anything. She freed her hand and opening her purse pulled out the car tab as they exited the hotel lobby.

The valet brought the car around and she got into the passenger seat. She composed herself while Neil was getting into the driver's seat.

She was quiet; trying to analyse what was happening to her. Neil switched on the radio and after trying two other stations finally settled on Vividh Bharati. She came out of her reverie listening to Mohammed Rafi's *Tum Mujhe Yun Bhoola Na Paoge*.

As they drove out of the gate, Neil looked at her and said, "I can't help but wonder…"

"What?"

"You are smart, witty and confident and yet… all of a sudden you become so shy."

She shrugged. She didn't know what she could say. She herself didn't understand it. Why was she reacting to him like this? She had never felt so shy with Ajay. She had enjoyed sex with Ajay, though it had never been earth shattering.

The same distance took them half the time at this time of night. At their hotel, Neil handed over the keys to the valet and they walked in.

"I have not heard from DK or the Commissioner," Neil sounded worried.

As they walked across to their rooms, Neil said, "I am going to call DK and then if required the Commissioner and find out what happened to the video."

He called after ten minutes and said, "The video has reached Vasantrao. The Law minister has given him till tomorrow to think about it. If Vasantrao agrees to stay out of the police matter concerning Prof. Dhotrey, the video does not need to be made public."

Then he said, "I'll see you at breakfast. Say at 8:00 AM?"

"Yes." Ishani said. "When will we know Vasantrao's decision?"

"Tomorrow," Neil said. "Hopefully before tomorrow ends. He might say he is still thinking and will need another day. We will not wait beyond Sunday evening."

CHAPTER 24

On Saturday morning, as Neil and Ishani walked across the lobby towards the coffee shop, Neil was greeted by the hotel receptionists with a lot of enthusiasm and queries about his health. He was not sneezing anymore, but his nose hadn't lost its redness. He talked to the two girls and thanked them for all the help.

After a solid breakfast, they left the hotel at 8:40 AM and made their way to Sameer Ranade's place. They crossed the bridge over the river and turned left. Ishani was not sure about the exact address but Neil was driving as if he knew exactly where he needed to go.

After driving around through small lanes for a few minutes, Neil stopped the car near a paan shop and asked for the address. The paanwala thought about it and said that they were on the wrong road. They needed to get to a road that was parallel to this one. But it was a one way road with traffic moving in the other direction. After some more conversation, Neil and Ishani decided that it would be best to park the car in the paid car park on this road and walk through aby lane to the parallel road.

It took them a few minutes to find the house, even after they were practically standing in front of it. It was an old, three storied house and its entrance was from the side. As soon as they entered the building through its thick wooden door, they saw a door on their left with the "Ranade" nameplate. There was a metal door outside and a wooden door inside. When they rang the bell, they heard some sounds inside and the door was opened by an old man.

"Yes?" the old man asked, looking at them through the grill of the outer door.

"Hello sir. We are looking for Sameer Ranade," Neil said.

The old man looked at Neil, then at Ishani and said, "He is in the garage. Go through that door," he said pointing to the garage door.

Just then the garage door opened and a young man in his late twenties came out. He must have heard the doorbell. He gave them a smile and said, "Hello." Then turning to the old man he said, "Grandfather, can you please tell mother to send some tea?"

"Yes, will tell her," the old man said and closed the main door.

Neil and Ishani walked to the garage and entered behind Sameer. He was slim and of medium height. He was very fair but deeply tanned. His hair looked like it had not been touched by a barber in a long time. He was wearing old, faded khaki shorts and a T-shirt that must have been dark green at some point.

The place didn't look anything like a garage. There were a lot of books on two shelves and even on a centre table. There was an old writing table in the corner. A desktop computer sat on that along with a couple of binoculars. They could also see many CDs stacked on the side.

"Please have a seat," Sameer said, pointing to the bed that was against a wall. Sameer pulled a chair that was in front of the writing table and sat on it.

As Neil and Ishani sat down, Neil introduced himself and Ishani.

Sameer acknowledged him and said, "Yes, we talked yesterday."

"We are both private detectives and are investigating the death of a woman from over a month ago," Neil explained.

Neil then explained the circumstances of Manjiri's death. Sameer listened attentively. "So you are trying to find out if someone saw something at the time of her drowning?" he asked.

"Yes, on the campsite or in the water. She drowned and died sometime between 11:30 PM and 1:30 AM."

Sameer Ranade looked down at his feet and then again up at them, "I am studying Indian foxes. So I go to places that have reported fox sightings." Then he started talking very lovingly about the foxes, "These are elusive creatures. They manage to hide from the human eye quite effortlessly even when they are moving about very close to us. It is very difficult to observe them. You almost never see them in the day time."

"So you watch them in the night?" Ishani prompted.

"Sometimes," Sameer said. Then he said, "But I setup cameras and try and capture their movement."

"So at Mulshi, did you record?" Neil asked.

"Yes, I did. I recorded for five nights. But I managed to capture them only on two nights—the 13thand 14th. I think they realized that the food that was mysteriously appearing was stranger they felt that they were being watched. I think they moved away from that area," Sameer said, with admiration for the animal.

"Did you see the complete recording of the previous night the next morning?" Ishani asked. How else would he know if his recording had captured something relevant to him or not?

"Actually, I don't have to. I setup a small contraption. When some animal, a fox or something else, eats from the food trey, a thin rope tied to it gets pulled. On the other side of the rope, I arrange an alarm clock such that when the rope gets stretched it pulls out the pencil cell inside the clock and it stops working.

"So if the clock stops it means there was some movement at the time at which it stopped. This gives me some indication of the time at which I could expect to have recorded some animal activity," Sameer said and smiled.

"I see." Neil said. "Would it be possible to see one of your recordings?"

"Sure. I can show you what I got from the night of the 13th," Sameer said and got up.

When Sameer indicated that the recording was ready to play on his computer, Neil and Ishani got up and walked over to the table. It was a night recording; Neil and Ishani concentrated on trying to figure out what they were seeing. Ishani looked at the slight movement of the water and some reflections danced on its surface. But the other shore, Wild Outdoor's side, was completely in the dark.

"Here, see! Two of them. The one on the right is a female. They are completely at ease." Sameer started talking about the small animals that had appeared in the frame. "See now, they are going to the food tray." He continued to talk excitedly about the animals for a few more minutes.

Ishani was feeling disappointed. "Do you have any recordings from the night of the 16th?" Neil asked.

Sameer shook his head and said, "I got movement only on 13th and 14th. So all the other recordings were useless."

"Would you have those or were those deleted?" Neil asked.

"I have not deleted them but I have also not kept track of them. Those recordings are on some flash drive."

"We would like you to look for the recording of the night of March 16th," Neil said.

"I'll dig through my stuff and see what I can find. Should I give you a ring when I find it?" Sameer asked. "It could take a couple of days. Some of my recordings are here and some are at the department. Right now, I am not sure where these recordings are." He looked at them and explained further, "I have been recording for the last three months; on an average I spend about fifteen days a month in the field. Out of those recordings only ten have been useful so I have a lot of useless footage to sort through.

"I hesitate to delete those thinking, 'What if one of them actually has animal activity even though the animal didn't touch the food?' so I have not deleted anything yet."

They left Sameer's house and walked back to the parking lot. Once they were seated, Neil started the engine and made his way towards the river. Ishani dialled the number for the car rental company and it was picked up quickly. "Rent easy!" said a person on the other end.

Ishani said, "We needed to talk to someone about renting a car. Where is your office?" The person would think she was a prospective customer.

She took down the address and closed the call. She then said, "I think we can go to this place before going over to QSoft. Turn left after crossing the river, then go over the fly over. Rent Easy's office is somewhere there. We can take the highway from there and go to QSoft."

"Yes, Ma'am", said Neil, touching his left hand to his temple in a mock salute. Ishani punched him on his arm lightly and he said, "What? Not only am I a driver but a punching bag too?"

Ishani stared at him for a few seconds and then opened the glove compartment. She looked inside, pulled out the contents and then put them back saying, "Where did I put them?"

"What are you looking for?" Neil asked looking at her with curiosity.

She gave him a deadpan look and said, "My boxing gloves."

He laughed heartily and she found herself smiling. He picked up her right hand, kissed her fingers and then squeezed her hand. Then he started whistling a tune.

When they went over the flyover, they started looking for Rent Easy. But it was not easy to find. After going around the block a couple of times, they finally found the place.

The car rental office was right next to a sweet shop. It was bigger and better maintained than what Ishani had expected. Neil parked the car a little ahead and they walked back to the entrance. There was a girl sitting behind a table; she looked at them and said, "Are you looking to rent a car or are you returning one?"

Neil smiled at her and said, "We are looking to talk to the owner."

"The owner? Regarding what?" she asked.

"We are detectives investigating a case and we need some information from him," Neil stated.

The girl looked at him and then she looked at Ishani. "I will check," she said and picked up the handset of the intercom on her table and pressed a couple of numbers.

Ishani looked around the small office. There were two other tables in the room about four feet behind this table. Behind those tables there was a wooden partition.

"Sir, there are two detectives here and they are looking for information they are saying," she said, into the intercom. She then listened to what the person on the other side was saying. "Yes, OK sir." She said and closed the call.

She then got up and said, "Come with me."

Ishani and Neil walked behind her. There was a sliding door in the partition behind the other tables. She slid it open and they walked through it into a decent sized office. It had a big glass top table and a few chairs in the front. Behind the table sat a middle-aged, portly man. As they entered, he got up and said, "I am Jitesh Taneja. Owner."

"Hello Mr. Taneja. I am detective Neil Bhargav and this is detective Ishani Sohoni." Neil made the introductions and stretched out his hand.

Jitesh Taneja shook Neil's hand and then he looked at Ishani. He said, "You are the one in the news."

"Yes. I am," Ishani acknowledged.

"Please have a seat", Jitesh Taneja said to them. Then he turned to the receptionist and said, "Pinky please send in some tea."

Pinky closed the door and Neil said, "Someone rented a car from you in January for a couple to go to Mahabaleshwar. We need the address of the person who rented the car."

Taneja looked at them, "Here is the number," Neil said and gave him the car registration number.

Taneja looked at the car number. He was going to say something but the phone started ringing. He picked up the call and talked for a few minutes. The conversation was with some irate customer. He finished the call and turned to them and said, "January, you said? What dates?"

Ishani gave him the dates. Just then Pinky came back and served them tea. Then she said, "Sir, Jagdish called. He will be late in returning from Mumbai so he can't go for the pickup at 12:00 noon."

Taneja, cursed under his breath and said, "Call Siddhu. See if he can do the 12:00 noon pickup. Then Jagdish can go in Siddhu's place."

Pinky said, "What about that car rented by the guy in Kalyani Nagar? He is still not picking up our calls."

Taneja scratched his head and said, "Keep trying."

Pinky closed the door behind her and they all sipped the tea. Taneja looked at them apologetically and said, "This is a busy time for business. I will not be able to look through the past bookings right now. Leave your phone number with me. I will search through the bookings and give you a call in the afternoon."

"Alright. Here is my card. I am also writing Ishani's number here. If you can't reach me, call her. But we need this information today," Neil said.

"Definitely, definitely. I'll call you in the afternoon," Taneja said looking relieved.

When they came out of Taneja's cabin in the outer office, the other two tables had occupants. The place looked busy. They nodded at Pinky and left the place.

Ishani looked at her wrist watch. It was 11:30 AM. They needed to be at QSoft by 12:30 PM. So they had some time on their hands. Neil seemed in a hurry though. He was walking so fast that Ishani almost had to run. He got to the car, opened the door and got in. Ishani quickly got into the passenger seat and said, "What's the hurry Bhargav?"

Neil started the car, looked at her with a smile and said, "We have a few minutes on our hands so I want to use the time to buy some stuff."

"Buy? What? Where?" Ishani asked. What did he need to buy? Clothes?

"Some snacks from Chitale Bandhu," Neil said and grinned.

Ishani laughed softly and said, "It's a good thing you are tall."

"What?" Neil said, then realizing what she meant said, "Ah! Well, I am told I am underweight for my height! So I really need all the food I eat."

"Really?" Ishani asked. He looked slim but not underweight.

Neil's phone rang and instead of asking Ishani to take the call, he parked the car on the side to take the call himself.

"Neil Bhargav," he said. Ishani waited patiently while Neil was on the phone. He was doing a lot of listening and very little talking. "I see," he said and looked annoyed. Then after few moments he said, "How sure are we of that?" He nodded absently. Then he looked up and said, "Aah. I see. That was quick." Finally he closed with, "Right. Tomorrow then."

He put the phone down and cursed under his breath. Then he looked at Ishani and said, "That was the Commissioner. Vasantrao called the Commissioner and informed him that Prof. Dhotrey will come in and let the police question him."

"Oh! That is good. Why the annoyance?" she asked.

Neil started the car again and joined the flowing traffic. Then he looked at her and said, "He will come in tomorrow. He is just buying time. Prof. Dhotrey and his sidekicks will destroy a lot of evidence today, any papers, photos and other things they can get their hands on.

"That means while we do get to question Prof. Dhotrey, we get very little that can be used against him."

"For our case, any information he gives us might be enough though, right?" Ishani asked.

Ishani got the feeling that he was hoping to catch Prof. Dhotrey as well. Neil said, "What he and the likes of him are doing to our education system is criminal! They are choking and slowly killing good educational institutes. They should get caught and punished."

He looked upset till he saw the shop he was looking for. He managed to find parking space right in front of the shop and they both went in to buy snacks. Ishani had guessed correctly that he had wanted to buy bakarwadi. What she had not realized was that he wanted to buy so many other things and in such large quantities. When they walked out of the shop, he was carrying about three kilos of sweets and savouries. He put the bags on the back seat and got back in the driver's seat.

"I'll send these across to Delhi with DK if he comes down on Monday, as he is thinking of doing." He said as he started the car. "My father loves this mango sweet."

"What if DK does not make it here?" Ishani asked.

"Then I'll have it on his behalf. I told you I am underweight, didn't I?" Neil said and chuckled at her expression.

As they got onto the highway and made their way to the IT Park, Neil said, "By the way, QSoft had a press conference at 9:00 AM this morning. They said that they were a law abiding company and would of course do whatever required, to help the police in the investigation."

"Meeting SSV yesterday, I thought he was sincere about wanting to do what was right," Ishani said.

Neil nodded and said, "I am sure he is sincere. But for big companies like QSoft it is not enough that the CEO is honest and sincere. He is not the only one taking important decisions. It is the whole leadership team that needs to be sincere and honest. They need to understand right from wrong. They need to have the courage to do the right thing.

"Someone from the leadership team took the decision to close this case after failing to understand that in the long run, running the investigation was in QSoft's interest as well."

Neil turned to look at Ishani and she nodded. He understood the issue well. Looking at her expression, he went ahead, "Many of these new companies, especially the ones that grow very fast, suffer leadership issues. They don't have enough senior, mature people. Moreover in the IT industry, even hiring senior people is not easy. The industry is young and has grown at a fast pace. So even if you wanted to hire senior people, you won't not find enough of them.

As a result, incapable people end up in leadership and decision making roles. These people can do much harm to the company; something many of these companies refuse to see or acknowledge."

"You have given this a lot of thought," Ishani said admiringly.

Neil gave a brief smile and said, "This is something I have heard from my father. Even though he has given up hope of me joining the family business one day, he continues to make an effort to educate me.

"I should call him this evening. I am thinking about him too much today," he said with a small smile, shaking his head.

"Do you see your parents often?" Ishani asked, without thinking about it consciously.

"I see my mother much more than my father. He is busy being a successful industrialist and businessman," Neil sounded scornful. "When I am in Delhi, my mother and I have lunch at some fancy place once a week. I go over to the big house a few times a month. I end up seeing my father about two or three times a month.

"Of course there are many functions and parties. I get dragged out to at least a half of these," he said with a sardonic smile on his lips.

"You are very rich, aren't you?" Ishani asked wrinkling her nose.

Neil looked at her and chuckled at her expression. He ruffled her hair and said, "My family is rich. I make a decent living, but I am not rich." He was quiet for a few moments. Then unexpectedly he said, "Divya and I had many fights about my profession. She wanted me to go into the family business. If not, she said, I should at least make use of the wealth that was rightfully mine. She didn't like having to manage on my earnings." He sounded bitter now.

"How did you decide to be a private investigator?" Ishani asked.

"Well, Sohoni, I will tell you that story some other time darling, because we are almost here," Neil said. He was back to being playful.

Ishani made a face at him and he said, "Don't go looking for your boxing gloves again now!"

Ishani laughed and shook her head just as Neil stopped the car in front of QSoft's entry gate.

CHAPTER 25

Their reception at QSoft was very different today. Dheeraj was waiting for them in the lobby. Once they were all seated in a conference room, Dheeraj pointed to a stack on the table and said, "I have the files of all the engineers recruited on campus last year. There is some data in the system that you can go through. If you like, I could print those for you."

"I'll take a look at the digital data. It should suffice," Neil said.

Ishani turned around to look on hearing a sound outside the door and noticed Atul standing there. "Hello folks," he said, entering the room.

Dheeraj got the desktop machine started and opened the employee management application while Neil and Atul had a discussion about food and ordered pizzas for everyone.

"These files are sorted by college name," Dheeraj said pulling the stack to the centre of the table. "We hired fifty five students from 12 colleges," Dheeraj was saying as he arranged the files in different piles. "The biggest number came from M.V. College, S. J. Institute of Technology and HIT. We hired ten from each of them. From the other places we recruited a smaller number of engineers. From three colleges we got only one student each."

Ishani saw the different piles and said, "Can we start by looking at the files of engineers that managers have had issues with?"

Dheeraj nodded and started pulling out the files. There were three from M.V. College, two from S. J. Institute and one from HIT. Ishani and Neil started going through the files. It took them a few minutes to understand all the information, especially because of the way it was all arranged.

"Can you show us the files of the engineers who are doing well? Let us see the difference in these two groups." Neil asked and Dheeraj took out four files and said, "These four."

All four of them were from different colleges and one difference Ishani could see was that all of them seemed to have better marks and grades in their 10th and 12th exams.

Neil was going through the files too and when Ishani looked at him, he said, "Did you notice that all the six not doing well are from rich families?"

Ishani realized they were from other states but had not realized their families were rich? She picked up a file she had just put down and opened it again. Neil started pointing things out to her which had made him realize that these kids were from rich families; names of schools and colleges, the postal addresses of the parents, parents' occupations, their hobbies, etc.

"As for the four doing well, two are from Pune, one is from Nasik and one from Delhi. The guy from Delhi is from a well-off family but the other three are from a middle class background," Neil pointed out.

Neil looked at Dheeraj and asked, "Dheeraj yesterday you were saying something about how engineers generally get allocated to the teams of the managers who interviewed them. That was not the case for the five or six that we looked at. What about others from this batch?"

"I'll check," Dheeraj said and checked in the system to take out the details of the allocation of engineers to projects.

By 4:00 PM, they had gone through all the files and Neil had made notes in his laptop. Engineers from the three colleges, namely, M.V. College, S. J. Institute of Technology and HIT were all allocated to projects managed by managers who had not interviewed them. Engineers from all the other colleges were allocated to projects managed by managers who had interviewed them, except in four cases. Those four were interviewed by the same manager and Dheeraj had informed them that, that manager didn't take any fresh engineers on any of his projects. Manjiri had been on a panel at M.V. College and she had selected two students.

Ishani was startled when suddenly Neil's phone rang. He picked it up quickly saying, "Neil Bhargav." Listening to the person on the other side, he mouthed, 'Rent Easy' to Ishani.

"From QSoft?" he said and all three looked at him. "Can you give me the number?" He noted the number on a piece of paper and said, "Thanks. If we need any more help, we'll call you".

He put the phone down and said, "Dheeraj, do you have a Rajendra Kulkarni on your roles?"

"Rajendra?" Dheeraj asked. Then he shook his head and said, "We have four Kulkarnis but not Rajendra."

"Hmm." Neil said. Then he picked up his phone again and unlocked it. Ishani was curious and said, "Neil?"

He looked up and said, "Let us see if Trucaller can help". He opened the application and entered the number he had noted down. All of them waited while the application searched. When the search was completed, the name displayed against the phone number was, 'Nitin QSoft'.

"You have a Nitin Kulkarni?" Neil asked looking at Dheeraj.

"We have two Nitins. One is Nitin Daga and the other is Nitin Parulekar. No Kulkarni," Dheeraj said.

"Nitin Parulekar!" Ishani exclaimed and all the three men looked at her in surprise.

Ishani picked up the file in front of her, flipped through the papers and said, "He has interviewed many of the people from these three colleges."

She opened file after file. "Of the thirty from the three colleges, seventeen were interviewed by Nitin Parulekar. Three out of six confirmed poor performers were interviewed by Nitin," Ishani pointed out.

Neil turned to Dheeraj and said, "He was present at the offsite right?" Then he looked back at Ishani and asked, "Is he the one who didn't tell you that he was alone in the tent?"

Ishani pulled out her notepad from the backpack and flipped some pages. She nodded and said, "Yes, that is right."

Was he involved in some sort of recruitment scam? Maybe Prof. Dhotrey paid Nitin to select students from their institute. Maybe there were other colleges, like M.V. and HIT who were also doing something similar.

Nitin was involved in the recruitment scam and Manjiri had started making noise about the recruitment process so maybe Nitin wanted to get her out of the way. If Nitin had rented the car, that meant Nisha and he were involved. And Nisha was scared for Nitin, not for herself. It all seemed to be adding up.

"We will need to make sure it was really Nitin who rented the car," Neil said.

Dheeraj was looking stunned. Atul seemed calm but he was obviously curious. Neil looked at them both and said, "We were trying to identify the person who rented a car in Jan from a car rental company called 'Rent Easy'. The person gave Rajendra Kulkarni as his name and said he was from QSoft." Then he asked, "Does QSoft rent from this car agency?"

"Yes, we do. We have a corporate tie up with them. We get a discounted rate because we provide regular business," Dheeraj said, still looking quite disturbed.

Neil got up and paced the small area behind the chairs. Ishani waited patiently for a few minutes and then finally said, "Neil?"

Neil stopped pacing and said, "I am going to ask Taneja to call Rajendra Kulkarni over to his place under some pretext. If one of you is there to recognize Rajendra Kulkarni when he comes over then things will move a lot faster."

Atul and Dheeraj were quiet.

"We will need one of you to go with us and identify the person," Neil repeated.

Dheeraj and Atul looked at each other and then Dheeraj nodded, "I'll be there."

Neil acknowledged and then picked up the phone to call Taneja. He explained what he wanted Taneja to do. Then they discussed what pretext they could use to lure Rajendra there before ending the call.

Neil put the phone down and said, "Taneja will call Rajendra Kulkarni and tell him that his signature is needed on a booking slip. That the auditors were going through his papers and so they were correcting whatever was missing." Dheeraj nodded at that.

"We should also have Inspector Pathare come over to Rent Easy's office," Neil said looking at Ishani.

"OK. I'll call him," Ishani said.

She dialled Inspector Pathare's number and waited. He picked up in a couple of rings and said warmly, "Hello Ishani. You are going to live a hundred years! I was just thinking about calling you." Ishani knew others in the room could not hear what he was saying, but she still felt conscious.

"Hello Inspector," she said and before he could say anything she rushed on to explain about Rent Easy and Neil's plan.

He said, "I see. OK. Let me know. I'll go over to the place. By the way, are you interested in going out for dinner? There is this Dhaba on the highway that serves great food".

She didn't want to go out with him but she didn't want to say an outright 'No'. So she did what she thought presented the only way out available to her. She pretended that she thought he was asking both Neil and her. "Sounds interesting. Let me check what Neil thinks," she said.

She thought she heard the Inspector sigh, but he didn't object. Instead he said, "I have also made a list of adventure sports shops that we could check at about the Swiss knife. I'll send you the details in a message".

Dheeraj seemed to be slowly recovering from the shock. He said, "Do you folks want to go through any more details? If not, I would like to put these files back."

"We'll need copies of these files. Scanned copies will do," Neil said.

Dheeraj nodded and slowly got up. He collected all the files and turned around with the big pile. When Dheeraj walked out, Atul looked at Neil and Ishani, "This is quite a shock for Dheeraj. While I had logically arrived at the thought that someone from QSoft was responsible for Manjiri's death Dheeraj had refused to believe it so far."

"We are not ready to conclude anything yet," Neil said shaking his head. "What we do have is a strong suspicion." He paused for a while and then said, "Tell us what you can about Nitin. We have talked to him and gathered some basic information. But how is he to work with? Did he and Manjiri get along? He is a married guy. Is there anything that you could tell us about his marriage?"

"Nitin has been working with QSoft for a long time. I think more than eight years now. He got promoted twice in quick succession after he joined the company but he has been at the same level for the last four years, as a delivery manager. He and Manjiri never worked together. Two very different people; I don't think they had anything in common. Their friend circles, their hobbies, everything was poles apart. He is your average middle class married man. His wife is very simple and they have one son," Atul said. Then he got quiet.

"Can you tell us anything about his views on things; what does he believe in?" Ishani asked.

Atul was quiet for a few moments looking down as if he was carefully choosing his next words. Then he looked up at Ishani and said "Money is important to him. He wants to discuss the year-end bonus every year. The pay-out doesn't change much so because of that he goes to Dheeraj and them comes to me to discuss his options. He also complains about his salary all the time."

"But there must be many people doing that, right?" Ishani asked.

"Umm" Atul said this as though he didn't completely agree, "A lot of people complain about their salary but not as much and not every year. Also the way he argues every year is quite annoying; especially coming from such a senior person".

Neil's phone rang again and he picked it up. Looking at the number flashing on the screen he said, "Rent Easy."

He listened for a few moments before saying, "I see. Please keep trying. Let us know as soon as you get through."

He disconnected the line and said, "The phone is switched off. He will keep trying. We might need to think of alternate methods to get in touch with Rajendra Kulkarni."

The door of the room opened and Dheeraj came in. He looked better than he did when he walked out few minutes ago. "Do we have to go to the car agency now?" he asked.

"No," Neil answered and explained what had just happened. "We can't keep waiting. Folks, please go ahead with whatever plans you had made. If I need to, I'll call you. We might setup the 'encounter' sometime tomorrow."

CHAPTER 26

It was after 5:00 PM, but it had not cooled down enough for it to be pleasant. Ishani was grateful that their car had been in the underground parking lot. The inside of the car was cool and she sighed as soon as she got in. Neil didn't seem to be affected. She looked at him and said, "It's hot! How come it does not bother you?"

Neil looked at her and shrugged, "I am used to extremes. Neither the heat nor the cold bothers me much." Then he smiled and said, "That first time we came here, I realized that you get bothered by the heat but I liked that you didn't complain about it".

"Well, I do complain about it. A lot!" Ishani said, "… but not to strangers." She turned to look at him, smiled sheepishly and said," Definitely not when I am trying to make a good impression".

"Well, that you did," Neil said and smiled.

As they drove out of the QSoft premises, Ishani said, "Inspector Pathare has sent names and addresses of five adventure sport shops. These shops have international brand equipment. He thinks one of them might be able to help with the Swiss knife."

She looked at the message the Inspector had sent. The five stores were in different parts of the city. She looked at the addresses and tried to see if she knew where each one was located. She could figure out only two out of the five addresses he'd sent. She said, "We can visit this one. It can't be too far from the hotel." She read out the address and Neil nodded.

She closed the message and saw she had another message from the Inspector. She opened it to find that it was about dinner. She sighed and Neil looked at her with raised eyebrows.

"The Inspector suggested a Dhaba on the highway for dinner. He asked if we would like to go with him. Do you want to go?" she said.

Neil shrugged and said, "I am sure his invitation is for one person." He gave her a crooked smile.

"He didn't specifically say. I assumed it's for both of us," she said. Then she felt she had to clarify, "I would like to go, but not alone. I don't want to give him the wrong impression."

Neil smiled at that and said, "OK. We'll go."

Ishani called the Inspector and told him that Neil and she would join him for dinner. It was decided that the Inspector would meet them at the hotel at 8:00 PM.

They had to ask for the directions a couple of times before locating the adventure sports shop. It was a small shop named 'Sahyadri Adventure & Camping', in a side lane next to a big mall. There were other shops next to it, a medical store and a general store, among others.

Right at the entrance, at the billing counter, was a girl of about twenty dressed in jeans and a t-shirt. She looked bored and not very interested in the shop.

"Do you have Swiss Knives?" Ishani asked to open the conversation.

"Actually I'm new here," the girl said in reply; then went ahead to say, "You can look around. We have lots of stuff. Backpacks, sun glasses…"

"We need to talk to someone about Swiss knives." Neil said firmly. "Who can answer our questions?"

The girl looked at him in fascination and said, "I'll call the owner."

"Good. Do that," Neil said and stepped into the store. Ishani followed him.

The girl didn't know much about anything, but there was a lot of adventure equipment to look at. In the crowded store, a small tent for two people was setup right in the middle making it very difficult to walk around.

The girl looked at them curiously before making the call. Then she called out, "The owner will come over right away. He stays nearby."

They made their way around the tent to the wall that had small items hanging on a stand. They found many models of Swiss knives by Victorinox.

No other brand. Ishani tried to think of some other brand name and couldn't.

"I think this is the only brand available in India," She said.

Neil nodded knowingly and said, "Yes. Not just India. Probably, worldwide."

"Yeah? But the one that was found in the lake is a different one." Ishani said.

"Yes, I know." Neil said picking up a torch and looking at it. "I think it must be an old one."

In a few minutes, the owner came on a scooter and parked it right in front of the store, on the wrong side. He was a man of about fifty, average in his appearance. He came over to them without even looking at the girl and said, "Hello. I am Mohan Rao, the owner. Tina said you wanted to buy Swiss knives."

Neil picked up a Victorinox knife and said, "Is this the only brand you sell?"

Mohan Rao misunderstood and said, "It is a very good brand. There are different types of knives. If you are willing to spend a little more, I can show you some very good models."

Neil shook his head and said, "Do you sell any other brand?"

"Any other brand?" Mohan said and then went ahead, "We only keep the best. This is the best."

"What are the other brands that you don't keep?" Neil asked.

Mohan looked offended. He asked, "Do you want to buy this one?"

"No. We are not here to buy anything. We are detectives investigating a case and we just need some information," Neil said calmly.

Mohan Rao's demeanour changed on hearing that. He straightened and said, "Detectives?" Then he looked at them closely. "You were in the newspaper!" he said looking at Ishani.

"Yes. As it says in the news, we are investigating a case," Ishani said in a matter-of-fact manner.

He signalled them to the counter and said, "Maybe we can sit and talk. Would you like a cup of tea or a cold drink?" For some reason he felt he needed to treat them with respect and show good hospitality.

"No. That is OK. We just need to know about the Swiss knives. Do you know any other brands? Do you know someone who will know?" Neil asked.

"I don't know any other brand. I have only seen this one." Mohan Rao said. "Let me be honest. I don't know much about any of the equipment that is sold in my shop. I have a hardware store. I had seen a shop in the camp area like this. I realized that we don't have anything like this in this part of the city and so I opened this store." He was being honest alright.

"OK. Can you tell us which adventure equipment dealers would know about different brands of Swiss knives?" Neil asked.

Mohan Rao scratched his head and said, "You can try 'Himalaya Trekking & Adventures' which is in Kothrud and maybe 'World of Adventure' in the old city."

"Yes, we have the names and addresses of both", Ishani said. Neil nodded, shook hands with Mohan Rao and they left the shop.

As they got out of the car at the hotel Ishani said, "I am going to get ready and then have a good cup of coffee."

Neil looked at her in surprise and said, "I was thinking exactly that! I'll see you at the coffee shop in 20 minutes?"

After a refreshing shower, Ishani wore a turquoise wrap-around skirt and tied its sash into a knot. She had chosen a cream sleeveless top to go with it. She combed her hair and tied it back into a pony tail. She wore sandals and put on her wrist watch.

As she walked towards the lift, her phone started ringing. She pulled out the phone from her small purse and saw that it was Geetu. She was smiling as she said, "Hi".

"Hi Shaani! I was hoping you would call today." Geetu sounded disappointed. "I waited all day. Finally I wondered if you were not well. After all, your friend was not well and if you had stayed by his side to take care of him, you might have caught something."

"Sorry Geetu. We have been busy, got back only about half-an-hour ago. I was planning to call you later in the night." Ishani said thinking she should have called earlier.

"How is Mr. Bhargav?" Geetu asked.

"He is fine. He is still sneezing a bit but the fever is gone."

"Good. So what are you two doing for dinner?"

"Going out with the Inspector from the Commissioner's office."

"Oh. OK." Geetu was quiet for a couple of moments. Then she said, "Why don't you both come over to my place tomorrow? I'll make nice paranthas."

"We might need to work; I am not sure right now."

"Why don't you check with the hotshot detective? I am sure he will like some good, home-cooked, Punjabi food."

Ishani chuckled and said, "I am sure he will. I'll tell him."

She disconnected the call and waited for the lift. She heard a door close and turned to look. Neil was walking towards her looking relaxed in khaki pants and a collared, army green T-shirt. He smiled on seeing her. Then he looked at her from top to bottom and his smile broadened. Ishani looked down at herself. What had made him smile like that?

"What?" She asked.

"A wrap around skirt."

"Yeah? So?"

"You can't ride on a motorcycle with this skirt, can you?" Neil said still smiling.

"Why would I ride on a motorcycle? I assumed we'll all go in the car."

"Good," Neil said and then putting his arm around her shoulder gave her a quick squeeze before dropping his arm. He said, "I had this horrible vision of the two of you riding ahead on his motorcycle and me trying to follow in the car."

Ishani turned her head to look at him and laughed out at his expression. "How about the two of you go on his motorcycle and I drive the car?" She said bumping his arm with her shoulder.

Neil chuckled at that just as the lift arrived and shook his head saying, "Not on my life!"

When they got off at the lobby, Neil said, "DK is coming over tomorrow evening. I'll talk to the reception and make a reservation."

They went to the reception and the girl there greeted them warmly.

"I need to book a suite," Neil said to the girl.

The girl said, "Sure sir. Let me check and see what's available. Do you want to move there tonight?"

"No. It's not for me." Neil explained about DK needing the suite for Sunday and maybe also on Monday.

Ishani waited patiently while Neil went about making the reservation. Then as they walked to the coffee shop, Ishani asked him, "The case isn't solved yet. And in any case you give him regular updates on the phone so why is he coming to Pune now?"

Neil shook his head and said, "He is not coming specifically for the case. He was supposed to come over for some business meetings in Tata Motors. He just adjusted the dates."

"Aah, OK." That made sense.

"But he is asking a lot of questions about the case. While he claims to be OK now, I don't think he has come out of the shock and sadness of Manjiri's death yet. I think finding the person responsible and ensuring their swift punishment has sort of become his mission."

They entered the coffee shop and looked around for a table. The coffee shop seemed quite busy on this Saturday evening. They found a table in a far corner. Once seated Ishani said, "Geetu wants us to go to her place. She asked me to tell you that she will prepare good Punjabi food."

Neil smiled at that and said, "We can go. Home cooked Punjabi food sounds wonderful."

The waiter came over and they both ordered coffee. Neil also asked for some sandwiches for himself. Ishani found herself shaking her head. When the waiter left Neil said, "What?"

"Sandwiches?"

Neil looked at his watch and said, "It's only 7:25 PM. It will be at least another hour-and-a-half before dinner. I am hungry!"

Ishani smirked and said, "That is OK. I am just surprised you asked for sandwiches. I thought you didn't like them."

"Oh I like them", Neil clarified, "But not as my lunch or dinner. They are good as a snack."

As they waited for the sandwiches and coffee and talked about the case. Once the waiter served their order and left, Neil continued from where he had left off, "Apart from Nitin, another person who doesn't have alibi is Hemant. He is someone who had a relationship with Manjiri, which she ended and he was angry and hurt about it."

"But the relationship had ended more than a year before the incident," Ishani pointed out.

"True. But maybe something happened between them recently that pushed him over the edge. Maybe they had a fight and what happened wasn't intentional." Neil said. "That's a possibility."

"The third person is Dilip; someone who reported to Manjiri and she was rather sweet on him," Ishani said.

"That is what everyone believed. But maybe there was something that he was not happy about. She had refused to promote him," Neil said.

Ishani just nodded and sipped her coffee. Neil ate his sandwich in silence for a few minutes and then said, "I think there are some important pieces to this puzzle that are missing. If we find those links, things will be clear."

After they were done with their coffee, Neil looked at his watch and shook his head. Ishani checked the time; it was ten past eight. "I know," she said and Neil looked at her. "My friend Nikhil is late. I am sure he is doing this just to keep you waiting you know!" Neil looked nonplussed and then laughed a little.

Ishani said, "I'll tell Geetu that we'll go over tomorrow." She made the call and talked to Geetu. Then looked at Neil and said, "So 10:30AM tomorrow?" He nodded and she conveyed that to Geetu.

Ishani looked at her watch again after a few minutes and then said, "Maybe I should call and check with Nikhil."

"Give him a few more minutes," Neil said. His phone rang. For some reason looking at the screen made him smile. He picked up and said, "Hi."

He listened for a while with a smile on his face and then said, "She is right. I did promise her that." The person on the other side was probably a woman and she was probably scolding Neil. "I don't think that is unreasonable," he said with a scowl. Then after another gap he said, "Let's talk about this when I get back to Delhi. This is still some time away."

Then he sat up and said, "Yes," and gave Ishani a guarded look. He listened for just a few seconds and said, "I'll call you once the case is over and we can talk about this at length. Right now I can't answer your questions." Then he laughed and said, "Yes. I talked to Ma. I'll call dad in a couple of days. No. I know! I will call him." He ended the call with, "Bye Ami".

He put the phone down, smiled and said, "My sister." Then he looked up and looking back at Ishani said, "Your friend is finally here."

Ishani turned to look at the door as the Inspector was walking in. He saw them and came over. He was dressed well in a pair of jeans that looked brand new and a checked, half sleeved cotton shirt. He smiled and said, "Sorry. I was stuck in an enquiry."

Neil signed the bill and they got up. The Inspector said, "How should we go? Ishani would you like to ride on the bike?"

Neil gave her a knowing look. Ignoring that, she said, "Let's take the car. We can all go together."

CHAPTER 27

Ishani stretched and slowly opened her eyes. She tried to guess the time but she had drawn the thick curtains last night, and it was semi dark in the room. She picked up the wrist watch from the side table and checked the time. Her watch showed 8:10 and she decided she had some more time to just lie around and relax. She picked up the TV remote, switched it on and selected the channel that played old Hindi songs every Sunday. Then she closed her eyes and smiled as one of her favourite songs came on.

She thought about the dinner last night and her smile turned into a giggle. When they had set off from the hotel, she had been worried looking at how the Inspector and Neil were treating each other. The Inspector had been very obviously tense. Neil had been more polished and if she had not watched carefully, she might not have noticed his stiffness.

Ishani had let the Inspector sit in the front seat. Neil had not been happy about that, but she had ignored the look he gave her and got into the back seat. The conversation had a forced feel to it and while no one was saying anything out of place, the tension had been obvious to Ishani. She had started wondering what she could do to make the men relax. As they got onto the highway, the conversation turned to cricket and by the time they had reached the Dhaba about ten minutes later, Ishani had felt that the two men had forgotten her presence.

Neil and Nikhil had talked about cricket like two experts. They had discussed different matches and different players. They had realized that their favourite players were the same. This discovery made them see each other in a different light. They had talked about Tendulkar, his style and his records for so long that Ishani had felt that it would have been better if she had stayed back at the hotel.

It was Neil who had noticed that Ishani had started feeling left out and tried to change the topic. But the Inspector had ignored his attempt at diverting the conversation and kept dragging the talk back to cricket.

When the Inspector had stepped away to take a call, Ishani had touched Neil's arm, smiled and said, "Don't worry about me. I am completely fine with letting the two of you go crazy talking about your favourite sport."

Before Neil could say anything, the Inspector had come back. Ishani had looked up and seen the Inspector's expression change. He had suddenly realized that Neil and Ishani were behaving very familiar with each other.

Neil too had noticed the Inspector's realization. He had gone out of his way to make sure that all three of them enjoyed the dinner and that the conversation remained friendly. They had talked about various topics after that and Ishani had ended up enjoying the meal.

It had been quite late when they got back to the hotel. Neil had asked the Inspector to join him for a drink or a coffee and the Inspector had accepted the invitation. Ishani had excused herself and gone to her room instead. It had been 11:35 PM when she reached her room. She didn't know if the two men had gone to the bar or the coffee shop and she didn't know how long they had stayed there.

She got up at 8:30 AM and dialled Neil's room number. He took some time picking up and said, "Hello".

"Did I wake you up?" Ishani asked.

"Yes. What time is it?" He asked. He didn't sound completely awake yet.

Ishani felt a very strong urge to go over to his room and snuggle close to him. She put that thought aside with an effort and said, "Its 8:30 Mr. Bhargav! Time to get up and get ready!"

"Hmm," he said, "OK."

"What time did you go to bed?" Ishani asked.

"Umm," Neil was still talking in a lazy tone. "I think it was close to 2:30 AM."

"I see… I am getting ready and heading down for breakfast. I'll see you there in an hour," Ishani said.

"Yes Ma'am," he said and Ishani felt he was smiling. "9:30 sharp Ma'am!" he added.

When Neil came in, he took one look at the fresh fruit and glass of milk in front of her and said, "Is that all you are planning to eat?"

Ishani made a face and said, "No. I just got this to start with."

After they both had more food on their plates, Neil said, "I called Taneja before coming down. He has not had any luck with reaching Kulkarni yet. I have told him to keep trying."

"Should we call Sameer Ranade once?" Ishani asked.

Neil shook his head and said, "Let's wait one more day."

They ate in silence for a while and then Ishani said, "So what did you and your friend Nikhil talk about till 2:30 AM?"

Neil looked up from his breakfast, a fork and a knife in his hand. He had a twinkle in his eyes when he smiled and said, "I was waiting for this. I knew you would call him my friend."

"Are you going to tell me?" Ishani asked trying to not show any emotion.

"I am thinking about it," Neil said. Then looking at her expression he said, "We talked some more about cricket. Then after a couple of drinks the bar was closing, so we went up to my room. After a few more drinks he got all serious and told me that he had heard that I was married. When I told him that in a way I was, he got angry and asked me why I was fooling around with you."

Either because of the way Neil was telling it or because it just didn't fit with her image of the two men, Ishani had difficulty believing his story. But Neil kept going, "I then ended up telling him about my impending divorce." Then he made a face and said, "More because I was worried about Nikhil doing me physical harm than anything else!"

Ishani shook her head and gave him a disbelieving look. But he went on, "After another peg, he asked me what you saw in me. And I told him I really didn't know!" He put down his knife and fork and with an earnest, searching look in his eyes asked, "What do you see in me, Ishani?"

Ishani ignored the question and asked, "How much did the two of you drink?"

"Oh. Umm, I wasn't really keeping count you know. We drank a little in the bar and then we took a bottle up and we had to finish that."

"Why did you have to finish it?" Ishani asked thinking that between the two of them they had drunk a lot of alcohol.

Neil just shrugged and grinned.

"Do you have a hangover?" She asked, looking at him closely.

"No. But your friend Nikhil—" He then corrected himself and said "I mean our friend Nikhil, might have one." Then he said, "He left his bike here last night. I insisted that he take a rickshaw."

"Thank you!" Ishani said a little sternly.

"He wanted to talk about you." Then after a pause he said, "In fact, a lot of people have been asking me about you."

"What people?" Ishani didn't know what he meant.

"My sister for one was asking about you," he said.

"Why would your sister ask about me?" Ishani asked.

"Because she heard from my mother that I am working with a woman detective that I am highly impressed with," Neil said with a grin.

"Oh!" Ishani said. Then because she couldn't resist she asked, "And what did you tell your mother?"

"I didn't tell my mother. DK told my mother," Neil said straight-faced.

"Oh," Ishani said again.

"Of course Ami, my sister had called to yell at me because she found out that I had promised my niece a big doll house for her birthday." Ishani remembered him saying that he didn't think that was unreasonable. "But then she wanted to know if you were beautiful." Neil said and gave her a deadpan look.

Ishani was dying to know what he had said, but she didn't want to ask him. She was debating about what to say next when Neil's phone rang. He picked it up and said, "Good morning, sir." He listened for a few moments and then said, "Alright. Sure."

He put the phone down on the table and said, "That was the Commissioner. Prof. Dhotrey called and said he would definitely come in by evening." Neil obviously had not liked the news.

"Do you think he will come in?" Ishani asked suddenly feeling tense.

Neil looked down at his empty plate. Then he said, "I think he must be looking for support from some other politician right now. Since Vasantrao has decided to throw him to the wolves, he must be approaching Vasantrao's opponents. If he gets that support he will not come in."

He picked up the phone and dialled a number. As soon as the call connected, he said, "Good morning DK," and he proceeded to tell DK what was happening. "Yes, please do that," he said and closed the call.

The mood had changed; their light hearted banter had suddenly ceased. In a few minutes, they made their way out of the hotel and towards Geetu's place. Neil was driving and Ishani gave directions. With traffic being really light, they reached their destination in twenty minutes.

Geetu lived on the seventh floor and had a great view from her balcony. She showed them around her place and then served them cold lemon juice. Then she showed them her music collection and asked them to play something before vanishing into the kitchen.

When Geetu came out after about ten minutes with some snacks in two plates, Neil was humming a romantic song looking at Ishani. Ishani was trying hard to look nonchalant but it was quite obvious that she was more than pleased. Looking at the two of them, it would have been impossible to miss the romantic vibes.

Geetu cleared her throat and said, "If you two want something to nibble on…"

She put the plates on the centre table and put one of the CDs Neil had selected into the music system. As the music flooded the room, she said, "Shaani can you come in the kitchen and help me?"

"Of course!" Ishani said feeling guilty that she had not volunteered. She turned to Neil and he said, "Go ahead. I have cold juice, hot snacks and lovely music to keep me company."

As they stepped into the kitchen, Geetu pointed to the stuffing she had made and said, "Aloo paranthas and kheema paranthas".

"Great!" Ishani smiled. For her, spending time with Geetu was what mattered; what they ate, not so much.

"You think your Mr. Bhargav will be pleased?" Geetu asked.

"Oh, I am sure he will be pleased!" Ishani said laughing softly. "He likes food," She said looking around the kitchen. Then turning to Geetu she said, "As you would have realized the other evening."

"Shaani…" Geetu started and stopped. Ishani turned her head to one side and said, "What?"

"Well," Geetu started again, "You were acting a lot more reserved around him the other evening. Today, anyone would who saw the two of you would think that there was something going on."

Ishani made a face, then sobered up and said, "That evening I didn't know that he was getting divorced." She turned around and picked up the serving spoon that was on the kitchen counter and held it in front of her face. She could see her face all warped in the image.

Geetu came closer and pulled away the serving spoon and said, "And?"

"Umm. We like each other," Ishani said and smiled because she couldn't help herself. Geetu raised her eyebrows at that. Ishani giggled and said, "A lot!"

"And?" Geetu said again.

"What is this and, and, and?" Ishani asked getting annoyed. "We'll figure out something. What, we don't know right now. We are not thinking about it what with having a murder case to work on!"

Geetu got quiet and turned around. Ishani felt guilty about her outburst. Her friend was obviously asking because she cared. She went after Geetu and hugged her from the back saying, "Geetu I am sorry. It's just that we really don't know what we are going to do. The only thing we have thought about is that once the case is solved, we will go on a proper date. Till that point we are trying to keep a distance."

"Hmm," Geetu said and sighed. "Your love life is never straight-forward, Shaani!"

"That is true!" Ishani said with feeling and both of them laughed.

At 1:15 PM Ishani and Neil were seated at the dining table. Geetu was in the kitchen waiting to bring out the first batch of paranthas. Neil was humming a song that was playing on the music system. While he was making an effort to look relaxed, Ishani could feel that he was anything but calm. Prof. Dhotrey not coming in was bothering him.

She was so lost in her own thoughts that when Neil said, "Ishani?" she looked up with a question in her eyes and then realized that her phone was ringing.

"Hello," she said, picking up the call. It was Sameer Ranade.

"Hello Detective," Sameer said. "I found the recording of that night and have gone through it." He sounded very serious.

"What did you find?" She asked eager to know.

"I think Bhargav sir and you should see this. Can you come over to my place at 3:00 PM?" He had found something!

"Of course," Ishani said, looking at Neil.

"OK," Sameer said, sounding quite sombre, "I'll wait for you folks."

Ishani put the phone down and told Neil about the conversation. Neil nodded and said, "Right."

Geetu came out and served a big parantha to Neil. The second one she cut in half; served one piece to Ishani and the other to herself. She sat down and said, "My maid, Sunita has got very good with paranthas. She makes them just the way I like them." She served a dollop of butter on Neil's parantha and another one on Ishani's. Neil looked at his plate and smiled. He looked at Geetu and said, "Thank you. This reminds me of my grandmother's paranthas."

He then ate a piece and said, "Oh this is very good!!"

Ishani tasted her parantha and said, "Hmm. Really good!"

The conversation was smooth and effortless, mostly thanks to Geetu. She kept telling them things about her son and some about her husband. Ishani didn't want to spoil Geetu's mood so she listened and responded appropriately. Neil, she noticed was doing the same.

After they were done with paranthas, Geetu brought out vanilla ice-cream which she served with freshly cut mangos. "Shaani this is especially for you!" She then turned to Neil and said, "When we were studying, in the summer, we invariably ate ice cream with mangos. This woman used to skip dinner and hog only ice cream!"

Neil laughed and said, "Is that why you didn't mention this earlier today?"

Ishani made a face at both of them and helped herself to more ice cream. Then she checked the time. It was almost 2:00 PM. "We should leave by 2:30 PM," she said looking at Neil.

"What is the hurry Shaani? Stay till evening. We can watch a funny movie." Geetu said.

"We'll have to leave Geetu. Something related to the case has come up," Ishani said looking apologetic.

It was 2:35 PM when they finally got up to leave. Neil shook Geetu's hand and said, "Thank you for having me over and for a wonderful meal."

Geetu hugged Ishani at the door and said, "Please come and stay with me once the case is solved."

They reached Sameer Ranade's house at 2:55 PM and Neil even found a place to park, not too far from the house. As they opened the small gate and walked in, the main door of the house opened and Sameer Ranade came out.

"Hello," Sameer said. "I think I have found something significant."

He had a key in his hand; he opened the lock on the garage door and took them inside. It was quite hot in the garage. Sameer switched on a small air cooler as well as the ceiling fan before switching on the flat screen monitor of his computer. He had already arranged his chairs around the computer. He looked very serious.

He talked as he selected the video recording to play, "I started watching the recording from 11:00 PM onwards. And for the first forty-five minutes nothing happened and then I just couldn't believe that I had unknowingly recorded something like this!" He started the video and asked them to sit down. He let Neil and Ishani sit in the two chairs closest to the screen and occupied the last one. He got quiet and let them watch.

Ishani and Neil watched with concentration. The time at the bottom of the recording indicated it was 11:47 PM. They saw a small object come in the view from the left end of the frame. It looked like a small boat with someone sitting in it, rowing. It was all dark and so it was very difficult to see clearly. The boat was a dark colour, impossible to say what colour exactly. But it seemed to have a light coloured stripe like a border. As it came in the middle of the frame they could clearly identify it as a boat. The person in the boat stopped rowing. Then he bent down and did something. He seemed to be pulling something from the bottom of the boat. Suddenly he looked up as if startled. Then the boat was rowed back to where it had come from and went out of the frame.

It looked like some person from the village, from the same shore as the one on which Sameer had stayed, had taken a boat into the lake in the middle of the night and then returned. There was nothing in that recording that would help them. Is this what Sameer had seen and called them over for?

Sameer had left the recording running. "The important part is ahead still," he said.

After a few minutes, another boat seemed to be coming in the frame, this time from the right side. There were two people in the boat. One figure was clearer as the person seemed to be wearing light coloured clothes. The other person was almost impossible to see as they were wearing dark colours.

The presence of the second person was clearer because of the first one. It was difficult to see clearly as it was further away from the camera than the first boat. Ishani checked the time at the bottom of the frame. It read 00:11 AM. The boat seemed to be rocking a lot; the two people seemed to be struggling with each other. Then suddenly, the one in the light coloured clothes was thrown in the water. It was not clear whether the person fell or was pushed. Then the person in the boat seemed to be reaching out to the person in the water. But again, it was not clear what the person was really doing. Then at one point it suddenly became clear that the person in the boat was pushing the person in the water away from the boat.

Unknowingly Ishani put her left hand on her mouth and watched in completely shock. The person in the water was still struggling when the boat was being rowed away back towards the other shore. The boat went out of the frame and they could see the person in the water struggling for air. Then after some time everything became quiet.

They had just seen the recording of Manjiri's murder!! The murderer was someone she had got on the boat with. But who?

The camera had not recorded any sounds but from the recording it seemed like Manjiri had not shouted for help. Why hadn't Manjiri shouted for help?

Sameer reached out and stopped the video. Ishani was stunned and couldn't believe what they had just seen.

"We will need this recording," Neil said. Ishani turned to look at him and found him looking grim.

"Of course," Sameer said. Since he had seen it earlier, Sameer was the one least affected.

Neil looked at Ishani and turning to Sameer he said, "Can we get some water?"

"Yes. Of course," Sameer said and went inside the house.

Neil pulled his chair around to face Ishani's. Taking both her hands in his he said, "Ishani? Are you OK? You look ill," he sounded concerned.

Ishani took a couple of deep breaths and closed her eyes just for a moment. Opening them she said, "I will be OK in a few minutes."

Neil nodded and sighed. He then got up and paced the small room. Sameer came out with two glasses of water and three glasses of what looked like fresh lemon juice.

Neil came and sat down on the chair and picked up a glass of water. Ishani reached out slowly and picked up the other.

Sameer pulled out the CD from the computer, put it back in its jacket and handed it over to Neil.

When they left Sameer Ranade's place, it was 4:15 PM.

CHAPTER 28

As soon as they got into the car, Neil started the engine and switched on the AC. Then he turned to Ishani and said, "I am calling the Commissioner. They should be able to use it to identify the person. Secondly, DK is coming over this evening and I don't want this disk to be with me when he gets here."

"Yes!" Ishani couldn't agree more.

Neil called the Commissioner directly and after a short conversation, he put the car into gear saying, "He will see us in his office at 5:00 PM".

They got to the Commissioner's office earlier than that, completed all the formalities and went to the main building. They expected to be kept waiting but the Commissioner was already there. He was not in uniform today. He was wearing light brown trousers and a cream coloured half-sleeved shirt instead. The casual attire gave him a softer look. It also made him look a little relaxed.

As they came in he gestured to them to be seated and said, "What have we got from the naturalist then?"

"It looks like he has managed to catch the act on video. I think it would be good if you watched it, Sir," Neil said.

"Of course!" said the big guy. Then he called someone on the intercom. Within five minutes a person came over and started the computer. The monitor was a big screen. Then Neil took control and put the disk in the machine. He played the recording from the approximate point from where Sameer had shown them. He then gave his chair to the Commissioner and he stood on one side.

"What kind of camera has he used? Night vision?" the Commissioner asked.

"Well, yes. But it is not the best quality," Neil clarified.

After that, they all watched in silence. This time around, because she knew what to expect Ishani was better prepared. She still found it upsetting to watch. She had not seen anything like this before. She was glad when Neil came and stood close to her as the second boat came into the frame.

When the significant portion of the recording got over, Neil stepped ahead and paused the video. The Commissioner was shocked. He was quiet for a few moments and then said, "Let's go back to the beginning."

When Neil took it back to where the first boat entered the screen, the Commissioner said, "Freeze the video when this boat is closest to the camera."

Neil did that and the Commissioner said, "Let's take a picture of this and enlarge it".

When the image was enlarged, they could see that the small boat had a thick yellow border drawn on it. They could not see the face of the person, but it was obviously a man. He seemed to be bare-chested. Under the yellow border, they could see a few white images on the side of the boat. They could have been letters in Devnagari. The lower portion of the lettering was under water and so could not be seen.

"I think those are letters of some sort. But what? Po, Ga, Ga"? Neil tried reading the letters.

Ishani tried to think of words that would make sense and it suddenly struck her what it probably was. *"Mogara!"* she said, realizing later that she had said it a little loudly when all the three men turned with a start to look at her.

"Mo, Ga, Ra," Ishani read out each letter separately.

"Yes, could be." The Commissioner agreed. "I am going to ask Inspector Morey to look for this boat. It might lead us to the man. He might have seen something that night."

"Yes," Neil agreed and then went ahead in the recording and paused the video when the boat with the two people was largest in the frame. Then he enlarged the image. They could not see the faces at all. Manjiri was wearing a light coloured t-shirt and shorts. The other person was wearing full length pants and a dark coloured shirt or t-shirt.

"Let's send this to the lab. They might be able to do something with it," the Commissioner said.

He then turned to the man who had come in and stood quietly throughout, "Let's prepare a report, make a copy of this and dispatch this first thing tomorrow morning."

"Yes, sir," the man said and left the room.

The Commissioner then went back to his desk and sat down. "Please come, sit down," he said to both of them. They sat down and he said, "The evidence is quite stark now. We have proof that it was murder and yet we don't know who committed it!"

The phone on his desk rang and he looked at it in surprise. Then he sighed and picked up saying, "Hello." He listened for a moment and then said, "Now?" and then, "Alright."

He put the phone down looked up and gave them a smile saying, "Prof. Ashok Dhotrey is on his way!" He sounded excited with the news. "I didn't actually believe he would come in!"

"Sir, are we sure he is actually coming in? He might just be saying that to mislead us while he makes plans to escape," Neil said, his eyes twinkling.

The Commissioner smiled again and said, "It was Inspector Pathare calling from just outside the gate. He said that Prof. Dhotrey just got out of his car and was talking on the phone. He should be here any minute."

There was a knock on the door and the Commissioner called out, "Come in!"

Inspector Pathare walked in. He too was in civilian clothes. He looked relaxed and cheerful. "Good evening, Sir," he wished the Commissioner and then turned to Neil and Ishani and said, "Hello".

The Commissioner asked him to take a seat. Inspector Pathare sat down and said, "Sir, should I call ACP Sathey? I think it would be best if he was here when we talk to Prof. Dhotrey."

Commissioner agreed and as Inspector Pathare was placing the call, turned to Neil and said, "I want to keep you two out of this; it would be best to let ACP Sathey handle this."

Neil nodded, "Of course, sir. Whatever you think would be best."

Then Inspector Pathare turned to Neil and said, "No luck with that guy who rented the car?"

"Not yet," Neil acknowledged.

The intercom on the Commissioner's table rang. The Commissioner picked up the phone and said, "Yes?" He listened and then said, "Alright."

He looked at the three people in the room and smiled broadly. "Dhotrey is waiting outside." He then said to the Inspector, "You have setup the room on the third floor right?"

"Yes sir," Inspector Pathare said getting up. "I'll take care of this," he said and left.

"Sir, apart from our case, we should also get to the bottom of the scam that seems to be running in these educational institutes," Neil said.

Ishani listened quietly as the Commissioner and Neil talked about the possibility of that happening.

After about twenty minutes, Inspector Pathare came back. He entered and said, "Everything is in place. I have made arrangements for him to be seated. I ordered tea for him."

"Alright," the Commissioner said. Then he picked up his phone saying, "Where is Sathey?"

"Sir, he will be reaching in a few minutes," Inspector Pathare said.

They had suspected that Inspector Pathare was the one passing on the information to Vasantrao. But he didn't seem to have any affinity to Prof. Dhotrey.

"What about the men who came with Dhotrey? How many are there?" the Commissioner asked.

The Inspector looked at Ishani and then back at the Commissioner and said, "Sir there are two of them. They are waiting outside. One of them is the guy who tried threatening Ishani."

Neil and the Commissioner sat up. They looked at each other and then the Commissioner looked at Ishani. She didn't know what he expected from her. But he seemed satisfied and said to Inspector Pathare, "Send him in here on your way out. You better get started with Dhotrey. Sathey can join you when he comes in."

Inspector Pathare seemed pleased with that and walked out firmly. After about two minutes, there was a knock on the door and when the Commissioner called out, "Come in," in his booming voice, the door opened. The big guy who had come to Ishani's hotel room stood in the door. He seemed to be hesitating, but finally walked in and stood at a distance from the table. He looked unsure and very uncomfortable. He had not looked at Neil and Ishani at all.

"So you have come with Prof. Dhotrey," the Commissioner said.

"Yes Sahib," the guy replied.

"What is your name?" the Commissioner asked.

"Tukya," he said in small voice.

"Tukya?" the Commissioner asked a little loudly.

"Tukaram," the guy said.

"Your parents named you after a great man and you do these kind of things?" The Commissioner said. Tukya was being scolded like a school boy.

The guy looked down and didn't say anything. The Commissioner then said, "You know one of our guests don't you?"

Tukya looked up and said, "Who sahib?"

Commissioner pointed to Neil and Ishani. Tukya seemed to notice them for the first time. He recognized Ishani and he actually looked scared.

"Sahib, I am really sorry. I didn't mean any harm to sister. I didn't do anything," Tukya said. He was really scared and seemed close to tears. A big and rough looking guy was behaving as if he was really a schoolboy, caught by the teacher for doing something wrong in class.

233

The Commissioner didn't say anything; he continued to stare at Tukya.

"Sahib", he said looking at Neil, then he looked at Ishani and said, "Sister, I am sorry."

"Why did you do it? Who asked you to threaten Ishani?" Neil asked. He sounded like he was asking a very casual question. But that seemed to help. Tukya relaxed a little.

"Not my sahib," he said. He meant Prof. Dhotrey. "He didn't know anything about it."

"Who then?" the Commissioner barked out.

"It was another sahib," Tukya said, his voice shaking.

"Who?" the Commissioner asked again.

"I don't know his name sahib. He knew my sahib. He asked me to only scare Ishani sister a little. He gave me ten thousand rupees," Tukya said.

"You don't even know the name of the person and you went to threaten someone for that person?" Neil asked.

"Sahib, I needed the money," Tukya said in small voice.

"Did you ask that sahib why he wanted to scare Ishani?"

"No Sahib," Tukya said looking sheepish. "He came to me, gave me ten thousand rupees and told me which hotel room sister was staying in. He told me when to go there."

"When did he pay you?" Neil asked.

"He was waiting outside the hotel when I got out," Tukya said. "I had not expected sister to run out like that and I had to quickly go down the scaffolding. I walked quickly out of the gate and walked to my bike. Sahib was waiting for me there."

"So you told him what happened?" the Commissioner asked. He continued to bark out his questions to Tukya.

"I told him that I had managed to scare the sister real good. That she would be leaving town the next day," Tukya said looking down. "I wanted the money and I didn't want him to tell me to do something like that again."

Looking at Tukya, Ishani felt sorry for him. "Tukya, will you be able to recognize the sahib? From a photograph?" She asked quite gently.

Tukya looked at her and nodded. Then said, "Yes, sister, I will." Then he folded his hands in a *namaskar* and said, "Sister I am really sorry. Please forgive me."

It all looked quite out of place to Ishani. Now that Vasantrao had thrown Prof. Dhotrey to the wolves, even his henchmen were in trouble. Prof. Dhotrey might even find a way out, but what about these folks? She couldn't help saying, "Alright. But you need to help us identify him."

"I will, sister," Tukya said and sounded sincere.

"Alright! Wait outside," the Commissioner didn't see any reason to soften his tone.

Ishani and Neil didn't talk much till they got into the car. As Neil took the car out and merged into the traffic, Ishani said, "I feel sorry for him now."

"The Commissioner?" Neil asked looking confused.

"No!" Ishani said with a short laugh. "Tukya!" Then she saw Neil's expression and realized he had understood very well.

"How are you doing Ishani?" Neil asked. When she looked at him, he went ahead, "You were quite shaken when you watched the video recording."

"Yes," she said and sighed. "You weren't affected by it?"

"I was. Of course I was," he said nodding his head, "But you looked ill."

"I am OK now," She said. Then she went ahead, "But I think I will not be able to sleep tonight." She gave a sad smile. "When I was in my last year of school, a young man had murdered his grandmother who lived in our lane. That night I stayed up and studied all night," she said wrinkling her nose, something she did when she was feeling embarrassed.

Neil looked at her and then reaching out he took her hand in his. He linked his fingers in hers and said, "It is OK. There's nothing wrong in being sensitive, even in our line of work. As long as you are not letting it affect your work."

They were quiet for a few moments. Then he said, "We need to make sure that we don't talk about the video recording with DK."

"Of course." Ishani said.

Neil turned his head to look at her and said, "I am a little worried about him. He will ask us a lot of questions and I don't want either of us to even hint at it."

"OK," Ishani said and squeezed his hand to assure him.

"What is the time?" Neil asked and Ishani turned their linked hands to look at her wristwatch.

"6:45," she said.

"DK's flight was supposed to reach at 6:00."

"From the airport, it will take him about half-an-hour to reach the hotel," Ishani said thinking back to last Sunday, when she had arrived in the city. Neil was a stranger then. She looked at their linked hands and smiled.

She thought ahead to when they would go on a proper date. Neil had said that they would not do what he wanted to, assuming that she would not be ready for it but Ishani couldn't wait for when the two of them would make love. She peeped at Neil and found him looking quite serious. He seemed to be focusing on the traffic.

Day dreaming about the date was all fine, but where would they go from there? After all, they lived in two different cities; two cities separated by a distance of more than thousand kilometres. She pulled out her hand from Neil's and he turned to look at her. But before he could say anything his phone rang. He looked at the screen and said, "It's DK. Can you please take the call?"

Ishani picked up and said, "Hello, sir. This is Ishani. Neil is driving right now."

After a brief conversation, she told Neil, "He is on his way to the hotel."

They reached the hotel in ten minutes and decided to wait in the lobby. Neil seemed to be deep in thought. Ishani looked at him a couple of times and finally said, "What is it?"

Neil looked at her and said, "I think it would be best for me to talk to DK alone first."

Ishani nodded in understanding and Neil went ahead, "I think you better meet him and then go up."

It would not be a bad idea to have some time to herself. She could just order something from room service and maybe watch something on the TV.

Ten minutes later, Neil said, "There he is," and got up. DK saw Neil as he was walking towards the reception and stopped.

Deenanath Kumar was broad shouldered and was wearing expensive looking clothes. He was not too tall but had a strong presence. He had what was generally described as a 'wheatish' complexion and he wore glasses in an expensive looking frame. He seemed to exude a quiet strength. She had seen his photographs in newspapers and magazines earlier, but in those photos you couldn't notice such things.

When Neil got closer, he said, "How are you?" and the two men hugged each other in the typical way that North Indians did. Though Neil had told her that he knew DK, she hadn't realized that the two knew each other so well; they were meeting like old friends. Then DK saw Ishani standing almost behind Neil. He smiled and said, "You must be Ishani."

Ishani stretched out her hand and said, "Hello sir."

"Hello Ishani," DK said giving her a firm hand shake. Then he said, "Don't call me sir. DK will work." He then turned to Neil and said, "Let me check in, then you can update me."

The check in was quick and when they left the reception, Neil said, "The suite is on the 8th floor. I'll go with you. I think we can give Ishani a break."

DK stopped and said, "Yes of course." Then he turned to Ishani and said, "But I hope you will join us for dinner, Ishani." He looked at his watch and said, "Should we say at about 8:30?"

Ishani said, "Yes. Sure." She looked at Neil who looked a little unsure. But his expression changed quickly and he smiled.

CHAPTER 29

In about half-an-hour, except for the video recording, Neil had given DK a complete picture of the investigation.

DK had asked a lot of questions and seemed satisfied with the progress they had made. He had stated vehemently that if the investigation had happened in time, by now the murderer would be behind the bars.

He had then talked about Manjiri too. Earlier, when he had talked to Neil, he had been careful. But now, it seemed like a dam had burst.

He said he cared for his wife, and she was a good companion in every way, but he didn't feel for her what he had felt for Manjiri. The world saw a happy family; a successful husband, a supportive wife, two well-behaved children. But DK continued to miss Manjiri.

When he had run into Manjiri last year in Bangalore they had sat up all night, just talking. He had considered dropping everything and going away with her. But then he had decided to be responsible; he had to think about his wife and children. However, he could not bring himself to stay away from Manjiri anymore. He had talked to his wife about running into Manjiri at Bangalore, but he couldn't tell her that they were in touch with each other. He definitely didn't tell her that he was going to Pune to meet Manjiri.

Neil felt sorry for DK. He also felt sorry for what Manjiri must have gone through. But she was gone now; her pain was over. DK on the other hand, was suffering a lot more. He would never be able to meet Manjiri again. Now, all he hoped for was to ensure that her murderers were brought to justice.

When the two of them entered the restaurant, Neil looked around for a quiet table. There was one close to the big glass window overlooking the swimming pool. He pointed to the table and when DK agreed, both of them walked over. They got seated and were handed the drinks menu.

DK turned to Neil, "What will you have?"

"A beer," Neil said. DK ordered whisky for himself. When the waiter left, DK said, "So how is it working with this Ishani Sohoni?"

Neil casually said, "She was a big surprise. To start with, I was unsure, but she is good. Very observant. Very logical."

DK nodded and smiled a little but it didn't reach his eyes. Then he asked Neil, "How scared was she when that guy forced his way into her room?"

Neil said, "She was shaken. That was but expected. But she recovered quickly and was focusing on the case in no time at all!" He was smiling as he remembered their conversation that night.

"You like her," DK observed.

Neil didn't deny it, "Yes. She has been a good partner on the case so far."

It seemed like DK was going to say something but he looked up and then said, "She is here."

Neil turned to look and waved to Ishani. Neil and DK were seated opposite each other and Ishani took the seat next to Neil.

"We just ordered drinks. Do you want something?" Neil asked, turning to look at her.

Like him she decided on beer.

"QSoft is cooperating now right?" DK asked, taking the conversation back to the case.

"Yes, they are," Neil said. "We met the CEO on Friday and he seemed genuinely interested in providing all the support we needed."

"I know the guy. I was surprised to know that QSoft had tried to hush up the case," DK said.

"Most people seem cooperative. Atul Vaidya seems keen to help us." Ishani said and Neil gave a brief nod. "Dheeraj Seth, the HR manager didn't seem very helpful, but now he has come around."

DK looked at Ishani and said, "Atul is the one who called and gave me the news."

Looking at Ishani, Neil said, "DK was telling me that in one of their last conversations on the phone, Manjiri had talked about the engineers they were hiring and that she needed to take up the matter with someone."

"Yes. She was quite frustrated," DK said.

He got quiet as their drinks were served and Neil asked for some starters. Neil looked at Ishani and found her looking at him. He raised his eyebrows at her but she smiled and shook her head, not saying anything. When he looked at DK, he found him looking at Ishani, full of curiosity.

DK raised his glass and said, "Cheers."

Neil and Ishani said, "Cheers."

Then DK said, "To Manjiri."

Ishani glanced at Neil and he shrugged.

"Did Manjiri talk about Nisha or Nitin?" Ishani asked.

"She had talked about a woman from HR who she said was incompetent. I think she did mention some name but I don't remember." DK said. "I don't remember any mention of Nitin in any of our conversations."

After a few moments of silence, DK asked, "And the police? They are helping?"

"Well, they are. But someone from the Commissioner's office is or was providing inside information to Vasantrao," Neil said. He gave Ishani a mischievous look and said, "We suspect that the mole is Ishani's friend, Inspector Pathare."

Ishani reacted exactly the way he had hoped. She gave him a mocking look, shook her head, smiled and said, "You mean your new found friend!"

DK was now looking at them with raised eyebrows.

Neil chuckled and decided to let Ishani explain this, "Ishani?"

Ishani gave him a bland look and then turning to DK said with a grimace, "Neil thought Inspector Pathare was trying to woo me."

Neil jumped in and said, "He very obviously was." He made a face and continued, "He took her out for lunch and then recited poetry to her!" He was glad to see DK lighten up. "Tell me DK, who does that?"

DK smiled and said, "Someone who understands poetry, probably?"

"His own poetry that too!" Neil said disdainfully.

DK actually laughed a little at that and said, "You sound quite horrified, Neil." Then he turned to Ishani with a smile and said, "So did the Inspector impress you?"

Neil could see that Ishani was unsure how she should answer this, so he decided to pitch in and said, "Thankfully his poems were not good."

"How would you know?" Ishani asked looking annoyed.

"Didn't you tell me that?" he asked. "Or did you just say that to make me feel better? Oh no!" He was going all out to get Ishani to drop her annoyance and help DK relax.

Ishani laughed softly and Neil wished, just for a moment that she was in his arms, in his room. Then she turned to DK and said, "Neil is right. I was not impressed."

Neil's phone rang and he saw thatit was Taneja of Rent Easy. He didn't say anything except, "Excuse me," and walked a little distance from the table as he connected the call.

"Hello detective. Taneja here. I kept calling and just now Rajendra Kulkarni picked up. I told him we needed his signature. He will come over before going to work tomorrow morning." Taneja sounded excited.

"That is great!" Neil exclaimed. "Around 8:30 AM or so?" he asked.

"Rajendra said he will come between 9:30 AM and 10:00 AM. OK for you?" Taneja asked.

"Yes. That is absolutely fine with us."

Neil called Dheeraj Seth as well as Inspector Pathare and told them to be at Rent Easy's office by 9:00 AM, to make sure they were all there well ahead of time, just in case Nitin turned up earlier. He walked back to their table to find DK and Ishani talking about him.

"He has always been fond of food," DK was telling Ishani, who was listening with a smile. DK turned to look at him and said, "We had given up on you." Then he smiled a little, "You were on the phone for so long that we started wondering if you were talking to your girlfriend."

"Maybe more than one girlfriend," Ishani added.

DK looked at her, smiled a little and said, "You are making him sound like James Bond or something!"

Ishani giggled and said, "Our own desi James Bond!"

Neil sat down and said, "Let me know once you two are done joking and I'll tell you what Taneja of Rent Easy said."

Ishani sat up and said, "What did he say?"

Neil gave them an update and said, "So Sohoni we have to be at Rent Easy at 9:00 AM in the morning."

Ishani mock saluted him and said, "Right Bhargav."

They ordered dinner and continued to drink some more. Now DK was relaxed. Ishani had become comfortable with DK and was being her beautiful self.

DK talked about Manjiri from time to time. In fact he seemed to find excuses to talk about her. Neil could understand the predicament he must have been in. He would not have been able to talk about Manjiri with anyone so far. Now here in Pune, where he had fallen in love with her, seated with two people who were working to bring her murderers to justice, he didn't want to hold back.

Ishani was listening attentively; asking appropriate questions from time to time. Her eyes filled up with tears a couple of times. Neil chose to stay quiet for the most part and watched the two of them talk.

Now Ishani's phone rang and she excused herself. Neil had noticed that the screen had said, 'Maa'. He watched her walk out of the restaurant and when he could not see her anymore, he turned his attention to DK who seemed to be watching him closely.

"I think the call is from her mother," Neil said, just to have something to say.

"Does she know?" DK asked.

"What? That the call is from her mother?" Neil said with a crooked smile. He knew that was not what DK was asking. DK didn't bother replying to that. He continued to watch Neil.

"That I like her?" Neil asked and then said, "Yes, she knows. And I think she likes me."

"Like her?" DK asked incredulously. Neil looked at him without saying anything and DK went ahead, "Are you sure it's nothing more?"

Neil sighed at that. He was madly attracted to her. He wanted to talk to her about important things and he wanted to talk to her about meaningless things. He had thought about going to bed with her and he had thought about waking up next to her. But he had avoided putting his feelings into words. Now DK was forcing him to do that.

"Neil?" DK said. When Neil looked up at him he said, "It is quite obvious you know."

Neil looked down at the table and DK continued, "I think she is in love with you. When you were on phone earlier, she couldn't stop watching you."

Neil smiled.

"Look at you! So pleased to just know that she was watching you; thinking that she too might be in love with you." DK smiled a little.

Neil dropped his guard. There was no need to pretend with DK. He nodded and said, "She is really something."

"She is smart," DK said agreeing.

"Yes that she definitely is! She is very good at her work too," Neil said.

"And doesn't get scared easily," DK pointed out.

"True." Neil was impressed with that. Also with the way she had talked to Tukya or how she had figured out the letters on the boat.

"She has a very good sense of humour and she is witty," Neil said and then wondered why he was listing out these things. What he felt for her couldn't be explained by a list of things he liked about her.

"You have not said one thing that is the most obvious," DK said. "She is very good looking."

Neil looked down and shook his head saying, "I don't know if that matters." Then he looked up, "I think she is very beautiful. But I think I find her so beautiful because of the person she is. That is what counts." Then after a pause he decided to say what he thought, "Divya has striking good looks. Everyone praises her for her looks. But I never felt like this about her."

DK nodded and said, "I understand that feeling. That is how I felt about Manjiri," he said softly. "I never got over that."

They got quiet as the waiter came and served their dinner. DK was the one to break the silence, "I met your father a couple of days ago. He knew you were here working for me."

"My mother must have told him." Neil said. His mother had wanted him to call his father and talk to him. He had thought about it a couple of times but had not called yet. She might have asked his father to talk to him as well but Neil knew that if he wanted to do something about the growing distance, he would have to take the first step.

"Your old man is not looking too good," DK said. "I asked him if he was feeling ok. He said everything was fine, in that typical way he does but he looks tired."

"I'll call him in a couple of days," Neil said. He could not just call him. He would need to be mentally prepared. He would like to not be thinking about the case when he called his father or about Ishani.

"He is very disappointed that you are going ahead with the divorce. He said he had hoped that after you two had calmed down, you would decide to make it work," DK said.

Neil sighed and said, "He wanted the marriage to work because it would be good for business."

Neil had agreed to get to know Divya to please his parents. She had seemed like the right match –she was right age, the family was well known and his father was keen on him marrying her.

Neil had just turned thirty. His friends had gotten married and some had already had children. Everyone around him wanted him to get married. He had dated a few girls but had not felt any strong emotion for any of them.

He had finally accepted that he would have to settle for an arranged marriage. That is when Divya had come into his life.

She was a very beautiful daughter of a rich businessman. She had done some modelling and then gone into interior design. She had decorated the homes of a few of her rich family friends in Delhi and then given that up as well. She had agreed with her parents that it was high time she got married; after all she had turned twenty six!

"Neil?" DK said and Neil came back to the present. "What happened?"

"No, nothing," Neil said.

"Coming back to you and Ishani," DK said and Neil immediately paid attention.

Neil noticed her walking in from the main entrance of the restaurant and said, "She's here." Then he said, "We have talked about going on a proper date once the case is over. Till then, we're not getting too involved."

"OK. Sounds all sensible and proper," DK said as Ishani reached the table.

She sat down sheepishly saying, "I'm sorry. That was my mother. She also made me talk to my father."

"That is OK," DK said. What had her parents wanted to talk to her about that made her look so sheepish? Her parents would be after her to get married. She was 31; practically over the hill by the standards of Indian parents.

Neil knew Ishani liked him a lot. In fact she had seemed as eager as he felt when they had kissed and when he had talked about a proper date. DK seemed pretty sure that she loved him. Neil vowed to make sure they went on a date soon. He didn't want to give her time to meet any good, eligible, marriageable men!

CHAPTER 30

On Monday morning, Ishani called Neil on his cell phone. He picked up and said, "Morning darling!" surprising her. He seemed to be in a cheerful mood. She didn't respond fast enough so Neil said, "I hope you are not going to clam up every time I call you darling, darling!"

Ishani chuckled and said, "I thought we agreed to wait till the case was over."

"Oh, you know what we decided to wait for." He paused and then laughed softly and said, "That we will wait for."

"Right! Then can we focus on the case for now, darling?" Ishani asked smiling to herself.

"Yes, Ma'am," Neil said. Then he sobered and said, "We need to leave by 8:30 AM. So we should go down for breakfast now. Are you ready?"

They made their way downstairs together. DK came in when Neil and Ishani were seated at the table with food in front of them. He looked better than the previous evening but his eyes were shadowed by dark circles.

"Good morning you two," He said taking a seat. He turned to Ishani and said, "I am very happy with the progress you folks have made on the investigation. I am grateful to Abhijeet for assigning his best detective to this case."

Abhijeet's best detective? Was that what Abhijeet had said? Or was that how DK saw it? "I don't know what to say," Ishani said honestly. "I am glad to be working on this case."

"I am sure, so is Neil," DK said with a knowing smile. What did he mean? What had Neil told him? Ishani didn't know what to say. Neil didn't say anything either, and it got a little awkward. But then DK went ahead and asked, "Do you think I should meet the Commissioner?"

Neil shook his head saying, "No, don't. Things are moving well. I think it is best that you keep your involvement remote."

They parted ways at the porch. DK had a chauffeur driven white Camry, which came over as soon as they stepped out on to the porch. He was heading out for his business meeting but he said he would have dinner with them. Ishani had thought he was heading back to Delhi in the evening, but it looked like he was staying.

They made their way to Rent Easy's office. Neil was driving and seemed lost in his own thoughts. The traffic was not too bad and they reached the place much before 9:00 AM. Rent Easy's office was open and Inspector Pathare was seated on a chair chatting with Taneja. Taneja looked a little uncomfortable, maybe because the Inspector looked tense. When Neil and Ishani entered Taneja smiled and relaxed visibly.

Neil looked around and then gave instructions to all, "Inspector, I think you should be inside with Mr. Taneja. We don't want him to suspect anything. Dheeraj, Ishani and I will wait at that tea shop across the road. As soon as he comes in, we'll walk over."

He checked the time and then said, "Let's get into position. Let's be ready for the possibility that he might come in earlier."

When it was five to nine, Ishani and Neil walked across to the small tea shop. Neil called Dheeraj, who assured him that he would be reaching in the next five minutes.

Neil and Ishani sat down across a table, just inside the entrance. The place only had benches and didn't look very clean. But this was a convenient place from which to observe Rent Easy's entrance. In a couple of minutes a waiter in a dirty-looking uniform came over and placed two stainless steel glasses of water on the table. He asked them what they wanted. Neil looked at Ishani and then turning to the waiter said, "Two teas."

"Do you want the plain tea or special?" the waiter asked.

"Special," Neil said.

Ishani checked the time. It was 9:07 AM now. There was no sign of Dheeraj yet.

"Relax Sohoni," Neil said and Ishani turned to look at him.

"I was just wondering why Dheeraj isn't here yet," she said.

At 9:12 AM, an auto rickshaw stopped across the street. They could not see the passenger clearly but it was a man in formal trousers. When the rickshaw moved away, they were able to see that it was Dheeraj. He looked around and then walked across. He entered and blinked a couple of times because he was not able to see anything. Then he noticed Neil and Ishani at the table right by the entrance. He said, "Hello. Sorry I'm a little late."

"No harm done," Neil said and moved inside on the bench to make room for Dheeraj.

Dheeraj sat down and said, "I didn't bring my car. I didn't know if I will get parking space. Also, I didn't want to park close to Rent Easy."

The waiter brought their tea and placed the two cups in the middle on the table. Neil looked at Dheeraj and said, "Want some tea?" When Dheeraj shrugged and said, "OK", the waiter nodded and went to get one more cup.

They all finished their tea, but they didn't see anyone entering Rent Easy. After some time, they ordered another round of tea so as to have an excuse to continue sitting there.

Around 9:50 AM, a rickshaw stopped right in front of Rent Easy and a man got out. When he paid the fare and turned, Dheeraj exclaimed, "It's him! Nitin!"

Both Neil and Ishani got up quickly. Then realizing that they needed to pay, Ishani said, "You two go ahead. I'll pay and come."

As the two men walked out, Ishani heard Neil tell Dheeraj, "We need to get him to sign as Rajendra before we catch him."

She made the payment as quickly as she could and walked out behind the two. When they got to the short flight of stairs, Nitin was standing at the table near the entrance saying, "I am Rajendra Kulkarni. Mr. Taneja wanted me to sign some form."

The girl at the desk was ready. She said, "Please sit down, sir." Then she took out a form and placed it in front of Nitin, who now had his back to the stairs.

The girl looked at the signature on the form and said, "Thank you, sir."

As Nitin got up, Neil and Dheeraj climbed the six stairs to enter the office. Ishani climbed two steps and waited.

Dheeraj said, "Nitin?"

Nitin was startled. He looked around and found the three of them looking at him. Just then the sliding door in the back opened and the Inspector stepped out followed by Taneja.

"Nitin Parulekar, I am arresting you for fraud. You have signed documents under a false name."

Nitin turned back to look at the Inspector. Then he looked at Dheeraj again and said, "Dheeraj please help me. You know me. I am not like that. This is only for renting a car. I have not used the name for any crime."

Dheeraj looked lost. Neil stepped ahead and shaking his head said, "You also used this name to book a hotel in Mahabaleshwar, didn't you?"

Nitin looked nonplussed. Then suddenly he turned and ran down the steps. All of them realized that he was trying to run at the same time. It was a good thing that Ishani was standing a few steps below because that gave her an extra second to react. She caught his collar as he was trying to climb down next to her. He pushed her and tried to rush away while trying to free his collar. In the struggle both of them fell down the stairs.

Neil and Dheeraj ran down and stooped next to her. Neil looked at her and said, "Are you alright?"

"I am OK," she said but didn't let go of Nitin's collar. Neil got hold of him and then said, "I have got him. You can let go Ishani."

As she sat up, a sudden pain shot through her left arm. She had fallen on her side and in the effort to hold onto Nitin, she had twisted her left arm. It hurt very badly.

The Inspector stepped ahead and looked at Nitin. Neil, held his collar and made him stand. The Inspector took out his phone, stepped aside and made a call.

Ishani got up slowly and walked aside gingerly. She looked at Taneja standing on the steps above and said, "Can I get some water?"

After handing over Nitin to the Inspector, Neil slowly walked over to Ishani and said, "Let me see." He touched her arm and Ishani cried out, "Ouch!" Neil took his hand off saying, "Sorry." Then he took her hand in his and massaged it a little. It was her shoulder and upper arm that was hurting. Then she realized that even her left hip was hurting.

Taneja came and said, "Water" and handed her a bottle. She sipped some water but standing independently seemed like too much of an effort. She reached out and held onto Neil's arm. Neil said, "Ishani?" and he stepped closer to her. Then he put his arm around her.

The Inspector looked at them and said, "She seems to be in a lot of pain. Take her to a doctor. I know a Dr. Phatak. He is only about a kilometre from here. I'll call him."

CHAPTER 31

Ishani became conscious of the phone ringing. Where was it? She opened her eyes and looked around. She couldn't see much, it was too dark. Then she realized that she was on the bed in her room and the blinds were closed. What time was it? She got up with an effort. Her shoulder and arm felt stiff. She winced and sat back. Then she focused and found her backpack next to the TV. The phone would be in that. She got up with an effort and walked to it. By the time she opened the backpack, the phone had stopped ringing.

She was looking at the screen trying to identify the caller when the hotel phone started ringing. She walked across and picked up. "Hello," she said.

"Hi! How are you feeling?" Neil asked.

"Not too bad," she said. "What time is it?"

"Its 8:15 PM."

"Oh," she was feeling disoriented. When you slept at unusual hours, you took some time to adjust on waking up. Ishani wondered if people who suffered from jetlag felt like this.

"How is the arm?" Neil was asking.

"Stiff, but not too bad. I would be ready for action tomorrow morning," Ishani said. She was becoming more alert with every passing second. "What happened today?" she asked.

"If you are up, let me come over. Do you want some tea or something?"

"Tea would be good," she said. Then she decided that she should freshen up. "Give me a few minutes."

"OK. I'll order tea and come over in ten minutes," Neil said.

Ishani tried moving her arm about and found that it was still painful. All the small scrapes she had on her side were stinging too. But mentally she was feeling better.

Neil had taken Ishani to the doctor recommended by the Inspector. The doctor had said that Ishani had pulled her muscle badly, but it didn't look like a fracture. Though Neil had wanted an X-ray done, Ishani was glad when the doctor had said it didn't seem necessary. But then he had advised bed rest for at least a day. He had also prescribed a muscle relaxant and painkiller which Neil had gotten on their way to the hotel.

At the hotel, Ishani had been in too much pain and Neil had hovered around taking care of her. He had ordered lunch for the two of them and forced Ishani to eat a little so that she could take her medicines. The muscle relaxant had made Ishani feel very drowsy. The last thing she remembered was Neil sitting by her side and saying, "You are behaving like you are drunk!" Then he had taken her right hand in his and asked, "Do you want me to stay with you? Or do you feel well enough to be on your own because I need to go to the Commissioner's office?"

Ishani had said, "I want you to stay but I don't need you to." Then she had found that very funny and giggled.

She didn't remember changing out of her jeans but now she was in her track pants and a crumpled top. She changed in to her wrap around skirt and a sleeveless shirt with a low neck.

Her hair was all tangled. She combed it with one hand and decided to try and tie it into a ponytail. When she tried to lift her left arm, the pain shot up from her arm to her shoulder and she had to sit down. She gave up and left her hair loose.

When she opened the door for Neil, she looked almost normal though her shoulder and the arm were swollen. Neil smiled a big smile looking at her and walked in saying, "The tea will be here any minute."

Ishani followed behind him and said, "Did you come in earlier and draw the blinds?"

"Yes, the street lights were turned on and they seemed to be hitting your eyes," he explained making himself comfortable on the bed.

"You got a spare key?"

"Yes, I needed to check on you," he said as if it was obvious.

Ishani sat in one of the sofa chairs and said, "So tell me now, what happened today?"

Neil sighed and said, "You do sound much better," He shook his head before going ahead, "And completely like the focused detective that you are." He grinned.

"That's good right?"

"I am not sure right now. You won't be doing and saying all the interesting things you did and said," Neil said. "I am almost disappointed. "

Ishani looked at him suspiciously. "What things?"

Neil chuckled and said, "I liked you better before I left for the Commissioner's office. You were asking me to join you in bed. You asked me if I would make love to you."

"What?!" Ishani exclaimed. Then tried to think back but it was all hazy. There was confusion in her mind about what had really happened and what she had imagined. Had she really done that?

Neil said, "I was so sorry to have to say no! What with the Commissioner expecting me and we having made a pact to stay apart till the case was solved!" he said, making a face.

"I…" Ishani was embarrassed. "Umm… I don't know what to say."

"You don't have to say anything darling. I am thrilled that you want it as much," Neil said and got up from the bed. He came close to her chair and bending down gave her a quick kiss. Then looking at her expression took pity on her, ruffled her hair and said, "Relax! I am just kidding!"

Just then they heard a knock. "That must be our tea," Neil said and walked to the door.

Ishani watched the waiter come in and put the tray on the table. Neil then walked him to the door and came back. She was still thinking about what Neil had said.

"Are you going to clam up now?" Neil asked coming over to sit in the other chair.

"No," Ishani said with a small smile. "But I am not like that normally."

"So maybe when we do go on the date that we keep talking about, you should take the muscle relaxant. I would love you to be like that," Neil said and winked.

Ishani found that very funny and laughed out. Then, as she bent to serve the tea in two cups she winced, "Ouch." She had completely forgotten about her arm just for a moment.

Neil said, "Tsch, tsch. Let me do it." He went on to serve tea for them making sure he added the right amount of sugar and milk in her tea before handing it over to her.

"Thank you," Ishani said with a soft smile. He knew how she took her tea exactly.

When he sat back with his cup in hand, Ishani said, "OK. Now tell me what happened today."

Neil nodded, "Hmm," he said and took a couple of sips before starting. "We questioned Prof. Dhotrey. His statement has been recorded but whether it will be kept on the record is another thing. Vasantrao called a couple of times during the day to find out how it was going."

"So what did Prof. Dhotrey tell us?" Ishani asked.

"As we got to know earlier he takes additional fees to ensure that students are placed in a good company of their choice. They could choose between one of the four companies that Prof. Dhotrey had a 'tie-up' with. Two to three people, in each company were a part of the scam. They ensured that those students got in. These two to three people of course got part of the additional fees charged. But then they had to go to a lot of trouble to make it work didn't they?" Neil said sarcastically.

"And in QSoft the people taking a cut were Nitin and Ajit Sinha," she added.

Neil put his cup down and said, "There were three people taking a cut. Nitin, Ajit Sinha and Nisha Khanna. They needed to involve the person heading the campus recruitment for sure. Such a scam wouldn't work without that person. In addition they needed at least one technical interviewer. In QSoft, that was Nitin. And they needed a person from HR too."

Neil paused. Ishani thought about Nisha's file; she thought about the expensive flat that had bothered her. All of that seemed to fall in place now. When Neil didn't say anything, she prompted him "Neil?"

"Yeah," Neil said. Then he went on, "There are two sides to this. There are people who seem to have a lot of money but not much of respectability. Now, some of these people would like their children to be a part of respected society. Politicians; so called businessmen who are working on the side-lines of the political system; corrupt officials. You know the types I am talking about.

"They would like their children to have degree from places that have reputed educational institutions like Bangalore and Pune. They also want their children to work in reputed industries.

"Where do you think they look for cushy jobs and high respectability? They look at the software industry and see people who have made a lot of money and are highly respected. They don't see the hard work that has gone into making them the way they are; the tensions these people have lived through and the risks they have taken. They think their children only need to get into this industry to someday become rich, the respectable way. And even if these children do not make the kind of money their parents have, they would still be well-off.

"Most of the kids of these rich people are not likely to be hardworking. So how do they get into good colleges? And how do they get into good software companies? Well, with the help of daddy's money, of course! Daddy has a lot of it!

"Daddy is not expecting them to struggle or fight for it! In fact many times daddy has no clue about the effort required to get a good education! So, daddy needs educational institutes that will admit these children even when they don't show any merit.

"If he is willing to pay for his child to get into one of these colleges, then he is also willing to shell out some more to ensure the child gets into the company of his choice!

"The fact that this will never work in the long run is beyond these parents' understanding. This is the reason why someone like Dhotrey is able to run the scam in the first place.

"Now, you're probably wondering why good educational institutions would accept students like these. But these educational institutes are started as business ventures by people similar to these rich parents. These educational institutes are the money-making machineries of politicians. Places like Bangalore and Pune are known for their educational tradition and for good institutes. But today, there are many institutes that have sprung up in these old education hubs which are nothing close to what good institutes are supposed to be.

"Some of these politicians are really smart. They start or support institutes of repute; but they also use those for money making. So you have institutes like those under the Gaikwad Group. The standard of teaching is high there and some seats are for merit holders; the deserving students. That helps to build and sustain its reputation.

"Ten years back, they reserved 50 per cent of their seats for merit students and 50 per cent for management quota students. Management quota seats are open for sale. You pay a high amount and you are in. Today, they proudly tell you that they have not changed this ratio. However, since then, they have increased the total number of seats from 200 to 2,000. Which means that, earlier they had 100 students paying high fees. Today they have 1,000 students paying high fees.

"Then Prof. Dhotrey came up with this brilliant scheme of guaranteed placement. Of course, this is not done openly. It is not offered to everyone. According to Dhotrey, it is really just for a small fraction of students; only about 30-40 students opt for this scheme every year.

So he is only collecting about Rs. 2.8 to 3 Crore. From this he has to pay the recruitment teams of the companies. So close to half of this goes in paying them. Then there are others in the institute that he has to pay. I think some money must be going even to Vasantrao, though that is not something that Dhotrey dares to say but he probably ends up making about 40-50 Lakh every year!

"That does not sound too big when we compare it to some of the scams we read about in the papers that go into thousands of crores but it is still corruption and in the field of education that too! And it is now affecting one of the industries in India that has so far made a good reputation for itself."

Neil walked to the window and lifting the curtain, looked outside.

"How did it exactly work, the recruitment of special students I mean?" Ishani asked because he had stopped talking.

Neil came and sat down once again and ran his hands through his hair a couple of times.

"Neil?" Ishani prompted.

"Dhotrey paid a certain amount for every special student selected. The amount was different for different companies. It depended on various things like how much of a struggle it was for the recruiters to make the arrangements."

Neil stopped what he was saying as his phone started ringing. "Hello DK," he said into the phone and then after a short pause said, "I'll check if she is feeling up to it."

Feeling up to what? Slowly Ishani had become aware of the pain; she didn't want to change or go down to the restaurant.

"OK. Sure," Neil was saying.

He disconnected and said, "DK just got back. He suggested that we have dinner in his suite." He looked keenly at her and said, "If you would like to. If you are in a lot of pain, then we'll skip that as well. But you should eat something so that you can take the painkillers."

Ishani didn't feel like doing anything really. But she was pretty sure that if she said that, Neil would insist that she stay put tomorrow as well. She wanted to be part of the investigation tomorrow; she didn't want to miss any more of it. So she said, "OK. We can do that."

Neil called DK and conveyed that they would be over in half-an-hour. Once that was done, Ishani said, "OK. Tell me how the recruitment of special students worked. You said Dhotrey paid a certain amount per student."

Neil said, "Right. In QSoft, he had to pay Rs. 4 Lakh per special student. Rs. 1.5 each to Ajit Sinha and Nitin; Rs. 1 Lakh to Nisha. Ajit's job was to plan the recruitment in such a way that when they went to the Gaikwad Institute, they select a committed number of students. He had to make sure he selected at least 5 special students in the lot.

"Nitin had to make sure that he was the technical interviewer going to Gaikwad Institute and interviewing the special students. But Nitin couldn't be the only interviewer. There would be other people going from QSoft; people who would conduct proper interviews unlike Nitin.

"Two things were done to overcome this hurdle. Firstly, the technical panel was told to focus only on technical interviews; leaving the candidate's background, hobbies etc. to be covered in the HR interview.

"Prof. Dhotrey had solved the problem of technical interviews very effectively. In fact he had also solved the problem of the entrance test. He simply had lined up some of the exceptionally good but poor students to take the tests in place of the 'special' students. He also got these students to appear for the interviews, when needed. He had offered then some relief in their fees as compensation.

"They preferred to send the special students only to Nitin. In case one of them got lined up with another interviewer, there were a couple of good students kept in reserve who would appear for the interview.

"Nisha's job was to make sure that in such cases, the application form that was sent to the interviewer at the time of interview, had the photograph of the person going in for the interview but the resume was that of the special student, in whose name the interview was being given. After the selection, she had to change the photograph on the application form. So at the time of the student joining the company, everything would seem to be in order."

"Everything worked till Manjiri came around and insisted that the person she had interviewed was different," Ishani said interrupting him.

"Yes. So now you see how someone like her could be a problem for Ajit and Nitin," Neil said.

"But would they kill her for that?" Ishani mused.

Neil shook his head saying, "We'll have to see what Nitin has to say today. Inspector Pathare was questioning him. When I left, he was still busy with Nitin so I didn't get a chance to talk to him."

Neil got up and arranged the empty cups on the serving tray before taking them to leave them outside the door. "You do that every time don't you?" Ishani said.

"Do what?" Neil asked walking back towards her.

"Every time we are done with the food, you promptly put it all out," Ishani said with a smile. She had relaxed in the chair and had rested her head on the back rest.

He smiled back and said, "Hmm," and came to stand close to her.

"What?" She asked.

"You are really not up to it right?"

"I am!" Ishani said sitting up. The sudden movement made her wince. Neil crouched in front of her chair and held her hands in his.

"Alright. I am not going to argue about this, but you don't have to prove a point you know," he said.

"I know. I am not trying to prove anything. I am feeling quite ok, and I am going to be a part of the questioning tomorrow," Ishani said.

Neil got up and said, "OK. By the way Ajit Sinha and Nisha Khanna were picked up late this afternoon. Also, Inspector Pathare sent a couple of his men to the adventure sport shops to get information on the pen knife."

"Oh!" Ishani said. "Did they find anything?"

"No luck. But one shop owner talked about some people he knew who travelled a lot and bought adventure gear from places like Germany and the US. I thought I would check with Mohan Rao too, if he knew someone like that."

He then held his hand in front of her. Not knowing what he wanted her to do, she looked at him with raised eyebrows. "If you are joining us for dinner, you need to get up now," he said with a smile.

259

She said, "Yes, of course," and grabbing his hand pushed herself out of the chair. She swayed a little but steadied herself with Neil's support.

"I am going to let you join us for dinner, but tomorrow morning I'll decide whether you need to stay back and rest," Neil said.

"Oh?" Ishani said. She was not happy with the tone he had taken with her. "You can decide how to involve me in the case and if you want you can choose to keep me out of it tomorrow but whether I stay back and rest is something that I will decide for myself!"

"Ishani," he said sounding exasperated. "Don't be stubborn about this."

"Why don't we discuss this tomorrow?" Ishani said with a fake smile and walked to the bathroom. She turned at the bathroom door and found Neil giving her a look that was part confused, part amused and part exasperated. She laughed softly, entered the bathroom and closed the door behind her.

She stepped out, after freshening up and applying a little makeup to hide the paleness.

Neil took a look at her and said, "You can't fool me by applying war paint." But he was smiling.

As they walked to the lift, Ishani's phone rang. It was Inspector Pathare and she connected the call immediately. "Hello" she said.

"How are you feeling now?" the Inspector asked.

"I am better. The pain has reduced," she said.

"Neil said that there is no fracture and nothing to worry about," he said.

"Yes, that is what the doctor said," she confirmed.

They waited for the lift and Neil was watching her with an unreadable expression. She smiled at him and mouthed, 'Inspector Pathare' to him. He nodded to indicate he had already guessed.

"OK. That is good," The inspector was saying. "Are you going to be able to come in tomorrow? We will be talking to Ajit Sinha and Nisha Khanna tomorrow. Today we did only some basic questioning."

What if Neil decided to keep her out of the questioning to force her to rest? "I'll see," she said. "I'll have to decide based on how I am feeling tomorrow."

She looked at Neil and found him looking at her intently. Just then she heard the bell indicating the arrival of the lift. So she said, "I am going to have to go now."

Ending the call, she entered the empty lift behind Neil and reclined against the side wall. She was feeling tired and washed out. She was really glad that she didn't have to dress up or be formal. Neil was watching her quietly. He had not said anything since they left her room. Ishani was wondering about it when they reached the 8th floor. When the lift doors opened, Ishani saw a luxurious lobby.

She stepped out and followed Neil. He turned around to find her looking at the décor with wide eyes and said, "This is the executive floor, with only suites. Quite different from our floor isn't it?"

They reached DK's suite and Neil rang the bell. DK opened within moments and said, "Come in." Ishani stepped in and was awestruck by the size of the suite. This was like a one bedroom apartment! A big one bedroom apartment with no kitchen. And two bathrooms. Why were there two bathrooms, Ishani wondered.

DK led them to the seating arrangement in the living room. The sofa looked very comfortable and Ishani was glad to sit down. Neil came and sat next to her. There was a small bar in the corner and DK walked towards it. "What would you like to drink?" He asked.

"I'll go with beer," Neil said.

"Ishani, how about you? Some wine? Or beer?" DK asked.

Before she could reply, Neil said, "No. Nothing for her. She is not supposed to."

Ishani knew she was not supposed to have alcohol while taking the muscle relaxant and was going to decline. But she gave an angry look to Neil. He looked at her and said under his breath, "You know you are not supposed to drink."

Ishani didn't want to argue in front of DK. So she just said, "Yes," with a tight smile and turning to DK said, "Can I have a Thumps Up? If that is not there, I would like a coke."

As DK went about getting them the drinks, Ishani knew, Neil was looking at her but she looked around the room and ignored him. She was annoyed with him for deciding things for her. He had let her make her own decisions; he had let her drive things for the investigation and even changed his opinion based on something she had said. But now, just because she was injured, he was treating her like someone who couldn't say no to an alcoholic drink!

As DK placed her drink in front of her she said, "Thanks."

The centre table was just the right height so that she didn't have to bend to pick up her drink.

She took a sip and put down the glass when she realized her phone was ringing. She picked it up and looking at the two men, said, "Can I please take this?"

DK said, "Of course. You can go in the bedroom, if you need privacy." She got up and connecting the call, walked into the bedroom. It was Abhijeet and she gave him a quick update. She mentioned she had taken a fall but made sure that it didn't sound serious. She wasn't sure if she should mention DK, so she didn't. He listened to her and gave her a few suggestions. As always, she felt good after talking to him.

When she walked back to the living room, she found Neil giving DK an update. She sat down quietly and listened to the same stuff that he had told her downstairs.

DK listened attentively and asked, "What happens tomorrow?"

"More questioning. Ajit Sinha and Nisha Khanna. They talked to Nitin today. But I don't have an update on that." Neil turned to Ishani and said, "Did Inspector Pathare say anything about Nitin?"

"No," Ishani said. She had not thought about asking him either. Maybe she was not as alert as usual. Maybe Neil had noticed that. Was that why he was telling her what she should do? She looked at him and when he turned to her, gave him a smile.

Neil said, "We have ordered food. Hope you will be OK with some sabji and naan." Ishani nodded, she was very hungry. She would be OK with anything right now.

Neil turned to DK and said, "Do you have any more meetings tomorrow? When do you fly back?"

DK shook his head and said, "No meetings tomorrow. I only had these two meetings." Then, turning his glass around a couple of times he said, "I am going to visit an artist tomorrow."

"An artist?" Neil prompted.

"Manjiri liked the works of this artist a lot. The last time we talked, she had said that she would like me to buy couple of his works for her."

Neil seemed surprised by this. "What kind of artist?" He asked after a while.

"Milind Mulick; he paints water colours," DK said, "He has a studio here. Manjiri and I had talked about visiting that on my next visit," DK gave a sad smile. "I am planning to buy some of his works." Then he looked at Ishani and said, "Do you know anything about paintings?"

"Not really," Ishani said. "But I don't like modern paintings much. That I know. Also I generally like landscapes."

"Will you go with me to the studio tomorrow?" DK asked sounding quite sad.

Ishani couldn't bring herself to say no. "Yes, sure."

CHAPTER 32

On Tuesday morning, Ishani woke up when the phone in her room started ringing. She struggled to get up and it was a while before she finally picked up the phone.

"Hi," Neil said softly. "It's me. How are you feeling?"

Ishani was not really sure yet but she said, "I am OK."

On Monday night, when they had come down after dinner, she had been in a lot of pain. She had held onto Neil's arm as she got into the lift and had not let go till she reached her room. Neil had insisted on coming in to help her get ready for bed. She had let him; primarily because she had no energy to fight. He had waited while she took her medicines, changed and got into the bed. Then he had given her a peck on her cheek and left saying, "Good night. Sleep tight and if you dream, dream about me."

Coming back to the present, she asked, "What time is it?"

"8:45," Neil informed her. "Let me come over". Before she could say anything he had disconnected.

Within a minute there was a knock on her door. Neil took one look at her and said, "Do you want your breakfast to be served here?"

"OK," she said.

Neil walked in saying, "I'll make some tea for you. Do you want to freshen up?"

"Yes, OK," she said.

When she came out, Neil had made tea. "I am going down for breakfast now. Should I tell DK that you will be ready by 11:00 AM?"

"You are really glad he asked me to go to the studio, aren't you?" Ishani asked.

Neil looked at her for a moment and then said, "Ideally I would like you to stay here. Rest. Watch TV if you like. Read a book." Then he smiled as she made a face and said, "But going to an art studio for about an hour is better than going to the Commissioner's office for the whole day for questioning."

"OK, sir. Whatever you say, sir," she said. But smiled a genuine smile when he gave her a look.

She sat in the sofa chair and picked up the cup. Taking a sip she sighed and said, "Thank you for the tea."

Neil ruffled her hair and said, "I'll see you in the evening."

She had her breakfast in the room and took the painkillers. She avoided the muscle relaxant; it made her sleepy and worse than that, it made her lose her inhibitions.

She met DK at exactly 11:00 AM and they made their way to the studio in the old city. Ishani looked at the different paintings and was glad that she had agreed to go with DK. She loved all the works she saw. She noticed that DK had stood in front of the same painting for quite a while and so out of curiosity walked over to look at that specific work. As soon as Ishani saw the paintings she knew why DK stood there mesmerized. It was a painting titled 'The Ripple Effect' and showed a woman seated by a lake at night. The tranquillity projected by the night sky and the dark water was almost overshadowed by the perceived loneliness of the woman. DK turned to look at Ishani and said, "Long ago, Manjiri and I had gone for a picnic to a place like this and looked at a star studded sky. This seems so much about Manjiri; as if she is waiting there for someone; for me."

Ishani felt very uneasy at DK's words and found herself worrying about him. DK purchased 'The Ripple Effect' and two other paintings of the by lanes of Pune.

At 1:35 PM, the two of them were in the restaurant ordering lunch.

"I am going to keep it simple," DK said. "Naan and a sabji. Some rice and curd. How about you?" He asked Ishani.

"That sounds good," she said.

DK ordered the food and then asked, "What do you think about the investigation Ishani? You have met all these people, does anyone seem suspicious to you?"

Ishani shook her head saying, "I knew Nisha Khanna was hiding something. She was very jittery." Then after a pause she said, "To start with, even Dheeraj, the HR manager was very reluctant. But later on he went out of his way to help."

They talked about the investigation till the food was served. Then DK asked, "What's next for you? Anything lined up?"

"I don't know yet," Ishani said. She had mixed feelings about going back to Mumbai. She was looking forward to sharing her experiences with Abhijeet. But after this case, she didn't know how she would feel about other investigations. Most importantly, she would not work with Neil; would not even see him on a daily basis.

"How would you like to move to Delhi? Have you thought about working for a business house?" DK asked.

"Business house? Doing what?" Ishani didn't know what he meant.

"For example, Beacon," he said. Ishani knew that Beacon was founded by DK and today it was a big group of companies, Beacon Auto, Beacon Electricals and Beacon India were three of its subsidiaries that she could remember. But what would she do there? She didn't have any background in mining, manufacturing or electrical equipment. What exactly was he asking?

"I am sorry, I don't know what I could contribute at Beacon," she said.

"We need people who are good at investigative work. The type of work we need you for would be slightly different," he said.

Ishani was curious to know what kind of investigative work would be required at Beacon but she liked being a private detective. "I like my work," she said.

DK nodded, "You have my number. If you want to know more about the job, please feel free to give me a call any time."

"OK. Thanks."

He shook his head and said, "No. Don't thank me. That is the least I can offer after what you and Neil are doing for me."

"We are only doing our job," she said feeling uncomfortable.

"Still. It means a lot to me." he said and wiped his eyes, "If you need anything, please know that you can call me any time." Then he saw her worried look and said, "Don't worry. I am OK."

The atmosphere had gotten too serious and sad. But Ishani didn't know what she could do to cheer him up.

As they walked out of the restaurant, DK said, "Neil told me that you need to rest. So let me not keep you."

"I am feeling quite alright now," she said.

"But taking rest won't harm you," he said with a smile and entered the lift as the doors opened. As they made their way up he said, "I'll be leaving around 5:00 PM so I'm going to say bye now."

"Bye," Ishani said and stretched her hand out.

DK's hand shake was warm and he said, "I am very glad to have you work on this investigation."

Ishani didn't know how to respond to that. She just said, "I am sorry we had to meet in these circumstances."

They had reached the 5th floor and as Ishani got out DK waved at her and gave her a smile. That smile was one of the saddest Ishani had ever seen.

In her room she changed into track pants and a loose t-shirt. Then she got into bed and switched on the TV. But as she flipped through channels, she found herself yawning. How could she feel sleepy again? She had slept for a good part of yesterday. Then she had slept more than nine hours at night. She decided not to think about it too much. Switching off the TV she slid under the sheets, made sure her pillow was comfortably placed and put her head down on it. She closed her eyes and nodded off.

When she opened her eyes she felt refreshed. What a power nap can do to you! She brought up her wrist to see her watch and couldn't understand the time for a second. The next second she was wide awake and getting up. The watch said it was close to 6:00 PM; she had slept for over three hours! She picked up her cell phone and checked to see if there were any missed calls or messages but there were none.

"When are you going to be back?" she messaged Neil. If it was going to take time, should she go over? Or maybe she could go over to adventure sports shops. She decided to go down to the coffee shop first; in the room she was getting restless. She freshened up, changed into her jeans and put on a good t-shirt. Then she checked her phone to see if Neil had replied. He had not, so he must be busy.

She opened the door of her room and found Neil on the door step, about to knock. Neil looked surprised and said, "Hi!" He looked at the wallet she was carrying and asked, "Where are you going?"

"I was just going to the coffee shop. I am feeling much better and I wanted to get out of the room." She didn't know why she was sounding defensive about it.

He smiled and said, "Come into my room. I'll freshen up; we can go down in ten minutes."

"OK," she said.

Opening his room, he walked in and put his backpack next to the TV. Then he turned around and looked keenly at her. "You are looking much better," he said.

"I am feeling much better," she said putting her wallet and phone next to his backpack.

She then turned to face him and put her hands on his chest saying, "Thank you."

He looked pleased and wrapped his arms around her. Pulling her closer he asked, "For what?"

"For being there. For taking care of me," she said slowly raising herself on her toes and wrapping her arms around his neck. She did feel pain in her left shoulder and arm but she ignored it. Not giving him a chance to say anything, she closed the gap and put her lips to his.

She realized his surprise just as she was touching his lips. But then he tilted his head and held hers in place so that he could kiss her properly. His other hand moved down to her backside and squeezed it gently. Ishani pressed herself closer and moved her right hand to caress his nape. His hand now snaked up inside her t-shirt and released the hook of her bra.

It was a rude shock when he suddenly started pulling away from her. "No," she said when he lifted his head. But he pushed her back saying, "Phone." Ishani had not heard it ring but she stepped back. He pulled out the phone from his back pocket that must have been put on vibrate mode. She turned around as he connected and said, "Hello."

She slowly walked to the sofa chair and sat down. "I see," Neil said. Then he listened for a while before saying, "When?" After another short pause, he said, "I'll come over. Say around 9:30?" Then he disconnected and threw the phone on the bed. He sighed and ran his hands through his hair. Then he slowly walked towards her but stopped at a distance.

Ishani calmed herself down with effort. "Neil?" she said. "I am sorry. I don't know what came over me."

He walked closer then changed his mind and sat in the other chair. He shook his head and said, "Sweetheart it thrills me that you want me. But I am trying really hard to keep a distance. If you throw yourself at me, I can't resist!"

Ishani didn't say anything; just nodded in agreement. Then she got up and said, "I'll go down to the coffee shop. Do you want me to order something for you?"

"Coffee and something to eat," he said and she walked out as quickly as possible.

After ordering a sandwich for Neil and coffee for the both of them, she waited patiently. Where had Neil said he would go?

Neil joined her in a few minutes. He sat down saying, "What have you ordered for me?"

"Chicken sandwich," she said.

"OK, good," he said and put his phone on the table. Then he stretched out his legs and said, "That well-timed call was from Inspector Morey. They have found a small boat with Mogara written on the side. He has brought in the owner of the boat. He's a guy from the village and is known to have some petty crimes to his name. Inspector Morey would like at least one of us to be there when they question him tomorrow."

"Oh!" Ishani said sitting up.

"It is quite possible this guy saw something," Neil said.

"So we go there tomorrow morning?" Ishani asked.

Neil looked at her and shook his head, "Not we. Me. I go there tomorrow morning."

"I am feeling alright now. I am not going to stay back and 'rest'!" she exclaimed.

He sat up and smiled at her, "That is the plan. I need you to start working, woman!"

"Oh?"

"I talked to Mohan Rao this morning. He gave me the name of a person who regularly travels abroad and buys adventure equipment from various places; US, Italy, Germany, Australia. His name is Rahul Purohit. He also advices Mohan Rao on some of the things he should look for; what people would like; where it is available etc. He has never talked about Swiss knives, but Mohan Rao thinks he would know about them."

"We go and meet Rahul Purohit then?" Ishani said.

"Not we. You," Neil said with a grin. "I talked to him just before I left the Commissioner's office. He said he can meet me at about 11:00 AM."

"When I was talking to Inspector Morey, I had forgotten about that. My brain was not functioning fully," Neil said. "But when I was in the lift, I remembered. You can go and talk to Rahul; especially since you are feeling so well now," Neil said stressing 'feeling well' and smiled a naughty smile. "I am willing to do anything right now in the interest of time. The sooner we complete the investigation, the better!" he continued with a twinkle in his eyes and Ishani found herself blushing.

She didn't know what had come over her. In her earlier relationship, she had enjoyed love making but she had never been the one to initiate it. Upstairs, in Neil's room she had had no inhibitions. She had not only initiated it, she had not wanted to stop even when she had realized that he was pulling back. It was so not like her! Now, she found that she couldn't meet his eyes and looked down at her hands.

Neil laughed softly and said, "Twenty minutes ago you jumped me, and now you are blushing just thinking about it?" Ishani forced herself to look up and he said, "You are..." he shook his head and then sat back. She looked around and found that the waiter was coming over with their order.

By the time the waiter left, Ishani had managed to compose herself. She said, "So, where do I meet this Rahul Purohit?"

Neil looked surprised at her question and her tone. He laughed softly, shook his head and said, "At his residence, in Aundh. I have the address."

Ishani took a sip of her coffee. Then she put the cup down and watched Neil attack his sandwich. "Boy, you are really hungry aren't you?" she asked.

He looked up and nodded. After he had finished half of the sandwich he said, "Haven't had anything since lunch and lunch was very light. Just a couple of wada pavs."

"Tell me what happened today."

"Let me finish eating, woman!" he said and proceeded to demolish the remains of the sandwich. Ishani waited patiently, sipping her coffee.

Once Neil had finished the sandwich, he sipped some of his coffee and said, "It was difficult to get Nitin talking. But once police were able to do that, he spilled the beans. He accepted that he was a part of the scam; that he was taking a certain amount for selecting Dhotrey's special students. The three of them, Ajit Sinha, Nisha and Nitin had a tie up in three other colleges.

"Ajit Sinha talked too. He accepted his part in the scam but refused to accept that he has actually harmed QSoft. It was entertaining to see him defend what they had been doing," Neil said scornfully.

"Defend what they have been doing? How?"

"Well. As per Ajit Sinha's opinion, companies like QSoft look to hire only the best, the brightest students. But there is a lot of work that is very simple, even monotonous and many times quite boring. Really intelligent, bright engineers don't want to do that work; not for long anyway.

"This kind of work can be done by people who are not really ambitious; are not seriously thinking about their careers. The 'special' students that this team brought in were a good fit for this work. It was important to make sure that they got those kinds of jobs; that they were not put on tasks that needed a lot of knowledge about the subjects or where you were expecting a lot of initiative and quick learning, interest even.

"While placing them on their first projects, Ajit Sinha personally took care to see who got allocated on which project. When they moved to a new project, the new manager would have a conversation with the earlier manager, would know the limitations of the person and take him only for those tasks.

"Even otherwise, when teams are big, if a few people are not doing good work, it does not matter. There are always a few over enthusiastic, bright people in the team who carry the team along; the weaklings don't have to get exposed.

"People like Manjiri are the problems in the system. When she took this person on her project, there were other bright engineers available for allocation, so why did she pick him? How did she choose this person?

"Ajit didn't mince his words and was quite vocal in expressing his strong dislike for Manjiri. He said things like, 'When she got an engineer who was not up to the mark, why didn't she just ask for a replacement? Why did she have to talk to people, create so much noise and ask to find out who had interviewed him? It was just bad luck that this kid was from the place where she had gone as a technical interviewer and she was supposed to have interviewed him! This has never happened before. People are better behaved than Manjiri. They don't start asking engineers to be fired; they don't go about doubting the process or their colleagues. How could she continue to create so much noise when it looked like she had been the one to select the bad apple? Shouldn't she have actually shut up then, thinking that it was her own mistake?'" Neil paused and shook his head. Then he sipped some of his coffee. He saw Ishani's expression and said, "He actually said all this."

After a pause, he said, "I have seen a lot of criminals trying to defend what they have done but I was still quite surprised today."

"And he actually believes that he has not harmed QSoft?" Ishani asked incredulously.

"It was convenient to think so. He was making 1.5 lakh per student. They got about 15-20 special students each year. It was a nice sum of about 25 or more lakh per year; over a period of about two to three months. This has been going on for the past three years with QSoft."

"All three have confessed?" Ishani asked.

"Yes, they have." He went on to sip his coffee and realized the cup was empty. He drummed his fingers on the table and then said, "But all three have denied vehemently knowing anything about Manjiri's death."

He saw the waiter and signalled for him. The waiter came over and Neil said, "I would like one more coffee," then he turned to Ishani and said, "Ishani?"

"No. Not for me," she said.

The waiter left and Neil said, "Ajit Sinha's presence at the recreation centre is validated from about 11:00 PM onwards. So he himself does not have anything to do with the death."

"Yes," Ishani nodded.

"Nitin has no alibi for that night," Neil said. "But your friend, Nikhil thinks Nitin is telling the truth when he says that he does not know anything about Manjiri's death."

"How is he still my friend? I thought the two of you became best buddies over a few drinks and cricket!" Ishani said.

"Your friend first!" Neil said with a grin. "He was quite worried about you, you know. He suggested we call you to see if you were doing ok."

Ishani made a face at him and didn't say anything. Neil chuckled and said, "Don't distract me!"

Annoyed, Ishani said, "What? I didn't do anything to distract you! You…"

"Alright. Alright," Neil said raising his hands, not letting her complete what she was about to say. Then he winked at her. "You are very distracting," he said with a smile.

Ishani smiled almost to herself, quite mollified by his statement.

"What about the SIM card?" she asked. It was the SIM card that had led them to Prof. Dhotrey.

"Aah! The SIM card!" Neil said. "When Manjiri started making a noise about the campus recruitment from last year, Ajit and Nitin started wondering about recruiting students from those colleges this year.

"They had given a commitment to Professor Dhotrey but then they went back saying that they were not sure they could keep their word for this year Dhotrey got really mad. He had made plans based on their support."

"They met on 14th March but Ajit and Nitin were still hesitant at that point. He gave them a deadline and said he absolutely had to have a commitment from them by that date. He had started threatening them with consequences. He said he had to hear from them before 17th March. Ajit then told him how they were going to go for an offsite and how they would not have connectivity as neither of them had a BSNL phone.

"That is when Dhotrey called his driver and asked for his SIM card. He handed it over to Ajit and told him that he expected Ajit to call him on 16th evening, no matter what.

"Ajit and Nitin felt truly cornered then. But they could not see a way out either. Ajit took the SIM card with him when they went to the campsite.

"On the night of the 16th, when everyone dispersed after dinner, he went down to the lakeshore and made the call he was ordered to make. But just when he had dialled the number on the phone, he saw Manjiri.

"He was quite startled to see her. She then started asking him how he was making a call. She was quite drunk and he tried to get her to talk about something else. But she would not change the topic. She kept asking him who he was talking to. She started getting louder and at one point tried snatching the phone from his hand. He got scared. He tried walking away to avoid her. Hastily, he opened the handset and took out the SIM card. He thought he put it in his pocket, but later on could not find it. It is only now that he has realized that he had dropped it on the lakeshore."

When Atul saw Manjiri, she had been saying, 'he has a phone'. But she had not been able to give the name of the person.

"By the way," Neil was saying, "Nitin and Nisha independently accepted that they are having an affair. According to Nisha, they are in love and are going to get married once Nitin divorces his wife. According to Nitin, he has told Nisha that he can't marry her though he loves her. He can't leave his wife and kids," Neil said smiling mirthlessly.

"They go away together on weekends sometimes. No one at QSoft knows about this. At home Nitin would say he was going to Bangalore for work or they were having a company offsite. Nitin had an arrangement with a friend and he used to take that friend's car since he couldn't possibility take his own if he was supposed to be going to Bangalore.

"When they were going to Mahabaleshwar, Nitin got to know just a day earlier that the friend's car was not available. He didn't want to change their plans, so he decided to rent a car. He didn't want to rent one in his own name. Still he went to Rent Easy so as to get a discount.

"The Commissioner, ACP Sathey, My friend Nikhil," Neil said glancing at Ishani and smiling when she smiled. "They all believe that the recruitment scam is what is linked to the death. Not the affair." Neil said. Then he got quiet and sat back as the waiter came with coffee.

When the waiter left, Ishani said, "Neil?" and sat up. The sudden movement caused her pain and she winced. "Ouch!" she said before she could stop herself.

"You are still in pain, Sohoni!" Neil said putting down his spoon and looking quite stern. "Why do you act as if you are alright? What are you trying to prove? That you are really tough?"

"No, I am actually OK, Neil," she said. "It's just that I will have to be a little careful. No sudden movements. Going over to talk to Raul Purohit will not be a problem tomorrow." She smiled just to reassure him. He didn't seem completely convinced but didn't say anything more.

"I wanted to talk to you about DK," she said. She was changing the topic but it was on her mind and making her uneasy.

"What about DK?" Neil asked. Then before she could answer he asked, "How was your visit today? Did he like anything?"

"The visit was very good. He bought three works." Ishani said and paused unsure about how exactly to say what she wanted to.

"What did you want to say about him?" Neil asked.

"Umm. Well..." she hesitated and Neil raised his eyebrows. She then told him about how he had looked at the painting titled 'The Ripple Effect' and what he had said. "He looked very sad today. Like he has lost his reason for living..."

Neil didn't say anything. He appeared lost in thought. Ishani wondered if she was over reacting.

Neil sighed and said, "When I talked to him before coming down to Pune, he looked even worse. He told me that the first couple of days after he got the news, he didn't know what to do. It hurt too much to know. It didn't seem like there was anything he could do. I think there was also a sense of guilt."

"Guilt?" Ishani didn't quite understand that.

"I guess somewhere he felt that he had not been there for her; not taken care of her." Neil explained. Then he looked at Ishani and said, "Not logical probably, but then many times logic does not dictate ones feelings."

After a pause, he continued, "Once he came out of the shock, he started digging for information and realized that it was not investigated properly. Then, having it properly investigated; finding out about Manjiri's death became a mission. The investigation gave him a reason to go on. I don't know what he is going to do once the investigation is over," Neil said and rubbed his eyes. Ishani stayed quiet, not knowing what to say. After a while Neil said, "It was good to see him go to the studio and buy paintings. Even if only in Manjiri's memory, he is at least taking interest in things. It is a positive step. I hope he has talked to Arpita Bhabhi." Then he looked at her and clarified,

"His wife. She is a very nice person; a very understanding woman. She has this quiet dignity. Even with all the money at her disposal, she has remained very simple. Their children have been brought up well."

Wasn't it ironic that even with a mature, caring wife and two wonderful children, DK felt Manjiri's loss so strongly that it seemed as if he had lost his reason for living?

———————— ❖ ————————

CHAPTER 33

Wednesday, 25th April turned out to be a very hot day. When Ishani stepped out in the porch of the hotel and asked the valet to call her taxi, it was not even 11:00 AM yet, but it seemed like afternoon.

Neil had left just after 8:00 AM to go to Mulshi. Before he left, he had come to her room to make sure she was up and about. Then he had argued with her about booking a taxi. He had put his foot down and said that either they booked a taxi for her or she would not go at all. She had said he was being dictatorial but he had not budged.

As she got into the air conditioned car, she was really glad that Neil had insisted on the taxi.

It took her a few minutes to find the place and it was 11:10 AM when she rang the doorbell next to the door that had Rahul Purohit's name on it.

The door was opened by a slim guy in his thirties who was about 5' 10" tall. He was in a pair of jeans and a dark blue t-shirt. He badly needed a haircut; he could also do with a good shave.

"Detective Sohoni?" He asked tentatively.

"Yes," Ishani said with a smile. "Can I come in?" She asked.

"Yes. Yes. Come in," he said and stepped aside.

Ishani entered the sparsely furnished living room and looked around. There was an Indian style seating area arranged on one side of the room and a simple wooden bench on the other. The dining area had a simple table and four chairs around it. There was half a wall between the dining table and kitchen. The place seemed very open and airy.

Rahul went to the dining table and pulled out two chairs. He waved his hand saying, "Please have a seat." Then he went into the kitchen and within few moments came back with a glass of water. He put it in front of her on the table and said, "It is getting quite hot now, isn't it?"

Ishani took a sip of the cold water and got to the point. She explained how Mohan Rao of Sahyadri Adventure and camping had given his name as an expert who they could consult to know more about adventure sports equipment.

"I don't know if I can be called an expert, but I am more than happy to help . I know a little bit about the equipment used for adventure sports since I do look for it wherever I travel. Fortunately for me, I get to travel a lot in my job. Countries like US, Germany, Italy and Australia. They have good equipment," Rahul said.

"What kind of adventure equipment do you look for?" Ishani asked.

"Well, I do a lot of hiking. Trekking. I also like to do some hard core mountaineering, mostly in the Himalayas. So I look for equipment that would be useful in my activities. Everything from carabiners and ropes; pulleys, axes. Even tents and backpacks; shoes, sleeping bags. Everything really."

"Swiss knives?" Ishani asked.

"Yes, Swiss knives, torches…" Rahul said.

"We need help to identify a Swiss knife," Ishani explained. "In Sahyadri Adventure and camping, and in fact in all the shops we went to, we only found one brand," Ishani said.

"Victorinox," Rahul said.

"Yes."

"That is practically the only known brand of knives available now. World over," Rahul said. The Internet searches that the Commissioner's office had run had said the same thing.

"What about a brand called Wenger?" Ishani asked.

Rahul shook his head and said, "They used to make Swiss knives. But they got bought out by Victorinox a few years ago."

Did that mean the Swiss knife they had found was old? But it had looked like it wasn't used much.

Rahul then said, "Can you tell me exactly what you need to find out? Maybe if I knew the exact problem you are trying to solve, I can help a little more."

Ishani nodded and said, "Of course. We are investigating a death that happened more than a month ago. A woman drowned in the backwaters of Mulshi dam and…"

"Are you talking about Manjiri from QSoft?" Rahul asked sitting up.

"You obviously know about the case," Ishani observed.

"Can you tell me why you want to know about Swiss knives?" He asked looking uneasy.

"A Swiss knife was found close to where her body was found. The knife has 'Wenger Titanium' written on the grip," Ishani said looking at his expression curiously.

Rahul looked ill now. "Do you know the model I am talking about?" Ishani asked.

Rahul nodded but didn't say anything.

"Do you know someone who might have the knife I described?" Ishani asked.

Rahul kept quiet for so long that Ishani had to say, "Mr. Purohit, you obviously have thought about something. I advise you to let me know what it is. It could be of value to our investigation."

He still didn't talk. Ishani waited for a couple of minutes. Then she took out her phone and started dialling a number.

"I am calling the Inspector working on this case Mr. Purohit," she said.

"No. Please don't!" he said. "I'll tell you what I have just realized."

Ishani put the phone down and waited for him to talk.

"Look, I don't want to get my friend in any trouble. It could very well be a coincidence, you know," Rahul said and stopped.

Ishani said, "Mr. Purohit, if your friend has nothing to do with the death then you won't get him into trouble, right?"

Then since he was still hesitating, she said, "Look Mr. Purohit, a woman died in suspicious circumstances when she was with her colleagues. Don't you think justice should be done by her?" When he still didn't talk, she went ahead, "If you have information which could help the investigation, you have to share it. Otherwise it could be considered as an obstruction of justice."

"OK. You are right," Rahul said. Then he said, "In the month of December, I had gone to Switzerland on work. There, in one of the stores, in the Christmas specials section they were selling Wenger Titanium Swiss Army knives," he said. Then he rubbed his forehead and went ahead, "I wanted to buy gifts for a few friends so I decided to look at them. But the titanium models are very expensive. I finally ended up selecting only one. It was the most expensive one. There in the special sale, it was being sold for 130 Euros. It was the Ueli Steck Special edition. It has a pouch of its own.

"I wanted to buy a big gift for a special friend. He always admired my adventure sports equipment and I thought I would gift this to him," Rahul stopped.

"Would you be able to identify the Swiss knife that you bought for your friend?" she asked.

Rahul gave a forced smile and said, "You would be able to identify it too." He sighed and then said, "As part of the special, they were etching whatever you wanted on one of the blades of the knife. I got my friend's initials etched on the blade."

After a long pause, Rahul finally said, "I don't think he would have anything to do with Manjiri's death. It could just be a coincidence that he happened to drop his Swiss knife at the same place," Ishani could see he was saying it more to convince himself. "Or someone could have borrowed it from him."

Interestingly, Rahul had not said that someone else might have had a similar knife.

"Mr. Purohit, I am sure all that is possible," Ishani said quite gently.

He nodded and sighed. "Dilip Araghade is the friend I gave the knife to," he said quietly and smiled a sad smile.

As soon as she left Rahul Purohit's building she tried calling Neil but his phone was not reachable. She then called Inspector Pathare but he did not pick up. So she made her way to the Commissioner's office. Now seated in her taxi which was moving slowly through the traffic, she felt restless. She moved her arm about a little and felt a little better. The pain had reduced considerably, but some positions were very uncomfortable. She put her head on the head rest and closed her eyes.

She had first seen the photographs of the knife when she was going through all the papers on the first day and the knife itself later on. The knife had been in the water and there were no fingerprints on it. She remembered opening the blades and looking at them. There were some things written on some of the blades—model name, brand name, etc. No one had realized that there were two additional letters that made up someone's initials.

At the Commissioner's office, she went through the security procedure and made her way to Inspector Pathare's office in the CID section. She had to wait for about twenty minutes for him to return to his office. While waiting, she sent a message to Neil and asked him to call her back when he could.

"Hello Ishani," Inspector Pathare said coming in just as the wall clock struck one.

"Hello," she said smiling.

"God it's hot!" he said and sat down. He picked up the intercom on his desk and asked the person on the other side to come in.

An office boy came in and Inspector Pathare asked him to get kokamsharbat for them. "Make sure it's chilled," he insisted.

When the office boy left the Inspector turned to her and said, "So what did you find out?"

Ishani told him how the Swiss knife they had found was quite distinctive according to Rahul Purohit. "He is almost sure it is the knife he has given to his friend. It has his friend's initials etched on one of the blades."

The Inspector raised his eyebrows.

"Can we see the knife?" Ishani asked.

The Inspector stepped out and within a few minutes came back with the knife. Ishani took the knife eagerly in her hands and opened the blades and then showed him, "See here. It says 'DA'."

Inspector Pathare took the knife from her hands and looked carefully. He whistled softly and said, "Interesting!"

"Dilip Araghade then?" Inspector asked sounding surprised.

She spread out her right hand and said, "Have we been going after the recruitment scammers for nothing so far?"

"All three of them say they have nothing to do with Manjiri's death," he said.

There was a knock on the door and the Inspector looked up. "Yes, come in," he said. The office boy came in with their sharbat. He put the two glasses on the table and withdrew. Ishani took an eager sip of the drink; it was cold and refreshing.

The Inspector went ahead to give a more detailed account of grilling Nitin, Ajit Sinha and Nisha. He stopped as Ishani's phone started ringing. It was Neil, "Are you still at the Commissioner's office?" He asked.

"Yes."

"Alright. It will take me about half-an-hour to get there. Can we talk once I get there?" he asked.

"Of course," she said. "I tried calling you and then sent you a message."

"I had no range in the village. For some strange reason, it didn't catch the signal even when I was in range. It's only now that it has started working. I am close to the city. So instead of talking on the phone I would prefer to do it in person," he explained. "Is the Commissioner in?"

"I'll check," she said.

In about twenty five minutes, Neil came and sat in the chair next to Ishani saying, "Hello." He gave her a big smile and said, "Please continue with whatever you were doing."

The Inspector returned the smile and said, "I was just making arrangements to bring in another QSoft person for questioning."

Neil turned to look at Ishani. Then turning back to the Inspector and said, "Another person? Let me see if I can guess correctly."

Ishani turned in her seat and looked at him and the Inspector said, "Yes?"

"Dilip Araghade," Neil asked.

"What?" Ishani was saying at the same time that the Inspector was saying, "What did you find out?"

"So I am right?" Neil asked.

"Yes!" Ishani and the Inspector said in unison.

"Well, you can fill me in on what you folks have figured out. But clearly I will have to tell you what I found out first," Neil said. "Do you want the long version or the short one?" He asked.

Having ensured he had piqued their interest, he sat up and said, "The owner of the small boat is one Chandu Bhoite. He is known to the police as a petty thief. That is why it was easy to pick him up.

"In February, Chandu managed to steal an idol from a temple in a nearby town. The idol is made of silver and weighs about five kilos.

"He was unable to dispose it off and was getting scared keeping it with himself. He didn't want to get caught. He had not thought about it before stealing it but because it was an idol from a temple, the case was being very seriously investigated.

"On the night of 16th March he had taken his small boat in the lake at night because he was planning to dump the idol in the lake. He wanted to dump it as away from the village shore as possible.

"But when he took his boat in, he saw another boat coming from the other shore with two people in it. So he rowed back. When he got back to the lakeshore he stowed the boat and made his way back to his place quickly. He didn't want anyone from the village to see him near the lake."

"So did he see something or not?" Ishani asked.

"He didn't see the murder and the boat was at a distance. Also it was quite dark so he could not see their faces. That means he can't recognize them. But he did hear them!

"He heard the woman saying 'Dilip', 'Dilip' a few times. The man's voice was low and could not be heard clearly. But he could clearly hear the woman."

For a few moments all of them were quiet. Then the Inspector said, "In the video recording that we have, it is impossible to identify the two people clearly. However the lab can check if the footage matches their faces.

"We were planning to send photographs of the four people who were missing between 11:00 PM and 12:30 AM on that night. Dilip is one of them. Now we will ask them to check his face first."

"What have you folks found out?" Neil asked.

While Ishani was talking about her conversation with Rahul Purohit, the Inspector excused himself and stepped out.

When Ishani completed her findings, Neil nodded, drank some water and asked, "How is your arm? Still painful?"

Ishani moved her arm about, smiled a little and said, "It's much better. A lot less painful."

Neil smiled back and just kept looking at her. She finally asked, "What?"

"Well it looks like our work for the day is done, Sohoni!"

"Yeah?" Ishani said.

Neil said, "Let's get out of here as soon as possible. May be you can send your taxi back."

Ishani was calling her driver when the Inspector came in, "The Commissioner will be here in half an hour. He would like you to wait." He then sat down in his chair and said, "It's quite late. So I have asked lunch to be arranged in fifteen minutes."

CHAPTER 34

At 5:00 PM they were finally driving back to the hotel. Ishani looked at the temperature displayed at the crossing near the observatory and exclaimed, "God it's a hot day!"

"41.3 degrees," Neil read. Then said, "Delhi goes to 45 degrees."

"Oh God! I can't even imagine that!" Ishani exclaimed.

"You don't have to imagine it; you can experience it. Come to Delhi," Neil said with a smile.

"To do what?" she asked.

"Come and spend time with me," he said.

What did he mean by that? "Neil, I don't..." She stopped as his phone started ringing.

He looked at the phone and said, "This is my sister." Then he said, "I'll call her back." But the phone started ringing again. It was his sister again.

They were at the hotel entrance now. Neil entered the hotel's gate and stopped the car. He picked up the phone and said, "Hello Ami."

He listened and his expression got serious. "When?" he said. "Yes, right away!" He looked at Ishani with unseeing eyes, "How is Ma?"

Neil looked grim; something was seriously wrong.

"OK," Neil said and cut the call. He then just sat looking ahead, his hands on the steering wheel.

"Neil?" Ishani said tentatively. "What's wrong?"

"My father has suffered a massive heart attack," he said tonelessly.

Then he put the car in gear and drove up to the porch of the hotel. Ishani got out quickly and followed him into the hotel. Inside the lobby she touched his arm and said, "Why don't you go up and pack? I'll ask the travel desk to book a flight for you and arrange for you to check out."

Neil stopped in his track and turned to look at her. He gave her a searching look and then just said, "OK."

After taking care of the two things, Ishani dialled DK's number. He picked up after only two rings and said, "Hello Ishani."

"Neil's father has suffered a massive heart attack."

"When?" DK said sounding concerned.

"I don't really know. Neil's sister called just now," she told him.

"I'll find out. I'll call you."

"OK, Thank you," Ishani said. "I am sorry but I didn't know who else to call."

"Don't worry, you did the right thing. Take care of Neil. He has been thinking of patching up with his father for some time. He must be cursing himself for not having done that yet. But things just happen the way they are meant to."

Ishani went up then and directly to Neil's room. He had put his suitcase on the bed and was keeping his clothes in it. He looked grim and didn't talk.

"Your flight is at 8:50 PM," she told him. He looked at her at that. "That was the earliest available flight," she said.

"OK," he said and continued packing.

Ishani looked around to see what she could help with. She went and opened the door of the closet and found some clothes on a shelf above the hangers. She brought them and put them on the bed next to the bag. Neil saw them and said, "Thanks".

Ishani went into the bathroom and found his toiletries. She put them in the pouch she found on the counter and brought that out. She put the pouch in the bag and Neil once again said, "Thanks".

Ishani stroked his shoulder and he turned to her. He took her hands in his and said, "I am really worried." Ishani nodded.

"I have been thinking about him for the last few days. I meant to talk to him but somehow kept postponing the call. Now…"

"Neil…" Ishani stepped closer, put her arms around him and hugged him. He slowly put his arms around her and snuggled close.

"Stay positive," she said. "It's going to be OK." She could feel how tense he was. "Would you like something to drink?" she asked. That might help him relax.

Neil lifted his head from hers and said, "Can you make me some coffee?"

"Yes. Right away!"

Neil gave her a tight hug and then let her go.

Neil started talking as he continued to pack, "He and I have had our differences for a long time. When I decided not to study engineering he was angry. When I said I didn't want to do an MBA he was really mad. Then when I said I didn't want to join the family business, he stopped talking to me.

"He disapproved of everything I did. Marrying Divya was the only exception. He was very happy about that. We got along well for a while. Then my marriage fell apart and he became very distant.

"My mother kept trying to get us to talk to each other and sort out the differences. But she stopped trying after a while."

Ishani could imagine how painful it must be for both Neil and his father.

When the coffee was ready, Ishani said, "Come, sit down."

He did and took the mug from her. He sipped a little coffee and said, "What is the time?" Ishani sat on the arm of his chair and put her arms around his shoulder. She checked the time and said, "It is 6:10 PM." Then she said, "I'll drive you to the airport."

"How is your arm?" Neil asked.

"Not too bad."

"I can get the hotel to arrange a car for me," Neil said.

"I'll take you," Ishani insisted.

Neil nodded. Then he said, "They will be questioning Dilip tomorrow..."

"I'll go. I'll give you an update," Ishani said.

"OK," Neil agreed. Ishani could see that he was uneasy about not having it all completed before he stepped out.

"I should call the Commissioner," Neil said.

"I can do it," Ishani said.

Neil shook his head and said, "No. I'll do it."

Ishani's arm was hurting while driving, but she was going to ignore it. Neil was very quiet and Ishani asked, "Do you want to call your mother or sister?"

Neil thought about it and then said, "I'll message my sister about my flight. I'll call her once I land."

He probably didn't want to call because he feared he would have to hear the worst.

Just then her phone rang. It was DK. She looked at Neil and said, "Why don't you take it? I had called him before I came to your room," she explained.

Neil picked up the call and said, "Hello," then he listened. "OK," he said. Then after a pause he said, "Yes. 8:50 PM."

Once the call ended, he said, "DK talked to my brother-in-law. They have put in a pace maker and he is on the ventilator. They will observe him for 48 hours before thinking of taking him off the ventilator."

"That is good, isn't it?" Ishani said.

"Yes, I think so," Neil said. He had obviously relaxed with the news and it made Ishani feel better.

They reached the airport at 7:30 PM. Neil insisted that she just drop him and drive back. He had to check in immediately anyway.

"Call me. Let me know," Ishani said when she stopped the car.

Neil turned in the seat to look at her. Then he touched her cheek softly and said, "Of course I will." He stroked her soft skin with his thumb, "I am sorry to have to rush out like this. I can't say anything right now, but I hope we'll see each other soon," he said and got out of the car.

CHAPTER 35

Ishani stayed up late waiting for Neil's call, but he didn't call. He sent a message around midnight to say that he had reached and that he would talk to her on Thursday. She had wanted to talk to him but told herself to be patient. He had said he would call…

On Thursday, she drove to the Commissioner's office. As she went over to Inspector Pathare's office, he asked "How is Neil's father doing now?"

"I don't know. I have not talked to him since he reached Delhi," Ishani said honestly. The Inspector looked surprised, but didn't comment.

He asked, "Are you sure you want to be present during the questioning? It won't be pleasant."

"What do you mean?"

"So far in this case, we have not had to use any force. Prof. Dhotrey talked because his godfather asked him to and because he thought he was protected." He thought? So he was not? "Nitin, Ajit and Nisha; we could make them talk easily. We didn't need to use physical force," The inspector went ahead. "But Dilip seems different. Since we picked him up late yesterday afternoon, he has not confessed anything."

There must be a way to break him. "Have we shown him the video recording?" She asked.

"No."

"We should show that to him and tell him that his face has matched with the one in the video. We should also tell him that we will show the video to his wife," Ishani said. She didn't know where that thought had come from, but it suddenly felt like a good idea.

The Inspector looked impressed and said, "Let us try that." He made a couple of calls to arrange that.

"These digital recorders have made things really easy," he showed her a small recorder and put it in his breast pocket.

Once they entered the main building, the Inspector turned left from the lobby and at the end of the corridor turned right. They entered a room and found a constable seated at the table. The constable saw the Inspector, got up and saluted him. There was a door leading to an inner room which was closed and a lock put on it. Next to the door was a Window but that too was closed.

"Open the door, Dhobale," the Inspector said.

The constable took out a key from the drawer and went to open the door. Once the door was opened the Inspector walked in and Ishani followed. The Inspector then closed the door from the inside and switched on the light.

The room had no other door or Window. There was a table by the wall opposite the entrance. Dilip Araghade was seated on a chair. He looked uncomfortable but quite alert. He watched as both of them sat down in front of him.

"You know Detective Sohoni," The Inspector said.

"Yes," Dilip said.

"Mr Araghade," Ishani began, "Tell us what happened on the night of 16th March. Let's start from the time when everyone was having drinks."

"We didn't drink," Dilip said.

"There were drinks there; people have gone on record to state that. We were also told that you normally drank at such events, but on that night you didn't," Ishani said sounding stern. "Why didn't you?"

Dilip looked nonplussed but didn't say anything.

"Why didn't you, Mr. Araghade?" She asked firmly once again. When he didn't say anything she softened her voice and said, "Was it because you wanted to have a clear head?"

"I was not in a mood to enjoy!" he snapped.

"Because you were planning to kill Manjiri, weren't you?" The Inspector stepped in.

"Of course not!" said Dilip.

Ishani and Inspector Pathare kept asking him questions. Dilip must have felt attacked from two sides. After about twenty minutes, there was a knock on the door and the Inspector got up to answer it.

"Mr. Araghade, we have a video recording, that you should see," Ishani said.

The Inspector had opened the door and there was a different constable standing at the door with a laptop. The Inspector took it from him and locked the door again. Then he walked across the room to the table by the opposite wall and setup the laptop. He then turned and said, "Alright. Come over."

Ishani waited for Dilip to get up then walked behind him. The Inspector had advanced the video to the point where the two people were seen struggling on the boat. They all watched quietly for a few minutes up to the point where the second person had started rowing back. Ishani was watching Dilip closely and noticed the shock register on his face.

The Inspector then stopped the video and said, "As you can see, you are caught on tape. Your face has matched the person in the video." After a pause, he said, "There is also a witness who heard Manjiri and you talk when you were rowing the boat."

Not giving Dilip a chance to think, Ishani said, "I am sure your wife would like to see this video recording. She would definitely be proud of what you have done!"

"You bitch!!" Dilip snarled turning to Ishani. His anger seemed to be directed towards Ishani.

"Mr. Araghade!" said the Inspector but Dilip was looking at Ishani ina fury and before either Ishani or the Inspector could stop him he had slapped Ishani hard across her face. Her head swam. Just for a moment, she couldn't see anything. She stumbled sideways but then got hold of the table and made an effort to steady herself. When she turned, she saw that the Inspector had punched Dilip and he was lying flat on the floor.

The Inspector turned to Ishani and said, "Call Dhobale."

Ishani nodded and walked over to open the door and call the constable outside. When he came in, Inspector said, "Dhobale, bring Mr. Araghade around if he is unconscious and lock him up again."

The Inspector then walked Ishani out of the room. Her cheek was burning, and she was sure it would have gone red. She touched it tentatively and winced.

The Inspector got her a glass of water and asked, "Are you OK?"

"This will hurt a little, but don't worry. Let's get his statement," she said.

The Inspector went back to the room and checked inside. Then he came back to Ishani and said, "Are you sure you want to go in?"

"Yes," she said and got up from the bench.

They both walked in to find Dilip on the chair, his hands tied behind the backrest and constable Dhobale standing next to him.

Ishani and the Inspector entered and the Inspector indicated to the constable that he could leave. The two of them sat in the chairs opposite Dilip once again. Before they could say anything, Dilip looked up at them and said gravely, "I didn't mean to kill her."

Ishani and the Inspector looked at each other and the Inspector said sternly, "Tell us everything."

"Can I have some water please?" Dilip asked.

The Inspector said, "Start talking first!"

Dilip sighed. He looked at Ishani and said, "Sorry," then without waiting for any acknowledgement he started talking about Manjiri. "Manjiri behaved as if she liked me a lot. You would think that would give me an advantage," Dilip said disdainfully. "But no! Oh no! She would not cut me any slack. She kept rating me as average! She didn't want me to have any advantages because she had a soft spot for me. She was over compensating for it.

"Whenever we were doing things together, any outing, lunch etc., she was very nice to me. She would ride with me in my car. She would crack jokes with me. There was a time when I thought it would go beyond being friends. But that didn't happen either.

"Forget it all helping me; it actually was a huge disadvantage! On top of that, everyone thought that whatever I was getting was because she was favouring me," Dilip paused. Ishani and the Inspector didn't rush him.

"She had an affair with Hemant," Dilip said without any prompting. "People whispered about it but of course no one knew for sure. On a whim I followed Hemant once. He went to her place and was there for quite some time.

"Just to check, I called Manjiri and asked her if she was home. I said that I wanted to talk to her about something and if she was home I could go over. She lied blatantly saying that she had gone out with a friend. The bitch was standing at her window when she was telling this to me!" Dilip said with contempt.

After another pause, he said, "Can I have some water, please? I am really thirsty." He was probably kept without food and water for quite some time.

"Once you complete the story," Inspector said with a tight smile.

Dilip looked at the Inspector in annoyance and then went ahead, "That evening, just before the camp fire, I heard Dheeraj talking to Atul about my possible promotion. Atul told him that Manjiri had clearly said I was not ready for the next level. With her strong refusal to promote me, I would not be promoted." Dilip still seemed angry about it.

"Then Dheeraj talked about sending me to the US on a project. Atul said that that too was not going to happen. Manjiri didn't think I could handle the work at a customer site. The bitch thought I was not good for anything! I felt hurt! And Angry!

"I had sort of known about the promotion but it came as a shock to me to know that she had also said no to letting me go to the US on a customer project!

"I was very upset. I didn't drink and I hardly had dinner. I went to the recreation centre, but felt restless, so I left the place and stepped out. I kept thinking about how I had lost opportunity after opportunity because of this one woman! What did she have against me anyway?

"As I walked towards the lake, I saw her alone outside her tent. She was looking for company and when I suggested we go down to the lake she was more than happy to do so. I had thought of talking to her; asking her why she behaved in such a two-faced manner with me.

"As we walked down to the lake, she was unsteady on her feet. I put my arm around her shoulder and walked carefully to keep her steady. She kept giggling. I didn't want her to make too much noise. So I kept quiet after a few comments.

"When we got to the lake, she looked at the boats and said that she wanted to go for a boat ride. I pointed out that it was really dark and she said that was perfect!" Dilip said and laughed contemptuously.

"In the boat, I tried talking to her; asking her about why she didn't think I could be promoted. She said she didn't want to talk about work in such a lovely setting.

"But I insisted and she told me that I was not a good manager. That I had a long way to go. She was not going to promote me till I proved my capability.

"I said she was spoiling things for everyone. Apart from me she was spoiling things for Ajit Sinha. She got really mad at that. She asked me if I knew what he was doing. I didn't know really; I had only seen him talking to Nitin about her. He had been angry. But I said, of course I knew.

"She got mad at that. She started calling me names 'Dilip, how can you say that? Dilip you know something is wrong and you want it to go on?'"

"I don't know why she was saying my name so many times! The bitch!" he said vehemently.

"When I got up in the boat, she too stood up, making it very unsteady. Then I took out my Swiss knife, I was not thinking clearly. She saw the Swiss knife and started walking towards me saying, 'Give it to me, give it to me!' She started struggling with me; the boat was rocking too much and at one point I just pushed her hard. I just wanted her to get away from me but she ended up in the water. At first I bent down to give her a hand but then something just snapped inside me! I pushed her away and started rowing back to the shore."

Dilip sighed and hung his head. After a long pause, he looked up and continued, "Your video does not show it, but before I got to the shore, I had calmed down and even started rowing back. I called out her name, but she was nowhere to be seen. Then I heard some sounds from the campsite. So I rowed back quickly and found Nitin standing on the shore. I told him what had happened and asked him to find help so that we could rescue Manjiri."

Dilip then started crying. "But he said she must be dead already. And if we told people what had happened then I would be taken in as the murderer! He said, he would not tell anyone. He would keep quiet. I didn't know then, why he would do that," Dilip stopped talking but continued to cry.

Neil had not called her. Neither had he messaged. Once she reached the hotel, she messaged him, 'How are things? Can you talk?'

Ten minutes later, the phone rang.

"Hello Ishani," Neil said sounding tired.

"How is your father?"

"He is still under observation. The doctor wants to do an angiography but his blood pressure is fluctuating a lot. That needs to stabilize for them to do the angiography."

"How are you doing?" Ishani asked.

"I am ok. I was worried about my mom but she has proved once again that she is a strong woman," Ishani could hear the admiration in his voice.

"Is the hospital far from your place?" Ishani asked.

"Yes. But it's manageable," Neil said. Then he sighed and said, "What happened with Dilip?"

Ishani told him about the confession but didn't mention how Dilip had slapped her. Neil said, "Maybe he needs therapy!"

They both were quiet for a couple of moments. Ishani didn't know what more to say at this point. Neil changed the topic and asked, "When are you going back to Mumbai?"

"Tomorrow. I am taking the train," Ishani replied.

"Was it Dilip who paid Tukya to threaten you?" he asked.

"I don't know!" Ishani exclaimed. She should ask Inspector Pathare this evening; she had agreed to have dinner with him.

"Ishani…," Neil started but then stopped. Finally he just said, "Bye. I'll call you."

In the evening, Ishani and the Inspector went to a restaurant close by. He looked at her cheek closely. It was slightly swollen and she had put on some makeup in the hope of hiding the discoloration. "I am OK," she said and smiled, "First it was my left shoulder, now my right cheek!"

"I am really sorry. I should have restrained him!"

"You didn't know he would turn violent," Ishani said.

"I didn't," he agreed. "But I am going to see if he has a history of getting uncontrollably angry and violent."

After placing the order Ishani asked him if Tukya had identified the person who had paid him.

"It was Nitin," Inspector said. "He had encouraged Dilip to not 'help' Manjiri. He was glad that she was removed from the scene. When the case reopened, Dilip got scared and Nitin offered to help. He said he could get rid of the detectives. Nitin didn't want the case to reopen either."

"Did Dilip know about the scam?" Ishani asked.

"No. Not really. He only knew something was going on and that Ajit Sinha was involved," the Inspector explained.

"When you questioned Nitin, he didn't mention anything or say that he knew anything about Manjiri's death," Ishani pointed out after a few moments of silence.

"He couldn't talk then because if he told us what he knew, it would be obvious that he was party to the murder. It's not just that he didn't inform the authorities, he encouraged Dilip to not get help!"

After that, almost by mutual agreement, they didn't talk about the case. When the Inspector dropped her off at the hotel he told her that when he was in Mumbai next, he would let her know. Maybe they could meet. Ishani said she would like that.

As Ishani got onto the train on the sunny Friday morning, she looked back at the twelve days she had spent in the city with wonder. It is not often that one can feel such a big change in oneself in such a short span of time.

She didn't know what she and Neil were going to do next. She had looked forward to that one date that they had talked about, not letting herself go beyond that. And yet, her disappointment at being denied that date was much bigger than what one would expect of a cancelled date.

She had voiced her concern about him being in Delhi and her being in Mumbai to him and he had said they would work something out. Did he still think that? She hoped so…

EPILOGUE

25 June 2012

When Ishani got off the local train at Grant Road station and walked out, the sky looked dark grey and it was very sultry. The train had not been as crowded as the one she usually took. After all it was barely after 4:00 PM.

She had been working really hard since getting back from Pune. Today, Abhijeet had sat her down and told her that she should relax a little; he had practically ordered her to go home early.

She walked home just the way she had been doing for the past month; since she had moved to this place. She had shared a flat in Boriwali earlier with two other girls. This flat that belonged to her uncle and was rented out to a family for about eight years before it suddenly fell vacant.

When Ishani got back from Pune, her uncle and aunt had insisted that she shift here. She couldn't afford the going rent and she didn't want to stay for free. So after a lot of back and forth, with her mother mediating between them, Ishani had agreed to shift here and pay the rent she could afford. The place was conveniently located and Ishani liked having the place all to herself.

She reached home in fifteen minutes and went up to the flat on the fourth floor. It was a spacious one bedroom apartment; quite airy with a lot of light and a small balcony attached to the bedroom.

Ishani closed the door and switched on the fan in the living room. She took off her sandals and put her backpack on the dining table on her way to her bedroom. She switched on the fan in the bedroom and threw herself on the big double bed.

She looked at the ceiling fan and sighed. Neil had called her ten days after she got back to Mumbai. In that call he had informed her that Dilip's face had matched with the guy in the video recording; a formality had been completed. He had also told her that Dilip had a history of domestic violence,

300

though his wife had never registered a complaint. He was pathologically violent; he got uncontrollably angry with women.

After that, he had called to tell her that his father was undergoing angiography and they had ended up talking for over an hour about various things. It had then become a pattern; one of them called the other and they talked about anything and everything.

Right after Neil went to Delhi, he had been worried for a while. Ishani could feel his tension when they talked on phone. But now his father was home after a successful surgery and Neil sounded quite cheerful. They had talked three days back; Neil had told her how his father and he were getting along.

Neil had not talked about their date so far. While Ishani understood that he would be in a different frame of mind right now, it did make her feel restless sometimes. But for now, she was glad that they could be friends; albeit long distance.

She pushed herself up and decided that she should go out and have fun! She took off her shirt and jeans; got into shorts and wore a funky t-shirt. She put on her floaters, put some cash in the pocket and left the flat.

She made her way to Chowpati which was a twenty minute walk from her place. She went directly to a stall selling pani puri. There were no crowds there yet, but in another half-an-hour it would get busy.

She took off her floaters and walked into the water. She stood there for a few minutes enjoying the waves lapping at her feet and then found herself thinking about Neil. She wished he was there with her. She thought about calling him and checked her pockets. She didn't have her cell phone with her. She shrugged and smiled to herself.

Half-an-hour later, she was still standing in the water with her floaters in one hand when it suddenly started raining heavily. She laughed at herself remembering another thing that she had forgotten—her umbrella.

She was drenched in minutes. There was no way to get a taxi from here to the flat. So she just started walking in the rain towards home. It was still raining when she reached her apartment building. She climbed up to her floor and almost bumped into the person turning away from her door.

"What the…," the person was saying as he dropped his handbag.

"Neil?!" Ishani said incredulously. Was he really here? What was he doing here? Why had he not called her? Her mind was a tumult of questions.

"You are soaked," Neil said. "Where have you been?"

"Chowpati," Ishani replied with a big smile, then she stepped aside and pulling a key from her pocket opened the door. "Come in," she said and walked in.

Neil followed in and put his handbag by the sofa. Then he looked around and said, "Nice place."

Ishani smiled and said, "I told you, you would like it, didn't I?" She had taken her floaters off and left them by the door.

Neil smiled and reaching out with his hand pulled her closer.

"I am drenched. I need to get out of these clothes," Ishani said.

Neil laughed softly and putting his other arm around her said, "Let me help you."

Ishani was thrilled to have him there. But she wanted to talk to him first; ask him a lot of questions; answer his.

She put her hands on his chest and said, "I think I will be able to manage." Then she smiled and put her hand on his cheek, "I'll not take long. Why don't you make yourself comfortable? If you want water or a cold drink, the fridge is in the kitchen." She saw that he looked disappointed. She stretched on her toes, gave him a quick kiss and said, "Let's talk when I have changed."

He let her go and said, "Alright darling, let us do this your way."

Ishani went to her bedroom, closed the door and got out of her wet clothes. She towelled herself dry and got into a flowery yellow, orange skirt and a white sleeveless top with lace. She combed her hair quickly and walked out.

Neil was standing by the Window. He turned around as Ishani walked out of her bedroom.

"Don't want anything to drink?" Ishani asked.

"No, I am OK," he said and walked away from the window. He sat down on the sofa and patted the place next to him. Ishani went and sat by him and he took her hands in his, "It's good to be here! I have missed you these last two months."

"Yes," Ishani said, "Me too."

Then she asked, "How did you find this place? And why didn't you call me to tell me you were coming over?"

Neil smiled and said, "Hmm. I decided to fly in and give you a surprise. That is why I didn't call you from Delhi. I didn't know this place. I went to your office and was told that you had left early today, of all days.

"Then Abhijeet wanted to know why I was in Mumbai. When I told him I was here for you, he wanted to know why. So I had to sit down and tell him."

"Tell him what?" Ishani asked. For the past two months she had been wondering what to tell Abhijeet. She had not told him anything so far.

Neil looked at her intently and then raised her left hand to his lips. He kissed it and said, "I told him that I am in love with you."

"You did?" Ishani asked almost whispering. "You are?"

"Yes," Neil said nodding his head.

"Really?" Ishani asked incredulously.

Neil laughed and only nodded. Then after a moment or two he said, "Anyway, then he wanted to know more. He wanted to know what I plan to do. So I told him that I would do whatever you wanted to."

"Oh!" Ishani was having difficulty taking it all in. It was too much.

"So he gave me your address and he tried calling you to see where you were. But you didn't take the call. So I decided to come over and check."

"I forgot my phone at home, my umbrella too," Ishani said sheepishly.

Neil kissed her hand once more. Then he got up and said, "You said something about cold drinks. Do you have beer by any chance?"

"Yes, you are in luck," Ishani said getting up and went to the kitchen. Neil followed her and stood in the kitchen door watching her.

As she went about getting the beer and mugs, he said, "Things have been hectic in Delhi. But things seem to be falling in place. I have had long conversations with my father and we are on much better terms now. His health is improving.

"That attack scared all of us. But it helped us get closer. My mother is very happy that he and I are agreeing on things a lot more. He has finally accepted that I am not going to join him in the business. I have agreed to be involved in the hiring process for the position of a CEO."

Neil stepped towards Ishani as she turned with two mugs filled with beer. She handed one to him and they walked out to the living room.

"Cheers," he said.

"Cheers," Ishani replied and took a sip. Neil sat down, looked at Ishani and extended his hand. She placed hers in his and sat down next to him.

He took a few sips and said, "My divorce came through two days back. I am a free man now."

Ishani turned to look at him. Then she carefully put down her mug on the table. Neil put his mug down too, smiled and said, "Maybe we should be drinking champagne, not beer."

"I am sure we could celebrate with beer too," Ishani said, her eyes bright. "How long are you in Mumbai for?"

"I don't have a plan. I could take up a case here so that we get to spend time with each other. Or we could both take a vacation," Neil replied.

"Here? In Mumbai?" Ishani asked, liking the idea of spending days with each other, doing whatever they felt like.

"Here if you want; or in Delhi. Or we can travel. Whatever you would like," he said and tucked her hair behind her ear.

"How about we start with that date we had talked about, Mr. Bhargav?" Ishani asked huskily.

"Sure. What do you want to do? Go out to eat?" Neil asked.

Ishani smiled a shy smile at that. "Are you hungry?" She asked but went ahead without giving him a chance to answer, "I was thinking about what you had said you would really like to do when we went on our date."

"Ishani," Neil said huskily and moved closer. He then held her face in his hands and kissed her. Ishani leaned back and Neil pushed her all the way down on the sofa, and stretched his body over hers. Ishani wrapped her one arm around his waist and caressed the nape of his neck with the other hand. She groaned when his tongue stroked hers.

When he lifted his head and looked down at her, she said, "The bed would be more comfortable."

Neil touched his forehead to hers and chuckled softly. "So, lead me to it darling," He got up in one fluid movement, extended his hand to her and pulled her up when she placed hers in his. Ishani smiled and holding onto his hand walked him to the bedroom.